P9-ASM-574

Born in 1978, **Mohammad Rabie** is the author of three acclaimed novels. His first novel, *Amber Planet*, won first prize in the Emerging Writers category of the Sawiris Cultural Award in 2012. He lives in Cairo, Egypt.

Robin Moger is the translator of *Women of Karantina* by Nael El-toukhy, among other books, and his translation for *Writing Revolution* won the 2013 English PEN Award for outstanding writing in translation. He lives in Cape Town, South Africa.

Otared

Mohammed Rabie

Translated by
Robin Moger

hoopoe
AN IMPRINT OF AUC PRESS

Map (on pages vi—vii) by Amr Kafrawy

First published in 2016 by
Hoopoe
113 Sharia Kasr el Aini, Cairo, Egypt
420 Fifth Avenue, New York, 10018
www.hoopoefiction.com

Hoopoe is an imprint of the American University in Cairo Press
www.aucpress.com

Exclusive distribution outside Egypt and North America by I.B.Tauris & Co Ltd., 6
Salem Road, London, W4 2BU

Dar el Kutub No. 25814/15
ISBN 978 977 416 784 3

Dar el Kutub Cataloging-in-Publication Data

Rabie, Mohammed
        Otared / Mohammed Rabie.—Cairo: The American University in
    Cairo Press, 2016.
        p.   cm.
        ISBN 978 977 416 784 3
        1. Arabic Fiction –Translation into English
        2. Arabic Fiction
        I. Title
        892.73

1 2 3 4 5   20 19 18 17 16

Designed by Adam el-Sehemy
Printed in the United States of America

Otared

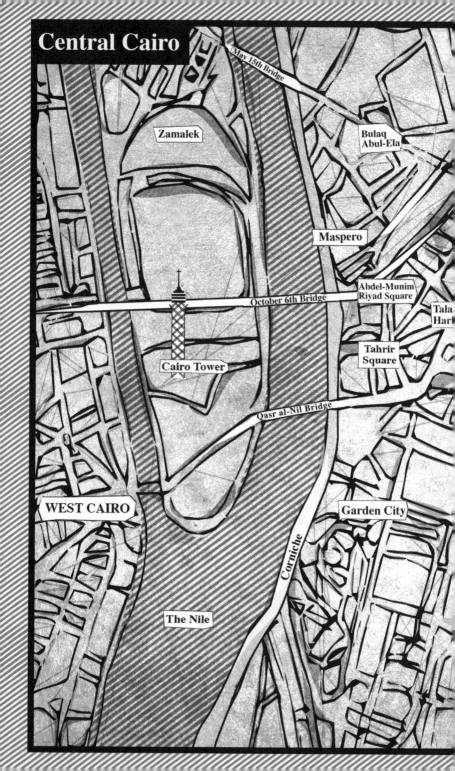

Central Cairo

May 15th Bridge

Zamalek

Bulaq Abul-Ela

Maspero

Abdel-Munim Riyad Square

October 6th Bridge

Tala Har[...]

Cairo Tower

Tahrir Square

Qasr al-Nil Bridge

WEST CAIRO

Garden City

Corniche

The Nile

Abbasiya

amses Street

July 26th Street

Tiring Building

Opera Square

Ataba Square

al-Azhar Bridge

al-Azhar st.

Bab al-Luq

Baron Palace

Abdeen

Salah Salim Street

EAST CAIRO

Muqattam

A Beginning

THIS LINE OF BLOOD PUT me in mind of many things.

It was traced on the wall, not quite vertically but leaning at a slight angle and at its apex looping sharply back to the ground. Small droplets hung down, running from the edge of the bend. It reminded me of an ostrich's tail feather, a column of water rising from a fountain, the glowing tracks of fireworks launched across the sky.

The butcher was a true professional. With his massive cleaver, he struck the calf's forelegs a single blow to bring the beast down, then passed the same blade over its neck, opening the rosy throat and an artery, and sending the blood jetting out in a clean line—dragged down by gravity, held horizontal by the pumping heart—only to meet the wall a few centimeters away and describe itself: the classic profile of airborne liquid, a shape about to be lost forever and then preserved, a stroke upon the wall.

Many people ate from the flesh of the slaughtered calf. They say raw meat stimulates the sex drive, or so I've heard, and certainly the rites have something rousing about them: the slaughter, the mingled stench of blood and dung, the skinning, the carcass hung up and butchered, the sight of dozens standing waiting for a cut of meat, of kids off to one side eating lumps of raw liver, still hot and soft, of a man rushing off with his plastic bag full of meat and smiling as he goes . . . and then me, sat watching it all in my white robe, relaxing after the exertion of many months.

1

The Eid al-Adha holiday: a fine opportunity to derail your diet, kick back, and find out what's going on out in the countryside; to ponder, too, the relationship between flesh and sex.

In the evening, the poor gathered in numbers, come to eat from the vast spread laid out for them. They sat on the ground around a spotless white cloth with empty bowls of various shapes and sizes before them, and then a charity worker came around, dishing two pieces of meat for each person from a huge pot carried by his colleague, picking them out with his bare hand, and not bending to place them in the bowl but waiting until the dish was lifted, then letting them fall—at which the pauper would immediately start eating. Boiled meat swaddled in fat: gray flesh, white fat. To me, it all looked revolting, but those doing the eating were thoroughly enjoying themselves.

On the wall before me a line of blood was traced like that I'd seen five days earlier, during Eid at my family's place in the country. On this occasion, it had come from the artery of a sixteen-year-old boy. Between wall and bed, in the narrow gap no more than fifty centimeters wide, his body was crammed into a most outlandish pose: head to one side, mouth squashed but open, the two arms raised with palms half-folded into fists and, stranger still, his legs also raised—knees up by his face and one broken, the lower half dangling forlornly from the joint and resting along the side of the corpse. On the opposite wall, clearly visible to the naked eye, was the line of blood. It looked to me as though the owners of the apartment had recently repainted the walls. The pale cream was even and flawless, unmarked by fingerprints, unscuffed by furniture: a wall in one color, a canvas or a blank page, and the line of blood showing its color ever stronger.

I was on my own. I'd rushed impetuously to the address provided to find officers from the Emergency Force had beaten me to it. Some stood dazed in the living room. Others were on the stairs outside the apartment. None had been into the bedrooms, just peeked past the open doors at what lay inside, and sure enough they'd been careful not to touch a thing—not out of any desire to keep the crime scene uncontaminated as the rules dictate, but because they were frightened. It was when I looked into the eyes of the first officer that I understood. I know what the eyes of a frightened police officer look like. It's impossible to put into words. We're the only ones who recognize it, who share it. Wordlessly, we confess our fear. We share the burden between all those who lie within the circle of trust. I'd been in the same position many times myself, prey to the same fear, had shared my burden with colleagues using that same look and, a few times, carried it alone, and I know the pressure it brings. I was informed that the father had killed his family and prepared myself for a lot of blood, but the officer's look told of something more. For an instant, some of his fear transmitted itself to me and I understood that fear would be with me for a long time.

The owner of the house was sitting in the living room in front of the television, his shoulders covered with a light blanket and staring at the screen. He seemed to be eating from a bowl held between his hands. In a well-stuffed armchair sat an elderly man, his hands in his lap and his head resting against the back of the chair, and I saw at a glance that he'd been dead for hours. The other man was watching an old film—Ismail Yassin cavorting in a shady dive and singing the praises of alcohol, the other patrons all warbling along—and wolfing from his plate with a spoon. The smell was deadly—rot, and excrement, and cooked meat, and vomit—and I noticed hardened lumps of shit beneath the dead man, on his chair and the floor at his feet, even as the other finished his meal, laid the dish down beside him, and went on watching the film. I realized then that my brother officer's fear had been an unvarnished response to the scene before him.

The officer told me that there were four more bodies: the young man in the first bedroom, his older sister in the second, and the mother and a young boy in the third. They had

3

been killed by thrusts from a kitchen knife, dealt out by the father now sitting in front of the television. The rigidity of the corpses and the smell of decomposition suggested that he had killed them two or three days ago.

The kitchen was in a state of chaos: pots and bowls all over the floor and table, a putrid stench, patches of dried vomit on the floor, and shit everywhere.

In the first bedroom, I stood transfixed before the corpse of the boy wedged between the bed and the wall, and after a minute had passed I realized that I was slowly losing consciousness. Losing it and conscious of it. I pushed out of the room and out of the apartment. It was on the top floor, so I climbed the stairs to the roof and there, beneath stars that choked on the filthy air, I threw up.

The nausea was overwhelming. Unable to stand, I sat on the grimy rooftop, trying to bring my stomach under control. The boy's bizarre posture, his rigid body, face turned to the wall and hidden from sight, were images that would never leave me, as though etched into my memory for eternity. And most regrettably, they brought back every corpse I'd ever clapped eyes on since starting in this job: wretched faces, slack mouths, half-closed eyes surrendered to death. I made an effort to suck in fresh air, something other than the rancid fug inside the apartment. I filled my lungs as full as they would go. A gray haze lay between the stars and moon and me, and looking up I saw, among those stars, the faces of a family. I saw their names spelled out beneath their pictures in the paper: Wife—Abir Abdel Haqq, 37; Daughter—Farida, 11; Daughter—Sally, 4. And my picture with them: Captain Ahmed Otared. Husband. Father. The article bore no headline, contained no details, just black lines beneath the pictures where the writing would be, nothing I could make out or understand, and yet I knew that this was an item about how I'd murdered them, without the faintest idea who they were or why I was certain that I'd killed them and had changed

4

their fate for a better one, even if it had been death. Then I saw that I would kill many people, and that a great number of people would be killed in whose deaths I'd play no part. I saw that people would kill their children and eat their flesh, and I saw that the man sitting, eating, and watching television had broken the last of the seals and set loose everything that would later come to pass. All this I saw and I understood nothing.

This was before I had entered the remaining rooms. Before I had seen the other bodies. Before I had seen what the man had recorded on his phone.

The investigation and confessions established that the father had killed his family with the kitchen knife, then spent several hours preparing for the next stage. He had laid out a small knife and various cooking pots, and proceeded to chop onions, peel garlic, and deseed a large quantity of tomatoes. Next, taking his sharp little knife, he had chopped off their lips, noses, and ears, prized out their eyes, sliced away portions of their calves and thighs, and dug out his wife's breasts. He had put the eyes in a small bowl, the ears and lips in a larger one, and the chunks of flesh in a third, while the breasts he'd laid in an earthenware dish. He had added the chopped onion, garlic, and tomatoes to the bowls, and then cooked it all in the kitchen. The smell of food had suggested meat being cooked for Eid, and the neighbors hadn't suspected a thing. The father had taken calls from family members, accepting their good wishes—had even called some of them himself—and when they'd asked after the family, he'd said that his son was out with friends, the other children were asleep, and his wife was in the shower.

But the father had been careful to solicit the approval of the grandfather, the man I'd seen dead alongside him. He told us that he had recorded much of what had happened on his phone and with a camcorder. We had already extracted all the recordings and added them to the case file by the time he told

5

us this, and with the footage we had it looked like this was going to be easy: a clean case with no complications, death sentence for the father guaranteed. If it hadn't been for the cooking business, it would have been a textbook case. Run of the mill.

Most of what took place was caught on camera. We found a clip of the father cutting up a section of his wife's thigh, and another of him slicing her breasts, as if giving a demonstration of his technique. There was a clip of him unhurriedly and calmly chopping noses, ears, and eyes—except for the eldest son's. He was left untouched. The father said that the boy had resisted fiercely, had died suffering, and so hadn't deserved to be cut up and eaten. Then there was another clip of him placing all the flesh in a bowl, adding vegetables and seasoning, and stirring everything together. A long clip of a steel saucepan with its Perspex lid, and the meat gently stewing inside; the longest of the lot.

But the most extraordinary set of recordings were those of the man's father—the dead grandpa swamped in his filth on the well-stuffed armchair.

The camera had been mounted on its tripod. The footage was of higher quality and clarity than the earlier recordings taken from the phone. Father and grandfather filled the screen, the former attempting to feed the latter from a dish in his hand. He was holding it in his left hand, bringing it up to the grandfather's face, and lifting out a spoon containing a small quantity of meat. The grandfather glared at him furiously, slapped at the dish, and shouted something in his face with such anger that we couldn't catch what he had said. By that stage in the investigation, everything was crystal clear, but we still needed an explanation or a clarification—a hint, at least—as to the motive, and the angry grandfather came as a surprise to us all. It was clear that the grandfather was immobile, that his old age confined him to the chair, and that he was aware of what his son was doing but had no way of stopping him. He knew that his son was chopping up his grandchildren

6

one after the other, and no doubt knew that he had cooked them. The most he could manage, it seemed, was to slap the dish and send it flying. It was all he could do.

In the next clips, the father was trying to persuade the grandfather to eat. Pressing him to eat. Whispering things we couldn't hear. We couldn't hear a thing he said, and couldn't imagine what a man might say to convince his father to eat the flesh of his own grandchildren. Initially the grandfather reacted angrily. "You're a liar," he was shouting. "Don't say that. . . ." The father spoke calmly, whispering, and the grandfather turned from anger to despondency, from shouting to weeping, and then to moans. The more the father spoke to him, the more he moaned, and the recording ended with the grandfather murmuring, "Enough . . . enough. . . ."

The next recording had been made a few hours later. By now a whole day had passed since the murders had been committed. Father and grandfather were seated as before, and the grandfather was trying to force himself to eat from the dish held by his son. He was gripping the spoon, bringing it to his mouth, and saying, "It's better for them. . . . Fine. . . . But I just can't. . . . It's not. . . . To eat them's not . . . to kill them. . . ." Then he began to whimper like a child, and ate the first spoonful.

Between each spoonful and the next, the grandfather wept. He was eating and murmuring, "It's best for them. A good father, a good grandfather. . . . They'll go to heaven for sure. . . . They won't come back here. . . ." Then he finished the first bowl, and after that he was silent, though he went on eating with a strangely mechanical air. In less than half an hour, he'd worked through five helpings, and the clip ended as he laid the empty dish in the father's hands.

From the autopsy, we learned that he had died from severe poisoning and had expelled a torrent of shit and vomit before he'd passed. The father must have watched him dying and not moved a muscle. The pair of them had been on a suicide mission to eat the victims: the grandfather had died almost

7

immediately, while the father had gone on eating even after we had entered the apartment. He had eaten and eaten, getting up to defecate anywhere and everywhere. Five whole days, and not a thought for keeping himself or the apartment clean. We later found out from the medical report that between them they'd consumed more than fifty kilos of flesh.

On the sixth day, a neighbor called the Emergency Force, bothered by a putrid stench issuing from the apartment next door. The father had calmly opened the door to the jumpy officers, then gone back to the television to finish the very last bowlful of a feast that had lasted all the days of Eid.

We all know the rules: not a finger must be laid on the killer. He is to be treated with great gentleness. Officers, recruits, and prisoners treat him as a dead man—particularly if he's confessed, particularly if he hasn't resisted or screamed at us. This is a man marching to the gallows of his own accord, so let him march.

During the trial, the judge didn't ask him much, other than the one repeated question: had he killed his family or not? The man confessed to what he'd done in the court's first session, and repeated his confession more than fifty times in the sessions that followed. Given the details of the case, the judge's boorishness and clumsy insistence on the point were completely out of place. The man had opened the door of his apartment himself and had surrendered to the police. He'd put up not the slightest resistance. He had confessed to the prosecutor and confessed to the judge. I could not understand why, every session, the judge repeated the same question: "Did you kill them?" When the judge asked him to put his confession in writing, the man produced one in his own hand, a large, clear hand with no mistakes or crossings out. Maybe he took pride in this document. There was one small detail that no one dwelled on for very long: his statement that the only reason he had murdered his family was that he'd lost a lot of money on the stock exchange.

8

But he showed no distress in the way he conducted himself—no feelings at all, in fact. Throughout the course of the trial, he was like the living dead, heedless of what went on around him. The prosecutor's sallies seemed ridiculous given the confession made in the presence of so many witnesses and repeated so many times, and the defense's arguments even more so. Everything about that trial seemed absurd. Even the judge, who insisted on hearing the confession more than fifty times, who demanded a written statement, who brought the accused out of his cage during the final session, handed him his written statement, and asked if it was his (to which he replied, "Yes"), then asked if it was in his handwriting (to which he replied, "Yes"), then asked for the last time if he had killed his family (to which he replied, "Yes")—even the judge was a joke.

Only the man himself didn't seem ridiculous, and yet quite how to describe him I could never figure out.

People were confounded. They all felt for the killer. This was a man of the bourgeoisie: comfortably off, a respectable job, didn't take drugs (just smoked), owned a large apartment in a classy neighborhood and two cars, his children at foreign schools and the eldest daughter graduated with honors from a private university. He was the beau ideal of the contented middle class, a man with a secure future, envied by many for his stable life and beautiful family. And yet not one of the stunned onlookers thought to ask why it had happened. Psychologists and sociologists offered no analysis. Of course, the pretext of losses on the stock exchange was very thin, too weak for the prosecutor to have advanced it as a motive in court, and were it not for the man appending it to his detailed account of what he'd done, it would definitely have been consigned to the trash. Television talking heads seized on his story, but no one asked what his real motive was, and discussions of the case were followed by pop songs, reports on fashion shows, and political debate. And though I might not have been that concerned by the true cause, even I knew "financial losses" was a fabrication.

I followed the case with great interest, attending every court session in anticipation of some surprise or dramatic turn in the course of events. I'd stare into the face of the man sitting in the defendant's cage, racking my brains for a complete memory of that face, but all that came to mind was the back of his neck and shoulders, and the blanket covering them. This was the only mental image I'd been able to retain. Even those images from the interrogations, with him sitting before me or beside me, seeing him plain with only the desk between us—they had gone for good, and nothing was left but the image of him sat before the television.

I was on my way to one of the trial's final sessions when my car broke down and I had to flag down a taxi to take me to the courtroom. I arrived late; the session had already begun. I can't remember if it was the turn of the prosecution or the defense. It was as good as over. All that remained were those formalities beloved of the Egyptian bench—and of judges everywhere—so that the matter could be elegantly concluded: a crisp life sentence; a duly solemn death sentence. Everyone knew that during one of the sessions the accused's case would be forwarded to the mufti, whose plea for clemency would fail to shake the certainty of the judge, who would then, in the next session, order the defendant's execution.

I delayed going in until I'd had a quick cigarette and a small cup of tea. I took a sip from the cup and it was bitter, no sugar, so I ordered some from the tea boy, who apologized with a smile and brought it to me with a little spoon. I stirred the tea and spent a few minutes looking at my phone. By now I was very late and estimated that the session must be halfway through. When I picked up the cup again, intending to finish it in a few quick gulps, I found a black beetle bobbing on the surface. A dead scarab.

My eyes fastened on the motionless insect. It hadn't been there before. Maybe it had fallen in while I'd been busy with the phone and had died, either drowned or from the heat of

10

the tea. I tipped the contents of the cup onto the floor, the finely chopped tea leaves swirling over the marble floor in the red liquid and the scarab rolling away. It started to move. So, not dead.

I asked the tea boy what he had ready to go—tea, coffee, anything. Someone had just ordered coffee and had walked off without taking it, he told me. As though it had been made for me.

He poured it calmly, picked up the little saucer that held the cup, and handed it over, volunteering the following: "That's a cup of coffee with hope stirred in. Hope's important. That guy who murdered his family lost hope, that's why he killed them. . . ."

As the session ended, I watched the man walk out of the cage. Hair combed, in clean white overalls, he walked the way he'd done since I first saw him, but it was only today that I saw what made his walk so distinctive. He walked with all hope lost.

AD 2025

1

WE TOOK TURNS SMOKING THE joint. The five of us finished it in under a minute: just two puffs each. We lit another. As usual, the hash was completely pure. Unadulterated. When cut and crumbled, the block left no marks on the paper; it broke easily between my fingers and had a pungent reek, exactly as my colleague in Narcotics had described the pure product from the eighties. He'd told me what used to happen during raids on hash storehouses.

The pair of us had been lounging by a roadblock on Qasr al-Aini Street. There were very few cars about, and a man walked past us smoking a joint. We could tell from the smell. My colleague laughed. "We'd know there was hash in a building just by standing outside. We'd walk down the street and the stink would leak out of the doors and windows and hit us, and when we got to the apartment we'd know it was the one immediately. The dealers could do what they liked, none of them could cover up the smell. When we caught a whiff, we'd smile and relax. From then on, it was up to the rank and file: they'd search the rooms for hidden compartments. They'd search cellars. Might even have to dig a bit to get the hash out. Sure—even the dirt piled over it couldn't stop the stink getting out. Later, the dealers were forced to mix it with a lot of cheaper substances, firstly to boost their profits, and secondly to hide the smell."

I didn't know them, these four. I was put in with them and now there was nothing for it but to share the hash. We were

15

stationed in one of the rooms on the penultimate floor of the Cairo Tower. In a few hours' time, this long posting would be over; two whole years it had been. We were an advanced observation post, the eye of the resistance looking out over East Cairo, an instrument of execution and assassination, snipers, the long arm of the partisans, and I, Colonel Ahmed Otared, was commander of the unit that had held fast for all that time. Even when, one after another, the officers had begun breaking down beneath the intense psychological pressure, even when three of them had committed suicide in a single day, not a hair on my head had been disturbed. I'd just sent a message to the leadership to send more snipers and a detachment to pick up the bodies. And as that detachment had made its way to the tower from West Cairo, I had been writing my report: attributing the suicides to the pressures of the job, to our dazzling success in taking out targets, to the absence of any psychological training for the officers, to the loneliness and isolation, and to many other things besides.

After that, I would send officers on leave once they had stayed three or four months, thereby maintaining a reasonably high standard within the unit, and most certainly preserving the lives of the officers. I had realized that everyone who stayed up in the tower underwent a gradual nervous breakdown, and everything I mentioned in the report really did contribute to this: in the end, no matter how much an officer believes in his work, killing a human being he doesn't know is a major undertaking. I was a sniper. I know. I know that images of the victims linger in the mind for a long time. That one's memory selects certain images to hold on to forever. Even mine—and I'm a professional—retains images of people I shot and whose identities I can't recall. I can't recall where I was or where they were. I can't recall when it happened or how I received the orders to kill them. And of course, there's that tableau of the three bodies heaped up on top of one another, framed by the circle of my scope. That one will stay fixed in my mind; it will never be erased until the day I die. So what of amateurs like them? Had it not been for the enthusiasm that sprang from their patriotic spirit, the Tower Group would not have had the slightest success.

The Tower Group was our official designation, and one that no one will ever find recorded in any official document. But it was the term 'hornets' which caught the imagination of the general public and became our *nom de guerre*. Truth be told, no one had the slightest knowledge of our presence, but they were aware that there were many snipers stationed throughout the city, on rooftops and up tall buildings. We left a clear trail—an officer walking down the street, then dropping without warning; a soldier sitting calmly at a café, his brains sprayed over the tables of those sitting beside him—and so it was that people came to conflate the Tower Group with the snipers scattered through the streets of East Cairo. We were all hornets to them, and certainly it never occurred to a soul that we were based in the Cairo Tower, the furthest point from everything, at the maximum range of our rifles and scopes. No one saw us and no one heard us, and with our suppressors we were veritable angels of death.

Initially, I'd assumed that the tower actually housed sixteen floors, but with time and much traveling up and down in the elevator, I realized that its capacity was very limited indeed. The massive structure housed just two floors (referred to as the fifteenth and sixteenth regardless), and atop the last of these an extremely narrow walkway ran around a vast central column, visible from many places throughout the city.

I climbed up to the sixteenth floor, whose own circular balcony commanded a view of the entire metropolis. I was looking out over East Cairo from an elevation of approximately one hundred and eighty meters. Its celebrated landmarks seemed stronger than people, stronger than time, stronger than anything. Even an architect sympathetic to modern styles would perceive their ugliness, accommodated

17

through long familiarity, and maybe this ugliness was the reason why they had survived despite the deaths of so many. The Maspero building, for instance, had no business surviving as it had. It was a gigantic-buttocked man squatting on the ground, his impossibly slender head and chest thrust up into the air. A Buddha erect. A Buddha deformed. To the north was the Ministry of Foreign Affairs, a tall European gent in an oriental turban, looming over the city, and at his back those numberless interlocked blocks of smaller buildings with no architectural style, or layout, or even specification in common, cut up by crooked streets whose widths would alter every hundred yards: the chaotic neighborhood of Bulaq Abul-Ela, its disorder a fitting backdrop for the infantile troublemaking that had broken out there years before. Then the Egyptian Museum, a clutch of decrepit idlers sitting on the ground, chatting in low tones. Inert for eons, shifting only to sip their tea, they lurked out of sight, loathing their own fraudulent history. The ruins of the deserted Nile Hilton, destroyed at the start of the occupation, was a drunken American tourist, fallen down and dead to the world, who had come to Cairo to find beauty in the shit around him, had searched long and hard, and found nothing, and even so couldn't admit that the place was a crapheap that harbored no beauty whatsoever— but blamed himself for failing to find the jewel buried in the dung. The Ramses Hilton, a vast whore hanging out over the Nile and hailing one and all . . . but no one went near her. And just as whores can be spotted by their filthy, frayed old shoes—as though they'd agreed among themselves that all their shoes would be like this—so the disorder of the street and the vendors outside the Ramses Hilton were its old heels. The intersection of the Qasr al-Nil Bridge and the Corniche was an unintelligible maze, a more byzantine version of its sister junction, where the Corniche met the October 6th Bridge. Then the Semiramis: a man, his wife, and their child. The man, having pissed at his feet, was just standing

18

there, neither moving away from the patch of urine, nor letting his family move. To his left was the Mogamma of Tahrir Square, bearing within itself the causes of all the sicknesses that plague Egyptians. It only showed me its flank because it knew I feared its chest, and head, and broad-notched belly. In front of it was the derelict Arab League: glorious rubble, stately ruins, whose demolition had finally laid Tahrir bare—it had been the only thing that lay between us and the square. It had come down the day after the Nile Hilton, but unlike the hotel, which had tilted over and fallen on its side without breaking apart, the Arab League building had collapsed completely, leaving a great mound of debris.

Nothing but chaos. I searched for some order amid it all, but whoever built Cairo seemed never to have contemplated it from a distance, never looked at the whole picture, but instead had taken each building as a discrete entity, standing alone; each one designed in isolation without regard for the structures that surrounded it. They had seen it from the perspective of someone at ground level—aiming to dazzle in an age before airborne cameras—not as a bird soaring through the sky. The architects who followed these founding fathers had continued to build in just the same way, and then those who came after had done likewise. Would I live to see it all destroyed?

For two years, this scene had kept me company. Today I would leave it.

The first thing we'd done was to divide the floor space of the old restaurant on the fifteenth floor into cubicles using plywood sheets as dividers, leaving the staircase up to the top floor accessible to all so that any one of the officers could get up there in an emergency. Each cubicle was occupied by a sniper. There he lived and slept and, when he was on duty, would climb to the top floor to watch over East Cairo. Over time, the number of officers rose and fell, corresponding to West Cairo's need for the Tower Group. Our mission: "To safeguard our surroundings." This elastic prescription had

19

always pleased me. Such flexible orders gave us the freedom to act in critical situations, although our job description went beyond conventional parameters, to include murder. I was left completely to my own devices; there was no rigid plan that I had to implement. I just had to adapt to developments and await orders, all of them most specific: assassinate so-and-so who'd be passing down the Corniche; shoot any five officers of the occupation over the coming month. There were even instructions to kill Egyptian police officers and civilians collaborating with the occupation. Plus our standing orders: to peer through our scopes at East Cairo and note any suspicious movements. As I mentioned, we were a post for advanced observation and assassinations.

Thick dust covered Cairo, a blend of car exhaust, a fog that seemed to come from nowhere, and maybe, too, smoke from burning agricultural waste that drifted in from surrounding villages and towns. Every few weeks, all these would gather together into a curtain that hid Cairo's distant buildings from our eyes in the sky—a curtain like the one I'd made myself to deflect prying eyes, like the mask I wore when aiming at targets.

Every morning, each man would take his rifle, adjust his scope, and take up his favored position—sitting on the floor with the rifle propped on his knee, or resting it on a slender bipod—while I went upstairs, up where the balcony curved around the tower's outer face and all Cairo lay revealed. I'd make a couple of circuits to take in the buildings and streets unimpeded by stone or glass: East Cairo and its celebrated architecture under occupation, and West Cairo's anonymous blocks—a few of which had been razed during the bombardment—free and under the complete control of Egyptians. Each time I went up to the balcony, the blockages and blockades would dwindle and Cairo become more accessible.

I was highest in rank, the unit's leader, who carried a rifle just like them. I didn't receive orders from another

20

commander, but had complete freedom to act as the situation dictated, with the exception of a few cases each month. For this reason, I didn't look through my scope that much, but whenever I tired of gazing down on the bigger picture I would raise my rifle to see the city's component parts through the sight. Not one of us had fired a bullet for nearly a month now. Things had settled down and life had returned to normal, as though nothing had happened, and then a week ago I received a message instructing me to vacate the position today. All week we had been getting ourselves together. We didn't even take up our observation positions with our customary commitment. These were our last days in the tower. Where to next? What would the next mission be? I didn't know.

I approached the edge of the balcony and leaned against the railings that rose over my head, facing East Cairo. Through my scope, I could see the five battleships lined up directly below me. I could see the sailors moving over the deck, lazily, as though they'd got nothing to worry about, as though they were not, like us, stuck. The flotilla in mid-river wasn't there for protection; it was a brazen display of force. Pedestrians on the Corniche saw it and no one crossed the October 6th Bridge without staring at the ships. They didn't do any real damage, as they had in the early days, and nor did they prevent it, and not a single Egyptian had ever contemplated attacking them. They were the occupation's immovable idols.

They didn't know where we were, but they knew we could see them, that we were watching them, tracking them through our scopes. They knew we'd dealt painful blows to their colleagues. We might have been in the tower, or one of Zamalek's many other buildings, or even on the Nile's west bank. Perhaps we were on a rooftop in the East Cairo that they occupied. To them, we were ghosts.

This was the first time I'd stood upright, facing East Cairo, in the light of day. We were out of range of the naked eye, but not of an eye that sought us through a scope. We wouldn't

21

stand staring scopeless at the city except by night. Though the sights' lenses reflected light, assassinations were carried out in minutes, too short a time to reveal our position. The observation mission took place on the fifteenth floor, where the revolving restaurant had been located before the occupation. The thick glass ringing the space broke up the sun's rays and kept our lenses from being seen. I remember how complicated it got in the final weeks: I'd update our routine every day in order to keep our position an undiscoverable secret, and I succeeded.

I remember my first day there. It was night when I reached the tower, and I wandered about for a while outside the grand entrance, looking up at the huge eagle that surmounted it, then got into the lift. Seconds later I was on the fifteenth floor. I climbed up to the top floor and looked out longingly at the five ships on the Nile. Full of eagerness, I took out my scope and inspected each one. I was breaking a number of rules by doing this, placing the position, if not the whole mission, in jeopardy. The next day, when the courier came with food and the first message, I gave him a letter requesting permission to destroy the five ships. What I'd written must have come across as overly excitable, for the day after that an officer from the resistance, a general, came to me and said a lot of things about the importance of the position and the importance of maintaining it unseen. He told me that the island of Zamalek was completely empty: no residents, no civilians. The residents had cleared out a while ago, during the violent bombardment that set the streets and spacious parks aflame. Only a few operatives from the resistance remained, and giving away their position in the tower was easily done: a bullet fired at the wrong moment, a glint of light on a scope's lens. One of us emerging onto the balcony in plain sight would be enough. No one, he told me, would ever dream that the resistance controlled the Cairo Tower and had retained it as a forward observation and sniping platform. He told me to ready myself for exceptionally difficult missions, and said that my job was to hold my position using guile, not gung-ho.

I walked around the balcony to the other side overlooking West Cairo, the lion-hearted sector the occupier had never managed to enter. Well, fine: that he had never tried to enter. . . . But even so, Giza was well guarded and the occupier couldn't get in. This half of the city we utterly ignored. We never bothered watching what went on there. Never bothered sniping anyone who walked its streets. Of course, it was just as forbidden to appear on the western side of the tower as it was on the eastern. Who could say? There might be spies in the free city as well.

A red dot of light appeared on the balcony wall, careering wildly in all directions. The source of the beam was very far away and being blown about in the breeze, but it was getting closer and would be here in a minute or less. It always took a few bullets before my own hands steadied. I remembered that the first laser dot I'd seen through my scope had also wobbled about violently; after days of training I'd come to hold my rifle as if cradling a baby, and the dot had sat more steadily on the target. Now, perhaps, it was no longer a way to gauge the accuracy of my aim, as is usually the case, but instead served as a signal to the target, letting him know that he was about to be struck by my round. The laser beam, fired out parallel to the gun barrel and coming to rest exactly on the point of impact—I no longer required it, but I went on using it as a final warning.

Slowly but surely, the red dot on the wall steadied. I stared at the horizon, searching for its source, but it was still far off and all I saw was the faintly trembling track of the approaching beam. A minute later, what I'd been looking for floated down and settled on the balcony floor in front of me.

A new drone, this. I hadn't seen one of these before. I opened the message compartment and extracted the small envelope that had been carefully placed inside. Whoever sent

23

me these messages was a true visionary: dispatching little paper missives inside a flying machine with a mind of its own. This drone had five tiny rotors, was lighter and smaller than the four-rotor model which had delivered all our previous messages, and was further equipped with a miniature laser, the message compartment, and a camera affixed to the under-carriage beneath a tiny glass dome that allowed it to swivel in all directions. In addition to all that, there was a thin tube pro-truding to the right of the camera. I could tell straight away that it was part of a weapon, and looking a little closer saw that it was connected to a magazine containing four 9-mm rounds. Now we had a drone with a gun that could shoot, a camera that could record, and a compartment for messages. A multipurpose tool: kill, deliver, spy.

I set the drone on the ground, and a few seconds later the rotors started to emit a low whine, like a harmless child's toy. It swayed back and forth across the floor for a bit, then flew through the balcony's railings and away from the tower. After a few months in the tower, these machines had become our silent companions.

I opened the envelope to find five small sheets of paper with our names on them, one name per sheet. I unfolded mine. It said I would be moving in an hour's time, the last man to quit the tower. I must make sure that everyone received their orders and that they evacuated the tower, then I was to head to East Cairo and be at the intersection of Ramses and July 26th Streets at exactly 10 a.m. There I would meet a member of the resistance who was to act as my guide.

I returned to the fifteenth floor, handed out the letters, and bade them farewell, asking them to leave immediately.

Now I was the only person left in the place. In a few min-utes' time, it would be completely empty.

I picked up my rifle case and descended to the ground floor, carrying a bag containing a few clothes, my mask, cig-arette packs, and some money—just a few pound coins. I remembered their cold, hard, metallic feel. Nothing else. No weapons, no ID card, nothing.

Selecting a spot next to the biggest tree outside the tower, I dug a little rectangular hole into which I laid the gun. The case would keep it free of damp and dirt for a long time. Then I backfilled the remaining space with soil. The tower was my safe place. One day I was sure to return, and when I did my gun had to be ready to go.

There weren't many routes between Zamalek and East Cairo, only the bridges that linked the two halves of the city: Qasr al-Nil, October 6th, and May 15th. As long as the battleships remained mid-Nile, preventing river traffic between the two banks, these bridges were the only crossing points. Of course, there were checkpoints at each one. Daily, I'd see those intending to cross from east to west and vice versa standing in long queues waiting to be allowed to go over. Through my scope, the checkpoint on the October 6th Bridge looked laughable. The officers and policemen had narrowed the road slightly using barriers, allowing no more than two cars through at a time, while a limited number of pedestrians could pass through a metal detector. The whole operation was a farce. I'd see the officer in charge sitting sprawled out next to the police car, the people around him all staring ahead, beyond the checkpoints, hoping to reach East or West Cairo on time. People here still took their jobs seriously. Even me—I was careful about my job: I'd obeyed orders and I had listened to everyone's complaints, faithfully forwarding them to the leadership in hope of an improvement in circumstances, for an end to the occupation.

I walked along, unburdened but for my lightweight bag and the few clothes it contained, treading lightly, my feet barely touching the ground. For a moment, I felt relief. I might even have smiled, and I tried to remember the last time I'd felt so secure, but it was so very long ago, so obscured by time I could scarcely recall it. I walked northward, parallel to the Nile, toward the October 6th Bridge.

Plants were everywhere here. The whole island was a garden run wild. How it had all spread and flourished unwatered and untended I had no idea. Trees and plants unpruned, flowers aplenty, boughs and stems beginning to break through the paving stones and asphalt, and all of it somehow unspoiled by the wrecked, burnt-out, and abandoned cars on every side. They were just details that made the scene complete. These cars of ours had been a wonder fashioned from steel and now were gone for good, their place taken by the plants, a glory that had lived on through bombardment, fire, and destruction, that had defied oblivion and stubbornly sprung back up. Many birds had built their nests here, as though our former presence had denied them life and stability. Our existence as peaceful urban citizens, our life on this earth, had ultimately been an impediment to that of the plants and birds, while the artillery was their friend: they lived in harmony with the falling shells, the bullets of the warring sides.

At last, I came to the on-ramp of the October 6th Bridge. I walked on a little way to where the bridge curved up over the Nile, and here I spotted a round breach in the body of the bridge itself, the entrance to the tunnel that spanned the river beneath the crossing cars. I climbed the wooden ladder resting directly beneath the hole and, before passing into the darkness, looked out at the island behind me, so perfectly calm and peaceful. At that moment, I might have been the last human on it and maybe, too, the last person ever to step through that hole into the belly of the bridge.

I moved into total darkness and sensed people standing there, silent, waiting for me to say something. Then one of them switched on a torch. A half-light came faintly from the hole at my back and picked out the shapes of four or five figures.

2

I STILL REMEMBER THE FIRST day. Two-and-a-half years ago it was: 3 March 2023, to be exact.

I was on leave, walking down Sharif Street in Downtown in search of a café to sit at. The street was crowded as usual. It was nearly 2 p.m.—Downtown rush hour.

Without warning, the National Bank collapsed and a huge mass of dust and debris rose up, concealing and choking everything around it. We'd subsequently learn that the bank had come down of its own accord and not from a rocket or artillery round.

Over the course of the next three hours, large numbers of warplanes would pass through the skies overhead, bombing selected targets: the Central Bank, the Ministry of Education, the Ministry of Health, the Doctors' Syndicate, the telephone exchange in Muqattam, the satellite dishes in Maadi, the Opera House in Zamalek, and army-owned buildings, factories, and warehouses the length and breadth of the republic—all of which we'd find out later. Communications were knocked out, and in the blink of an eye we were back at the beginning of the twentieth century. No internet, no mobiles, no landlines, and no television. Nothing but radio. *Voice of the Arabs* continued to broadcast its regular programming schedule, with soothing music taking the place of its hourly news bulletins.

After three hours of pinpoint bombardment, we heard the following report from the BBC:

The armed forces of the Republic of the Knights of Malta have inflicted severe defeats on the Egyptian armed forces, and the Arab Republic of Egypt is now under the control of the Fourth and Fifth Armies of the Knights of Malta. The Egyptian constitution is henceforth suspended and the constitution of the Republic of the Knights of Malta is promulgated in its place. Parliament, the Shura Council, the Military Council, the Egyptian Council of Motherhood and Childhood, the Egyptian Council of Civil Rights, the Egyptian Human Rights Council, and the Egyptian Council for Technical Support for Preventative Measures have all been dissolved, the Egyptian Constitutional Court abolished, proceedings at all Egyptian courts suspended, and the Egyptian General Intelligence Directorate absorbed into the Fourth Army of the Knights of Malta. The president of Egypt has stepped down, the current prime minister removed from his post, and the government disbanded. Finally, operations by all branches of the Egyptian armed forces have been halted.

At 9 p.m. that evening, we'd hear the name of Egypt's new military ruler, Field Marshal Paul-Pierre Genevieve, and learn of his first decree: appointing Dr. Khalifa Sidqi prime minister and directing him to form the new government. The morning of the next day, 4 March 2023, all the papers would run more or less identical headlines, the most significant of which would be *al-Ahram*'s front-page lead: *Dr. Sidqi tasked with forming new government amid reports of the abolition of Information Ministry.*

In the week that followed, while the new prime minister set about selecting his ministers *(so that the government can confront the dangers and difficulties that lie ahead for Egypt)*, some four hundred and fifty thousand soldiers and officers from the Knights of Malta's twin armies entered Egypt, sailing up the two northern branches of the Nile to the towns of Damietta and Rashid,

28

spreading out across the entire Delta region, and moving to occupy Suez and Port Said from the Suez Canal. Armored divisions established themselves in Damietta and Rashid, then in Mansura, Damanhur, Tanta, al-Mahalla al-Kubra, Ismailiya, Zaqaziq, Menuf, and finally Cairo. Just the Delta, though: not a single Maltese trooper moved south of the capital. The south was utterly ignored.

Occupation patrols started up in these cities and towns, their mission to maintain order following the disappearance of the police and the army's defeat. It was said to be the most successful military operation in history, with the Egyptian army's equipment and bases completely destroyed within a week of the Maltese forces' deployment. Most soldiers and officers, without leadership, weapons, or communications equipment, went home, all hope of mounting a resistance gone. At week's end, with Maltese units deployed throughout the Delta and in Cairo itself, the prime minister announced that:

Egypt abides by all international treaties and shall continue to subsidize comestibles and fuel, pay the salaries of government employees—including employees from the Ministry of Defense—and, in light of recent international developments, looks forward to a successful future with which it shall dazzle the world.

During this time, Egyptians offered their occupier no resistance, and when communications networks were brought back after a week offline, news spread that twenty civilians had been killed during the Maltese deployment—a very small number when weighed against other wars—while there was nothing at all about military losses, nor about the former government or president. Photographs and reports on the subject of the Knights of Malta's two armies and Field Marshal Paul-Pierre Genevieve were everywhere. Very quickly, life returned to normal.

As proof of the Maltese Knights' naval power, the swiftness and maneuverability of their boats and launches, and to underline their control of Nile traffic, five light battle cruisers moored in the river between the island of Zamalek and Cairo's east bank. The boats were dwarfed by the massive buildings looming over the Corniche, but everyone knew what these dwarves were capable of.

I was living in Doqqi back then and working at the Qasr al-Nil police station in Garden City on the other side of the river—the east—and, like all the other policemen in East Cairo, I stopped going to work. West Cairo and its sprawling hinterland didn't seem to be of the slightest concern to the Knights.

For all that time, the word 'occupation' was never once glimpsed in the papers. It was never heard.

Very strange, that. I mean the journalists' ready acceptance of the occupier and the fact that they put up no resistance. Everyone acted like the whole affair was forgotten and went on with their daily lives—cooperating with the Knights of Malta's traffic patrols in the occupied cities and waiting obediently in queues for long minutes while their licenses were checked and ID documents perused—and then, two months in, the military ruler declared the Egyptian courts open for business once more. The news was met with great acclamation and was widely regarded as Maltese recognition of the splendor of the ever-splendid judiciary. The prosecutor's office treated the Knights as it had once done the Egyptian police, as the authority that maintains order and brings cases to court, and as keepers of the peace, and the judiciary treated them in the same way. The Knights of Malta, it appeared, were considerably more competent than we were and, truth be told, the Interior Ministry's performance had reached its lowest ebb some time before. People had stopped making complaints and had come to accept the thefts and kidnappings with equanimity—after a while, there was nothing left to steal or anyone worth snatching. Maybe that was why the Knights of Malta's task proved so very easy.

Nine months of calm, and then Colonel Mohamed Ahmed Abdallah was appointed minister of the interior. Colonel Abdallah had formerly been deputy minister in charge of prisons. In his acceptance speech, having first taken the oath before Field Marshal Paul-Pierre Genevieve, he invited all former employees of the ministry to return to work, asking that they conduct themselves irreproachably and set the interests of the citizens above all others. A most moving speech.

At once, a media campaign got underway, demanding that the men of the Interior Ministry return to their posts in order to serve the homeland and its citizens. The press, yet to use the word 'occupation,' came out in support of the minister. Much was penned about the 'majesty of the state,' fallen into decline since the police had gone on strike, about our responsibility toward the country in which we lived, about lifting the burden from the shoulders of the Maltese armies, who were sacrificing much to safeguard security within Egypt's borders when their real job was to secure them against foreign aggressors. There were calls for the next Police Day—25 January 2024—to be the date they went back to work, and the campaign was dubbed 'The Police Return on Their Feast Day,' but it never spread beyond the confines of the papers and television. There was no sign of support for their return on the streets—not the slightest interest in what was happening.

Sure enough, on 25 January 2024, Maltese troops handed control of police stations and security directorates, as well as the ministry building itself, back into the hands of the Interior Ministry.

I was at a crossroads, with two clear choices: return to work under the occupier or refuse to countenance the idea, as I had done all along. Up until then I'd been receiving my salary as usual, and of course giving up the job for good would have entailed a major dent in my finances, for in the normal course of events a police officer has no income save his salary and I myself truly had no other.

Things were still pretty much stable. Of course, Cairo was full of the checkpoints set up by the Knights. Their soldiers spoke Arabic like Tunisians, and English in many different dialects, and they and the inhabitants got by one way or another. As I saw it, we had sunk as low as it gets, content with a bunch of mercenaries as our occupiers and with no hope of getting rid of them. Just shy of half a million men from various countries, all of them now citizens of the Republic of the Knights of Malta, and we, all pride set aside, were welcoming them as guests into our country.

This republic had no territory to its name. What history it possessed went back to the remnants of that crusading order which had taken control of Malta and then been expelled, leaving it in limbo until it adopted Rome as its headquarters. A state without citizens, just twenty thousand affiliates and four hundred thousand members. . . . And then, just prior to March 2023, the whole lot, members and affiliates alike, became citizens of the Republic of the Knights of Malta: the bureaucrats, officers, and soldiers of many nations now a mighty and many-branched fighting force.

Their leadership determined that Egypt was a land where they could all settle down, and so they set out, sailing from points all over the globe to battleships and aircraft carriers moored off the Egyptian coast. It could be that the nations of the world had encouraged them to do so, to bring an end to the hollow bluster and stupidity with which Egypt had long conducted its international relations. The republic was a state without a political or administrative system, just two vast, highly trained armies drawn from a range of ethnicities and nationalities. Land pirates, to use a choicer term, and landless, so patriotism never featured in their thoughts: they'd chosen to leave their countries behind them and settle here.

I gave a lot of thought to what had happened and was convinced that they had known we wouldn't resist. And, of course, that they'd be able to beat the Egyptian army outright. That accomplished, the rest was just a jaunt through a fertile land, green and populous.

I refused to work. Something beyond all understanding was taking place around me. A serene madness afflicted Egyptians, allowing them to accept everything which had happened in recent months, and the same madness claimed the police. I'd do anything, I decided, but I'd never work for the occupier. Even as the majority of my former colleagues were going back to their posts, and stations, and salaries, dissenters such as myself were almost too few to mention. Maybe no more than a thousand officers. I was in about as bad a state as could be when a Maltese armored car was blown up on Ramses Street. An hour after the explosion, the Egyptian resistance announced that this was its first operation and would not be its last. I realized then that I was not alone.

The pace picked up thereafter. The resistance carried out assassinations of occupation soldiers, blew up their armored cars and tanks, mortared their bases, and launched missiles at their jets. In the space of a week, more than one hundred Maltese officers and soldiers lay dead, and at the end of it I received a call from an old colleague asking to meet up. The request was friendly, and down the line his voice seemed devoid of enthusiasm or excitement. Sitting at the café surrounded by people, Major Karim Bahaa al-Din asked me to join the resistance. Just like that, simple as could be, and I wasted no time making my delight clear and accepting his offer. What Bahaa then said was truly gratifying: the resistance was made up of former police officers plus a very small number of former army men, who were not kept fully informed and were regarded as second-class members, entrusted only with suicide missions or high-risk operations. There was, in addition, an even smaller number of civilians, prompted by patriotic fervor

33

to carry out foolish but nonetheless effective acts with the aim of ending the occupation. They spied or passed on information, that was all. They didn't know the police officers, the names of the leaders, or the meeting places, and they weren't armed, though any one of them who wanted to volunteer was handed a blade and let loose on the enemy. Set up like this, the Egyptian resistance was our paradise: a perfect instance of the Egyptian police service's acumen, its members' devotion to the service of their homeland, and their wary reluctance to bring outsiders into their circle, even if they were true patriots and loathed the occupation, as many regular citizens surely did. We all knew the reasons—the uncountably many reasons—why we alone should occupy the most important positions inside the resistance. For instance, civilians are essentially weak, they prefer their little families and trifling pleasures, and they aren't trained to use weapons, to work in groups, or to take responsibility. Even when they are—like army officers, for example—they inevitably lack the ability to think clearly in a tight spot. Karim said that the army guys had developed this limitless, suicidal bravery, its source their shameful defeat and a desire to compensate for their grave sin against the nation. They were in a continual and incurable state of torment, he said, and they were prepared to kill themselves in the cause of wounding a single occupation soldier. That seemed right and proper, and I reflected that by the time the occupation was over—and I'd no idea when that would be—we would have got rid of all of them. In the end, who wants the army to run the country again?

The resistance belonged to us, and to us alone: a huge organization run by the cream of the cops, whose first and only purpose was to expel the occupier. The fact is, I couldn't have cared less about the army officers. They were finished the first day of the occupation, and they'd stay that way unless we said otherwise. What bothered me was the credulousness of the civilians in our ranks. From a colleague of mine, I learned that

34

they were just throwing their lives away, and it was only when I saw that the overwhelming majority of Egyptians were living under occupation in perfect contentment that I felt sympathy for them—there are people who still care about this country, I told myself.

Following this first encounter, another colleague asked to meet me. A brigadier general this time. I didn't recognize him and I hadn't ever heard his name, and I even had my doubts about whether he was an officer at all, but my fears vanished when I saw him walking over to where I sat in the restaurant in Heliopolis. He moved very slowly, as befits an officer whose mind is busy with thinking, not with throwing his body around. This was how a brigadier general walked, and this was how he sat, and no sooner was he sitting, in fact, than he told me his name and a little about the work he'd done with the Interior Ministry. Brigadier General Adel al-Shawarebi, a mid-ranking figure in the leadership of the resistance, who despite his poker face and dead eyes warmed up considerably after just five minutes of conversation, as though he'd been waiting to get comfortable with me just as I had been with him. We talked a lot about the state of the country and when I voiced my surprise at how long the occupation had lasted and the resistance's almost total invisibility, he said that this was infinitely preferable to getting civilians involved: their abstention would only emphasize the role we played in military operations inside the cities. We were currently engaged in a guerrilla war, he said, and no one was better suited to that than us. I interrupted to tell him that my sole condition for signing up was that this structure be preserved unchanged: police officers at the center and army officers and civilians on the periphery and powerless. He laughed and said, "If only the civilians cared!" and that the leadership couldn't involve them even if it really wanted to. The real problem was the army officers, which was why they were taking care to dispose of them through high-risk operations. This tactic would never

35

change, and it seemed that the army officers themselves were well aware that this policy was being applied to them and to them alone, and that moreover they appeared to be perfectly satisfied with the arrangement. "In the end, we're at war, and in any war there are casualties. Why shouldn't those casualties come from the side that lost us the country in the first place?"

His words put me at my ease. Then he told me that they wanted me as a sniper. I mustn't take too long making my mind up and I would begin work in short order.

I thought back to my time as a sniper with the Airport Police and Public Protection Authority. For ten years, I'd held that rifle, gazing out at the world through scopes for hours on end, and after a brief struggle had surrendered to the temptation to spy on people. And I'd shot four of them.

"We know you never miss," said Colonel Adel.

And really, I never had. Even after leaving Public Protection and going to work for other branches of the service, such as homicide, I'd never missed. I'd practice out in the desert east of Cairo and from time to time go off to Sinai "to hunt gazelles." I'd never aimed at the gazelles—I would zero in on the black rocks that covered the open ground. Hunting gazelles I regarded as beneath a man who'd hunted men; stones were more honorable by far. My companions on the first hunting expedition made fun of me, but they quickly realized I couldn't be screwing up every time and that I must be deliberately leaving the gazelles be. Even in Sinai, I'd never fired wide.

I remembered the long vigils: the stillness that comes while waiting for a viable target to appear, reporting in that a target was available, waiting the few moments for the green light to be given, the stillness of the instant that followed, and the bullet vanishing into the target. I'd always had my breathing under control. Never had to puff and pant to pull in more oxygen. My throat never dried up. Adrenalin never surged through my veins. Aiming and firing as easily as running a hand through my hair. Glorious memories, for sure.

36

I agreed on the spot, and made it clear I was ready to go to work without any conditions or reservations. The only difficulty was that I didn't own a weapon at present and the resistance would have to provide me with rifle and scope. He smiled and said that this was not a problem.

In the six months that followed, I killed many people, many more than I'd killed as an officer of the Interior Ministry. Previously, the people I'd shot had been attempting to force their way into the places I protected, or trying to assassinate or assault the people I guarded. Simple, clean operations with no complications. As a key operative in these missions, I had known exactly what was what: waiting for my orders in accordance with standard procedure, firing the bullet that kept the person I was protecting safe. Working for the resistance, everything was different.

The risk was far greater. I was exposed to enemy fire at all times, at risk of arrest and trial for murder, or for resisting the authorities, or for being in possession of an unlicensed firearm. Joining the resistance was patriotic, but it was against the law, and murder was a crime as it had always been. But it was necessary to get rid of the occupier.

I took up positions on rooftops all over the city, until I came to know the features of each roof and flight of stairs by heart. I used many versions of my beloved Dragunovs, from advanced Romanian models to perfect Chinese-made imitations, and for several days I worked with one particularly beautiful Russian variant. In the six months before I climbed the tower, my darling Dragunov was my constant companion.

For those six months, I killed officers and soldiers from the twin armies of occupation, and I killed those who collaborated with them: Egyptian policemen, former Egyptian army officers, government workers, and ministers.

I killed the minister of culture as he left an art exhibition in Garden City. I was set up in the building where the exhibition was being held and I watched him emerge, bid goodbye

37

to the artists, and get into his car. I let the car move off down the street, then fired three shots, the first passing through his head, and the second and third penetrating the back seat and lodging in his body. I hit the minister of the environment with a shot to the head from a standing stance. The rifle was resting on a parked car in the street outside his residence. I fired the bullet, dropped the rifle, and calmly walked out of the street. No one gave me a second glance. The resistance was at its strongest back then, and no one dared look me in the face. I killed civilians, those who had regular dealings with the occupation soldiers: heads of companies and institutions that provided them with food and equipment. They had the wherewithal to provide protection for themselves and their families, and assassinating them had become all but impossible without a sniper's rifle. I killed lots of them. I killed an officer after he had taken a first and last sip of coffee, and I killed the waiter who set the cup before him. The waiter remained frozen in place for several seconds after the bullet struck the officer; he must have known the next one was for him. I accidentally killed a civilian when I shot an officer and a round passed through his chest and hit the man in the thigh. I saw his thigh bleeding heavily, and I saw him crawling in an effort to escape, and I knew he would die from loss of blood. I killed the Egyptian wife of the commander of the Cairo Military Zone. I killed her as she stood there at a public gathering to receive guests' good wishes for her honeymoon and a happy marriage. I shot her in the head from a building at a distance of less than twenty meters, and at first no one realized what had happened, so I went on firing and killed five people I didn't know, then shot at random into the crowd. I killed a total of twenty individuals that day. I killed the former Egyptian chief of staff, the man who'd been responsible for the Egyptian army, the very army that had been wiped from the face of the earth in accordance with a precisely executed plan. Planes, tanks, armored cars, troop carriers, trucks—anything with an engine was destroyed on the first day while this fellow sat at his desk trying to get through to the Americans and failing. Pissing his military pants, no doubt, as reports came through of the army's rapid collapse, and no one picking up. It had been 1967 all over again. A grim day. I was going to shoot him in the head as he walked his granddaughter to school but I shot out his liver instead, leaving his granddaughter bent over him, trying to stanch the bleeding with her hand. I fired on anyone who approached to try to assist them and I fired on the first ambulance to reach the scene a full hour later. The man was dead by then and his granddaughter had stopped crying and was now staring at his bloody body, the sticky softness of the gore beneath her fingernails lubricating the palm with which she rubbed his dead hand. For the duration of that hour, I was at risk of being discovered, killed even, at the very least of being arrested, but the former chief of staff deserved the torment of blood loss, of the heat leaving his limbs, and the sight of the fear in his granddaughter's eyes, of the final spasm. I was tormenting the man and I was happy.

These were months of sprinting, climbing stairs, leaping away over rooftops, and of weighing up situations. Should I leave the rifle or carry it with me as I make my escape? Will the pedestrians notice me? Will an occupation soldier shoot at me? Do I really have to kill this one, or is it pointless? Is killing this one a punishment or a message?

In my power to kill people there was a measure of the divine.

3

I WAS APPROACHED BY A young man smelling of soap—he seemed to me to have just had a bath and shaved—and gripping a long-barreled shotgun of local manufacture in his two clean hands. His nails were carefully clipped and filed. I looked like a beggar by comparison: I reeked of sweat, my clothes were filthy, and my hands were smeared with the soil I'd dug up not long before.

For those like me with no papers, the inside of the bridge was the only way to move between Cairo's two halves, despite the risks. You could lose your money and your possessions. You could lose your life. But crossing over the bridge was impossible. For me, the checkpoints were traps. And the toll down here wasn't high: just a single pack of cigarettes. Cheap to them and cheap to me. I was going to cross as a regular citizen. They had no idea I was with the resistance, and I couldn't tell if they were with the resistance or just thugs protecting their source of income. I was carrying nothing of any value and the journey was a very short one, just a kilometer or so through the bridge.

Calmly, the young man said:

"Price of entry is one unopened packet of cigarettes. No weapons here. If you're carrying a weapon, chuck it down that hole, now. No talking to the pedestrians and no looking at their faces. If you're carrying a mask, then put it on; otherwise cover your face with a scarf or a sheet of newspaper. If you don't have those, then here's a paper bag you can put over your head. This

41

is for your own protection. Don't reveal your name or identity to any of the pedestrians or vendors, asleep or awake. The inner bridge isn't just a passage like it used to be—it's a place where lots of things are bought and sold. I won't forbid you to buy anything from the vendors, but all purchases are made at your own risk. Don't come to me complaining that you've been robbed or cheated. Now, on your way."

I placed the cigarettes in his hand. I took the mask from my bag, put it on my face, and fastened it to my head with the leather strap. Now I was ready to cross.

The darkness pressed in on every side. Nothing could be seen ahead. To my rear was the youth and the fading scent of his soap, his comrades clustered around him, watching me. With their clubs and short swords, they looked like real guards. What little pale light came from the hole fell across the lower halves of their bodies. I took a few paces forward and distant sounds reached me from the depths of the tunnel. There were scattered gleams of colored light, the rattle of blades and chains.

The first thing I saw was a woman. She looked to be about sixty years old, her features obscured by a piece of cloth wrapped around her face, like a turban covering her entire head. She wore nothing else, and the sagging flesh of her breasts and shoulders gave away her age. Her appearance was overwhelming. The sudden nakedness and the covered face threw me completely off balance. I'd never before seen a naked woman in a public place. Without thinking, I lifted my hand to my own face, checking that the mask was fixed in place. I felt properly secure now. She was stroking her thigh with her palm, and then she squeezed her right tit and in a hoarse, unruffled voice asked: "Five for five?"

I walked on, expecting the worst.

I wouldn't have guessed that the bridge had been built with a tunnel like this inside it: two walls, a floor, and a ceiling, all cement. Vast cables and pipes stretched the length of the tunnel along the ground, clearly visible to the passerby through gaps in the long wooden planks that covered them and that had almost certainly been placed there by those using the tunnel to protect against the risk of electric shock should the cables fray, and in order that the pipes wouldn't spring leaks or break if trodden on. There were a number of shacks on both sides of the passageway, a meter across and two meters high, and over the entrance to each one hung a blackout curtain, blocking what little illumination was given off by the lights that dangled from the tunnel's ceiling. Some of the curtains were lowered, and some were raised to show what lay inside. Curiosity got the better of me. I hadn't laid hands on a woman for a long time, and the warmth of the place and the ever-present sense of danger urged me to stop. Outside what I judged to be the most orderly of the shacks, I halted. There were no pedestrians nearby, and a thin girl sat on a raised chair outside the curtain. In the wan light, her legs looked soft and smooth. Her face was small with regular features, and embellished with the dark red of her lipstick. She wore a light robe whose open neck displayed her throat and cleavage. "Five for five," she said, and though I didn't understand what she meant, I nodded to seal the deal and followed her inside, and she lowered the curtain behind us.

There were pictures of naked women stuck up on the walls. I was standing, looking around, and trying to avoid the girl's eyes. Working rapidly, she undid my belt, tugged down my trousers, took my cock in her mouth, and sucked it until it stiffened. Then she sat me on the mattress and rode me. When I tried removing her robe, she checked my hand, gripped the hem herself, and in a single movement pulled it off to leave herself completely naked before me. She clutched her breasts as she bounced wordlessly around on my cock, and I stared hard at her chest and shoulders, in awe of a sinuous grace I'd not sampled for so long. I squeezed her breasts and she bounced faster, trying to escape my grip, but I wouldn't let go, and lifting my

43

gaze I saw her face clearly for the first time. Her right eye looked wrong, staring off to one side and not moving like the other. She picked up speed and moaned. It was all an act, but because she moved so rapidly, the surface of her dead eye dropped out onto the mattress, revealing a truly damaged orb beneath, and then I realized that it must have been some sort of artificial covering. Stunned, I released her breasts, and she lowered her good eye, then closed it, and now it became clear that the eyelid of her damaged eye was missing or not working; a single gray eye stared out at me, its surface marked by faint crooked lines: a blind eye, unseeing but open wide, its upper lid torn and lashless. She moved closer to hide her face from me and ran her fingers through my hair, and as usual I couldn't sense that I was nearly there, and at that very instant I came.

She got off my lap, retrieved her eye-cap, and returned it to its socket. Then she took a plastic cup and filled it from a bucket in the corner, splashed water over her vagina a couple of times, put on her robe, lifted the curtain, and went out. I was sitting on the mattress, slowly deflating, the sperm drying on my trousers and thighs. I saw blood smeared thickly over my penis, sticky and starting to dry. I had no idea where it had come from, and adolescent nightmares flashed through my mind: had she stuck a razor up herself? But what had happened was more a cause for disgust than fear. She was menstruating. Someone walked by the shack and paused for a moment to peer in beneath the raised curtain, and I saw his eyes smiling behind his mask. An Ismail Yassin mask. The narrow brow, thick lips, big teeth, and broad grin gave it away. I was still wearing mine. I was safe. I quickly got up, straightened out my clothes without wiping away the sperm or blood, and emerged to find that Ismail Yassin, interested in neither myself nor the girl, had wandered off. Standing outside her shack, she called out to me, "That's three for three, then," and I stood there, trying to work out what she meant. I stared at her breasts beneath the robe and grew flustered: I wanted

44

another grope, but the thought of the blood held me back. "Come on!" she said, "Three minutes for three pounds!"

I passed by many whores, none prettier than the menstruating girl. Though one-eyed, she was the most beautiful of the lot. Next time, I'd make sure to wear a condom. She might have some disease, I fretted, AIDS maybe, and I wondered if I'd been infected.

I walked for ages. I heard the sound of cars overhead. On this section of the bridge, the cars could speed along with no checkpoints to stop or slow them down. I thought back to before the occupation, to those endless hours stuck in traffic on the October 6th Bridge. I'd look around at dozens of others waiting just like me, would watch them staring straight ahead with no purpose in mind. There was no waiting now. The number of cars passing between the two halves of Cairo had declined dramatically, and even with the checkpoints holding it up the traffic didn't grind to a halt as it used to.

Contrary to the dire warnings of the guard by the tunnel's entrance, the place was perfectly safe, and my mask kept me at a remove from those around me. They were selling all kinds of contraband down here: hash and weed, white pills and colored pills in all shapes and sizes laid out on low tables, bottles of cheap booze, small plastic bags of fermented bouza, imported porn mags. There were no shacks for prostitution in this section. This was the tunnel's commercial center. Business was more respectable here.

The further I walked, the fewer vendors there were, until I reached a section where there were no vendors and no whores, just pedestrians like myself. All the faces were covered with masks, or paper bags, or the tail of a headscarf. A few, as I did, wore specially made masks, and these people were somehow different, as though their masks were not really hiding who they were. Wearing the same easily recognizable mask all the time is essentially pointless: you swap your face for your mask, and it becomes part of your identity.

45

My first steps in Cairo for two years. The time I had spent in the tower had left me cut off from the latest developments. When had wearing masks become a normal thing to do? Or was it just because we were walking through the bridge?

Vendors reappeared, this time hawking little pharaonic statues, which were—it goes without saying—forgeries, though they insisted they were authentic. I overheard one man arguing with a potential customer, trying to convince him that a stone head was real.

Toys next: dolls, and cars, and colored balls. I had assumed the tunnel would be a marketplace for contraband, but almost anything could be sold here, it seemed. When I saw white underwear laid out on the ground, I remembered my unwashed cock.

The tunnel narrowed. I heard someone tell his friend that they were very near the exit, and minutes later daylight could be seen filtering palely through a square hole in the floor. It was like the place was upside down, lit by windows in the floor rather than in the walls or ceiling. For a moment, I forgot that I was walking in a tunnel suspended in the air.

I lowered myself down through the square opening and was assailed by the din of cars and crowds, and an overpowering stench of urine. The ladder was attached to a column against which people were wont to empty their bladders, and over the years the urine had formed a vast black stain that reached halfway up the concrete stem and spread further still over the ground. The stain was dry—I didn't see it glistening as liquid would—but it gave off an intolerable smell. This, together with the various sights of a man eating a round of bread, drool coursing down his chin, a fellow clearing his nose down in the street, and a third guy gripping a short sword and brandishing it threateningly at the passersby, brought the bile into my throat and I puked. I was in Galaa Street, in the neighborhood they call Isaaf.

I walked along slowly, trying to get out from under the bridge to where there was air to breathe. I could see the bright

46

sunlight striking July 26th Street and I wanted to reach the intersection between July 26th and Ramses before I lost consciousness. I had to meet someone there. It was nearly 10 a.m. now. I'd be there in five minutes, no more.

An old man stopped me. He was naked and barefoot, his legs so grimy that his toes could hardly be made out through the blackened filth, and he muttered inaudibly, spittle running down into his beard. He looked at me and whispered in terror, "We are all dead. We are all in torment." I held his gaze for a while, then went on.

For five minutes I loitered outside the Isaaf Pharmacy and then a woman wearing a niqab approached me and asked, "Otared?" I was silent for a few seconds before I replied. She nodded and walked off, and I followed her, feeling hopeful. I was afraid to look back at what I'd left behind.

She walked down July 26th Street toward Downtown. It was at its most crowded and there was no space to move on the sidewalk, but she made her way through the throng as though she were used to it. I tried getting past people by shoving them or dodging. They divided into those who held you up by dawdling and those who were advancing in the opposite direction. The vendors set up on either side occupied a sizeable chunk of the sidewalk, and the space left for pedestrians had narrowed to less than a meter. I couldn't see the woman clearly and I trailed her at a distance, forever trying to get closer through the pressing crowd.

Then the sidewalk widened a touch, the crowds thinned out, and I drew up alongside her. I asked where we were going and she didn't reply. She walked until we came to Ataba Square, went on to al-Azhar Street, and took a side street, then began turning down alleys of diminishing size until, though close behind her, I almost lost my way.

This was my first time out and about in Cairo for a long time. No changes worth mentioning to the apartment blocks and buildings. The cars were the same and the crowds no

47

smaller. But the people were less familiar. Incessant cries rent the air. Squabbles were breaking out in every street, outside every shop, a stream of insults let loose to amuse, to humiliate, to threaten. Fights with fists and knife thrusts. I counted four men puking on the pavement, then stopped counting. I saw someone lying on the ground, blood running out from beneath him. No one went over to cover his body. Back in the day, someone would borrow a newspaper and cover the body with it, holding it down with small stones around the edges, and any blood there was would be enough to stick the paper to the corpse. Now they left the dead body exposed to all and sundry.

The woman climbed the stairs of an old building and opened the door of an apartment on the first floor. In we went. The niqab was removed to reveal a man with a pencil mustache. He lit a cigarette and said, "Won't you remove your mask?" I'd grown used to looking through the narrow eye slits and to the mask's weight on my face. I lifted it off, and my sense of security disappeared, and the fear came back, but I didn't let go of it. I clung to the only protection I had here. Up in the tower, I'd been safe. Now I was out in the open. The man peered into my face for a moment and settled onto a chair. I sat facing him and, seeing no reason not to, put the mask back on. I was a regular civilian now. I'd left the Interior Ministry a while ago and nobody had my back. Everyone I knew there had either left, or died, or joined the resistance, and anyone who'd stayed on as an officer was my enemy, no doubt about it. I was in danger, therefore, and my mask was my only protection. Though I was currently in a safe house belonging to the resistance and sitting with one of their communications officers, the sex change trick he'd played made me wary.

He smiled. "Someone will drop in on you tonight to give you a message and a date. There's an important meeting taking place and you should be there. People like yourself are thin on the ground these days, and maybe you don't realize how vital

48

you are. You can leave now if you'd like, but you must be back before midnight. And whatever happens, hide in the crowds if an officer should ask to see your ID. Kill him if you must. Technically speaking, you're a dead man. After all, you've killed a lot of people in the past few months and, who knows, you might be killing more quite soon. Police officers these days are traitors, as you're aware, so there's nothing to hold you back."

I had no idea if the man sitting before me was an officer or not. The era of proud and upright officers was past, and so much brass had been stripped from shoulder boards it was no wonder people's backs were bowed. Most likely his role in the resistance was to pass on times and dates, to meet people and escort them to safe houses, but he would have no experience with weapons, or explosives, or real police work. He rose, said goodbye, and left.

I was exhausted. Wandering through the apartment, I came across a big, clean bed in one of the rooms, and I stretched out on it and immediately relaxed. In minutes, I had surrendered to sleep. For a brief instant, I thought of the semen and the blood. I wanted to get up and wash after my draining journey, but I was already going under.

I was shaving with an electric razor. I'd used one before—ten years ago perhaps—and hadn't liked it much. Now I could hear that familiar metallic whine, but I couldn't feel it buzzing against my skin. Ten years ago, I'd been in a room in a hotel, whose name I couldn't recall, in Berlin. Well, I wasn't in Berlin now. Ten years ago, I'd visited the place, bought an electric razor in the street, and when I'd got back to my hotel room and tried it I hadn't been impressed. Now, though, I was in Cairo, it was 2025, and I was sleeping in a small room in a strange apartment. I was asleep and, if I wanted to be rid of the razor's whine, I must wake up.

Suspended in midair was the smallest drone I'd ever come across, slightly smaller than an unfurled hand and hovering motionless by the ceiling. Six slender articulated legs hung down from the gleaming black body, and above it two huge black wings spread out—or rather, not wings exactly, but two hard casings under which the wings hummed. I was still sprawled out on the bed, so I sat up and serenely the drone drew closer. Its low whine was what had woken me and I realized how accustomed I had become to the absolute peace and quiet on the top floor of the tower. Accustomed to sleeping undisturbed. The drone landed beside me on the bed. For a few seconds, as the four translucent wings performed a few last upward flicks, the casings stayed raised, then they settled back flush with the body. I picked up the drone. It was very light, under a hundred grams, I guessed, or maybe less. Less than fifty, even. Astonishingly light and precisely engineered, and because it was a beetle—a scarab to be exact—I was instantly fond of it. I have a strange partiality for insects; an appreciation for the way they move and work, perhaps, for their ability to hold their own against humans. I turned it over, searching for a message and considering how I could keep hold of it. But I'd break it for sure if I kept it with me. This was no rugged weapon like my rifle, which could withstand being shunted around, neglected, and abused, and nor was it my mask, which had been scratched and marked in many places but remained solid and robust. This was a fragile toy, quite unsuitable for a man so disorganized and careless as I was. On the drone's underside, I found a little button. I pressed it and a hatch opened to reveal a small hollow in the belly. In the hollow, I found a sheet of paper. I took the paper, closed the hatch, and placed the drone back on the bed.

The message gave the address of an apartment in Abdeen, a time, and nothing else. I didn't spend much time worrying over this unanticipated terseness—I'd been waiting for a message and here it was, with all the information I required. I had to be there at 7 p.m. and it was now 4. Three hours were enough to wash and get over to Abdeen.

50

The drone started moving on the bed, skillfully scaling the rumpled covers. I hemmed it in using my leg, the pillow, and the wrinkles in the bed sheets. With a pair of hair-thin antennae, it felt out the slope of the pillow, tested a wrinkle, then approached my leg. And without any hesitation at all, it climbed up onto my knee, changed direction, and crossed over my knee onto my thigh. There it paused, neatly cocking its head toward my face, and started to dance. Was it aware that I was testing and teasing it? I knew drones were intelligent enough to move and fly, to make it past obstacles and reach their targets, but anything more was beyond the capabilities of a basic model, let alone interacting with its controllers like a pet. And even if this drone could act like a pet, I wasn't its controller.

Scarabs are amazing insects, I think, and drones are more amazing still: they use hardly any power, they're minuscule, and all their complexity stays hidden away beneath their metallic shell. In my opinion, mankind's first truly creative act was to build these drones. My little scarab tapped my thigh with its two back legs, flipped once in the air, then settled back down on my leg. It was showing off to me. It flipped again, spread its wings, and hovered there, perfectly balanced.

A little performance for Mr. Otared.

I went into the bathroom and closed the door. Cold water, and not a trace of soap in the apartment. I stood beneath the shower for a few minutes, then dressed in the same clothes I'd been wearing. Outside, the drone hovered right in front of the bathroom door as though waiting for me, and as I emerged a thought occurred: was it watching me? And just like that, the happy moments I'd spent in its company were wiped out. I was being watched, then, and I couldn't do a thing about it. Of course, I could smash it, but if I did that, then the meeting would be cancelled and my association with the resistance would be over. I knew there was someone watching me, and the person watching me knew that I knew it. There was nothing to be done. If the watcher was a cop, then he had to know that I'd be suspicious of the drone. Maybe he was some callow operative from the resistance, a new recruit, or maybe he was an experienced officer who just wanted to let me know that he could get to me. Message received, in any case. From now on, I'd adopt the standard wooden expression: no flare-ups of any kind. The drone flipped in midair whenever I looked at it. It wanted to impress me. What irritated me was that I had initially been taken in by its games. My sixth sense had deserted me and I'd only realized what it was long after it had arrived.

Sooner or later, man will construct drones like this one not to serve him, not to cook for him, not to drive his car—nor will they become our masters, for that's just the naive science fiction of crass filmmaking—but rather to worship us. There will be drones ready-made to be raped to keep the rapists busy, and others configured to resist. Configured with voices that scream and plead. We will beat them, and they will weep, and the drones' owners will string them up on lampposts to flog and torture them. We'll set fire to them, perhaps, as punishment for things they didn't do. We'll catch the smell of roasting flesh, pumped out of special compartments in their sides, and even better, we'll be able to program them to beat us and turn us on. To rape us, perhaps, so we can sample the delicious agony of our orifices being violently abused, enjoy the strokes of a whip wielded across our backs by a mechanical arm, and then . . . then, we'll shower and dress like civilized men and women, and walk the streets, toting our robot rapists in little bags.

6 p.m. The number of people on the street not less but more; likewise the number of occupation army drones in Ataba and Opera squares. The sheer quantity of checkpoints made it impossible to walk through Downtown, and so I crossed Opera Square in the direction of Gumhuriya Street on my way to Abdeen. The statue of Ibrahim Pasha was still disfigured—its head had been stolen at the start of the

52

occupation—and if anything its lower half looked as if it was getting smaller by the day. They said people stole bits by night, would climb a ladder with a saw and cut. Tiring work, but the statue seemed to invite theft. Ibrahim Pasha pointing out at the horizon. We had cut off his head, and hand, and arm, and we wouldn't stop until we'd done away with the whole thing, down to the horse's hooves. We wouldn't leave a single atom on that plinth.

A huge balloon bobbed over the statue, and midway up the rope that anchored it a gigantic advertising board was swaying in the wind. I couldn't make it out at first, but looking closer I saw it was an advert for a television show. *Tomorrow: Hope.* Just reading the title told me everything I needed to know. Shows like this one had been common currency for at least twenty years, all of them talking about Hope and Tomorrow, Tomorrow and Hope, the Tomorrow that lies in Hope, or Hope in Tomorrow, and then the cycle would start over and we'd be back to a show about Hope and Tomorrow. Even after the death of Hope's biggest huckster—the author of hundreds of books on self-help, positivity, and the like—from the inconceivably vicious double-whammy of AIDS and bone cancer, people still looked to Tomorrow with Hope. Which is why rapist drones were the solution.

I walked down Gumhuriya Street, a little calmer than the square behind me and less crowded than Downtown's interlocking grid. Then, without warning, something flew up behind me, whizzed over my right shoulder, and came to a halt in midair about a meter in front of my face. Another drone? No, it was the same one I'd left at the apartment. Maybe it had followed me all the way, or maybe it had been looking for me and had only just found me. It hovered in front of me as though asking permission to come along. Had drones become sentient? Fine. I had no objection to being watched. I just wanted to go on my way, that was all. I nodded, signaling my consent that it accompany me. *Let's see if it understands. . . .*

53

What happened next was genuinely extraordinary: it flipped three times in the air, completed a single circuit around me, and came to rest on my right shoulder. I walked on. It was so light I could hardly feel it was there.

I gave passersby the name of the street and building number, and got directions off several of them. They all described the same route, but I asked more than one to make sure. Three in a row gave me a shortcut. At last, I found myself in a small alley that terminated at a small building; an alley branching off a wider street and containing no shops or large buildings, but squat residential blocks, none more than three stories high. 6.45 p.m. I wouldn't go up until the exact time. I'd wait in the dark for fifteen minutes. I'm the king of waiting.

The choice of the building at the far end of the narrow alley suggested extreme stupidity. This was a trap, not a safe place to meet. Who was going to escape from a building like that if the police raided? The alley was perfectly still and silent, the ideal setting to sniff glue and inject, a place for streetwalkers.

The scarab flew off my shoulder, made for the streetlight, and hovered beneath it for a moment.

A man was hoisting up a naked leg and pressing its owner against the wall of one of the buildings, pushing her body into the wall, his trousers and underwear slipping down off his bare ass, jabbing her repeatedly with his cock, as she held her face up and away from his panting breath and gazed nervously at the alley's distant entrance. What they call a quickie. I hunt in places where dirty deeds are done.

He finished up in no time and the whore started adjusting her clothes, taking two steps backward into the circle of light beneath the streetlamp. She had taken off one trouser leg to make it easier for the man, and now she was trying to put it back on again. The man pissed against the wall and shook his cock. But where was the cash? Could you get one for one, as well? Was there new slang for the trade? I don't know why I was so bothered, so angry. Was prostitution going to put paid to my dreams of a happy future? Was Ahmed Otared rediscovering his high moral principles after one quick tour through the streets of Cairo? The drone returned to my shoulder, but this time did not keep still and crawled slowly across my collarbone. Tell me, dear drone, if you'd be so kind: does my anger come from my Hope in Tomorrow?

So far, the man and woman had been silent—and I had held my tongue, too, hoping to watch undiscovered for as long as possible, if only for the sake of a little entertainment and to kill time. For some reason, she slapped him, the sound of the slap ringing out into the emptiness, and he responded in kind, a violent blow that gave off a muffled report. Suddenly, the drone fell still, as though it were listening or watching, but I was distracted from the drone by what the man and woman were doing. She was scratching his face with her nails, and he began to punch her hard. At last, he managed to get her off him, at which she picked her bag off the ground and started rummaging around inside, searching for something. As she did so, he advanced toward her nervously and jabbed her in the arm with a short-bladed knife. There were no screams. His face was bleeding, and she took the knife thrust in complete silence. He backed off a couple of paces as she took what looked like a small handgun from her bag. At a glance, I could tell it was a weapon made here in Egypt, a basic zip gun, knocked up by a metalworker in his workshop to no blueprint, and untested—conceivably one of just ten that he'd put together and sold to anyone wanting a small, cheap, unlicensed firearm. The barrel being brandished in the man's face had kinks that were clearly visible even in that wan light. The weapon bucked gently in her hand and little holes spread over the man's face, and chest, and the wall he'd been pissing against earlier. A shotgun cartridge, then. Usually not fatal, but at such close range it just might be. Would certainly take out an eye if a pellet hit it. The man held himself together, didn't cry out, and she took another cartridge out of her bag

55

and tried feeding it into the barrel. He came closer, apparently able to see only some of what was taking place in front of him. With his left hand, he grabbed the zip gun and tried to wrench it from her grasp. His right hand was out of my line of sight, but eventually he managed to pull his knife out of the woman's arm and started stabbing her hysterically in the face. At the fifth or sixth blow, the woman dropped to the ground. She had reloaded by now, and this time she extended her arm and brought the muzzle right up to the man's body. There were about ten centimeters between the mouth of the barrel and his crotch when she pulled the trigger. The man jerked upright and his trousers caught fire, a pale flame licking up where the shot had gone in. The pellets had clearly hit a major artery, because I could see he was bleeding heavily and hear the sound of the blood splashing onto the asphalt. He kicked her a few times, then brought the knife up to her neck and started cutting. A few moments passed, then a fountain of blood spurted out over her head and hair. The pair of them were now indistinguishable from one another, their features obscured by the blood and wounds that covered their faces. She had loaded the gun a third time and now she lifted it up to the man's face and inserted the barrel into his mouth. The man didn't try to move his head away. He could have done, but he was too busy sawing at her neck. For a few seconds, the woman held the pose, arm raised in the air as the man worked away at her throat. Then, finally, she fired.

The drone flew off my shoulder and went over to where the two bodies lay locked together, then returned and, dancing in front of my face, inviting me to follow, made for the door of the building where the meeting was to be held and smoothly passed inside.

It was 7 p.m. I entered the building and calmly climbed the stairs.

4

ONE EVENING, I'D RECEIVED A message informing us that a technician would be coming to produce a mask for each of us. He would be at the tower in no more than two hours. The message requested that we be clean-shaven for the cast to be taken.

At first I didn't understand what was being asked of us. True, we carried out our orders to the letter, as though we were still officers with the Interior Ministry, but what did masks have to do with the task at hand? The whole thing was absurd.

The technician asked me to lie down on the floor and placed two thin tubes in my nostrils. He covered my head, my hair, and my neck, then poured a cold, damp paste over my face, waited a few minutes for the paste to dry, and lifted the mold. Inspecting the inside of the mold, he told me that this wouldn't be the final one, that he would make another mold from which to cast the mask. I was on my way to the bathroom when he asked what design I'd like. "Hold on," I said, "Let me think about it."

We had treated the business with the masks as extracurricular entertainment—something frivolous but fun. Our unusual situation meant we welcomed any distractions at all, but I was considering motivations greater and more profound than providing distractions to the troops; the leadership had some undeclared objective in all this. I held my counsel and told myself we'd find it all out soon enough.

When I went back in, the technician had finished making molds for everybody. They had also chosen faces for their masks. All had gone for comic actors. One had picked Fuad al-Mohandis and had asked for the actor's famous black-framed spectacles to be added as well. As I thought about what I'd like, the face of Buddha floated before my eyes.

If it was a memory, it was a very obscure one. I couldn't recall having seen the face anywhere before. A picture of him in a magazine or newspaper, perhaps? Maybe I'd watched a documentary about him. In my mind, Buddha was associated with wisdom, but really I knew nothing about him. Was he a prophet? A god? Did he worship cows? I had no idea why I asked for a Buddha mask. Later, a few people would come to call me Buddha. For some in the resistance, it became my *nom de guerre*, but my personality would be more readily associated with mystery than wisdom. Others would assume that by making this choice I thought myself superior to everyone else—to those who chose celebrities for their masks. I later found out that all the snipers received masks made especially for them by professional sculptors, and learned, too, that this was a privilege granted only to the elite—to those who had killed, or were about to kill, large numbers of people.

When the same technician came back to see me, he took the mask from a wooden case and very carefully handed it over. And as I put it on, and felt the cold metal's touch, and discovered that it didn't fit exactly over my features, I asked him what the point had been of making the mold in the first place, and he said that the purpose of the mold hadn't been to capture every detail of my face, but to get a rough idea of my measurements. "This is a mask of solid metal," he said, "an alloy of aluminum and other lightweight compounds. It's inflexible but affords protection for the face against small fragments of shrapnel."

Mask in his hands, he said, "Don't worry, it will never fit your face exactly. It will never become your face." Well, he had been wrong about that.

For several days, I wore it just a few minutes at a time before taking it off, and then the period I spent masked grew. I would go days with it on, would wear it in place of my face, would forget that I had a face of flesh and blood. I would gaze into the mirror, unconcerned by the sight of my gleaming, immutable metal reflection—knowing that it wouldn't age, that it was immune to changes in the weather and the aging effect of cigarettes. Taking it off every few days to shave, I would become afraid—so afraid to look at my own face while shaving that I had to ask a colleague to do it for me. I'd tremble when I came to bed. Against my will, I would lay it aside and would feel as though I were standing naked before millions. I would put out the light and, masked, walk over to my little bed, and I would not remove it until I was under the covers. And I would lay it beside my head in readiness for when the daylight came. I would put it on the moment I woke. For months on end, I would do this. And then the madness reached its peak, and for a full six weeks I slept with it on.

With time, I came to realize that I wasn't substituting the mask for my face as I'd first thought, but putting a barrier between myself and everyone around me, though they were my colleagues and friends, the people I believed in and trusted most of all. Like me, I saw them go into decline, hanging onto their masks, refusing to take them off for extended periods of time. Once his face had become familiar, I wouldn't smile to see Fuad al-Mohandis. I would develop the strangest ideas about the characters around me. Would completely forget all the conventional associations of those laughing, smiling, frowning masks and would forget, too, the original faces. I would create imaginary faces for their bodies, and whenever we received a group of snipers whose true faces I had never seen—just their masks—their actual personalities wouldn't come into it at all: nothing would stick in my mind but details of those borrowed identities. I would reach a point when featureless masks—with no noses, ears, lips, or eyeholes, just a

59

grille of very fine wires that the wearer could see through while his own eyes remained completely obscured—would leave me in a state of complete bewilderment. We were breaking down without being aware of it, throwing up barriers around us and ensuring they were buttressed and maintained.

It went further. I lost the ability to aim unless I was masked. It happened when I was lining up a target standing by the Maspero building. The officer was waiting for a car to pick him up; it was as rare an opportunity as you could get. According to protocol, I shouldn't have waited or hesitated. We had standing orders to snipe soldiers and officers on sight. I took off the mask to get a clearer look through the scope's narrow, round eyepiece and as I got back into position and searched around for the target I found that he was looking straight at me. The target, at a distance of approximately a kilometer, was staring into my eyes with a defiance that my hands shook to see, and if it hadn't been for the last vestiges of common sense, I'd have assumed he was actually looking at me and that he recognized me. I moved back from the eyepiece in a daze and put on my mask, then looked through the scope to find that the man had turned his face away and was looking at the Nile. Much reassured, I took aim again and fired. I didn't kill him because he was an officer of the occupation, but because I was convinced that he had seen me.

After taking out that target, I never again removed the mask while taking aim. The mask had become the secret to my precision, and maybe, without my realizing it, the secret behind the accuracy of the entire Tower Group.

For days and days, I studied East Cairo from behind my mask. I felt no need to hide behind the scope and heavy rifle. I did not give in to curiosity and inspect all the little details that the scope would let me see. Up here I was immune, protected by height, distance, and my mask. I was an ancient Egyptian god with a borrowed face, whose true features no man could ever know, do what he might. A Greek god, full of contempt for the world that he'd created—killing whomever he chose, deserting whomever he chose, sleeping with whomever he chose, impregnating whomever he chose. And the day a drone came with a message, telling me that my colleagues and I were now free to select targets and snipe without checking back with the leadership, I felt that my divine status had been confirmed, and I told myself that what was to come would fulfill me utterly.

Now I had the green light, the five battleships became easy pickings: close range, immobile, and, should we so desire, quite sinkable. And that was why we ignored them. Long-distance, arbitrary targets in East Cairo were now our main concern, and bulky drones brought us vast quantities of ammunition. We'd abandoned our beloved Dragunovs and now relied exclusively on two models: the McMillan Tac-50 and the Barrett M107. We must have poured thousands of half-inch rounds into East Cairo.

I killed the minister of foreign affairs. I received a message telling me his car would pass along the Corniche within the next quarter of an hour and that it would be stopping at some point between the Semiramis and Maspero. On tenterhooks, I tracked the black Mercedes and, as it sped toward the Maspero building and I realized that it was going to go on without pulling over, I had no choice but to fire five rounds into the vehicle. At last, it did stop, but only thanks to my bullets. Nobody got out. I killed the minister of information. I was watching the outside of the Maspero building through my scope when he stuck his head out of one of the windows, chattering away on his cell phone. A happy coincidence indeed. I don't think it was more than three seconds between my spotting him and opening fire. I killed what could have been a general from the Fourth Army of the Knights of Malta who drove past in his armored car and got out to inspect a checkpoint. His mustache and eyebrows were what got my attention—the mismatch between his salt-and-pepper

61

hair and the lone lieutenant's star on his shoulder. I killed him, and I'm still not totally sure whether or not he was a general in disguise. I killed a former colleague, a major in the police, who was sitting on a balcony at the Semiramis. He was dressed in civilian clothes, slumped beneath an umbrella, drinking beer straight from the bottle and smoking. I recognized his face but couldn't remember his name, just that I'd graduated a few classes ahead of him, and I supposed that if he was relaxing like that on a hotel balcony he must have done well for himself under the occupation. So I shot him.

One hot, listless day, I aimed my rifle in the general direction of Bulaq Abul-Ela and opened fire at random. Three hundred rounds buried themselves in the district's buildings, and I had no idea if I had killed or injured anybody. Then I turned the gun on Tahrir Square and fired through a gap between the twin wrecks of the Nile Hilton and the Arab League. I hit a large number of cars, and buses, and pedestrians until the square had cleared completely, and then I went on firing into the deserted space until my gun jammed.

I didn't stop to consider what I would say to the leaders of the resistance to justify my actions, or to think about the reprimand I'd get. I didn't care about my fellow snipers, standing around unable to understand what I was up to. And when I was done and I turned to face them, I saw only the immobility of their masks, kept on to hide their quaking eyes.

5

EVERYTHING HERE WAS OLD, AND I don't just mean that the furniture and walls had seen twenty years come and go—they were so old and dusty I couldn't tell which era they belonged to. It wouldn't have made much difference if we'd met in a tomb.

There were five of us, including the leader of the resistance, Major General Kamal al-Asyuti. I had met him once before when I'd been an officer at the Interior Ministry and I'd later learned that he was our leader. He looked thinner than I remembered him. His cheekbones jutted, his front teeth stuck out, and his eyes bulged. White hairs outnumbered the black. Then there was his aide, Brigadier General Suleiman Madi. Him I knew well, and I knew his story. He'd been a detective his whole career, had never transferred to another department—the very essence of an officer who dedicates his life to police work and cares for nothing else, not even the standard pastimes of hunting and marksmanship, not even research. Suleiman Madi was a one-dimensional man without dreams, ambitions, or expectations—nothing more or less than a work machine. I'd been astonished to hear that he had not carried on as a cop following the occupation and had chosen to join the resistance, evincing a patriotic zeal quite at odds with his character. Then I had started to notice his methodical fingerprints all over the resistance's actions and the violence meted out to the recruits and officers of the Interior Ministry. The last two officers I didn't know, but the presence of the organization's two most powerful figures gave an indication of this meeting's importance.

We stood, since sitting on the filthy chairs was out of the question, and a lamp on the table illuminated the room and cast its light onto us. The meeting, it seemed, was going to be an ordeal for everyone.

Al-Asyuti spoke first. "So, the drone wasn't lost after all," he said, pointing at my shoulder. Suleiman Madi, the aide, looked over at me and nodded: "We dispatched it to inform you about the meeting but it never returned. We assumed it had been broken or stolen, and we weren't sure if the message had reached you or not. Don't ask me why, but it appears to have become quite attached to you."

Was Madi trying to make a fool of me?

"How can a drone disobey its orders and attach itself to someone?" I asked.

"It rarely happens and then we have to reprogram it to factory settings. It'll operate normally after that. Anyway, we have no choice. Drones are scarce these days."

Al-Asyuti looked around, studying our faces. With a sweep of his hand he said, "Everyone's here. Let's begin."

He appeared to be in a considerable hurry and infirm as well, having trouble holding himself upright. Why I felt sorry for him I don't know. He stared absently at the floor as though searching for something he'd misplaced. To us three, Madi said, "We're missing one officer, but his mission is a little different from yours, so we can start without him. In any case, we have absolute faith in you, just as we do in him."

He turned to me.

"Incidentally, he's in charge of the drones. In a few minutes, he'll be here and he'll take that one off your hands."

For a few moments he was silent, gazing at us each in turn, then: "The resistance has tried everything to drive out the occupier. You know what we've done. You have been our long arm in these operations and not one of those many assassinations

64

would have been possible were it not for your skill and bravery. Civilian casualties were unavoidable and we have never blamed you for them. If anything, perhaps there should have been more. At the end of the day, the occupation is still with us and civilians are going to have to make more sacrifices. Why shouldn't we become that land of five million martyrs?"

Smiles appeared on everyone's faces. Al-Asyuti remained completely silent, completely preoccupied—with us in body, but his mind elsewhere.

Madi went on: "You're the cream of the resistance snipers, and the mission to come will be the hardest any of you have undertaken. By hardest, I don't mean technically difficult; I'm talking about the ethical side of things. Each one of you will have to debate this with yourselves, but I hope you will stay pragmatic and level-headed. This kind of opportunity doesn't come along that often. We're standing atop a volcano of public rage and we mustn't let the chance slip."

Public rage? Where? I hadn't noticed any in the last few hours. There wasn't any rage out there at all.

"The occupier now has more experience of how the resistance operates and our assassination rate has dropped off. Become ineffective, even. Worse still, the occupier's begun taking out our people. He's gotten smarter: arresting our operatives and executing them in public. Naturally, people sympathize with our martyrs, a sympathy we simply must exploit, and that is why, over the past few months, we have been changing course. Our objective now is to push the population to overthrow the occupier. We're going to engineer a new grassroots revolution."

I understood perfectly. In recent years, the people had been led, sheep-like, into uprisings, revolutions, and demonstrations. We ourselves prompted them to revolt against a previous revolution that others had led them into, and every step of the way—with every incitement to take action or encouragement to desist—we were assisted by the media.

65

"Four months ago, we initiated an ambitious strategy to bring people onto the streets. We have stirred up alarm at social collapse and caused them to fear the occupier. We have talked at length about water being unfit to drink, about the diseases being spread by prostitutes, about the extent of the moral decline that has taken hold since prostitution was legalized, about civilians being murdered at random and their bodies tossed on rubbish dumps, and we've stressed to them that it is the occupier who bears responsibility for keeping them safe and well. All this we've achieved using our men on the ground and online, and we've exploited the zeal shown by a few civilians, their sincere desire to expel the occupier (and also, perhaps, their imperfect understanding of our plan), and we've let them help us out, though without any kind of formal agreement. What has delayed us considerably has been our inability to persuade the media to take our side. The entire media has sided with the occupier. The Interior Ministry going back to work was clearly not the best thing to have happened—the media went over to them and abandoned us and, most unfortunately, have shamefully exploited the issue of collateral damage incurred during assassinations, directing the filthiest accusations against the resistance, which is perhaps the reason the people hate us."

What was the point of all this talk? Madi was setting the stage for something, but just what I couldn't tell.

"But we shall never, ever give up. We shall persevere until the occupier has been driven out completely. In a few days' time, you shall ignite the revolution that will sweep him away."

This was over the top. When a police officer loses his cool and gets excitable, you can be sure disaster lies ahead.

"The civilians know we're bastards and that we kill them, but when all's said and done they'd rather have us than the occupier. Not because we're patriots or fellow citizens, or because we speak the same language. It's simply that we will go on killing them as long as the occupation endures. They

66

can work out for themselves that once the occupier's gone we'll leave them be. Do you know how many citizens have lost their lives at the hands of the occupier over the last three-and-a-half years? Three hundred thousand. Not much, really. It practically amounts to an oversight. Do you know how many we've killed in the same period, whether as collaborators or as unintended casualties of our operations? Many more than that. And in the days ahead you'll be required to kill still more. This is our moment. . . ."

Major General al-Asyuti was peering about. He heard what was being said, yet he didn't hear. With us and not with us. Serenely and incessantly fiddling with his hair, his nose, and his beard, while his eyes roamed around the room. For a moment, his aide fell silent, waiting for a comment from his audience, or maybe to emphasize the importance of what came next.

"We have taken a number of steps to prepare the way for this revolution, and now that the people are more aware of the true nature of the dire social and economic reality of life under occupation, they are panicked. The thought of war profiteers keeps them up at night; the casual killing terrifies them. They yearn to be safe and secure, and they don't want to be forever fretting about their children and loved ones."

What was new? People had been yearning for that for the last ten years.

"But one final step still remains. It appears that provoking mass panic about declining morals is not enough to mobilize the people, and if we wait any longer the panic will subside and we won't be able to whip it up again. Moral panic, like any form of terrorism, is a fraud. People only spot the lie long after the fear has got its claws into them, but once they've seen through it it's impossible to convince them of it again. It's up to us, it seems, to go one step further. Instead of engineering a fake crisis, we must give them the real deal. Pure panic."

This looked like it was going to be bad, but surely it wouldn't be as bad as Madi was making out?

67

"In a few days, at a set time, the streets are going to be full of murder. It will be a crime without punishment. In every street in Cairo, the casualty rates will soar. No escape from the gunshots, the gangs of thugs, and the speeding cars, running pedestrians down. There will be no looting of shops or homes, just murder—killing without rhyme or reason. The fragile barrier of security, the wall that the Interior Ministry struggles so hard to preserve, will collapse without warning, and it is at that moment that the people will have no option but to rise up."

I knew what he was talking about. It's exactly what we had done all those many years ago, on that so-called Day of Rage, back in 2011. We hadn't done it to push them into an uprising, though, but to avenge ourselves, the police, upon them.

"Your mission is easier than that of the others. You will take up position at specific locations on the top of certain buildings. You'll receive enough ammunition to kill hundreds. Your task will be to kill the greatest possible number of people in the street. You will be our vanguard, the first to open fire. And rest easy: there are no restrictions to what you can do—select your victims with total freedom. Men and women, children and the elderly, it's all the same. It will be easy because you will be concealed. For the teams on the street, the mission will be more difficult. Some of them are courageous colleagues of yours and will face real peril. These men are potential martyrs."

His words stirred an old memory. Here we were carrying out the same plan we'd fallen victim to years before.

"We shall make sure that it is your bullets that kill first. Then the thugs and extremists will appear, to kill people with blades and clubs, prompted and directed by our operatives on the ground. Primitive warfare. So: people will first of all fall victim to your bullets, fired from unknown locations, and then to a deluge of swords and staves. We'll take them to the outer reaches of terror."

And not a single question. My two fellow snipers, it seemed, hadn't a thought in their heads. They were younger than me

68

and I knew nothing about them, but surely they had minds of their own, yet confronted with everything that had just been said they didn't respond, let alone object. Fine then. I was silent because, although I knew that what was going to happen would lead nowhere (not to revolution, not to anything), I didn't want to appear at odds with the leadership's decisions. But what about those two? Did they know what I knew? Were they prepared to carry out the mission in full? Were they genuinely persuaded by what Madi was saying? Would they be ready to kill a family member if one happened to wander across their sights?

"You will receive full information about your sniping positions in the next few days. Be ready to go to work at any time, and make sure you are present at the safe houses allocated to you between the hours of midnight and sunset. This period, with the exception of tomorrow, is when the messages will reach you. Be ready at all times."

Would the debate start now? Wasn't anybody going to ask about the morality of this?

Al-Asyuti looked at us. "Everything clear? Are there any questions?" He waited for a response, then, with the tone of someone calling an end to business, said, "God be with you. It seems we'll have to wait a while longer for our tardy friend. Give him a call, Madi, we don't have much time. You men can all relax. This meeting is over."

No questions, then. The meeting had been a resounding success.

We stayed standing, but loosened up a little, lit up, then in lowered tones began to talk among ourselves. Major General al-Asyuti spoke to Suleiman Madi in a louder voice and the two other officers whispered back and forth, while I stood silently, waiting for someone to address me. That's how it used to be in meetings before the occupation; these friendly chats did much to reduce the tension. Things were always difficult, and personal interests were forever intruding into meetings and the decision-making process. Casual conversation had a magical effect on the permanent atmosphere of suppressed irritation.

Talking to them, I learned that the two snipers moved fairly freely around East Cairo, returning home daily or every few days. Al-Asyuti lived in West Cairo and only rarely ventured out. It seemed to me as though he were handing over control to the enthusiastic Suleiman Madi. Al-Asyuti's calm, his air of being absent, made me wonder about his effectiveness and ability to lead. Ranks evidently weren't in effect here, or at least no longer as tightly observed as they had been in the ministry. There was no real system now. We were officers, and still thought of ourselves as officers, but the whole discipline thing was out of the window. Laughter rose up in response to a joke, and before it had died away one of the snipers asked Suleiman Madi, "But didn't this happen before—killing people during the January troubles?"

Madi's chuckle slowly died away and he was still smiling when he said, "Not that old story."

There were muffled giggles. The troubles of January 2011 had been a disaster, and the Day of Rage on 28 January would live long in the ministry's memory as a black day.

They were thinking back to what had happened, I could tell. We'd known the people were a time bomb, permanently on the verge of going off in your face, and were certain that bullets were the best way to deal with it when it did.

"The January troubles were different," Madi continued. "The shooting was our attempt to frighten people and get them to go back home. To defend the police stations. It had the opposite effect entirely. I don't know what the leaders were thinking back then. There was confusion over everything we did. Of course, there weren't any explicit orders to fire. That never happened. The idiotic way things worked back then, giving orders like that could land you in court and maybe prison. A few years after 2011, all that was done away with of course, and killing was permitted to dispose of terrorists, troublemakers, fifth

70

columnists, and demonstrators, with the unconditional support of the people, the prosecutor general, and the judiciary."

Indeed. Truly wonderful days.

"Everyone knows when an officer is supposed to shoot, don't they? What happened in January was that the officers got it completely wrong. But why are we discussing January and not what came after? August 2013 was the real epic. The Battle of Rabaa, when we crushed the Brotherhood with the blessing of the overwhelming majority of the people and without the slightest feelings of guilt or regret. Or March 2018, when we opened fire in Manshiya Square in Alexandria without receiving orders, without any prior agreement among ourselves. Perfect timing. Four thousand dead in six days and no one brought to book. And don't get me started on September 2019. That was a real day out. Al-Azhar Park and the Faculty of Engineering at Ain Shams University. Thousands of teenagers on a sit-in protest at both sites for some silly reason—I can't even remember why. And because the planning for that operation had been especially meticulous, we dropped more than two thousand of them in two hours. We used a 'mince the legs' strategy that worked a charm: if you don't fancy killing a protestor, then just dip your sights and shoot at his knees. He won't be going on any more demonstrations after that. He won't be getting out of bed. September 2019 was a demonstration of our control over public spaces and the universities, and of our capacity to mobilize and occupy a number of locations simultaneously. Of our capacity to break up any gathering, demonstration, or protest. Followed up by some truly heroic work by the prosecutor. Sure, we used live rounds, but no one stepped forward to point the finger. Confirmation of the threefold power of the Interior Ministry, the prosecutor's office, and the judiciary. That day, we achieved everything we set out to do and we managed to tame the people forever. After September 2019, we knew none of us would ever be prosecuted for killing a citizen during disturbances.

71

There would never be any repeat of the January courts, gentlemen. The prosecutor had understood that all that had been a huge error, and the judges hadn't hesitated to set us free, silencing the agents and traitors. At last, everyone came to accept that we were their long arm; that if it wasn't for us, the judiciary would have no dignity to speak of and their rulings would never be carried out. On many occasions, on many days—in January and August, March and September—we showed ourselves to be heroes, courageous, proved that we were worth more than the average citizen, that our lives were worth more than his life. Indeed, we showed that the life of the average citizen was worthless when measured against the value of safeguarding the state. But rest easy. We're planning to take back the state from the occupier, and if killing citizens is permissible in order to safeguard the state, then it's a positive duty when you're setting out to reclaim it."

For some minutes, nobody said a thing. Madi, I believe, had a lot more to say. He was grave and eager, and it was as though he was trying to add a lighthearted touch to his former excitability when he gave a bark of laughter and said, "Reverlooshun!" At which everybody dissolved in laughter.

Through the booming laughter, someone said, "Marters of the reverlooshun!" and al-Asyuti gave a chuckle, finally snapping out of his reverie. The laughter fell off a little and Suleiman Madi said, "It's all a consequence of our own actions, gentlemen. If we hadn't opened fire in January, none of this would have happened. Maybe we wouldn't be standing here now, and the army would definitely never have turned on Mubarak. But one thing has changed: we now know when to shoot them down and when to let them rise up. Brothers, people called what happened a 'revolution' and, in their minds, that's how it's stayed for years. Thank God they woke up in the end and changed the term to 'troubles.'"

That was true. Everyone had felt a great sense of relief when the name changed.

Madi spoke calmly now. "It seems we're in agreement. The process is much clearer now. We are trying to recreate the January troubles. We anticipate that people will attack occupation patrols and police stations. This time, the police will not resist the attacks, but will leave them to burn instead. Do they have instructions to do so? Certainly not. Do we have an understanding with them? Certainly not. But I know they will abandon the police stations to be looted by the crowds. Don't worry. In a few short days, we shall celebrate the anniversary of the old 'reverlooshun.'"

"And when we're done, maybe one of them will write a poem!" I said, laughing.

"Maybe," Madi replied, "There are plenty of fools about."

Then he smiled and turned to the youngest man there. "Do you remember any of the poetry from the January troubles, Lieutenant Ali?"

A nervous grin spread across the man's face and he half-turned toward al-Asyuti.

"Don't you worry," Madi said. "We're not in any official meeting now, and I shouldn't think the major general will object to a little fun."

"I didn't hear any at the time, sir," said Lieutenant Ali, "It was years later. We used to hear that stuff from our classmates at the academy and then afterward we'd recite it."

Al-Asyuti said, "All right then, poet, give us what you've got. . . ."

Lieutenant Ali cleared his throat, then raised his arms aloft like the poets do. "Slaughter me and leave me slain / It won't restore your state again." As he declaimed, he was brandishing his finger in the air like a pistol and I couldn't hold back a grin. We had killed them and we had got our state back. "In my blood, and by my hand / I write a new life for my native land!" Now he was mashing his chest like a woman in the throes of sexual abandon. We cracked up, and finally I remembered the poem. It was a poem written by an obscure poet called Safaa al-Muweilhi in honor of the martyrs. I'd never forget that name. The lieutenant was still going: "This blood of mine or this Arab Spring . . . ?" He trailed his fingers down between his thighs and wiped at his crotch, then raised his palm to his face, opening his eyes wide as he inspected it. "Both are the hue of menstrual blood!"

Al-Asyuti laughed a lot, then, coughing, asked: "Did the poet really write menstrual blood?"

But the young man couldn't answer and we couldn't hear. The laughter was so loud that we worried we'd be found out. If the floor had been cleaner, I would have fallen down. I remembered the whore's blood on me down in the bridge and I thought to myself that she must have been one of the "reverlooshunaries," her eye taken out by the birdshot my colleagues had unleashed, that we'd maimed her like we'd maimed others. And now, the struggle, and the demonstrations, and the dollars she'd been paid for her treachery were all finished, and there she was: a whore in a bridge that I fucked for three pounds. A truly fitting end for a traitor.

Still laughing, Ali raised his hand to excuse himself. This was the time we had waited for: vengeance for the January troubles preoccupied us to this day. Bit by bit, the laughter faded, then someone fluted in effeminate tones, "Marters of the reverlooshun . . . ," and a fresh wave broke out.

We heard a knocking at the door and, when one of us went to open it, in walked a young man carrying a large bag. Had the laughter given us away? The man was frowning but when he saw me he grinned, then looked at the scarab on my shoulder and nodded. "Looks like it's in love!"

"Looks like it's dumped you!" I countered.

So this was the officer in charge of the drones. The two snipers asked if they might leave and, after Suleiman Madi had spoken briefly to both of them, they shook hands with everyone and departed. The drone technician set his bag on the grimy table, opened it up, rummaged around inside for

74

a while, then took out something resembling a long needle, a device like a cell phone, and a bunch of cables. He made straight for me and introduced himself. He was Major John Mokhtar, he said. He'd have the drone back under his control in less than a minute.

This was shaping up to be an unusually cheery day despite the two bodies lying outside the building and the unhappy memories that had momentarily claimed us. The major apologized for the drone's behavior. This was the best one he had, he said—extremely light and with low power consumption. It could convert solar energy to electricity and do the same thing with physical motion. That was why it had clung to my shoulder while I walked. A technological marvel, he said, but for some reason it had decided to ignore the remainder of its mission and keep me company.

Madi had his response ready. "It's no joke, Saint. You lost control of the drone. Others might be controlling it without our knowing. Isn't it possible that someone might be spying on us right now?"

The gravity of what Madi was suggesting passed me by. "Saint?" I asked John.

"That's the nickname they've given me because I haven't killed anyone yet."

"How's that possible?" I asked. "We've been under occupation for three years now. Have you really not killed anyone in all that time? An officer's not a officer until he's killed, my friend."

The Saint ignored me, a thin smile on his lips. He had finished connecting the drone to his device and was fiddling with it when he said, "Don't worry about the drone. It can't be used to spy on you. With this type, it's impossible to take full control of its movement. We can only set the target location and it finds its own way there. It avoids roadblocks and flies over buildings, or it can hide until the sun comes out in order to recharge. The drone doesn't let anyone restrict its movement. It will escape the first chance it gets and can immolate itself if it feels threatened. Ah! It seems the error was my fault. The command log seems to be saying it was me. Basically, I was negligent and forgot to give it the command to return, which is why it stayed with you. The extraordinary thing is that it actually kept you company instead of shutting down or flying off into the city."

"What's extraordinary is that it was playing with me," I said. "Like a pet I'd raised myself."

The Saint smiled. "It's an incredible development. Drones can learn now. They can store any actions they see and imitate them. It must have seen a dog playing with its owner or something along those lines, then analyzed what it saw and decided to copy it."

He finished with the drone and looked at us. "All I want to say is that its presence here among you should be no cause for concern, and if you'd rather spare yourself the worry you could simply smash it, just as you could have done with earlier models. But no one did."

I was inspecting the drone in the palm of the Saint's hand, when I heard Major General al-Asyuti ask, "Do you want to keep it?"

"I wouldn't mind."

I didn't think there would be any harm in keeping it.

I asked the Saint what it was called, and he said, "Burhan."

"Leave it here, John," al-Asyuti said. "It'll keep the colonel entertained."

The Saint shrugged, then took a series of objects out of his bag and said, "This cell phone contains the program to control the drone. In the normal course of events, Burhan will stay with you and will probably rest on your shoulder most of the time. Don't expect too much. He's never going to open his mouth and say, 'Burhan at your service, sir!'"

I slipped the phone and the connecting cable into my pocket and turned to Kamal al-Asyuti and Suleiman Madi to ask if there were any other orders. Al-Asyuti gave a gentle smile and waved me away. I should enjoy my next few days in Cairo, he said, but I must be ready at all times. He reminded me that tomorrow was my only day off. Madi approached me. He told me that the Saint could help me get hold of lots of things and to call him if I was ever in need. Then he handed me a sealed envelope. It contained cash, he said— not much, but quite enough to live on for the next few days.

Cash at last! It had been months since I'd paid for anything. Those living in the tower had food, and drink, and hash delivered to them, and there'd been no need to carry any money. I remembered that I didn't have any hash on me, then thought of the major. Would the Saint be able to get me some or would he think me a spendthrift, squandering government money on good times?

Burhan—that's right, it was Burhan now—went back to hovering quietly over my head, and when I left the apartment and went downstairs, he became more active. He looped faster and started to flip in midair, then found a new game: flying ahead a short distance at high speed, then holding his wings still and tucking them beneath the casings, at which his body would fall for all of a second or two before he reopened his wings and beat hard to float back up. Burhan was delighted that we were going back outside, it seemed.

On the sidewalk opposite, four men stood smoking, one of them gazing at the ground while the others played with their phones. My instincts told me they were up to no good, out to burgle an apartment or break into a car, to snatch a woman or a child. Their movements betrayed nerves and their preoccupation with what they were holding was unconvincing. But why should I care? I wasn't an officer now and I had to prepare myself for the revolution ahead.

It was nearly 10 p.m. A headache was inching through my head. I recognized the usual signs: perfect mental clarity for a few seconds, followed by a headache, then hammer blows of pain striking the back of my skull every few minutes—I would barely have recovered from the first when the next struck. I must have hash. Regular painkillers might not get rid of it and, if I did take them, they might send me off to sleep, and I had no desire to rest. Hash, though, would make me forget the headache, would leave me calm, capable of laying plans for what was going to take place a few days from now.

I took out the phone I'd been given at the meeting to search for the Saint's number and discovered that his was the only name saved in its memory. I called him. He asked me where I was, then said he'd be down in just a minute.

Two of the smoking men went into the building opposite. The other two stayed put, waiting for something. From the building's narrow entrance emerged a massive individual, his jutting belly and two huge arms clearly visible, and his face hidden in the shadows that fringed the street. He seemed to be making sure of his surroundings. He looked at the street and at me. For a full minute, he didn't stir, then he went back in. I turned to my right to find the Saint standing there, watching the man as I'd been doing. That man, he told me, guarded the door of the brothel across the street. Then, slipping his arm through mine, he led me out of the alley.

We heard waves of pounding electronic music, a blend of human screams and animal shrieks—I thought I heard a pig and the sound of a dog howling in pain—interspersed with short musical loops and synthetic drumbeats, metallic and harsh. The source of this din came closer as we walked along, as though I was slipping down a huge metal slide with nothing to check my speed, and then we were right beside it and I heard a voice whispering between the bursts of sound, "Water . . . I'm thirsty . . . ," and then we were moving away again, the music gradually dying away and the voice ever fainter: "Water . . . I'm thirsty. . . ." That voice was a sample, taken from an old film, perhaps, or a television drama where the lead actor asks someone for water. Maybe a dying man requesting a last drink. It occurred to me that the animal sounds were the sounds of copulation, a fat pig covering his sow, a bitch howling beneath a street dog's thrusts, the sounds of a female in ecstasy or a male approaching the point of ejaculation. I asked the Saint about it. "It's the new electronica. The guy who makes it is about forty, not a kid like you might expect. You must have heard of him. Abadir—a very distinctive name. He's been around for more than fifteen years, but he's always developing his music, never settles on one style. Those are the sounds of animals being killed. Abadir usually makes recordings in the street, then layers them over his music afterward: pavement sellers, passengers on the metro and public buses, government workers shouting at citizens—he captures all sorts of sounds and adds them in."

The Saint fell silent. I was amazed by how wrong I'd been. Although there were similarities between cries of sexual congress and the screams of the dying, the conclusion I'd jumped to was unsettling.

"Abadir recorded a donkey expiring in the street after being hit by a car," the Saint went on, "and as usual he mixed it into his music. The track was a huge hit, so this time he decided to record the sound of pigs being slaughtered. As you no doubt know, the police discovered a huge pig farm out in al-Marg in North Cairo and they were worried about the swine flu spreading again, so they slaughtered them all in a single day. Because they were scared of being infected, and to cut down on costs, they forced the owners and the workers to carry out the executions. Forced them to batter their skulls with hammers till they were dead. Abadir recorded several hours of the sounds the pigs made as they were being bumped off. It's a great track, and it ends with this incredible crescendo. Abadir said he was recording the pigs shrieking while they were being bludgeoned, and then, in among the screaming, he started picking up the sounds of the farm workers weeping. They were hitting and weeping. Then the shrieking died down, and the pigs gave up and stopped trying to escape, and the workers stopped crying and just surrendered to the killing frenzy. And then, slowly but surely, they started screaming from sheer euphoria—the dirtiest insults and abuse directed at the pigs. Abadir said he saw one of them hammering at a pig with the most incredible violence. The pig's skull had already been completely smashed in, and there was just no need to go on pulping the flesh and bone. When the man stopped and turned around, Abadir saw this huge damp patch on his trousers from his crotch down to his knees, and on his shirt up to the belly. The guy had come in his pants. Near the end, Abadir recorded a voice muttering in perfect Arabic, 'Water . . . I'm thirsty . . . ,' and he used that recording to end the track you've just heard."

The Saint's words distracted me from my headache and I asked him how I could get hold of the music. The curiosity was killing me. "Couldn't be easier," he said. "When we get home, I'll transfer the files onto your phone and give you some speakers so you can listen to it when you're on your own."

We walked on in silence. All I could think of was the hash. Saint John might be a stoner, but then again he might be a proper saint who'd never touched the stuff in his life. The streets were calm, free of pedestrians, cars, and occupation patrols. On we went, and not once did he ask me what I wanted or where we were going, and only when the periods of pain were longer than the periods of clearheadedness did I ask about the hash.

He said nothing for a while, and I told myself that I'd lost nothing since I had nothing to lose in the first place. Without looking at me, he said, "Getting hold of hash now will be difficult. The dealers reckon it's easier to move about during the day. The night doesn't hide them, but the crowds that come out in the day do. I'll take you to a dealer tomorrow morning. You won't get anything now. Only karbon."

He pulled a regular cigarette pack from his pocket, extracted a single, neatly hand-rolled specimen, lit it, and took a drag, then blew out a cloud of intensely thick, white smoke and reached out to hand it to me.

At first, I assumed karbon must be the name of some kind of high-quality hash—you only share the good stuff with friends, after all, to avoid embarrassment if the friend turns out to know his varieties and to demonstrate your generosity, sincere or sham. But with the first drag I knew it wasn't hash. The taste and smell were completely different from what I was used to; it didn't burn the throat and lungs, or make me cough, and the smoke didn't fill my nose with that pungent smell, didn't branch out through my chest, bringing tidings of the calm to come. This stuff had an unfamiliar, organic smell. For some reason, I thought of grilled shrimp—thin shells seared on the flame. Then there was a blend of other aromas, none of which I could identify. This was something different.

I took three drags and handed it to the Saint, who glanced at me as we walked along and asked, "So, what's the news?" I thought for a moment and said that current affairs didn't interest me any more, and he laughed and was just explaining that he'd been talking about the karbon when suddenly I found my head surrounded by a dense black cube.

Like marble, the cube was heavy, but it wasn't cold to the touch. It was completely without temperature, in fact. I reached out my hand to feel its square sides and found them absolutely smooth and regular, the edges and corners sharp beneath my fingertips, and yet I couldn't see a thing, or hear a sound, or utter the simplest word. I tried breathing, but there was no air inside this box—the cube was completely sealed, and my head was not so much inside it as part of it. Then the cube expanded, absorbing my neck, and chest, and belly, then further, down to my feet, and now I was completely cut off from my surroundings, not thinking of the Saint, or my mission, or anything else, but I could see myself, wedged beneath a vast mountain of pitch black and whispering, "Water . . . I'm thirsty. . . ."

Then everything went away and I lost awareness. Awareness, but not consciousness; I remained awake, my senses disordered, and I discovered that I had forgotten everything that had gone before, that my head was emptied of its memories, that I couldn't recall my name, or language, or even what I looked like. For a brief instant, I recalled that there were many things in the world outside the cube, but what I had been before I entered it I could not say. I was within the cube, in the nothingness that came before creation or the nothingness that came after its obliteration. It really didn't matter, for the two nothingnesses were one.

Then I heard the Saint. Talking about something. And just like that, my surroundings returned and with them the headache, fainter now and on its way out.

Without warning, the Saint halted, so I halted, too, and he looked at me, smiling. "You just had a karbon trip!" I stared at him, amazed at everything that had happened—the black cube, the sensory shutdown, leaving the physical world—then looked at my fingers and saw the cigarette there, reduced to clinging ashes, and I said, "What *is* that?"

Then the black cube clamped down again.

6

THE BURLY OFFICER FOUGHT HARD. He took two rounds from my pistol, then the third jammed in the chamber and wouldn't budge, and I was in the process of removing the magazine when I found the man pressing down on my neck and trying to throttle me.

He was bleeding heavily and his blood covered my chest, soaking my clothes. How could he still be alive, I asked myself, and cursed the hour I'd agreed to take on an idiotic mission like this. This was before the Tower Group was set up, back when assassinations were still carried out in person rather than at a distance, and killing a brigadier general from the Knights of Malta should have been easy enough. A Helwan automatic, a silencer, and a few rounds were usually enough to see these jobs through, but this brigadier general was more bull than man. He'd realized he was fast approaching the end, I concluded, and had resolved to kill me, to take me with him to hell, and I had a wild thought that the pair of us would be resurrected together in this very pose: his blood jetting from the twin holes in his chest and drenching my body, his eyes glaring into mine, his hands trying to break my neck. I was on the very brink of giving up but decided to give it one last try. Drawing the short dagger from my hip, I started stabbing him repeatedly and at random. I might be a professional sniper, but I was no good with a knife. However, by my great good luck all the blows struck him in the penis and crotch.

There I was, in the man's private quarters, him bare naked and the woman, naked as he was, sitting on the edge of the bed. Egyptian, judging by her brown skin and curves—and her state of undress, readily apparent despite the many sheets and covers heaped up on the bed and over her, indicated she was a whore as well, a pro. As I stabbed away at the man I thought that I might give her a few thrusts of my own should the opportunity present itself. As my vision began slowly but surely to fade, I turned my hand, shifted it upward between our two bodies, and opened his belly from left to right. His resistance crumbled instantly and he dropped, perfectly motionless.

The struggle had lasted a few seconds. Neither of them had made a sound. He was busy trying to kill me and she was dumb with terror, not to mention keen to extricate herself from the situation with the minimum possible damage. I was exhausted, about to pass out, but I wanted to visit one final humiliation on her. I recovered my pistol from the floor, removed the magazine and the jammed round, slipped it back in, and waved her over with the barrel. When she came over, I grasped her shoulder and forced her down in front of me, resting on her knees. With one hand, I pulled down my trousers, resting the pistol against her head with the other. She knew what I wanted.

I was panting, choked, still feeling the fingers gripping my throat, while she sucked and sucked. To no avail. I'd come erect for a few seconds, then start fighting for oxygen again. As she worked away, I was pressing the silencer's muzzle against her head. The pistol was pointing straight down and it struck me that if I opened fire the round would penetrate her head and pass down her back, completely shattering her spinal column. As a sniper, I reckoned I was a good enough shot to take out each and every one of her vertebrae in this way. Then it occurred to me that this wasn't sensible; it was quite likely that the bullet, having passed through hair, skin, skull, and brain, would hit the limp dick in her mouth.

84

Immediately, I pointed the barrel away from my penis. You'd have to be crazy to use a Helwan for this type of mission. You might get an accidental discharge if the gun fell on the floor, the barrel could warp if you fired too many rounds in a row, or you might fire a bullet at a whore's spine and end up shooting your cock off.

I got bored of what she was doing and, as she worked away, I began to remove my clothes. It was tricky. I got the shoes and trousers off using my left hand and my feet, then did the same with the shirt, though to take it off completely I had to transfer the gun to my free hand. The blood had saturated the shirt and gone through to my skin, but there was no time to wash or even wipe it off, so I put on the brigadier general's clean shirt, which was lying on the bed. The whore understood what I wanted to do and, without leaving my cock, she reached out, grabbed the man's trousers, and helped me put them on.

Despite her persistent efforts, I couldn't get it up. Her silence and her ability to suck my cock with me drenched in blood and the corpse lying next to her astonished me. Because her response seemed so natural, I couldn't think of anything to do that might humiliate her further. Indeed, what she was doing didn't seem humiliating at all. Now I'd killed the man and was soaked in his gore, humiliation didn't seem to mean very much.

She must have thought I wanted to kill her. She started begging me to let her live while she stroked my penis with her hand, not realizing that her wretched face and silly words were doing nothing to get me aroused. She wept as she told me she had children waiting for her at home. All that, and there she was, rubbing my cock and waiting for it to stand up—nothing doing—and then she broke down in tears, saying she didn't know anything, that she didn't know my name, that she'd forget my face the moment I left and would say she hadn't seen it because I'd been wearing a mask.

I left in a state of collapse, panting from the strain.

85

I was walking rapidly, my heart thudding. I tried to appear normal so as not to draw attention to myself. Someone might notice the blood congealing on my chest beneath the shirt, and maybe, too, the fact that the clothes I was wearing didn't fit me, were far too baggy. I was extremely nervous, and my throat was dry, and when I passed a café and spotted a cup of water on an unattended table, I drank it down without a second thought. Then, on the café's television, I saw members of parliament voting on the new prostitution bill. People were sitting, following what was happening in slack-jawed silence. Their minds must have been full of conflicting thoughts and emotions: that's right, the whores are going to get a union; the trade will be licensed; my sister and my wife could go and work in a brothel; if I catch them at it, I'll kill them for sure; you'll see, there'll be ID cards with 'Profession: Prostitute' on the back; it's all because of the occupation, see; yeah, all the fault of the limp-wristed army, the reckless resistance, the "reverlooshun"; yes, we're a nation of pimps; prostitution's the solution; the law will protect them, see if it doesn't; the cops will protect them; well, I'll have more of a chance to try out what skills I have on a real woman instead of being stuck with myself; better start manufacturing condoms in my bedroom—those things will sell by the million; I knew it, the members of parliament are pimps. . . . I thought to myself that the whore I'd left back there would never find herself in a similar situation again.

I was one of the first to object to prostitution being legalized. My position wasn't the product of religious faith, or a commitment to exemplary morals, or the like. The argument I made was that it was impossible for two people to have a relationship completely devoid of love. The first time I stated my case, it provoked raucous laughter from those around me—former Interior Ministry colleagues who'd become comrades in the resistance, my few friends, strangers at cafés. They all offered the same, unvarying response the moment I made

86

my views known, particularly in closed-door meetings with the resistance: a stream of sarcastic comments that verged on the insulting. My belief in the patriotic cause was another line of attack. How, I wondered aloud, could one fight the occupation without a moral compass of one's own? True, I didn't actually buy this idea myself, but it seemed more credible than the love thing. Yet the mention of morality prompted even louder laughter. Safeguarding Egypt, or the state, or our values, or love were all arguments we might use to justify our desire to kill, blow up, and destroy, but they had no place as a reason to ban prostitution. Rather, they were a good argument for legalizing the trade and looking after it, for encouraging tourism and protecting the honor of respectable girls. We only ever regarded people as potential criminals. Even the ones who kept their mouths shut were liable to switch at any moment to the antis, to the camp of those who transgressed against the law and the state—back when such a thing had existed. The bitter cynicism directed at my sentimental and moral arguments seemed to me to be a frank admission on my colleagues' part that their position was unsupported by any form of logic or rational thought. Each of us had his own silly justifications and private reasons for his beliefs, and the truth is I never had any real conscientiously held reason for objecting to the law. Maybe it was an automatic response with no thought behind it.

There had been an organized media campaign to get people behind the bill and ensure they didn't object. Al-Azhar's sheikhs, university professors, and intellectuals were silenced. They were the most fraudulent and insincere people around, their inconsistencies and lack of credibility sufficient to irreparably damage any cause they might back. Meanwhile, free rein was given to media figures to gradually begin addressing the matter at hand—weighing the pros and cons of legalization and broadcasting endless segments comparing the experience of European countries with Egypt's own. Statistics were bandied about in the press, on radio, and on television, clearly showing the decline in instances of rape, harassment, public disorder, and robbery in those countries that had legalized prostitution, and lengthy accounts were given of the stability, peacefulness, and settled relationships of young people who had experienced premarital sexual intercourse. Sex no longer their overriding obsession, they had space for other considerations, more appropriate to long-term marital ambitions, such as the personality and interests of their partner, their patience, their ability to make something of their lives. All this was linked to low divorce rates in countries where prostitution was legal, to which, of course, was added that most distinctive Egyptian anxiety: the fear of a population explosion. It was explained that prostitution would do much to reduce rising birth rates.

With their shiny suits, smooth chins, and slicked-back hair, the media types had the people on a platter, the very people who greased themselves up in a heroic effort to efface their own identities and replace them with something closer to— more in line with—that of the presenters. Oily fish gobbling their oily prey. Then someone discovered that prostitution had been legalized in Egypt under the monarchy but no one was talking about it! We were so terribly civilized in the first half of the twentieth century! We had permitted prostitution, and the honorable gentlemen of the police had overseen the whole process in their capacity as upholders of the law. But then the coup of 1952 had swept all that cultivation to one side and cast the country into an abyss of darkness and backwardness. I was considerably surprised. Since when had the media been so certain that 1952 was a military coup? Had history changed without my knowing?

But getting off to a bad start, it seemed, didn't mean all hope was lost.

A number of brothels opened within the first month. Fliers were distributed by hand in the street, and elegant neon signs appeared on each brothel advertising the name of the establishment and its rates. They occupied entire low-rise residential buildings, all of them in the cramped alleys off Sharif Street in the center of East Cairo, with the majority located in and around the Stock Exchange district. Abandoned buildings for the most part, uninhabited and in very poor repair, and it seemed as though these sad dwellings must surely house sad women, too—but when I entered my first ever brothel a few months later, I found that things were not like that at all.

The entrance was air-conditioned, chilled after the heat of the street, and the stairway clean and carpeted, giving an impression of comfort quite different from the unforgiving solidity of the usual marble cladding. On the ground floor, a door stood ajar bearing a sign that read 'Security,' and next to the door a second, arrowed sign with the legend 'Upstairs.'

I was confronted by a stream of people coming down the staircase, while a second stream accompanied me up. The place had more people descending and ascending than clients and whores in the rooms, and all of them were staring at the floor and avoiding looking at one another. I glanced quite innocently at their faces, but no one met my eyes. Some men were carrying plastic bags and briefcases, and others were empty-handed. There were young men, the middle-aged, and the elderly. There were soldiers from the Knights of Malta's armies and Egyptian policemen, some currently serving and some former officers, the latter identifiable from the broken look in their eyes. There were men in formal attire with gleaming brogues, and men dressed simply, or in tracksuits, with dusty shoes, wracked with shame and demoralized, no trace of the manly vigor you'd expect to be thick in the air. Eunuchs, listlessly answering lust's call.

On the first floor, four doors stood open, one per apartment. I went through the first and was taken aback by the lighting, which seemed to fall on nothing but the whores' underwear, making it glow. The whores were standing by the bedroom doors. You couldn't make them out in any detail, but their bodies were clearly beautiful and strong.

That day, I went into every apartment in the building and examined every girl who stood by the door to her room. The limitless variety took me by surprise—black girls, Egyptians, and foreigners, thin girls and fat girls, and clothes more varied still: nurses' uniforms in shiny white rubber; militia outfits (also shiny); two-piece lingerie sets; bras large and small; outfits with colored feathers, and gleaming pearls, and fairy lights blinking on and off; men's shirts worn with nothing on beneath (the most arousing of all); southern peasant robes displaying cleavage that teased and tempted you; factory workers' overalls, very short and very tight; bras of soft fabric housing jutting nipples; Superman and Wonder Woman costumes; a policeman's uniform with a truncheon stuck in the belt; an army officer's with a plastic rifle slung from the shoulder; the distinctive dress of an officer of the Knights of Malta; an English game hunter's outfit with a pith helmet and a stubby black whip in hand; a very loose and very short instance of a Delta peasant's traditional attire; a judge with a shiny pink ribbon of office; a pigtailed schoolgirl in big, black-rimmed glasses; an early-twentieth-century dandy in black suit and tarboosh, a thin black mustache penciled onto the beautiful, female face; and reams and reams of underwear and nightgowns.

On the fifth floor, all the freaks were gathered: real whips snapping through the air at regular intervals, stun batons that crackled and glowed with soft blue sparks, shoes with towering heels both thick and thin, the tiniest possible bras, the stiff dildo that a whore wore at her waist and waggled to entice the passersby, a crown of red, yellow, and black feathers and a tail-piece of very long feathers poking out behind (I couldn't see any leather straps holding the tail in place, but when the whore turned around and bent over I saw they were fixed into a black plastic plug protruding from her anus). There were flat-chested girls with massive buttocks, and others with huge breasts and flat

90

behinds. Girls so young they seemed as if they'd come of age just yesterday, and women with slack tits that had nursed many children. By the end, I had seen them all and I hadn't wanted one.

Overwhelmed, I hurried downstairs, as though fleeing these dozens of female bodies that had failed to arouse me in the slightest. Coming to the ground floor, I saw Farida for the first time. And somehow I knew I would spend the night with her.

She was mounting the stairs with unfeigned boredom, holding a bag that might have contained clothes or a costume like the ones I'd seen upstairs. I stopped, trying to catch a glimpse of her features, and I smiled, because I'd had a purely adolescent thought: that this girl would leave her terrible job and marry me because she loved me. I'd forget her shameful past and she'd ignore all my faults. But she didn't look at me. I was just another john going up and down the stairs on Sharif Street.

Later on, Farida told me that she had thought I'd finished what I'd come for, so she hadn't looked at me, sparing me the glance she turned on clients to catch their attention. Farida wasn't so very beautiful. She had a skinny body and sallow brown skin that hinted at some permanent medical condition or malnutrition. A boyish figure, but for a broad ass that seemed to belong to another body altogether. But I was captivated by her short hair, and likewise by her prominent cheekbones and her long, almost pharaonic face. She stopped and stared at someone coming down behind me. I heard his slow tread on the stairs, muffled by the carpet, and—detecting the beginnings of a mocking, not flirtatious, smile—the fellow shuffled past me. An old man, squat and bald, carrying a huge bag full of children's teddies and dolls: Winnie the Pooh, Piglet, Tigger, and Rabbit, plus others I didn't know, and red plush hearts like those sold for Valentine's Day, the whole collection nearly spilling from the vast bag. I looked at him in astonishment, furious at him for ruining the moment, and she watched him flatly as he passed her by. "The man wants a nanny," she declared.

91

I followed her up to the first floor, where she went into one of the apartments, then into a bedroom at the back. Beset by the glances of her fellow whores, I waited until she reemerged, dressed in an outfit that covered her body from top to bottom. It was a very thin, translucent shift of fine black thread, like the fabric used for those semi-transparent lightweight tights, and it showed off the slenderness of her legs and waist, the broad curve of her behind, and the modest rounds of her two small breasts, whose nipples she covered with her forearm in compliance with house rules *(Nipples may not be shown outside the rooms)*, while the hand of her loose arm reached down to shield her cunt—a substantial fig leaf that went with her two big feet. Later, I would see her breasts and notice that her left breast was missing its nipple, and I would discover the small scar that took its place. This was the cleverest ruse in the whole joint: she was naked and yet not. Wearing something that exposed her body, yet still covering what might otherwise be seen clearly. A mature woman, yet slight as a teenager. Her hair was light brown, yet it gleamed in the darkness. A face sharp as a boy's, but with lips that urged you on.

A strange mixture. The body halfway between a boy's straight lines and a young woman's lushness; an aura that coupled simplicity with seduction. I was utterly intoxicated.

I entered the room behind her and silently thanked the pimps in parliament who had sacrificed everything to bring us the joy of these exquisites.

92

7

THE SAINT MUST HAVE ESCORTED me to the street where I was staying. I could see his back drawing away from me. He turned, smiled, and waved, then hurried off. I can remember nothing of what preceded that moment, nor anything that came after, but there is a vivid memory of waking up, all weariness and exhaustion gone, as though bone and muscle had been replaced while I slept.

Burhan buzzed around me and a zephyr from his beating wings tickled my face. I was in a state of rare contentment, and it seemed to me as though all my problems were gone. Not solved, but completely disappeared, without trace and never to return, and like any experienced drug user, I attributed this effect to the karbon I'd smoked the day before. The sunlight dazzled me. On the bed by my head sat the phone. I picked it up and saw that it was almost 9 a.m. Then, that the phone's contents had been changed. There was a new icon on the screen—a musical note—and beneath it, 'Abadir.' I clicked on it and a menu opened of what I immediately recognized to be sound files: songs or tracks. Running my thumb down the screen, I came to one labeled "Beneath the Hammers' Steel" and for a moment the portentous title seemed almost absurd, but that music I'd heard yesterday was still echoing around my head, and this was it. The Saint had added it to my phone like he'd promised. I set the track to play, then started searching for the speakers he'd mentioned. Burhan knocked against

93

something, and when I turned to look I saw him sitting on the table, and beside him a set of speakers, and as I picked them up he flew into the air and did a flip. I plugged the speakers into the phone and the sound came pure and clear.

A whole hour went by. I listened to three of Abadir's tracks, held fast beneath a bombardment of pounding beats, as though ten huge drums were being battered one after the other, no more than a tenth of a second between each one and the next—each second a sequence of drumbeats strung tightly together. I'd never heard the like before. I pictured a little pig submitting to a brute's hammer, taking the blows without trying to flee, then whispering a plea for water. And I pictured the brutish man dropping his hammer, then bringing it water and letting it drink, and when the pig's thirst was quenched resuming his battering. Was this from the karbon, too? Death had become strange to me.

The Saint's call cut off the music abruptly and the phone's ringtone blared out from the speakers. He was waiting for me downstairs, he said, and I asked him to come up and wait for me while I dressed. As I ended the call, I tried to remember what had happened the night before. I couldn't remember him adding the music to the phone, nor what we'd talked about after the second hit of karbon.

I opened the apartment's door and went back inside to wash. All my clothes were filthy, and I began feeling and sniffing them to see which were the least offensive. I had just picked some out and was heading for the bathroom when the Saint walked in, greeted me with a smile, and sat down to watch Burhan.

I washed, and emerged to find Burhan circling around the living room in an orbit whose center was the Saint. The Saint stood there, peering at him every time he flew past his face.

"I'm testing him," the Saint said. "Looks like there's nothing wrong with the wings or any of his mechanisms. Burhan's okay."

"Should I be testing him, too?" I asked.

"No need. In any case, Burhan's mission is nearly over. You won't be needing him after the revolution." His certainty that a revolution would take place surprised me. I didn't make any comment, not wanting to get into a long debate about the people, the revolution, the state, and the occupation. I'd tired of all that stuff long ago.

The Saint said, "How are you today? Did you like the karbon?"

"Definitely, but I don't fully understand what it does. I'd like to try it again."

"You don't want us to go and buy hash, you mean?" He smiled. "Out with the old and in with the karbon?"

"I don't know yet," I said. "I told you, I don't really understand what happened to me and I want to experience it again. But you never said—what is karbon? Is it made in a lab?"

His smile widened. "It's made in labs, for sure, but not the neat and clean laboratories you're thinking of. But we can go to a karbon lab. There's one by the foot of the Muqattam hill. Just fifteen minutes by car."

Of course drug labs were dirty. Did he think I was new to the job?

"Will they let us in?" I asked. "They're going to let two police officers take a look at what they're up to?"

"You're forgetting that we're not officers any more. They don't know anything about me other than that I'm a friend of the lab owner. And by the way, the owner's a former officer as well."

"In the resistance?" I asked.

"No, he decided to drop all that shit and make a living off karbon. He lives for the stuff."

"Fine," I said. "No problem, then, let's go. Let's forget the hash and try to get to the bottom of karbon. Once again: what's it made of? Flowers or leaves of some kind?"

"You'll see for yourself."

We went out together, walking until we'd left the alleys and narrow lanes behind, and finally came to al-Azhar Street, jam-packed with cars, its sidewalks aswarm. "We'll take a taxi," said the Saint. I didn't answer and turned to my left to wait for an empty cab, when I noticed a crowd standing about a hundred meters off, the people clustering on the sidewalk and part of the road, constricting it still further, the cars having great difficulty squeezing through what free space remained. They were all looking up at al-Azhar Bridge, which rose up in the center of the street and ran parallel overhead. I couldn't see what held their attention, but the Saint tapped me on the shoulder and said, "Let's go and see what's happening over there."

Up on the overpass stood a completely naked man wearing a yellow mask. After a few seconds, I realized that it was SpongeBob: yellow, square, with big white eyes and a childish grin, and in the center a hole where we could clearly see the man's smiling face. He stood there, cars speeding past at his back, leaning his belly and elbows against the metal railing and spitting on the people below, shaking his hips at them, grinning. Next to him lay a thick rope, one end tied to the low rail, the other in a noose about his neck. The man had got himself his own private gallows, and on a grand scale— al-Azhar Bridge, no less. People were flinging abuse at him, and snorting derisively, and answering his shaking hips in kind. When he laughed at them and waved, they laughed and waved. When he stuck out his first and middle fingers to signal for a cigarette, one of them tossed him a pack, and the man deftly caught it, then took out a cigarette, and put it between his lips. He cocked his thumb to indicate a lighter and someone threw him one. The man lit the cigarette and calmly started to smoke, then he raised his leg, swung it over the bridge's railing, and very cautiously set his foot down on the edge of the bridge's outer lip. Next, he brought his second leg over and stood there, gripping the rail in both hands until he had his balance, then let go, grabbed his flaccid penis, and

96

started urinating on the people down below, the cigarette still in his mouth. I thought I saw him shut his right eye as the smoke stung it—and then he jumped.

The man's body swung sharply back and forth, his arms hung slack at his sides, and a thick stream of piss guttered from his cock. The rope sawed at his neck; then it cut into it and the wound began to bleed heavily, the blood covering his chest and belly then mixing with his urine, and the whole cocktail spattering down onto the ground and the spectators. I looked at the crowd and saw that they were standing and staring with great intensity at the swinging body. The blood dripped down onto the faces of some, but they paid no attention. One lifted his hand to wipe away drops that had fallen into his eye, then went back to gaping at the body. They were silent and focused, but unmoved by what they saw, like students at a lecture.

The cigarette still hung from the corpse's mouth—still burning, the smoke floating up past his mask, held in place despite the violent motion of the body, and I thought that the butt must have stuck to his lower lip, the way cigarettes do when you leave them in your mouth for any length of time. The cigarette was still alight when I saw the first stone fly.

Then everyone followed suit, pelting him with stones from the ground, pieces of wood, bags of trash, shoes, tomatoes, and after a minute or so I heard the sound of gunfire and turned to find a man leveling a zip gun at the corpse and firing a second time, and a third, and a fourth, and then I realized that he wasn't aiming at the corpse but at the rope, trying to sever it. The rope hung down from the bottom of the railing and no one standing on the bridge would be able to reach down far enough to cut it.

Then lots of people lifted their guns and started shooting at the rope, and the tiny pellets spread out to hit the body and the bridge, and to bounce back and strike the people who stood there, unmoving, and the body was spangled with pellets now, and then the rope broke, and the people sprinted for the corpse.

The Saint grabbed my arm and pulled me away from the crowd. "We have to get away from all this," he said. "No taxi's going to come down this street for at least an hour. Did the guy really have to commit suicide right now?"

"You care that much about the timing?" I replied. "The man killed himself and that's all there is to it."

"Of course I care. He lost this world, and the next, and that's his choice. But given the gridlock his suicide's going to cause, I'd say he got it wrong."

Which was perfectly logical, I thought, though the phrase 'he lost this world, and the next' was not. I said, "Quite right, and the guy really has lost the next world . . . but you can't say he's lost this world. How can you lose the shit we're in now?"

The Saint laughed. "There's still pleasure to be had down here. Life's not all shit. Maybe we're in paradise and we don't know it!"

I thought that perhaps the Saint was testing my faith by talking about this world and the next. *Is that what you're doing, Saint? I don't like those games, my friend.* We had walked on down al-Azhar Street a fair distance from the crowd, and the cars had completely vanished from the road, when the Saint said, "Even in the worst prisons, there's pleasure. There's pleasure in the State Security lockups, my friend. That's why nobody ever commits suicide in prison."

The Saint really was a well-meaning fellow—or perhaps I wasn't understanding what he was getting at—but his mentioning suicide and State Security reminded me of the 'State Security Dilemma,' which had been very popular with us officers years ago. I asked him and he denied ever having heard of it. We were close to al-Hussein by now, and the usual crowds thronged the sidewalks by the mosque.

"It's a riddle, famous among the officers—I've no idea how you haven't heard it before. I first heard it a long time ago, as part of an attempt to answer a big question: why don't people kill themselves in prison? Anyway, these three Salafis—Mohamed,

Mahmoud, and Ahmed—are being held at State Security head-quarters. Every day, they're tortured in all sorts of ways, then they're taken back to a single cell where they sleep till the next day, when they wake up and the torture begins all over again. This goes on for a long time, and then one night Mohamed wakes his cellmates up. He's beaming with delight and he tells them he's found a solution to their terrible dilemma. He says that they're being tortured beyond endurance, and that they've got no secret information that they could possibly confess. The fact is they're perfectly prepared to confess to anything, but the torturers never let them know the thing they're meant to be confessing to, and so Mohamed thinks the torturers must be doing it for their own pleasure."

At this point, the Saint broke in, laughing. "Fine then! So here's a Salafi who realizes that some of the officers in State Security are enjoying themselves. Didn't I tell you we might be in paradise?"

I ignored him and went on: "If that's the case, Mohamed says, then the torture will only end when they are dead, and for no other reason. Mohamed volunteers to be the first killer: he'll kill Mahmoud, and then Ahmed will kill Mohamed, and that way they'll be free of the torture, and surely God will forgive the killers for their heinous crime, which they only committed in order to relieve themselves of the agony."

The Saint broke in again. "What about the last Salafi? Does he commit suicide?"

I continued: "At this point, Ahmed objects. They are leaving him to a terrible fate, he says. He has no problem with one of them killing him, but he won't be the last killer, living on under torture until he is sentenced to death. So Mohamed tells him he can commit suicide. God's certain to pardon his great sin because he wasn't choosing to kill himself willingly."

The Saint was fully engaged. "But it's a trick!" he cried. "A suicide can never go to heaven, even if he kills himself in a noble cause like that."

I was on the point of asking him if it really was such a noble cause, but I went on: "And that was Ahmed's point as well. He says he doesn't have the guts to kill himself, and even if he was presented with a religious edict saying he could, he still wouldn't do it. For the second time, he says he's willing to be killed by one of his cellmates, but he won't let himself be left till last."

I fell silent. The story was over but the Saint, it seemed, didn't get it. "Then what?" he asked. "What happened to them?"

"Nothing. None of them did anything and to this day they're still being tortured. The point, my friend, is that prisoners don't commit suicide precisely because they're looking forward to a better life when they get out, or after they're dead, perhaps—or even because life in prison is preferable to life on the outside."

I lit a cigarette.

"Did you know that Salafis believe the torture they undergo in prison is a kind of cleansing of their sins? They think they'll go to heaven as a reward for their suffering on earth. Basically, that we get them into heaven ourselves by virtue of the things we do to them. And of course, if they die from the torture or if we shoot them, they're martyrs, and they go straight to paradise."

Smiling, the Saint asked, "And will they?"

"Of course not! They're insane, they're killing machines! It's just that they're unarmed. Hand them a weapon and see what they do."

The Saint's smile disappeared and he looked down at the ground as he walked on. For a moment, I imagined that he was mulling over what I'd said and what I'd done while stationed up in the tower. Would the people I'd killed really be going to heaven? Was I an angel of mercy, dispatching people to paradise? Had I ever killed anyone who deserved it—or was I just an instrument, its purpose to deliver people from this loathsome world? I could find nothing to say and I saw that I was just the same as those I'd described as killing machines—that I was conflicted and foolish—but that I had been given a gun, and I wondered to myself what Burhan was thinking as

100

he sat there on my shoulder, drawing energy from my movements and storing it away.

But the Saint made no comment. We had come to Salah Salim Street, and silently we crossed over to the other side.

We walked through the tombs, heading to Manshiyat Nasr. The crowds pressed in and I thought to myself that the dead here outnumbered the living, and at my first glimpse of the tombstones terror gripped me. But with each step taken and each tombstone passed my indifference returned, and the tombstones became stones once more, the ground just dirt, and beneath it mere lifeless bones. The smell of the fine dust filled my nose and I spied two groups of people, gathered by a pair of graves and burying two bodies. Tears, and prayers, and Quran recitals, and little leaflets, farewells, and pleas not for justice but for mercy, entreaties for a timely reconciliation with the departed, since life without them was insupportable, since life itself was insupportable . . . and the solution? That we depart this world in expectation of another, less full of torment—of a hell less full of torment than this world. At least in hell we would know that we were being tormented, would be certain that we were paying the price for our sins here, and that this price would be paid out in the end, and that better lay ahead—all contrary to what we'd seen today and knew for a fact: that worse was to come.

And I saw spent syringes strewn upon the ground, and the many bottles of many different cough medicines, and bones both old and new—whether human or animal, I did not know. We walked on, and the dead in their caskets beneath us looked up at us and wished that we might stop and talk, if only for a while. But we were in a hurry, and we did not stop and talk to them.

Without warning, the Saint spoke up. "People only commit suicide in very rare cases, friend. As you said, they live in hope of a better existence in some place other than this. All men dream of eternal life in heaven."

He fell silent for a moment, then: "But suicides have their logic, too. If they're atheists, then they're not expecting anything after death and what might happen there doesn't bother them. All they care about is being delivered, liberated, from this world. If they're believers, then they are going to think they will be in hell for eternity because of their sins, whether they commit suicide or not. In either case, they commit suicide because they have lost hope: the hope for a better existence in this world or the next. They see what we are blind to. Simply put, hope robs us of our sight."

It had been a long time since I'd considered such things. I was about to embark upon indiscriminate mass murder, but it was the Saint—who had never killed a soul—who was thinking on these matters. Had I lost my faith?

He went on. "Maybe we'd see the world differently if we knew we were in hell for ever."

"And the man who jumped from al-Azhar Bridge?" I asked. "Was he a believer or an atheist?"

The Saint laughed. "Well, of course I've no idea. Maybe he saw something you've never seen. Knows something you don't. You can't pass judgment on someone who pisses on passersby, then jumps bare-naked and breaks his neck."

Where had the days of the classic suicide gone? The note to the lover, the bottle of poison, the rope from the ceiling, the sleeping pills, the wrists slit lengthways, and, of course, the severe depression leading up to the final act?

We were through the tombs and Manshiyat Nasr appeared before us. The Saint was tired of walking, it seemed, and he flagged down a tuktuk to take us to the other side of the neighborhood. As he clambered in, he said, "We'll drive through Manshiyat Nasr to the foot of Muqattam. We're pretty close now, it won't take more than ten minutes."

Farida was still on my mind and I'd see her today, for sure. I'd wasted my first day in East Cairo but today I had nothing to do. I'd go back to Sharif Street and look for her.

Burhan, who I'd forgotten all about, suddenly flew off my shoulder and landed on the Saint's head. The Saint laughed and made no comment, and the tuktuk driver glanced at us in the mirror and smiled. Then Burhan returned to his perch on my shoulder. For some reason, the Saint's words echoed in my head and I thought to myself that both the suicide and the Saint—and maybe Burhan, too—knew what I did not.

The tuktuk stopped when the last buildings appeared ahead of us. Cairo's outermost point: Manshiyat Nasr, the tombs, Salah Salim, and the rest of the city behind us, and before us the vast cliff face of Muqattam. We walked for a while over uneven ground, the base of the cliff ahead of us and not far away—though very far from any buildings, roads, or humans, and surrounded by a broad expanse of wasteland and an electric fence—the Knights of Malta's rocket launchers sat ranged across a hillock. It was from this point that they had bombarded West Cairo. I looked behind me and saw the ghost of the Cairo Tower far, far away, enveloped in a miasma of dust and smoke, and I had no idea if it was empty or if someone was stationed there.

The Saint started scaling the hillock's sloped side, now and then resorting to his hands to help him climb. In a state of great excitement, I followed him until we came to a narrow, level platform about a meter high that looked like a table, missing only chairs and a feast. I noticed a trace of water on the stone surface, as though the clouds had rained over just this tiny patch and it had not yet dried. We went down steps carved out of the stone behind the platform, and I saw a hollow, like a narrow little valley, into which the Saint walked with me following after, and then, as if by magic, there was a brand new door set into a sandy, yellow rock wall. The Saint knocked, the door was opened, and we went in.

A cramped tunnel led to a cramped chamber in which a man stood carrying a Kalashnikov with its safety catch engaged.

103

He seemed perfectly calm, but when he caught sight of me he flicked the safety catch off, and his eyes and trigger finger tensed. The Saint raised his palm in the man's face and said, "Relax, he's with me," but he didn't relax, just gripped his gun. We stood there until another man came and searched us for weapons. He searched us with the scrupulousness and courtesy of a veteran cop. I know what a policeman's hand feels like when he searches you without wanting to humiliate you, and if it hadn't been for the man clinging to the Kalashnikov I would have asked him his rank.

We passed through another door and down a long passage, which branched into many more passages and tunnels. We were underground, the walls and ceiling of solid Muqattam rock, rough to the touch—the roughness of age and immutability. I was now properly lost in the network of impossibly narrow shafts. I couldn't remember which way we'd come, and I certainly wouldn't be able to make it back alone. No weapon, and I didn't know anyone here except the Saint; my survival depended on his.

"Ready?" the Saint asked. "We'll be going into the first room where they collect the raw material."

Then he opened a door and a powerful, organic stench rolled out.

Numerous barrels were set on the ground and a man stood among them wearing rubber boots reaching to the knee and jeans, while his unclothed upper body revealed his extreme skinniness. He turned to us, then went back to inspecting the sieve in his hand, passing his fingers through a large hole in the mesh and trying to gauge its width.

Curious, I went over to the closest barrel, looked in, and found that it was full of little scarabs—hundreds and hundreds of black beetles covered by a thin layer of soil, some of them attempting to flee by scaling the inner walls of their barrel but slipping back down the smooth surface. I froze, trying to understand what was going on.

The Saint lit a cigarette and told the man he'd put it out in just a second, then went over to another barrel. "This," I heard him say, "is how Egyptians started consuming karbon. . . ." He stuck the hand holding the cigarette into the barrel, moved his arm around as though searching for something, then pulled it out. A fat red ant was stuck on the tip of the lit cigarette, beating the air with its spindly legs as it tried to flee. The Saint lifted the cigarette to his mouth, eyes fixed on the ant in case it fell, then took a very long drag; the coal glowed and the ant convulsed. I saw it drumming its front legs against its head. The Saint took another drag, and halfway through the ant stopped moving. A pungent smell filled the room, the smell of a red ant burnt to death. Then the Saint took a third drag, and the corpse curled up completely and became a black dot, bearing no resemblance to the creature it had been. He let the cigarette fall and stamped to extinguish it. "That's the lowest grade karbon," he said. "The ants. What you smoked yesterday was the best—the sacred scarab of our forefathers."

8

I WAS PREPARING THE JOINT *al fresco*, the bright sunlight bathed my skin, and I felt unusually happy and at ease. It was a beautiful morning and it made me forget how dull the days were, suspended up here in the sky.

At the top of the tower, a man could think terrible thoughts: jumping into the Nile, not in order to kill yourself but from a yearning to embrace the water. I'd fantasize that, after falling from that great height into the Nile's broad span, I would be saved, would survive, would plunge down a few meters, then bob back up, relishing the cold water, and maybe swimming over to the five battleships and banging on their hulls with my fist, a challenge to the Knights of Malta's sovereignty, then back to the banks of the island to find my companions waiting. I'd think about firing indiscriminately on pedestrians along the Corniche. Those people didn't care about the battleships; perhaps they were in favor of the occupier staying. Thousands of cars passed down that road each day, thousands of pedestrians, gazing over at West Cairo, free from the control of the Knights of Malta, and knowing that over there someone was holding out, someone who might be sacrificing his life to expel the occupier, and yet they did not join him. Cairo was a truly corrupt city. Whenever news reached me of rebellions in the Delta, I wondered at the tame creatures who lived around me and did not resist. I thought of opening fire on the windows of the television building that rang with

107

praise of the Knights of Malta all day long. The official home of government broadcasting deserved to be bombed without any warning being given to those inside.

I thought how afraid the Knights of Malta's soldiers would be if we took to killing them, then grilling them over coals and eating their flesh. Maybe then they'd leave, not out of fear of dying, but for fear of ending up as shit in Cairo's sewers. And I thought that all that had happened and was happening was ordained, and yet we went on resisting regardless.

As I fixed the joint, I was staring at a drone drawing away toward West Cairo. A short while before, we'd received a smaller than usual block of hash and orders stressing the need for restraint for a twenty-four-hour period, during which time we were completely forbidden from firing on East Cairo. We immediately realized that a group from the leadership must be moving in the east that day, and might be passing down the Corniche or slipping into the television building, and they were concerned we'd hit them or worried about security measures being tightened up, standard procedure after one of our attacks. The order for restraint was very encouraging, suggesting we were building up to some exceptional action. Would the mounting pressure really force the Knights of Malta to leave? I pictured them bewildered: wanting to leave, but having nowhere else to go. Perhaps we'd throw them out and they'd occupy another country, oppress another people. I didn't much care. I was bored of being up here. Every day, I'd weigh the benefits of what I was doing and then I'd go back to thinking that there was no other way.

With the first drag, I realized that the hash was spiked, mixed with a large quantity of other chemicals. This was unusual, but I carried on smoking, keen to try a different high. Whatever had been added, pills or otherwise, the effect on me was dramatic.

Following the fourth drag, the chemicals had overwhelmed the hash. I lay stretched out on the ground on the top floor, the

108

heavens above my head aglow, marveling at the insistent light and the purity of the sky, while the metal spikes tilting outward from the top of the balcony's railing looked to me like a monster's claw with a thousand talons, and I pictured those talons closing on me and my companions, closing in and crushing us all, without hope of escape. Looking over at those who were with me, I saw them similarly stretched out on the ground or with their backs against the balcony's wall, all of them silent, and then I was visited by very short bursts of total awareness of everything around me, moments when my senses were fully alert: I could clearly smell the reek of hash smoke filling my nostrils, the scent of the soap I'd washed my face with two hours before, and the anti-inflammatory cream one of us had rubbed on his shoulder. The most distant sounds were perfectly audible: window shutters being closed in a building overlooking the Corniche in West Cairo; starlings gathered in the branches of a huge tree by the zoo and chirruping with wild hysteria. And somewhere in Imbaba, a brawl—twenty men slapping with their hands, and then the real fight, when voices fell still, insults were choked off, and it was out with the blades, tots and teens hurling bricks and stones at the combatants, and then the sound of shotgun blasts from zip guns and the reports of Egyptian-made automatics, and an ironmonger roaring in rage in a street nearby as he fished out guns he'd finished making just yesterday, putting them in a hold-all to be distributed to one side in the battle. And car horns blaring as they circled Tahrir Square in East Cairo, trying to escape that circle of hell, endless minutes of the drivers' and passengers' lives lost with no hope of recovery or of putting them to use. I saw the cars creeping forward before they were hidden behind the massive edifices of Talaat Harb Street, which blocked them from view but not from my gaze. I saw all things in outline, the sizes and dimensions of cars and pedestrians described without color, or shade, or surface: outlines that meant I couldn't tell their make and number, or the bulk and height of those that rode inside. I saw the shapes of bodies walking behind buildings, and I could hear them as clearly as if I were moving among them—an irreducible tangle of human sounds and voices. Slowly, though, these moments of heightened consciousness faded into the long periods of disengagement that followed. Were these really bursts of consciousness, or was I completely out of it, just dreaming that I heard, and saw, and smelled it all? And I thought to myself that they had sent us this spiked hash to make sure we were properly intoxicated: living corpses, incapable of action.

With difficulty, I got to my feet, staggered over to the railing, and tried waking one of those slumped on the floor, but he didn't move or answer me. I called his name, but got it wrong. "Ali?" I tried to remember who he was, but couldn't, and started kicking him gently in the leg. Slowly, he turned to look at me, made no response, and just then my head cleared, and I knew we were in grave trouble; our first lines of defense were high as kites and unable to do a thing. Hash calmed us down and helped us to relax, but this stuff had robbed us of our faculties. I walked around the balcony to the other side and looked out over West Cairo. Everything was as it should be, or so it seemed.

Suddenly, I heard a sharp hiss, like a firework taking off or the air being let out of a tire. I couldn't tell where the sound had come from. I peered around and a thought occurred to me: maybe we were in hell. Maybe that had been the Devil farting—a tongue of flame and a sound to make you jump. I stared out, ready for a pillar of fire to appear or a line of flame to cross the heavens, but all I saw was a small, dark object plummeting out of the sky at a tremendous speed. Baffling. Then light flooded the spot where it had landed and there was the powerful, unmistakable sound of an explosion, and intersecting balls of fire blossomed out and became black smoke. West Cairo was being bombarded for the first time since the beginning of the occupation.

I raced around to the other side of the balcony, to East Cairo. As I ran, I tilted my body toward the main body of the tower, and the balcony's fence flashed by me, its railings flickering past my eyes. It seemed to take forever to get there, and I lifted my wrist in order to look at my watch, and remembered I hadn't worn one for many years, and then I came to a halt. I must have run two circuits around the tower, I thought, and I hadn't yet reached my colleagues lying slumped and stoned. I must go back in the opposite direction if I wanted to get to the east-facing side. The tower's balcony was a circular maze with no way out. Then I looked out to the horizon, and I saw that all was peaceful and that nothing was out of the ordinary—the Nile flowing sedately north, indifferent to any shit that might be taking place on its banks—when I heard one of my colleagues scream my name.

Momentarily sobered, I sprinted over, closing the distance in a couple of seconds. The snipers were standing by the railing, looking out over East Cairo. They were staring at the battleships anchored in the Nile directly below us. I stood next to them and heard one say, "There, at the edge of the city," and he pointed east.

The rocket's exhaust trail could be clearly seen. It began at the base of the Muqattam hill, rose up until it had passed over our heads, then gradually disappeared. Even as he pointed, another rocket launched, tracing a second white line across the sky parallel to the first, and then a third, and a fourth. My supernatural awareness was fading once again, it seemed, as if the hash high and the chemicals' unexpected impact were ebbing away as I tracked the rocket rising up over our heads and vanishing into the sky, and I could see nothing but a glimmer, like a tiny star exploding by day. Then it dropped quickly toward West Cairo and the rocket's body opened to release hundreds of little objects, small bombs that would complete the descent, widening the area of impact and the damage done. They hit a number of buildings and flattened them,

111

even as the bodies of the third and fourth rockets broke open, spilling the cluster bombs that would make sure this patch of West Cairo was utterly destroyed.

And I heard the sound of things being demolished, and of particles of soft dust, of the moans of the dead, and of souls ripped from their bodies—though which was ripping which, I couldn't tell—of women weeping, their hands slapping their cheeks as the fire consumed their children, of cars speeding by, then stopping, the drivers sprinting heedlessly toward shattered homes, shunting the rubble aside in terror, and thousands beneath the wreckage pleading for water or for death, of doctors bellowing, asking for things I couldn't understand, of boys on motorbikes lifting up bleeding bodies and gunning away, stony-faced, in search of a hospital, of workmen from the south calling out the names of their friends as they heaved the debris away with their bare hands, of a man lighting a cigarette, then smoking it with equanimity and enjoyment, his body lying beneath tons of concrete, and brick, and wood, no hope for him at all, saying, "Why not enjoy yourself before you die?" of a woman crying, "At last!" as she surrendered to a freefall as rapid as the bedroom door, ceiling, and floor that plummeted down around her, of someone calling out from the mosque's minaret, and no one understanding him and so leaving him to rave, of dogs howling and not understanding, barking and not understanding, running and not understanding. And I did not understand.

When night fell, the rockets were still being launched from the edge of East Cairo, and white smoke trails were replaced by the jets of flame spat out by the rockets as they disappeared into the darkness. Half West Cairo in ruins. The drug was still working, and it looked as though it wouldn't stop any time soon. None of the members of the resistance on the ground made a move and no citizen of East Cairo stirred to attack the rocket launchers or stop them, and I later learned that that day had been the calmest in East Cairo since the occupation

112

began. Not a single Maltese trooper was harmed, and the public acted as though what was happening was perfectly normal. One of my colleagues, slumped next to me in an attitude of surrender, said, "Even if we'd been fully awake, we wouldn't have done a thing."

I watched East Cairo through my scope, looking for just one soldier, a single officer, to bring down. The rifle was steady in my hands, but I was not, and I saw thousands standing by the Corniche, watching the bombardment of West Cairo with an extraordinary lack of emotion, as though it were some imaginary city being bombarded in sound and light on a movie screen. The vendors moved through the crowd in perfect safety, and many of them sat down in the middle of the road as if taking a break from some grueling exertion. No one crossed any of the bridges to help the inhabitants of the west.

By the following morning, the black smoke from the fires had traveled a considerable distance south: a vast cloud of darkness stationary over what was left of West Cairo and an unbroken tail trailing away from the city. Life went on in East Cairo as though the day before had been just like any other. Cars sped down the Corniche, their passengers glancing casually at the ruins of their neighbor, and by noon, crowds had gathered where they'd stood the day before—leaving work and coming to stand and see what had happened, hoping that the city would be bombarded again today.

By dawn, I'd sobered up, though a faint, scarcely perceptible effect could still be felt. My companions were waiting for the next drone to show up with the day's orders, but it never came. The twenty-four hours was now up and we were free to start shooting. We readied all the ammunition, climbed to the top floor, and turned our guns on East Cairo.

I shot at those standing and walking along the Corniche, the closest road to the tower. I pointed the gun in their general direction and fired. I didn't aim at anyone in particular. I shot at the cars that drove by, killing a number of drivers, and the vehicles piled up in the road. But none of this stopped them. After sunset, thousands trekked down to the Corniche for a reprise of the previous day's scenes, and to me it seemed as though they weren't there to watch the West Bank smolder, but were waiting to be shot at.

I ordered everyone to cease firing. Then I instructed them to take aim at the furthest stretches of the Corniche and blaze away indiscriminately. We hit numerous buildings in Bulaq Abul-Ela, around Tahrir, and in Abdel-Munim Riyad Square, then started picking our targets, taking out anyone we caught passing through those distant areas and hitting the cars with many rounds. I didn't know why I was doing it, but I was happy. Enjoying myself, even. The pleasure and contentment I'd felt the morning before returned. No drone arrived asking us to stop. None of the civilians or occupation soldiers turned to look at us. Many of them must have guessed that up there at the top of the tower were snipers murdering people, but they didn't care and made no move to stop us. After three hours of shooting off half-inch rounds, our ammo ran out. The rifles were panting in our hands, but we were in raptures.

Gradually the crowds broke up. By midnight, the Corniche was free of vehicles and foot traffic, and East Cairo was sound asleep. Not the troubled sleep of a city traumatized by the many bodies that had fallen that day, but an indifferent slumber. The hundreds of corpses scattered before us were testimony to the lethargy and brutishness that afflicted the place. Even the corpses themselves were stupid and dull; no one who'd stared into their open eyes could sympathize with them. This was the first time Egyptian citizens had been indiscriminately targeted. Previously we'd hunted down those who collaborated with the occupier and senior government officials, and maybe killed one or two others unknowingly by accident, to zero-in the scope, or even for fun (how could a day go by without any shooting?), but today was revenge— and tomorrow would be, too, and all the days to come.

The smell of burning still hung in the air and, because we were as close as could be to the black cloud suspended over our heads, we covered our noses and mouths with strips of wetted cloth to block the airborne ash and dust. I was checking the day's haul through my scope when a group of nine or ten individuals appeared, wearing rubber masks of characters unknown to me, though I did pick out a poor imitation of actor Samir Ghanim. The masks' broad grins, arched eyebrows, and staring eyes suggested comic actors. One of the men bent down, reaching out his hand to that of the nearest corpse, looking for a ring or watch to remove, and then going for the clothes, rummaging for cash, which he took, and on to the neck and ears, for jewelry, which he stole, and then throwing everything he'd found into a plastic bag held in his left hand. All this happened quickly, hurriedly, though it didn't appear that they were afraid of the police or anything like that, but rather that they were rushing to strip the greatest number of corpses in the shortest time possible.

A bigger group came in their wake, wearing black trash bags that completely covered their necks, and heads, and hair, their eyes visible through irregularly ripped holes. I saw the bags plaster to their faces as they breathed in and puff out as they exhaled. The group was looking through pockets and bags, taking papers, ID cards, phones, watches, cheap rings, bags, shoes, and belts—everything the first group had left behind. Having searched the dead with frantic haste, they left, leaving nothing behind but the corpses' clothes.

Next came a small gaggle of teens. No more than five. Fifteen or sixteen years old, say, bare-chested and very scrawny. Their skin gleamed in the low light, either from sweat or something they'd smeared on themselves. I couldn't tell. Many tiny scars could be made out on their bare chests, and stomachs, and arms. Their heads were wrapped in sheets of newspaper and the pages of magazines, with only a single hole for their eyes. One of my colleagues said that people called them 'cockroaches.' I remembered what they called us: hornets. This lot were more squalid still. They stripped the clothes from the dead, one corpse at a time, leaving nothing behind, and giving special attention to the female bodies: lifting arms, clutching at breasts, and pinching thighs. Two teamed up to raise the legs of a young woman and part her thighs, then they started peering at her crotch.

I was really very tired by now, hardly strong enough to keep watching through the scope, but then one of them gave a violent jerk and I saw what he was up to.

He'd discovered that the girl was still alive. She lay there, sluggishly, limply moving her arm. She was signaling: requesting aid or asking for death. The cockroach stripped her of her clothes, shoved his trousers down, then flogged his cock erect and pushed it into her, clutching her upraised thighs. He was fucking her at a quite incredible pace, like some kind of purpose-built machine plugged into the mains, and the rest of the cockroaches gathered around. They were smoking through the sheets of newspaper they'd taken for masks, poking the cigarettes through the mouth-holes and puffing out smoke while they watched the machine at work. One of them stepped forward, felt the woman's head, and neck, and arm, then signaled to the machine that she was done, she'd died. His gestures were unmistakable, and the cockroach suddenly fell still, his cock still in the corpse, and let her legs subside, unopposed, on either side of him. Then it was mere seconds before he was back to pumping, and thrusting, and gripping the thighs, and then he was done, and the rest of the cockroaches could take their turn.

The corpses were spread out along the length of the Corniche, thicker in some areas and thinning out to none in others. I began combing the street through the scope to see what was going on, on the lookout for more thieves. More people started showing up, searching the bodies. They weren't masked or dressed alike in any way. They moved slowly

116

between the dead. Looking for their relatives, of course. They just looked at the faces—wouldn't touch the naked bodies or rifle through what clothing remained. Just looked at the faces, weeping. One large group walked together. They carried pictures in their hands and held them up to the faces of the dead. One woman walked along screaming in anguish, not looking at any of the dead faces, just wailing on and on, inconsolably, and when the others had all departed she remained, screaming intermittently until dawn. There was a man, carrying a small girl on his arm. Five or six, she looked. He was stooping over every corpse, turning the head to show her its face. He would point at the face and talk to her, and she would shake her head, then coil her little arm about his neck and bury her face in his shoulder. At each body he stopped, not leaving a single one without first pointing at its face and addressing the girl in his arms. But she always said no, moving her head very slightly, almost imperceptibly, at which the man would move on to another body and stoop.

9

THE FRESH AIR OUTSIDE WOKE me up. The smell of the insects had been acrid and unfamiliar, and I wasn't sure if I disliked it or not, but I was sure that I'd never take karbon again. Did people realize they were smoking ants and scarabs, cockroaches and beetles?

As we came away from Manshiyat Nasr, I told the Saint I was going to Sharif Street. He said he'd accompany me if I'd no objection. And I didn't, so long as he didn't come with me into the room. Truth be told, I wanted him there to be my guide should I fail to find Farida. Two long years of isolation, cut off from all communication, were time enough for homes and hearts to change. The Saint would help me, for sure. Maybe he knew an officer there, or one of the brothel owners, or a pimp, but I was sure he'd find her. Burhan clung to my shoulder as usual. Feeling somehow threatened, perhaps: compared to his friends in the barrel, Burhan was enormous, and he'd have been a prize find for any karbon dealer.

We had to get a taxi. We flagged one down near Manshiyat Nasr and the Saint told the driver, "Downtown. . . ." The atmosphere inside the brand new cab seemed sterile: the cold breeze from the air-conditioning vents had no smell. I'd forgotten about air-conditioning. Up in the tower, you breathed nothing but pure polluted air.

The Saint, seated by the driver, turned to me. "The whole country's smoking karbon these days." Talking about karbon without a thought for the driver surprised me quite a bit. Not that it really mattered, but conversations about drugs always used to be a private affair.

The Saint went on: "You don't remember what happened yesterday, am I right? That's one of its effects, my friend, and that's what people like about it. To put it simply, you turn into two people: you're completely sunk in darkness—no imagination there, no hallucinations, colors, or memories; you forget everything, you won't even remember your name—and on the other hand, your body and mind engage perfectly with the world around you. You were walking with me and we were talking. You were a perfect gentleman: talking politely, complimenting me, getting embarrassed when I swore. You don't remember it now, of course, and that's another of karbon's effects: anything that happens after you've taken it won't fix in your memory; it won't stay put in that mysterious part of your brain, because it's never stored there in the first place. All you recall is being lost in the darkness for a minute or two, though you're gone for at least three hours. Karbon makes people cleave closer to reality. It uncouples imagination from reality. Karbon users never make mistakes at work, never get bored, never drift off into daydreams and lose sight of the job. Their words and responses are carefully weighed against the questions they're asked: they flatter when they have to and rarely go on the attack. If hash is banned in the workplace, then karbon's a positive requirement—these days, it's the only reason to be good at your job."

I no longer cared about the driver listening in. What the Saint was telling me was bona fide magic. If I were king of Egypt, I'd legalize the stuff.

"The only thing is that it blocks inventiveness, creativity," he said. "But who ever complained of a lack of creativity?"

"Does that mean you're two people now?" I asked him. "I don't quite get the way it works."

"The Saint who's talking to you now is the practical, appealing version: the uninventive, optimistic, cheerful, hardworking me. The other version, in the darkness, is squatting motionless, perfectly suppressed: no voice, no impact on my actions."

"And because your memory won't be storing anything that's happening now—this conversation, I mean, getting into the taxi, the route we take, maybe events for many hours to come—because of that, you won't remember any of it when the karbon wears off? You'll just come out of what you call 'the darkness' into the real world, and that will be it?"

"Exactly," replied the Saint. "That might not sound like fun, but what's fun in this life anyway? Everyone's trying to get out, even if it means going somewhere dark where they're not aware of anything. It's still better than what we've got."

I glanced at the taxi driver, waiting for him to intervene. The conversation had opened up and he was surely going to have to have his say soon.

"It also makes those around the karboner much more open. Anything you say and I hear now I won't remember later. Whatever I'm aware of now will be wiped out when I come back from the darkness. By the way, you went into the darkness, right? What did you call it?"

"I didn't think of it as darkness," I said. "I thought it was blackness at first, then I saw that it was nothingness itself."

He laughed: "Nothingness itself! First time I've heard that expression. You found yourself in nothingness."

"That's right, nothing around me: no light, no objects, no smell, no sensation, no thoughts even. That's nothingness. No other word for it. Aren't you in nothingness right now?"

The Saint shut up briefly and shifted in his seat, looking out through the windshield. Then he said: "Maybe it is nothingness, but I've no idea where I am right now. I've no idea what's going on where I actually am. But I remember where I was the previous times, and it's nothingness. No other way to describe it."

"What about you, driver?" I said, trying to draw the man into the conversation. "You tried karbon?"

121

The Saint turned to me again. "If the guy hasn't interrupted us up till now, then that definitely means he's on karbon. That's the only explanation for such a courteous, unassuming manner." Then he turned to the driver: "Isn't that right, friend?" The driver nodded and I saw the ghost of a smile.

I wasn't going to take any karbon now, though—I wasn't going to be under the influence when I met Farida. Why forget? Didn't I say that I'd never use it again? Then I had a thought: "Saint?" I said, "Is someone who smokes karbon 'karbonized?'"

"Not quite," he replied. "We say 'karboned.' Like, 'I'm karboning' or 'we're karboned' or 'did you karbon today?' Then you can say, 'he's a real karboner, he karbons every week,' or 'that office worker's a full-on karbonator, he karbons every day,' and so on."

"Do the office workers really karbon every day?"

"Everyone karbons every day, friend. The whole country's karboned. You're never going to stop that or even reduce it. Do you want to know when it is that people come off the karbon? It's when they go to Sharif Street, when they smoke hash, or drink, or sleep with their wives or lovers. When they hold executions in the public squares. On execution day, you'll see what you've never seen before."

"I've seen it," I said.

"As regards our conversation this morning, people these days believe that what happens to criminals before they're executed absolves them of one third of their sins, the executions themselves remove another third, and the final third is canceled by what follows. What comes after death isn't a torment for the dead, of course, but for us: a charitable endowment in the form of suffering for others."

I had only ever witnessed the one execution, in Tahrir Square. I'd heard of people being sentenced to die in Ataba, Ramses, Abbasiya, and Roxy, but I never saw anything or knew what had happened. "What comes after execution?" I asked him: "I've only seen one of them."

122

"Of course, you were up in the tower. Which one did you see?"

"The first one, when they impaled five guys on stakes."

"It was different then. People were terrified. They weren't used to watching executions and didn't know how to deal with it. Maybe we'll get to see one or two in the days ahead. In any case, they announce the time and place the sentence will be carried out a few hours in advance. Who knows?" he went on, "maybe some of us will be carrying out executions soon."

True. We'd be carrying out a mass execution soon enough. Then we'd see how people dealt with it.

The car entered Sharif Street. The driver hadn't opened his mouth once. Stretching his arms, the Saint said, "I didn't ask for Sharif Street right away. People going there are usually after the brothels, and the cab drivers take roundabout routes to push up the fare. Because they're already ashamed of what they're there for, the passengers never like to argue and the drivers take advantage. This one's karboned, though; I knew it almost the instant we got in. That's why he won't cheat us and why I told him where we were heading when we were halfway here: as you can see, he took us the shortest route possible."

The Saint rummaged in his inside jacket pocket and produced a small leather bag. He opened it and extracted the contents, saying, "You see why everyone has to be karboned?"

The Saint had taken out a mask made of fabric. He unfastened the straps at the back. A soft mask, light to the touch, like silk. He put it on and tightened the straps around his head with both hands. It was the face of Anwar al-Sadat—the broad smile, great big gleaming white teeth, and dark skin.

"If you've got a mask, you should put it on now," he said. I took my mask from my bag and put it on, quickly as was my habit, and as I did the Saint cried, "What's that? That's the Buddha, right? That's the loveliest, most beautifully made mask I've seen in my life! More lovely than that mask of Maryam Fakhr al-Din even!"

123

I adored Maryam Fakhr al-Din's face. There was nothing ugly or even the slightest bit average about it in my view, and after she'd grown old I would look at her creased face and smile regardless: I knew those wrinkles and folds were the price to pay for her former beauty. "Who wears the Maryam Fakhr al-Din mask?" I asked the Saint. "Someone famous? Do you know her?"

I heard a chuckle from beneath his mask. "No, no, it's a notorious sissy who works in a brothel called the House of Martyrs at the end of this street."

I lifted my gaze and saw the brightly lit street, a treat for the eyes. Everyone, without exception, was masked.

The Saint went on: "What's lovely about it is that the mask isn't colored like mine, but black and white, just how the young Maryam Fakhr al-Din looked in the old movies. We're passing Studio Masr, where male clients wear Shukry Sarhan masks and the women are Leila Murad."

None of us spoke. I was trying to drive the old movies out of my head, but the storm of images was distracting me from the thing I'd come here for. I surrendered to the endless stream of footage and stars. We were passing by a building with Studio Masr written on its window, and I spied garishly lit portraits of famous actresses and singers facing out into the street. Then I noticed that their features were somehow wrong and realized that these weren't pictures of actresses and singers, but of masked whores instead. The likenesses scrolled by: Amina Rizk, Fairuz, Zeinat Sedki. . . .

I was on the point of asking him about the House of Martyrs, when we drove past the remains of the National Bank building, the one that had collapsed at the start of the occupation. The Saint nodded at it: "That's the place for the cheap tricks. Pay a pound and you can do what you like down in the vaults beneath the rubble. A lot of guys are drawn here by a thirst for adventure. Imagine it, lying down in a steel vault, thick walls, but very cramped inside—and the girl on top of you, or under you, and your bare body scraping against the cold, rusted metal. Your back, and elbows, and knees all scraping harder the more aroused you become, and you and her both sweating till you can smell the damp rust beneath you, then suddenly the steel gives way, and the vault buckles beneath the tons of cement that have been piled up over it for the last three years, and you die, pulverized, locked in that sordid pose."

I'd frequently imagined dying in poses much more sordid. That was nothing compared to what I'd pictured. I'd seen myself being resurrected in my former body; being reborn as a man with two bullet-holes in his chest and gripping my own throat; reborn with hundreds staring at me through their scopes, crosshairs on my chest, the lasers settling on my face and transforming it into a scarlet moon; reborn with a man demanding retribution, a man I had shot from behind and whose face when he visited me was a featureless blank, without eyes, or nose, or mouth—maybe just two holes to breathe through, nothing more— and who would say nothing, just point, and everyone would understand that I was a killer. But no, those ones had needed to be killed. They were killers themselves, or traitors: I killed them to keep the state safe, to keep Egypt safe. I would be reborn and I would be proud.

We reached the end of the street, right by the Ministry of Religious Endowments, where we encountered a man of massive dimensions. A giant. The first thing I noticed about him, after his sheer size, were his enormous breasts—great round tits worthy of a grown woman. He wore black leather trousers, high-heeled shoes, a cheap blond wig, a lacy black bra, and nothing else. He was smoking a cigarette and distributing flyers for brothels. His arms were at odds with his hair and his fingers, which were finished off with glossy black nail varnish. Anyone coming from Bab al-Luq would meet the man as they entered the street: a guardian, or a guide to newcomers.

The layout of the place had changed, I noticed. The brothels around the Stock Exchange had disappeared and the ones on Sharif Street had moved in to replace them, and I understood that it was going to be impossible to locate Farida. Satisfied that the Saint was karboned and wouldn't remember a thing, I approached the man in the bra and asked him what I should do if I wanted to locate a particular girl.

His response was delivered in an exceptionally gravelly voice, and I noticed that everything about him was big, and that he stank of cigarettes though he stood outside in the fresh air. I saw that his lipstick ran over the line of his lips, that he'd painted them clumsily and carelessly. He did his best to be pleasant, peppering his conversation with "Sir," and "My good friend," and the like, and asked what brothel Farida worked at, what she looked like, and when I'd last visited her. When I told him it had been two years, he laughed and said that was a long time indeed, that prostitution sent young kids to the grave, that a year here was like ten elsewhere, and that maybe I should go for someone else since Farida had most likely left Sharif Street. "But I can get hold of her, no problem," he said, and took his phone from his pocket. "Five pounds." I looked over at the Saint and he nodded. I paid the man the five pounds and waited.

Several calls later, he informed me that Farida was in Room 82 on the eighth floor of a brothel called the House of Forbidden Love, directly after the intersection of Sharif Street with Abdel-Khaliq Tharwat. The Saint said that we had passed it on our way. I'd now given up pretending and was gaping openly at the man's breasts. Thousands of others must have had the same thoughts. Were they implants? Surely he'd gotten implants because he wanted to turn into a woman—a first step to be followed by many more—but then he must have failed, or got fed up, or just stopped for no reason at all, and his chest had remained as it was. I was about to move on when, in tones of the utmost gravity, he said: "I was born with two huge tits. Bigger than my mother's."

As we retraced our footsteps to the House of Forbidden Love, I surveyed my surroundings. There were almost no cars in the street, but it was chock-full of pedestrians. I saw masks of famous figures, carefully made and faithful to their faces— Anwar Wagdi, Mahmoud al-Khatib, even Rafik Hariri—then cartoonish masks of others: Omar Sharif, Hassan Fayek, Mayada al-Henawi, and Alaa Al Aswany. Those without masks, and there were lots of them, had wrapped their heads in newspaper: some punching out round eyeholes so they could see where they were going, while others had made no holes at all, their heads bobbing along inside perfectly sealed hoods. How they could see where they were going I had no idea. Still others had wound worn cloth over their faces, or faded sacking. My mask was, as the Saint had pointed out, the most graceful and elegant of all.

Jammed on the first floor was a lift, enclosed not by walls but by thin metal bars that exposed the interior of the cabin. It hung there, suspended from flexible, plaited steel cables, while the space between the bottom of the lift and the ground floor was filled with a three-meter-high pile of trash: plastic bags, documents, newspapers, condoms, medicine bottles, packets—no organic waste at all, as though someone had sorted the trash before dumping it—the whole vast heap odorless, yet striking for its incredible array of colors and shapes. Near the bottom, a plastic sack which had once contained food was sticking out, and on it, the sell-by date: 9/10/2011.

The cop wasn't sitting in his ground-floor room where I'd expect to see him, but atop a well stuffed armchair on the exposed tiles of the filthy entrance hall, uniformed and reading a paper, with a cartoonish mask of Ronald Reagan over his face. I climbed the stairs and made straight for the eighth floor.

The bedroom door was locked. I asked Farida's neighbor, perched on a bar stool, if she'd seen her. Inside with a client, the girl said, and I felt a little better. Farida was here. I wasn't going to get caught up in a long search for her. The

Saint was circling the apartment, appraising the poverty in the whores' faces. Low-rent clothes, dirty shoes, crumbling walls, and glum faces. No clients, and whores by the dozen, gasping lasciviously and making sounds from deep in their throats like mewling cats. Farida's neighbor only spoke to let me know Farida was inside, but the rest of the girls started squirming around to catch my eye, and when they noticed that the Saint seemed interested three approached him. He quickly came to an agreement over the details and they all went into one of the girls' rooms.

At the very same time, the door to Farida's room opened and three cockroaches came out. Their loud shouts and laughter were clearly audible, but muffled by the sheets of newspaper wrapped haphazardly around their heads. They reminded me of the corpse robbers I'd seen stripping clothes months ago: the same skinny young bodies covered in scars. The three of them were laughing, and shouting, and letting off ringing snorts, in a frenzy of high spirits, bouncing around hysterically, sprinting off and deliberately smashing their bodies into the walls, into one another, into the terrified whores who stood there trembling. The women didn't utter a word of protest and—as Burhan circled by the corridor's ceiling as if avoiding some anticipated aggression against his person—the cockroaches ran noisily to the stairs and went down shouting, their howls growing quieter with every floor they descended.

With the exit of the three boys, everything became completely calm and Burhan returned to settle on my shoulder. As the rules had it, I should wait until Farida opened the door, ready for another trick, but I couldn't bear to wait and I knocked—and when no answer came, I turned the knob and gently opened the door.

With Farida, there was no embarrassment between us, no fear of what I might see, however upsetting. I was opening the door and remembering the blood of the suicide I'd seen that morning, sprinkling onto the bystanders, and them not moving, and then the man standing beneath the bridge, wiping the drop of blood from his eyelid and going back to staring at the body, and I readied myself to see Farida bleeding and trying to stanch the flow, to be bleeding from the nose and mouth, and from a wound by her missing left nipple. I thought this so I wouldn't be shocked, no matter how horrible the scene, and I went in and saw what was left of her. Farida's skeleton draped with skin. As it always did, her left breast with its missing nipple caught my eye and the bones beneath her face, more prominent than ever, hurt my heart. She was sitting on the floor, back resting against the wall, and panting. Her arms were slack by her sides. I came in and she said nothing, just looked at me instead: a glare, tongue-tied by the effrontery of this person who had entered without asking, and when there was just a meter separating us she stood up, quivering with rage and exhaustion, getting ready to curse me and throw me out. I removed my mask so she would know me, but she didn't know me. I took her in my arms, watching her astonished eyes stare into my face, and her trembling features. Her arms went rigid and she held her face away from mine, pressed back against her shoulder. She wanted to get a better look. She stared into my face as I clung to her, and she tensed against my embrace—not from revulsion, but to make certain I was really there. She stumbled over her words: "Are you . . . Karim?" I didn't know who Karim might be, nor did I care. Then she screamed, "You're Ahmed! You're Ahmed!" I stifled a sob of rage and she surrendered to a bitter wailing of a sort I had never heard before.

Oh, Farida . . .

Terror gripped her and she stayed trembling, arms still rigid, unable to return my embrace. I sat down. Sat her on my lap. Held her until she was still and calm, and in five minutes she had dozed off. She was wearing that distinctive shift of hers but it was torn in a number of places. I changed her clothes, picked her up, and walked out of the apartment

129

calling, "Saint!" and when he didn't reply I went back to the room he'd entered and thumped the door with my foot. "Saint . . . Saint!" I couldn't stay any longer. The whores had started milling around me, frightened now, but they might pluck up enough courage soon enough. Without further ado, I gave up on the Saint and left the apartment, left the whores behind me, waving and calling, "Saint . . . Saint . . . ," and hurried downstairs, eight whole floors, and the whores, hearing their coworkers calling, coming out to stand at the doors to their apartments and cry, "Saint . . . Saint . . . ," standing on the stairs looking down the central well around which wound the steps and calling, "Saint . . . Saint . . . ," and I exited the building to melt into the crowds, hearing their cries fade and dim, "Saint . . . Saint . . . ," without the slightest understanding of why they mocked me so mercilessly, nor why they laughed their whorish laughs as they mimicked me, why each one mocked me as though revenging herself on us both.

I walked through the crowds on the sidewalk, trying to keep myself under control—no running, no jostling the passersby, no panting—all so as not to attract attention, and Farida a bundle of bones and skin in my arms, no chance of stopping a taxi anywhere near here (the driver would think I'd snatched one of the whores), and Burhan flying before me like a guide; unwilling to stay put on my shoulder, he'd decided to lighten my load and taken wing. On I went, eyes fixed on Burhan, until I came to July 26th Street, where the real crowds were with their clamor and aggravation. So intense was the crush that I felt completely cocooned. No one could spot me here. Burhan would disappear into the throng, like he was parting it, then bob up a meter over people's heads as though awaiting my decision. I stopped by a building's entrance and heard the pig whisper, "Water . . . ," and if I'd had a hammer in my hand I would have left Farida on the ground and smashed skulls until there wasn't a human being left living in the street. My throat dried up, and I heard myself whisper, "Water. . . ," and I looked up to the heavens and prayed that they pour rain on our heads so that I might drink and the people would flee the downpour. I prayed that it might rain anything, anything at all, but the heavens denied me everything, even shit.

At last, I made it across the sidewalk to an uncrowded spot by the curb and, without my flagging it down, a taxi pulled over in front of me. I got in immediately and told the driver, "al-Azhar Street."

Farida lay in my lap, her feet jammed against the car door and my arm around her shoulders. I inched sideways so her body could stretch out the full width of the back seat, pressing up against the other door and resting her head on my thigh. Then I took off my mask. I studied it for a moment. Its imperturbability and blankness chilled me. How, amid all our flaws, could the metal remain so flawless? And I placed it over Farida's face: exposed and pale, half asleep and half unconscious.

Inside the taxi, in the darkness split every few seconds by the streetlamps' yellow glare, I saw Farida's open eyes staring out at me from behind the mask. The mask was utterly invisible to me—all I could see were her eyes, and I expected them to be tear-filled or blinking, but they were cold and still.

It had all been exhausted—my indifference, my calm, my cynical detachment from what was happening around me; even my rage had run dry—and now nothing was left but the desire for revenge: on the silent figures that prowled the streets, on the brothels' johns, on the people shouting songs on the sidewalks, on those who were gathered in circles in the midst of the crowd, bouncing and chanting rhyming slogans of which I didn't understand a word, on the street dogs and the pigs, on the docile cows, on the snakes scaling the walls and sliding along with a smoothness that cut at the sidewalk and cut me to the quick, on the cockroaches, abroad in every street with their slippery, naked, menacing bodies. The car drove past many people. I'll kill them all one day. And I thought that were I to start counting all those upon whom I'd

131

revenge myself, I would never finish. And I told myself that my patience was spent, and that my vengeance was just, and that the Day was at hand.

I wanted a closer look at Farida's scrawny body, stretched out in surrender on the bed. I placed my hand on her lean belly, her jutting hip, her small breasts, her thin neck, her gaunt cheek. I was caressing her, my heart thumping. She was awake, and looked into my eyes for a few moments before her gaze drifted off around the bedroom. *Farida, are you afraid?* But no. Whores don't fear strange places, locked rooms. I was scared she'd speak, that she'd get up before I'd had my fill of her recumbent body, and that if she spoke I would break down beneath the burden of her drowsy, ethereal voice. Farida was more than I could bear. I remembered the panic I'd seen on her face when she saw mine, her open mouth and the big teeth that I loved but that reminded me of the teeth of the dead, their bodies laid out on trolleys to be washed, and this image of her—slack-mouthed, neck aquiver—hovered before me and would not disappear. Even though her face was here, now, beneath my hand, and I could feel her pallid, sick skin beneath my fingers, the memory overpowered the present. Then Farida closed her eyes and swallowed, her breathing became regular, and she slept.

I was unable to sit still, pacing the room like a prisoner. Burhan clung to the wall, head down, as though sheltering from my rage and waiting for what I'd do next. That's right: I would kill them all for sure, would do it happily. If only I had a weapon.

I remembered the bag of karbon I'd bought that morning, the paste of sacred scarabs, and I remembered the Saint, though he was most likely still in the bedroom with the girls— he wouldn't care what had happened and would forget it all tomorrow morning. I had no rolling papers, so I emptied out the tobacco from a regular cigarette, filled it with the karbon,

132

and nipped off half the filter with my teeth. I did what felt right. I smoked that cigarette with a voraciousness I myself found hard to believe and even before I'd finished, the blackness hit me.

In nothingness again, this time cold, as though sinking down through oil that grew denser and denser as I descended, and warmer, until its temperature matched my body's and I could feel it no longer. And I asked myself how it was that I could be in nothingness and still be, and that if I was, then this was not nothingness, and I tried searching for something, anything, around me. I didn't look, but I searched, though looking and searching meant nothing in this blackness. I was trying to break this idea of nothingness, to find something so that I could at least be certain that I *was*. Then it came to me that everything that is, is in motion. Even if I were dead, even if I were dust, even if I'd left earth for space, for a blackness like the one in which I found myself now, I would still be in motion, however slightly. My internal organs would be, for sure. But I knew then that I was perfectly still, that my heart was still and did not beat, that my lungs did not fill with air, nor empty, that the blood sat clotted in my veins, and I knew that I was nothingness, like the nothingness around me—I was nothing at all—and I tried recalling what had happened that day, where I was and what I was, but I had forgotten language and memory.

10

BURHAN WAS WHERE I'D LEFT him yesterday, clinging to the wall, Farida was still asleep, and I was sitting beside her, looking at her. All was calm.

I couldn't remember what I'd done after the hit of karbon. Maybe I'd slept beside her without touching her, and maybe I'd been unable to keep my longing for her under control and had slept with her. The memory of her trembling face still possessed me; my desire for revenge was still there. How far I'd distanced myself in just one day from the resistance, from my hatred for the Knights of Malta, from assassination missions, from preparations for a popular revolution that would drive the occupier away. The public had become the personal, and if enough members of the resistance had changed like I had, then the occupation would last forever.

We would kill people, there was no doubt about that. We'd been killing them for years and it no longer bothered us. We would kill them and nothing would happen. We would kill them and they would not rise up. Would not move to smash and burn the occupier's bases, would not attack the soldiers and officers in their headquarters or the annexed Egyptian army barracks located far from the population centers where civilians could not get at them, and we ourselves didn't have strength or weapons enough to try it. It all seemed farcical, as though we'd be killing people just for the fun of it. I wanted to forget the whole affair, and live with Farida, and marry her. She'd leave the trade and I'd work as a bodyguard for some famous, imperiled individual. I could be head of security for a firm or factory. These were the dreams of people who craved stability, but stability had ended years ago and it wasn't coming back. I thought to myself that we had never had stability—that it was a fantasy without foundation. There are always going to be surprises that derail you from the course your life is taking, that take you into a maze of paths that never end, where you'll live in a state of constant fear, searching for an illusory stability, moving through the maze, trying to get out in hope of a better, untrammeled life. Then you emerge from the maze and find yourself in another maze, bigger and more complicated, from a little prison to a larger prison, and there is nothing else but this. Our stability is a prison—yet we prefer it because, unlike a maze, it's simple.

Would I go back to being an officer at the Interior Ministry after the occupation? Would the Egyptian army be rebuilt? Did the remaining officers have the ability to control the borders, to raise the flag once again over Egyptian dominions?

For centuries, we'd lived under occupation. We'd never fought back, and if we had seen how other nations fought we'd have understood that we had welcomed the occupiers one and all. It's said we only welcomed an occupier so as to drive out the one before—as though, under the right conditions, occupation could be desirable—and then as soon as we'd expelled the final foreign occupier, the questions began: was it a revolution or a military coup? Were we a socialist state or a capitalist one? Did we only care about ourselves or should we unify with the Arabs? Was it a setback or a defeat? Were we waging war or waiting? Liberalization or law of the jungle? Peace treaty or treachery? Terrorism or state terrorism? Were we fighting terrorism with fire or with enlightenment? Was Mubarak a skilled skipper or a chuckling fool? Had Mubarak's family brought back the monarchy or did the man respect the constitution? Was this dynastic succession or a son helping out his father? Was it revolution or unrest? A popular uprising or Brotherhood

136

putsch? Would the Brothers rule us forever or would we revolt against them? And then, all over again: was it a revolution or a military coup? Would we tough it out or rise up? Would we abide by the constitution or give the man a mandate to rule for eternity? Would he run against another dummy or take on a proper opponent? Was this unrest or revolution? Is corruption still rampant or is that just a feature of the modern state? Shall we amend the constitution so he can rule us for a third term or make him prime minister instead? And then nearly half a million Maltese Knights had showed up and put an end to all this confusion, all this unintelligible back-and-forth, these debates and discussions, and everybody stopped raising questions, even though we'd heard not one clear answer in decades. What we got was a frank and open and real and honest and beautiful occupation. Unarguable. No more minorities, no more mistreated blocs, no more opposition, no more parties, or fractured parliaments, or flawed elections. We were all against the occupation and no one lifted a finger. When a few individuals took action and set up a resistance whose backbone was made up of former police officers, not one citizen took the slightest interest or offered to help. When people were gunned down by the Knights of Malta, they made no protest; when we killed them ourselves, they did not accuse us of being mad; and when, a few days from now, I killed them, they would shrug their shoulders and walk away. We'd lost the ability to keep going and had turned into speechless lumps. Apathy had killed us and we no longer had it in us to take a stand, as though we were paralyzed or dead. But even the dead protest and feel regret. On the Day of Resurrection, the people shall weep with remorse for what they have done; those in hell shall scream from the severity of their torment—they shall not stand so smug and unresisting when they are tortured there. And Major General al-Asyuti thinks that they will rise up just because we kill a few thousand of them? This man, born in the time of nationalism, assumes that people hate the maze. He doesn't see

137

that they've all sat down and slept there; they've settled there and buried themselves within it, beneath its walls. He doesn't understand that they fell into despair long ago and that now they have gone beyond it.

But if my maze was to be the price of waking Farida, I would happily have paid it. *Wake up, Farida! I want to hear your voice and see your eyes.*

And then I heard a faint knocking at the door. A man I didn't know, wearing a huge mask in the shape of a horse's head that covered the upper half of his body, his arms sticking out from the sides of the neck. He handed me a small white envelope and left without saying a word.

The message was clear: 'At 7 p.m., send them to heaven. The Tiring Building, Ataba.' I'd have to play a lot of this by ear, it seemed, but things were in motion.

I didn't know exactly where the Tiring Building was, but Ataba was only a few paces from the apartment. I'd walked the route hundreds of times, but I'd never seen that building.

There was still plenty of time, but I had to go to Ataba to look for the place, then check it out to see where I'd be taking up position, then look for the gun, make sure it was working and zeroed in, and maybe test it out on a few targets. All before 7 p.m. I had to stick to the time and place, but other than that I was free to improvise. For the last two years, all my missions had been like that: just the basic information.

My tour around the neighborhood lasted less than half an hour. I bought food for Farida, water, tea, sugar, clothes I reckoned would suit her, and soap for her to shower, then I walked home to find her still asleep. There was nothing for it but to wake her.

At first, her voice was weak, maybe because she'd slept so long, and the first thing she said was, "Don't worry, I'm fine." Then she closed her eyes, rolled over on the bed, and slowly sat upright. I hugged her. I needed to feel her arms about my body when she was conscious, and she didn't let me down, clutching me to her, her fingers running over my back. I had to go now, I told her. I'd be back tonight. I told her she mustn't go out at all today. Everything she needed was here. She must just be patient until I returned. Immediately, her expression turned to one of coquettish irritation, the sham vexation I loved so much, and I smiled, remembering how she used to make that face whenever I said anything she didn't like. Not that she ever had any real objections, of course; she was just signaling a delicate displeasure without the slightest intention of changing what I would do. This was her way of registering protest, which is maybe why I was so attached to her.

Farida, I shall return victorious, but I do not promise you that it will all be over soon.

She padded off barefoot and I saw that in my haste I'd dressed her in men's clothes: a shirt I hadn't buttoned, trousers with the fly unzipped. Maybe nobody in the street had noticed the men's clothes flapping on her body. Maybe nobody had noticed us at all. She walked toward the door of another bedroom, clutching the trousers so they wouldn't fall, the long sleeves of the outspread shirt hiding her hands, and when she reached the door she peeked inside, retreated, and headed for the bathroom. In the short trip between the two doors, she took off the trousers, and shirt, and what was left of the outfit of lightweight fabric. She went into the bathroom and I saw her straight back, the vertebrae I longed to touch standing proud beneath the skin, and the broad buttocks—yes, still broad—that underpinned it all.

In the bathroom, she sat completely naked on the toilet and I heard the sound of urine hitting the bowl. I smiled and she said I'd better leave—it wouldn't smell nice. I smiled again, because I'd embarrassed her. Farida was still shy, despite everything.

I thought that I should stay with her, that I should abandon the mission, and the resistance, the whole lot, that maybe I should leave the Knights of Malta alone and return to a regular existence with a regular woman.

139

She emerged naked, stepping elegantly over the shiny tiles, her big feet at odds with her thin shanks and, as always, I raised my eyes to her big hands, so out of place at the ends of her scrawny arms. I had been crazy to abandon Farida and stay up in the tower, but this time I would definitely be back. I certainly wasn't going to disappear for two years. Still, I asked myself if she would wait for me.

I embraced her naked body. I longed to take my clothes off and feel my skin next to hers, for her to take my stiff cock between her thighs as she always did, to scratch my back and neck with her nails, to slap and grab my ass, to squeeze it and tell me how lovely it was, while I laughed and she became more playful still, walking around me and bending down to peer at it, and saying, "Really, your ass is lovely!" *But the country calls, Farida.*

I said goodbye and she smiled. She'd wait for me, she said, without any note of blame, or anger, or desire for a fight—as though two years had not passed since our first meeting, as though we had become lovers again in that instant. She hadn't demanded any explanation for my absence and I hadn't demanded any explanation for her terror the night before. This is what happens to us when we see the disasters piling up remorselessly: all the sordid things we do become forgiven.

Out I went, seeing in my head the cockroaches, heads covered in sheets of newspaper, chests bared, bodies thin, crashing down the corridor to the stairs, all crudeness and overexcitement. I wanted to go back and kill them, and it struck me that in their own way they had been committing suicide. They were striving for death, enraged to the utmost degree, without the slightest hope: all they wanted was for us to see them so—in despair—not that we might pity them, but rather that we might grieve at what they'd come to.

I stood outside the building and put on my mask. This was going to be a long day and I had to have protection from the outset.

140

Ataba Square was a few minutes away, and while my mask was on I didn't want to seek directions from passersby—that would shatter the solitude I had chosen for today—but I was considering removing it and asking when I remembered my cell phone and the maps.

Within a minute, the Tiring Building had appeared in the middle of the screen, at the center of a horizontal slice of Ataba and the surrounding area, accompanied by links to articles and reports on the building, and a plethora of pictures of the place from street level, showing the decorations on its balconies and on the dome, which was surmounted by a giant sphere. An historic building. I wasn't interested.

I walked until I came to Ataba Square and, glancing around, realized that the building was much more easily spotted than I'd imagined: an old place, its most prominent feature the dome—beneath which was written 'Tiring' in Roman script—and above it a huge globe of pale metal borne on the backs of four human figures.

The choice of building was perfect. Standing in or beside the dome, I could cover a broad expanse of ground. Hundreds of people passed the spot every minute, and I'd need limitless ammo if I was to kill them all. In front of the building were gathered a large group of pavement sellers hawking cheap goods, and lots of people were weaving between the tables, inspecting the wares, and moving on. An impromptu marketplace, with customers and vendors. Plenty of human beings to snipe. I was looking the place over when Burhan suddenly stirred and flew off toward the building.

No one noticed him. It was 5.15 p.m. The crowds were at their height and business at its busiest; not much buying and selling, but lots of vendors, and passersby, and people fingering the goods. Burhan cut through it all. One or two turned and pointed, laughing. Another, acting the fool, ran a few paces after Burhan, shouting, "Grab him! He's good for twenty smokes!" Meanwhile, I was walking calmly in his wake

141

and telling myself that people were truly ignorant, but it was no fault of theirs—who could guess I'd be climbing up there and killing them in less than two hours' time? Maybe they wouldn't move even if they knew: each one standing there, waiting for the bullets to hit.

I followed Burhan and went inside, to be surprised by a vast, crumbling staircase, a sign of a splendor that had been erased by the passing years. I mounted the stairs and the sunlight retreated. In the gathering gloom, the stairs were hard to see and objects I couldn't make out and piles of rubble prevented me climbing quickly for fear that I'd stumble. On the first floor, Burhan jagged off to the right, into one of the apartments. He was zipping through the air, as if hurrying me along. This time I followed him at a sprint, heedless of anything that might trip me, and he turned into a room that was in complete darkness. I switched on the phone's light and went inside.

I pointed the light toward the sound of Burhan's beating wings. His buzzing was a great comfort to me. He was hovering over some wooden and plastic boxes, and the moment I glanced at them I recognized two cases containing sniper rifles, and beneath them a number of smaller containers full of ammunition. Thousands of rounds this time. I opened one of the gun cases to find my favorite rifle, a beloved Dragunov, in pristine condition, still smelling of grease from the factory, and possibly never fired. It was the Polish variant on the classic Russian model, more accurate than its Romanian equivalent. I shut the case and picked it up in my left hand, took a couple of ammo boxes beneath my left arm, and, lighting the way with my phone, I turned around. What I saw terrified me.

In the far corner of the adjoining room was a gallows: a thick rope terminating in an empty noose and hanging from a short horizontal wooden beam, which was attached to a tall, upright post. For a moment I froze, then I set my load on the floor and walked toward it.

The gallows' upright was fixed into a large wooden platform raised a few feet off the ground. Three steps, then I was standing on top of it. The wooden boards creaked loudly and my skin crawled, and with every step they creaked more and more until I thought the platform would collapse beneath my weight. But what amazed and frightened me most was the swaying noose. It was rocking violently as though someone had just set it in motion, or as though someone had been strung up minutes before . . . and yet their body wasn't there. Directly beneath the noose was a square hole, pitch black, which seemed to be waiting for me. Here the body would drop, falling from life into death. I stood motionless before it for some time. I wanted to hold the phone's light up to it in order to see what was inside, but something held me back.

Carrying my boxes, I exited the room and continued on up the stairs. What was left of the daylight and the glow of the streetlamps stole inside to illuminate the vast space. Up I climbed, much shaken by the sight of the gallows. I managed not to think about what it was doing there, or who the last person to use it had been, or why the noose was swaying, and made up my mind that I would not go back to get the other rifle and the rest of the ammunition.

I had reached the dome. I was standing on the roof of the building, with the dome in front of me and the streets stretched out beneath my feet. I could see everything. Nothing blocked my view but the next-door building, and I decided to keep going until I was stationed not on top of the dome but inside the huge metal sphere above it. I took the rifle from its case, filled three magazines with rounds, then, hefting the ammo box and the gun, ascended the narrow walkway that ran up and over the dome's summit. I was right up against the four statues carrying the sphere, but I couldn't tell whether they were meant to be angels or devils, and neither did I know whether the sphere was meant to be the earth, or the universe, or something else, bigger than them both. Looking over my

143

shoulder, I saw my quarry drifting over the asphalt, waiting for me. I eased my body beneath the sphere and up into the large opening in its underside. I was now standing between the four statues, with my chest and head inside the sphere and the rest of me outside—as though I were holding it up like them.

Inside, I found a chair fixed to a framework of metal rods whose ends were attached to the inner surface of the sphere. The chair was suspended in its dead center. It was hot inside, thanks to the sun, which had been beating down on the sphere all day, and I told myself that it would cool down soon enough and that I wouldn't suffer too much from the heat. I clambered up into the metal frame and sat down. The chair, I saw, could turn on its axis; it moved, and there were tiny openings let into the surface of the sphere that allowed me to track pedestrians down in the street without a soul able to see me. An ideal contraption for committing mass murder. No lamp penetrated where I sat and I could barely see around me without the aid of the phone's pale light, but there was no way around it: I had to use up these ammo boxes, every one.

I took aim at a young man messing around on his phone. Playing some game. The target was in plain view, no more than a hundred and fifty meters away, very close indeed by the standards of my beloved Dragunov. He was wearing a white shirt, all the better to highlight the blood from his wound. I aimed at the middle of his chest, just above the hand that fiddled with the phone, and—making allowances for the recoil, the slight breeze, and the acute downward trajectory—I fired.

It might have been the most accurate shot I'd taken for a long while. I was used to firing from the top of the tower, where the shortest distance between the target and me would be over a kilometer, and here I was, shooting over an eighth of that range. From the shot that took out the young man, now fallen to the ground, it looked like this was going to be easy. Five people gathered around, bending over him but not

144

touching him, and I gave myself a little test. I fired at them, then swiveled the chair and leveled the rifle at another target, this time a woman in her fifties walking along with the crowd. Nothing to make her stand out, but I wanted to kill her and I didn't know why. I shot and she fell down, motionless. Then I killed a middle-aged man smoking a cigarette. I shot him in the face. Then I killed a young man, one of the vendors standing beneath the overpass, and he fell forward onto his wares, knocking them to the ground. Then I swiveled back to face the pavement vendors by the building, and stood upright, braced against the metal frame that held the chair, so that the rifle's barrel could point more sharply downward. It was easy to keep my balance, and the standing position gave my rifle more room for maneuver. For a while, I surveyed the scene through my scope.

I killed the most moronic one. I shot him as he shouted out his wares, wildly bellowing, "I'm robbing myself!" by way of explaining his low prices. I fired as he started to utter the word 'robbing'—"Robbeeeee . . . !"—and, suddenly full of eagerness, I made to shoot the vendors alongside him, but I was out of bullets. I quickly replaced the empty magazine with a full one.

I killed a woman picking up clothes and turning them over. From her expression, it didn't look like she had the slightest intention of buying. I shot her hand as it flipped the clothes, and she screamed and grabbed at an item of clothing with her other hand, so I shot that, too, and she snapped out of her madness and went careering between the tables, trying to get away. I shot her in the head.

9 p.m. The rifle had jammed four times and I was getting tired of trying to unstick it, so I went downstairs, retrieved the second gun, and went on shooting. There was more than enough ammo—still two full boxes by the dome. I wasn't bothered about counting up the remaining rounds. It was clear that I'd get bored of the whole thing before they ran out.

145

I killed a man walking along the overpass. I shot him in the leg, and he fell down and started crawling toward the edge, then tried to get his body over the metal barrier. He wanted to drop down, but I saved him the bother by shooting him in the head. I killed the man who pulled his car over—to try and save him, I assumed. For some reason, I hesitated briefly before opening fire, and watched as he pulled a knife out from beneath the seat of his car and began to butcher the dead man. I didn't understand why he would slit a dead man's throat—could the man have been alive, despite the bullet to his head?—and I didn't care, and I fired three rounds into the knifeman. *I'm the one who kills people here.* And I killed the man whose car collided with the stationary car and toppled off the overpass, hitting the ground with a massive crash. He staggered out of the wreck and I aimed at him, and I was laughing, laughing so hard that I shook. I tried keeping it in, but it exploded out of me, so that the rifle nearly fell from my hands, and then it struck me that the man might try to flee and that I had to kill him, and that his name was Amin, and I pulled myself together, and pointed the rifle at Amin, and fired two rounds into his chest. And I killed a southerner called Gowhar, dressed in a broad-sleeved robe. I shot him in the neck with a single bullet, and he took to his heels, bleeding, and I let him go because I knew he'd die in a few minutes and that nobody would be able to help him. And I killed Ali Khalil, an old man. Why he was walking about down here, I couldn't tell. I shot him in the head and he dropped, still breathing, and I shot him again in the chest because I knew that he was to die shot twice. And I shot Kamal Hussein, forty-two years old. I aimed at his head and fired two rounds, one after the other, and he died before he hit the ground. And I looked for Samira al-Dahshuri. She'd be walking beneath the overpass, I knew, and I swept the area through my scope, and when I saw her I fired without hesitation into her liver. It had been cirrhotic for years, and maybe she felt the bullet ripping through it and killing her. Maybe that is why she hunched over and peered at the spot as she died.

And I killed Ziyad Mohamed Bakir with a single bullet. I killed Shehab Hassan Abdo Abdel-Magid with a shot to the head. I killed Karim Medhat Wahba with a shot to the right side of his chest. I killed Mamdouh Sayyid Mansour with a round that went into his stomach and exited through his back. I killed Mustafa Zeinhom Rabie Mohamed with a shot to the chest. I killed Mohamed Khaled Mahmoud Qutb with a bullet in his left eye. I killed Ahmed Ihab Mohamed Abbas Fuad with a shot to the temple. I killed Ahmed Hussein Ahmed Hussein with a shot to the head. I killed Ahmed Sharif Mohamed Mohiedin Dahi with a shot to the chest. I killed Islam Essam Mohamed Fathi Mohamed Sharif with a shot to the head. I killed Amira Ahmed Mohamed Ismail with a shot to the chest. I killed Rami Gamal Shafiq Ahmed with a shot to the chest. I killed Ramadan Sidqi Aboul Ela with a shot to his stomach. I killed Rumani Matta Adli with a shot to the right side of his chest. I killed Sameh Mohamed Gamal with two shots: chest and head. I killed Mahmoud Merghani Mohamed Ahmed with a shot to the head. I killed Nancy Rifaat al-Sayyid Hassan with a round in her right eye. I killed Mustafa Fathi Mansour Darwish with a bullet to the face. I killed Mohamed Ibrahim Mohamed Khalil with a bullet to the heart. I killed Mumin Eid Hassanein Abdel-Muati with a shot to the head. I killed Heba Hussein Mohamed Amin with a shot to the head. I killed Abanoub Awadallah Naeem Khalil Girgis with a shot to the head. I killed Ashraf Mousa Higab Mousa with a shot to the temple. I killed Girgis Lamai Mousa with a bullet through the neck. Nothing easier than shooting necks. I killed Mustafa Kamal Ibrahim Amer with two rounds, in his chest and his belly. I killed Emad Abdel-Zaher Mohamed with a round that passed through his right eye and exited through the right side of his head. I killed Mahmoud Ramadan Nazir Abdel-Hamid with a bullet to the stomach.

147

I killed Ibrahim Rida Abdel-Hamid with a shot to the head. I killed Khaled Mohamed al-Sayyid Mohamed al-Wakil with a shot to the chest. I killed Mohamed Othman Abdel-Ghani Mohamed with a shot to the stomach. I killed Ayman Anwar Abdel-Aziz Abdel-Gawad with a shot to the chest and another to the belly. I killed Youssef Fayez Armanious Ibrahim with a bullet that penetrated his back and lodged in his chest. I killed Safwat Mohamed Mohamed Said with a shot to the right side of his chest. I killed Mahmoud Shehata Mohamed Shehata with a shot to the stomach. I killed Sayyid Farag Masoud with a bullet to the neck. I killed Mahmoud Ibrahim Mohamed Khafaga with a shot to the head. I killed Imam Kamal Mohamed Abdallah with a shot to the head. I killed Mabrouk Ahmed Abdel-Fattah Bahr with a shot to the left half of his stomach. I killed Sharif Yehya Atris Suleiman with a round to his left eye.

I killed Mohamed Ali Mohamed Sami with a shot to his temple. He stood in the street among the corpses and looked up at me as though he knew exactly where I was. Standing there, motionless. He raised his right hand, pointed his forefinger at me, then placed it against his temple and held the pose. After all those killings, it was quite possible that someone might discover my hiding place and run away or take shelter behind a wall, but Mohamed did not flee. He did not move. He stood there, waiting for the bullet. He knew that I'd answer his request, that I'd shoot him wherever I chose.

I glanced at the clock on my phone and saw that it was 10 p.m., and I heard the sound of Burhan growing louder, beating the air with his wings, the buzzing more intense than I'd ever heard it. I put down the rifle and turned around, searching for him. He was hovering off to my right and flying about as though panicked, swooping up to my face, then stopping before he got there. Me in the center of the sphere and him circling around me, then swooping in and away with an uncharacteristic lack of grace. The cramped space inside the

148

sphere was stifling him. He went over to the inner wall and hovered next to it for a moment, then surged forward and bumped me lightly in the face. I heard the clink as he collided with the metal mask and heard myself asking apprehensively, "What's the matter?" Back he went, then surged forward to strike me a second, more forceful, blow. I nearly toppled over and asked, "What is it, Burhan?" though I knew he wouldn't answer, and he flew out of one of the small windows as though running away. I took off the mask, so worked up I was gasping, breathed deep to draw in more oxygen, and regained my seat at the sphere's center while I calmed down. Then I heard Burhan approaching at high speed and held my breath. He came in through the window like a bullet and smashed into my temple, and I fell from the chair, crashing to the bottom of the sphere, then dropping out of the hole to collide with the top of the dome's unyielding curve.

I tried to cling onto consciousness. This was no time to be passing out. I put up a fight and started thinking about the mission, and the occupation, and the coming revolution, and how I despaired of any change—and then I felt a complete conviction, a true belief, that not a single soul would rise up. I knew that the revolution would not happen. And though I considered everything I had done to be pointless, I was taking my revenge on them all.

Burhan floated out of the sphere at a more customary slow pace and came up to me. He landed on my chest and fell still. For a few seconds, I fell unconscious.

I was lying between the legs of the four statues, the metal sphere over my head. My beloved Dragunov, which had not fallen with me, hung from the chair by its leather strap, swaying gently. I remembered Farida, alone at home, and I realized that I had killed many people. I was fine: a few mild aches in my back and neck, and a slight dizziness from my head striking the dome. I was thinking of getting moving, getting back in the sphere so that I could carry on shooting, when Burhan

149

walked leisurely up my chest toward my face. *If only you had a face then I would know your intentions.* In the gloom below, I heard people's cries rise up, mournful and wracked with grief because I had stopped firing. I heard them chant, "Where have you gone? Come back and shoot!"

Then the darkness covered me.

AD 2011

1

INSAL HURRIED OUT OF THE house on his usual route to the school, though not at the usual hour. It was 7 p.m. when he left, having received a call from the school's security guard. The man's anxiety and his fretful tone had moved Insal.

The guard said that Insal had to come to school right away. There was a problem he was unable to deal with—a young girl left at school until this late hour—and no one answering when he tried to call: the principal not picking up, the other teachers all protesting that they were too far away and there was nothing they could do, the girl's father not responding on any of the numbers listed under his name, and the guard unable go home. That the guard had chosen him was, thought Insal, an indication of the man's desperation—when he said he had tried calling others and failed, Insal believed him. His wife, Leila, hadn't objected. Go, she told him, go and see what's going on down there, and if she hadn't said this so sincerely he would never have gone.

Insal returned home carrying an utterly drained and fast-asleep four-year-old girl. He explained to his wife how there was nothing for it but to take her in, just for the night. Confronted by the girl, Leila hesitated. She felt sympathetic, a sympathy doubtless rendered more acute by the child growing inside her. As mothers do, she had visions of a future: in these, her fetus was now a boy of four, who had for some reason lost both his parents and been adopted by a kind-hearted family. So in the end Leila welcomed the girl with an open heart.

There was a lot of gas in the air that day. People wept. They were frightened, but it was the gas that made them weep. Their tears flowed, their noses ran, and some of them choked. The cops on the ground were teaching the protestors and troublemakers a lesson while the overwhelming majority sat back in their comfortable living rooms, surrendering to great waves of laughter as they watched events on the television, belching idly and indulging in that great pastime: mockery. *Who do they think they are, taking on the regime?*

By day's end, everyone who'd taken to the streets had been swept off them. The police deluged them with gas and they took to their heels, and in some neighborhoods the cops charged after them. Many were detained and the rest ran home. Most assumed it was over that night, but no: vengeance had blossomed at last.

No one realized that what had happened and what would happen thereafter was preordained, that the hell they lived in was perfectly normal, was in fact a hell that recurred elsewhere and often, and that all these things were a punishment.

The next day, the world's illusion was at its most intense. Everyone was taken in. A few thought that deliverance was at hand, but it was a false deliverance, a salvation from stupid things of their own devising. The majority surrendered to the illusion.

Zahra awoke very ill indeed, so sick that Insal called a doctor to the house, terrified of losing this stranger's child. The doctor reassured him and said that all she needed was two days' rest and strong medicine.

Insal stayed away from school that day, while the principal kept himself abreast of the girl's condition via telephone. He informed Insal that he was trying to get in contact with her family, but was having no luck. At sunset, he phoned to tell him what, after much effort, he had managed to learn.

Zahra's mother was dead and no trace could be found of her father. It seemed that he was either handicapped or unwell. There was no one at her father's house. The man had vanished, and when the principal asked his neighbors to take the girl in, to his despair they all refused. The principal was searching for other relatives of Zahra's, he told Insal, and if no relatives could be found then he would arrange to have her sent to a refuge in a few days' time.

The next day passed without any improvement in Zahra's condition, but when she woke on the Friday morning she started asking for her father.

That Friday, Cairo caught fire.

As Insal and Leila had been expecting, Zahra filled their home with the sound of weeping. In vain did Insal try to explain to her what had happened—every time he was about to start he stopped: how to explain to her what he didn't know himself?—and so instead he began consoling her every and any way he could. And he started to lie. He claimed that her father was away and questioned her about her other relatives.

He asked her about grandmothers and grandfathers, about aunts and uncles, but she denied knowing any of them, and when her crying became truly unbearable, Leila brought the interrogation to an end and picked Zahra up, murmuring to her and accusing Insal of getting her worked up.

Leila sensed Zahra's alarm. The fear of a four-year-old can't be imagined; it's a fear that can only be seen and felt, transmitted through a trembling body to adults, where it grows and metamorphoses into a sense of inadequacy and powerlessness. Zahra was in a state of constant and steadily gathering fear that peaked, then climbed higher still: fear on fear. She had no idea what was happening outside, and neither did Insal or Leila. No one knew of the wounded out in the street—and, of course, the dead knew nothing. Yet despite the almost total ignorance from which everyone was suffering, ignorant Zahra's terror mirrored that of the few who knew the truth.

After hours of crying, and calming, and attempts at feeding, Zahra slept, and husband and wife stayed up, transfixed before the television, anxiously catching up with the latest developments.

Many souls had been claimed that day, and many had been injured by birdshot that stung the skin and lodged beneath it, that could be fatal when fired directly into the face, that wrecked eyeballs whenever it struck them. Everyone thus wounded would think himself a hero. Those who'd been injured and hadn't died would regard the pellets as a splendid badge of honor, retained beneath their hides, and would see no further than that. A few months later, their wounds would be a mark of shame.

Hope roamed through the crowds in the streets, reaping them, chewing them up, and spitting them back out in a state of joy. They glimpsed only the fringes of their torment and thought it glory.

Three grim days the little family spent without Zahra's father making an appearance, and the principal concluded that he had been injured, or gone missing, or died. Just one of thousands. Things were more complicated now, and Insal and Leila had a discussion, finally agreeing that they would take Zahra in until a member of her family came to light.

The pair of them spent the three days in front of the television, watching the footage, listening to much talk about the numbers of dead and wounded, seeing the battle unfold between the two sides. As he flicked between channels, Insal thought about the girl's missing father. The man might be injured and in hospital, lying in a coma, or actually dead, his undiscovered corpse sprawled out somewhere—behind a trashcan, on the roof of a tall building, down a manhole, in a pile of garbage. Maybe someone had taken him to hospital, and he'd died there, and right now he was lying in a morgue. Maybe he'd died on the way to hospital and the ambulance had taken him to the big morgue at Zeinhom. And now he gave a shiver of fear. He'd have to go to all these places and search for him, search for a body or a corpse. He reached out his hand to Leila's belly, and drew strength from her.

156

2

IN THE MORNING, INSAL AWOKE and sat up in bed, trying to dispel the last vestiges of sleep. Casting a glance at Leila and Zahra, he saw that they were more or less as they had been the night before—Leila holding Zahra in her arms, and the girl's arm stretched out around Leila's body to hold her close—but Zahra was now upside down, her feet by Leila's face and her head at her belly.

Insal got up, laid out a clean set of clothes, and took a shower. He hadn't washed yesterday, had slept without eating supper. He stood beneath the jet of water as though ridding himself of something, or readying himself for something, for a plague that would strike him down. Today he was going to Qasr al-Aini hospital to look for Zahra's father among the injured and dead. This morning, Insal thought, he had better fortify himself. He would walk through the crowds, would take a stroll through his peaceful neighborhood, would stand on the street corners and observe the few trees and palms. He would avoid the towering heaps of refuse. He wanted beauty before he gazed on ugliness. He wanted to look on the living before he saw the dead, the hale before the maimed. His anxiety got the better of him and he hurried out of the shower, dressed, and went down into the street.

People were staying at home in a state of constant fear. Only a few courageous souls ventured out, on important business they couldn't let slide, to the squares where the protests were being held or to the market, while an even smaller minority walked the streets untroubled by what was happening all around them—knowing everything, but not caring.

Insal wandered aimlessly down streets and over intersections, and people started stopping him and asking him where he was going, demanding to see his identity card, and then apologizing, excusing their behavior: the city going up in flames, thieves everywhere. And Insal? He didn't understand. He didn't understand at all.

Again and again, Insal halted in front of groups of young men so they could check his ID: group after group, at every road junction, street corner, and café, until he was tired of stopping. He wanted to walk with nowhere in mind, to leave all his cares on the sidewalk, to unburden himself step by step, and these men insisted on stopping him and reminding him of everything that weighed him down.

A decrepit old man walked by, dressed in the tattered garb of the madmen who roamed the city streets, a huge pack of dogs trotting after him—street dogs, some small and slight, others big and bulky with floppy ears, all missing tails, and paws, and eyes, and clumps of fur. They scurried along in the dog man's wake, staying close. He was looking for something, looking into people's faces, staring for a few seconds before moving off and continuing his search.

Insal went on, keeping clear of the other pedestrians. He passed a grocer's and the colors and shapes of the fruit on display refreshed his weary soul. He purchased an orange with the idea of squeezing it for juice: he loved the acid tang on his tongue. He bought an apple, thinking to cut it into little chunks for Zahra: she could eat them from her little hand. He bought a banana, to peel for Leila: were bananas good for pregnant women?

The dog man approached him. For a few seconds, they stood facing one another on the sidewalk. The dog man was in his way, and whenever Insal tried to get past, the other moved to block him. The dogs surrounded them, circled them, yawned. "These are false pleasures," the man said. "You have taken your first steps now, and it shall be but a few short days until you see all. I tell you: take pleasure in what is false, for you shall not see it again."

Then the dog man went on his way.

They caught the thief in the street. That's what they thought him: a thief. Because he hadn't any ID. He was beaten and tortured, and when he grabbed hold of the knife that one of them was trying to stab him with, they all took to their heels in terror, the man remaining behind, grasping the knife and unable to believe what had happened. He ran off, tossing the blade as he went, and Insal stepped in. He grabbed the man and held him fast for a moment. The people caught up with the thief. That's what they thought he was: a thief.

By the time they put the noose over his head, he'd been dead for several minutes. He felt nothing when they strung him from the lamp post. They would leave him like that for hours until someone came at night to cut the rope and the body fell to the ground.

Insal stood beside the hanging body. Its hand was close to his face, the thing he could see most clearly: slack, half-gripping air, a deep cut on the back. The only cut. The nails were clean and the fingers well formed. Unable to resist, he looked up at the face. Here he was, looking at a hanged man for the first time.

He went home, exhausted. Just an hour he'd been walking, but it had left him a wreck. How could he go to the morgue today after all that? How could he pick Zahra up and carry her inside through the square metal doors?

Leila and Zahra were asleep. He closed the bedroom door on them and went out into the living room. There, he beat at his temples. He tugged at his hair. He covered his mouth with his hand and started to scream. He jumped up and down. He bit his fingers. He gripped his shirt and tugged at it violently, trying to rip it. Then he started slapping his face with a relentless rhythm, a slap every two seconds, one slap after another, striking harder with each one. His head rang from the powerful impacts, his view of the living room jolted violently, and by the end each blow seemed to flood the scene before him with a bright light, which would soon fade as the sight of the darkened room returned to his eyes. These flashes of light calmed Insal. They were moments when he was totally cut off from the world, far from the streets, and the hanging body, and Zahra, and Leila. After a quarter of an hour of violence, he settled. His breathing grew regular and his distress dwindled. He went back to wake up Leila and Zahra.

Insal was worn out when he reached Qasr al-Aini hospital. Amid the chaos, he asked where he might find the wounded, the missing, and the dead, and staff directed him to the registry, where the names of the injured were recorded. A man asked him for a name, searched for it in the register, and—when he couldn't find it—told him to go to the morgue, where bodies were waiting to be identified.

Considerably unnerved, Insal stood outside the doors and, before going in, remembered that he didn't know what the man looked like. He'd never seen him before, not even a picture of him. He felt a flash of regret for being so hasty and for not calling the principal, but he put it to one side. He was outside the door to the morgue now and he had no choice but to go on. All he knew was the man's three-part name, as listed in the school's records. The morgue attendant stood outside the massive door, waiting for visitors. His face impassive, his words clipped, he asked for the missing person's details: all three names, what relation he was to Insal, the place he went missing, and when he was last in touch. Insal gave him the name plus the usual lie, that the man was a cousin on his mother's side. After a short search, the attendant said that the

160

name wasn't on the list, but Insal might like to go in and look over the bodies since, in addition to those whose names were known, there were many anonymous bodies. Maybe the missing man was one of them.

Insal agreed, without the first idea who he was searching for. He went in and started moving between the bodies bundled together on steel trolleys and staring at the faces of those stretched out on the floor. They were much disfigured, with wounds to chests, and limbs, and faces. Some were naked. It looked like these ones had been identified. They were to have their chests sliced open to determine the cause of death. Their nakedness suggested surrender. The others—clothed, bloody, torn, and in a few instances even burned—had yet to give in. They were still waiting for friends and relatives to strip them and cut open their chests, waiting for the doctor to hunt for the cause of death, to extract the bullets and shrapnel. The expressions on the faces varied (fear, panic, surprise) but all had one thing in common, clear to the naked eye: indifference—the last thing the dead had felt as their souls departed their bodies.

All were men, he noticed, and he felt certain that there must be women laid out somewhere else, naked, too, no one allowed to see them but fellow females. Decent in death as in life.

He found the bodies of twins, astonishingly alike, their injuries the only thing that separated them. Both had died from gunshot wounds to the chest. They had been placed on a pair of tables side by side, the same expression on their faces, their arms at rest in the same pose, and their hands identically positioned: forefingers crossed beneath middle fingers. Their lower lips sagged down to reveal teeth blackened by cigarette smoke, and there were hairless lines through both their left eyebrows. The lines looked deliberately made, by a barber or by the twins themselves, to further emphasize the sacred resemblance. But doppelgängers in life did not necessarily mean doppelgängers in death. The bullet holes were disposed differently over the two chests: one had three clean

161

holes clustered by the collarbone on the right-hand side, while on the second two could be seen, one in the middle of the chest, the other by the belly, and then a third that seemed to appear, then vanish. Insal was confused. Was that really a bullet hole, or some trick of the mind? He was dead, that was enough. Both were dead and neither were Zahra's father. But near perfect interchangeability forced Insal to the conclusion that this was a single body killed twice.

He couldn't shake the thought. Could these two bodies be vessels for a single soul that had hopped from one to the other when the first man had died?

Before today, Insal had never seen slain bodies, just the dead: the bodies of people he knew who had slipped quietly away after sickness or in their sleep, beneath oxygen masks in hospital beds or in intensive care units. He'd seen one or two lying on the road under sheets of newspaper. He'd seen a body that had been run over by a car before passersby could cover it with their papers—had seen it from a distance, so hadn't made out the details of the dead man's face. Today, though, he'd gazed into many faces, trying to find a man he didn't know.

These were wounds in his soul that would remain unhealed until the day he died.

He went on moving from face to face, and in the end could see no logical reason for what he was doing, yet still he went on from face to face without the power to stop, and when he'd finished his first circuit of the faces around he went again, slowly inspecting each one, their features imprinting themselves on his memory the instant he saw them. He found this reassuring: perhaps he'd see the man's picture somewhere, at a relative's or even in one of the school files, and he could search his memory for the likeness. He was transferring the flesh bundled on the tables and floor into his memory, afraid lest their features be lost, afraid lest they be lost to the dirt.

The morgue attendant asked him if he knew who he was looking for. Did he know his face? Insal's repeated circling, combined with the clichéd fabrication he'd given him earlier, had aroused his suspicions. Insal was briefly at a loss, then he answered in the negative. The attendant didn't object or turn him away. None of those who came looking knew those they were searching for, it seemed. The attendant asked him to bring along a relative of the missing man—maybe they would know. That's what the law required, he said. What Insal was doing right now was against the law. Then his tone changed and his expression softened a little. He said that the dead were better off than the living these days, that many people would come here and identify their dead, and would then be killed themselves and thereby be spared the suffering of their loss.

But Insal was thinking of Zahra and her father. He wanted to find the man, even if he was dead. He told the attendant that the missing man had a four-year-old daughter and that she was the only person who could identify him. She was the only member of the family that he knew. Calmly, the attendant said that he must bring the child to identify her father, if he was here.

Insal froze. He said nothing in response, and assumed the man was mocking him, but the seriousness of his expression gave the lie to his suspicion. What was happening was wonderful, the attendant said. It was the only solution, no matter how strange that might seem.

He said that he knew precisely why Insal felt sorry for the girl: because he thought that the faces of the dead would stop her sleeping. Insal mustn't worry, he said, a child's memory was exceptionally unstable—she'd only retain the image of her slain father's face for a few weeks and then she would forget it utterly. And as for the other bodies, she'd remember them for a few days afterward, then they, too, would vanish from her mind, their place taken by other memories, other

163

images, more terrible still—or kinder. Intensely grave, he said, "Who knows? Maybe there's some kind of mercy in seeing the faces of the dead."

Insal left the morgue, not understanding what was happening all around him. In his head, he sketched out grim visions of his scheduled visit with Zahra. He pictured her entering the hospital all alone while he waited behind at the door, and he pictured her tiny form, so small, disappearing into the massive entrance, then climbing the stairs to the right. . . . Picturing what came after that became difficult.

The attendant envied all those outside—those who fired the bullets and those who received them—and wished that he might deal with the bodies only. Their relatives were more than he could handle. Chaos reigned in every corner of the morgue, and the attendant knew that many had buried their dead, that at that very moment many more were burying unidentified bodies, and that only a very few were here, moving between the corpses. They were the ones in true torment. He knew that the young woman over there would take months to find her brother, even though her brother lay dead in a hospital nearby. He knew that this other girl would find her brother alive the very next day, and that months later he would be killed and she would not have to search for him, for he would have died before her eyes. He knew that this father would find the body of his son tomorrow, and that after a few months of ceaseless grief he would follow him to the grave. He knew that no one would locate these three bodies, that no one would even search them out, and that they would be buried without friends or family in attendance, as strangers. And the attendant surveyed the faultless arrangement. Inspected, for the thousandth time, the plan's perfection. These strangers, tormented by the sight of other strangers.

The people out in the streets were angry. Murder was abroad. Unknown assailants dealt death from above and below. They believed they were throwing off injustice, and they believed that the tyrant was fighting them. Indeed, the tyrant believed he was winning. And the people thought likewise—that they were winning. But there would be no victory today. There'd be no victory here, ever.

Insal had no understanding of what was happening around him. Like the others, he thought injustice was being driven away. Although he had never sought to be any part of events, had never had any desire to join a demonstration, he left the hospital that day and joined one without meaning to.

Walking along in the midst of the chanting crowds, he saw them dropping to the ground for no clear reason. A man stood there, frozen in place for an instant, then collapsed. Down went that man—and then the arms of another man, who'd been waving and chanting, dropped to his sides, and he fell on his face, thumping into the ground. A red rose suddenly bloomed on a temple and the face vanished.

Insal took fright and started to run, not knowing what he ran from, but he saw people pointing to the skies, and screaming, and sprinting away from whatever they were pointing at, and he followed the line of their forefingers and saw a perfectly ordinary building, and when he heard the people shouting, "Sniper!" his gaze automatically went to the roof, looking out for a figure. Then he saw a little flash and someone next to him, who had just that instant been screaming out, fell to the ground. Insal sprinted away.

He took shelter by the corner of a second, larger building, just as a sniper's round tore into the other side of the wall. Insal saw neither the round nor the effect of its impact. On his side of the wall, the corner was undamaged. The bullet hadn't penetrated it. The concrete must have absorbed the impact. The other side of the corner had been totally disfigured: a hole surrounded by devastation, a bullet wound in the building.

165

He rested on the ground with others. He'd never heard such a noise in his life. A cacophony of screams, gunfire, and the reports from muffled explosions came to him from all sides. He had crossed this square many times in his life and had never seen crowds to match the chaotic mob now before him. He saw many people rush over to the fallen. To rescue them. Insal stretched his legs out in surrender. The reek of the fallen demonstrators' blood was pungent and fresh, and he recalled the way the blood had tasted when he'd knock a tooth out as a child.

The rescuers spotted a man lying on the ground, a quarter of his head gone—his right eye, half his forehead, and his temple—and they peered at what was left and saw that it was empty, without a brain, just a dark hollow devoid of flesh and sinew, and then all of them instinctively clapped their hands to their heads to make sure, to check that their heads were still whole and that their brains were still in place.

A man cried out plaintively, "Fucked! The world is fucked!" A second man asked him what was going on ("Who's killing who?") to which the first snapped, "Well, whoever's killing us, they aren't human. Who knows what they are?"

Then many people swarmed around Insal, wanting to lift him up and carry him to an ambulance, but he told them he was fine; he soothed them and he soothed himself. He only wanted to get moving and get home, he said, and after a few minutes he took advantage of their numbers and melted into them, heading toward the metro, fleeing from the heavens.

As he made his way to the metro, he thought to himself that Zahra would suffer greatly when he brought her to the morgue the next day.

In the streets, the people were weeping from rage. They had seen the blood plain before their eyes.

And they were threatening their enemy with vengeance, raising angry fists, chanting threats of execution. They were not in confusion: they believed that they spoke the truth, that

166

they were on the right path, and that they, for all that, were a minority; that while they stood firm in the face of the tyrant and his horde, the majority stood with the tyrant. Yet they believed, too, that their victory was ordained and near at hand. And not one of them knew that all this was fantasy. They did not know that hope was an illusion.

They would shoulder the burden of a vengeance that would never be satisfied, and they would be tormented as no one had been tormented before.

3

IN A WIDE STREET NEAR Insal's home, heaps of refuse rose up in piles to form a clutch of pyramids, the product of the trash collectors' months-long strike. At first, a little mound took shape in the middle of the road, and then everyone who threw out their garbage would launch it to the top of the mound, and the mound grew taller until it had become a great hill as high as the Giza pyramids.

Then a second pyramid appeared, and a third, and a fourth, and then there were seven pyramids stacked down the road's center, and it was dubbed Pyramids Street. And for some reason, people forgot that it had been they who had built them.

A man was walking there, trailed by two girls, one eleven, the other a child of four. The man had come from nearby, from beneath the overpass on the main road where he slept each night, while the girls had come as fugitives from an insane father. They remembered little, had no need for memory in the first place, for what was to come would be sufficient to leave the most terrible impression on the older girl. She knew that what was to come was terrible and knew, too, that there was no escaping it, and she surrendered to this knowledge absolutely. This sense of inevitability was her only comfort.

The man started rummaging through a little heap of garbage down a side street. The great pyramids were no good for picking. He did this every day, extracting whatever he could

169

eat from the smaller piles. Whatever was not yet rotten—its stink gone and the mold just beginning to spread—he would eat before it turned completely, before it fell apart or changed color. He'd pick out an apple to sniff, to detect the underlying hint of mold before the rot claimed the whole fruit. If he saw a scrap of decomposing bread, a piece of fruit putrefying at the edges, he'd bite off the decayed part, spit it out, and eat the rest. The garbage man.

The older girl mastered her natural delicacy and started picking through another pile. A minute in, she found a whole loaf, still fresh and supple. From his pile, the garbage man took a stale loaf, which he placed in his plastic bag to be sprinkled with water. Then the little girl found the remains of a chicken, white flesh still sticking to the breastbone. She lifted the morsel to show it to her older companion and they both smiled, but the garbage man could find nothing but his bone-dry bread. He watched them enviously, then realized that they were encroaching on his territory, that they would be sharing his pickings. Other stomachs would be digesting his food.

He spoke harsh words to them and waved his arm angrily, but they didn't flee. Moving quickly, the older girl picked up a stone from the ground and threw it at him. It missed his face and he advanced on them with his massive frame, striking the girl a single blow that laid her out unconscious. The little girl stared at her and didn't understand.

People were beside themselves with panic back then, making the rounds of the bakeries and markets while young men stood out in the street armed with staves, every man suspecting his neighbor, suspecting his brother, then embracing him once more, apologizing and confessing his error. The wound had opened, they were saying, and the pus was seeping out; they were in a time of trial by error, but were determined to see it through to the end. *No going back today. No retreating whence we've come. We shall never be unjust again.* And with every ignorant breath, their hope redoubled.

170

Neither regret nor rage surfaced in the garbage man's expression. His face was rigid. It hadn't moved for years. Even when he begged for food, it didn't shift. He would try instead to soften the tone of his voice, adding gentle groans and sighs, sometimes whistling, and these sound effects did indeed make him more appealing. The face, though, remained immobile.

Many years back, the garbage man had lost the use of his right eye, and its white orb acted like a magnet on the eyes of others. The bread that was always in his hand—a whole loaf or scraps, the thing he found in greatest abundance and his most prized possession—made people, wretched as they were, contemplate his dreadful condition.

The garbage man made sure to eat whatever he found on the spot. He'd eat fragments of fruit and vegetable peelings, would crunch bones between his back teeth and suck out the marrow he adored, however cold and stiff it was. But bread he treated differently. Bread he liked to keep with him, then search for a source of water to wet the loaf and eat it. He liked it soft. The garbage man kept a number of loaves stowed in his pocket, beneath his shirt, in the plastic bag by his bed; whenever he got hungry, he would take one out and start to chew it. The garbage man got hungry in his sleep. He'd wake, throat dry, down two swigs from the bottle at his side without sitting up, then take out a loaf, wet it with a few drops, tear at it until he was full, and go back to sleep. He always made sure the loaf and bottle were beside him before he slept.

The garbage man was a repellent pest. He'd tour the buildings, whose occupants he knew by name, calling out to them and sticking honorifics before each one. If he didn't know a name, he'd call, "Dear friend!" buttering up the people seated slumped in their apartments, and they'd throw down coins and scraps of bread. Others would stick their heads from windows and shout, "Go away!" The garbage man made a racket when he raised his voice, shouting out a different name every three seconds, and for anyone in earshot it was a nightmare.

But this boisterous routine was only a fallback: the garbage man only begged for food when he could find nothing in the trash. The people here were stingy. They ate everything. They ate the flesh, and the skin, and the bones, the rind and core of their fruit. All he could find was onion skins and the soil-matted hanks of their roots. Onion skin scratched his throat when he swallowed it. And now the two girls had shown up. There was not enough bread to share.

Insal passed the garbage man. He was moving along, swaying ecstatically. "Dear friend! A fine day to you!" he called out. Just that, mechanically repeated five or six times. Insal ignored him and noticed the two girls crying on a sidewalk nearby. The older girl had come to and was weeping softly, and the little girl wept to see her cry.

Insal thought to himself that killing these girls, and Zahra, and the garbage man would not make the world a better place, but it would bring relief to many.

Completely out of the blue, the garbage man strode up to the girl he'd slapped and began patting her shoulder. She was too weak to resist.

The garbage man wasted no time. He took the girls back to the place where he slept, his little home beneath the overpass. In a spacious, low-roofed area under the on-ramp, the garbage man had erected cracked wooden boards, making walls to shelter him from the wind—a cramped space hidden behind a heap of black trash bags, which protected him from the prying eyes of passersby and the police. He lay down. Four square meters. The space contained a small pillow, newspapers piled everywhere, and a small, colorless mattress. There was a powerful stench of rot, the sound of cars overhead on the overpass, and from beneath his fetid body, the moans of the older girl. The garbage man had never slept with a child before. Had never experienced such softness and delicacy. He wasn't accustomed to have the woman under him give such gentle, muffled sobs.

172

The older girl was weeping bitterly. The pain was unendurable, but she didn't cry out, just moaned, afraid of waking her little sister, who lay asleep in one corner of the tiny hut. The garbage man thought: *If she didn't want me, she'd fight back. She'd scratch my face and hit me, but she wants it.* And when he lifted his face and gazed into hers, her tears and fearful expression amazed him. He slowed, then stopped, watching the calm come to her face, then resumed his thrusting with sudden violence, reveling in the pain and muffled cries. Eagerly, he carried on.

Outside, people were caught up in the world's illusion. They were being killed in every street and alley, and the snipers were working diligently at their task. Insal was lying in bed, trying to sleep, but he would only manage a single hour before dawn came.

Zahra was yet to adjust to the apartment. Her frequent weeping made Leila tense, but there was nothing for it but to put up with the fatherless girl. And slowly she recovered from her illness, an illness that had muted the shock of her father's disappearance and the sudden materialization of this family she knew nothing about.

Leila created her own torment. She pursued the visions that had begun the first time that she'd seen Zahra. She imagined her own child living far away from her in an orphanage, her boy amid a mob of street kids, the most handsome and polite. Then out on the street: trotting barefoot with torn clothes, clutching a plastic bag, and inhaling the viscous glue within. Or living with a relative who persecuted and terrorized him, who spread a sheet on the bare ground for his bed, who got angry at him, say, and made him sleep without any supper. All these tragic fates had passed through her mind before her child ever came into the world. There, in her womb, the fetus hung suspended between life and death. A new soul was taking shape, awaiting the perfect moment to occupy the tiny body and settle there until it saw the light.

173

And Leila was constantly afraid. For Insal, searching the hospital morgues for the body of a man he didn't know and had never seen before; and of him, of his ongoing neglect, his perpetual abstraction, forever distracted from her by things that were quite unimportant (even the search for the body didn't matter), though the situation didn't allow her to object. And for the girl, too, who asked tearfully after her absent father. She had no idea how to rid herself of these fears.

Zahra was moving about the house, chattering to herself and her missing father as she went, describing what she saw and repeating his name over and over, telling him about the size of the chair, the color of the curtain, the unforgiving hardness of the door. She inspected the carpet, lay down, and sank into sleep.

Zahra hated the smell of the apartment, and Insal's smell, and Leila's. But the smell of Leila's unborn child was nice. Zahra liked it a lot.

Leila had received her husband frantically when he had returned. She had asked him about his trip to the hospital, about what he'd seen there and about Zahra's father. Had he found him?

Insal had been in no condition to confront Leila with everything he'd witnessed, and nor, for that matter had Leila been in any state to listen to descriptions of corpses, but she had to know about Zahra's coming trip to the morgue. He had given an abbreviated version of what had happened and had tried explaining how important it was that Zahra come with him. He had predicted that Leila would take fright at his words, so her response was unexpected when it came.

But no mother carrying her child inside her can ever be wholly sad.

That night Leila embraced Zahra as the child slept—there was no avoiding it—and the smell of her alarm trickled into the girl's nostrils. At the very same instant, the same alarm made its way to the fetus resting inside her. Zahra sensed the grief in the two bodies and woke up. Leila hugged her.

Insal lay motionless. He had not told Leila about what had happened to him: running from the sniper's bullets, the people swarming around him, wandering the street for an hour through a maze of ricocheting rounds. He had not told her about the morgue attendant and the bodies.

On his return to the apartment, weighed down by his body, Insal had walked straight to the bedroom, surrounded by a halo of odors, a vast number sufficient to confuse anybody—so what chance had little Zahra to tell them all apart? The smells of the corpses' indifference, of their joy at deliverance and their regret at departure, then smells from all the people Insal had touched that day: panic, hope, and fear. Smells that Zahra had never come across before, that she'd never inhaled. But one in particular stood out. The smell of a stranger, perhaps? No, this was the scent of someone she knew well, of someone Insal had met. Very familiar but somehow changed.

Zahra had been between sleep and wakefulness when she heard Insal come home. She could make out a lot of talk, but didn't understand what he meant by the words 'morgue' or 'hospital' and didn't grasp that she would be accompanying him tomorrow to see what was in that morgue. Perhaps if she'd understood what Insal was saying, she would have known that her search would one day be over.

Now Leila slept, pressing Zahra to her, her little face to her chest, her feet tucked between the older woman's thighs. That night, Leila held two souls. Insal, meanwhile, could not sleep, and gazed at Leila's face and at Zahra's body, her head flipping from side to side every few minutes.

Late into the night, Zahra's hand touched his cheek. She felt the short, groomed hair of his beard against her palm. She was half-asleep but let her hand run over his cheeks, and eyes, and nose, then did it a second time, and a third, brushing over every inch of his face. Then at last she surrendered, and her arm flopped to her side.

175

*

Battles raged outside. Many were killed and a great number were wounded, most of whom died shortly afterward. Anyone abroad in any of the public squares would have seen one or more bodies lying on the ground, patches of dried blood beneath them—and had he tried to move them, or even paused beside them, he would have been killed on the spot. The dead were traps.

The dogs roamed everywhere, muzzles raised to the wind, searching for the scent of the dead. When one of them caught a trace of it nearby, he would track it until he reached the body, then howl—calling his pack and the dog man, who came along, pulling his gray cart, to lay the body inside it with the others—and then move off, answering another howl that rang from the next street along.

4

ONE OF THE DOGS FOUND ANOTHER body beneath a tree. He sniffed it thoroughly and barked loudly until four more dogs arrived, which sniffed the body with him and barked to mark that the body was theirs. "A dead man!" they barked. "Another one dead! The man has died! He's dead! He must be buried!" Then the pack's howl went up, "Dead! Dead! Dead!" until their master hurried up, pulling his wooden cart.

The dog man searched long and hard for an ID card, for anything that might give a name, but he found nothing. Many in this country had no ID; many were too low down the scale to own one; many had lost theirs on purpose (their names a stain on their characters, marked down on the list of bad boys—the list that leaves you in a permanent sweat, wary and on the lookout); many had no interest in the whole affair: documentation, registering, the state, paperwork. He was one of them. This was a body that gave off the stink of bitterness, and the dogs snuffled and sampled a smell they hadn't encountered for a long time. This was a man who had died overwhelmed by grief—and what was more, a body with no identity or features, a body with a shattered head, skull fragments mixed with flesh, nose now far away from the eyes, and eyes only identifiable by the bright white that stood out against the flesh and blood around them. The blood ran gleaming over the eyeballs, which were whole and undamaged, spared the mutilation that marked the face.

What saddened the dog man deeply was the dusty scalp. To the dog man, this was evidence of suffering. The coats of the dogs and cats that lay dead in the street, or abandoned to the maggots in the trash, were like this: stiff with dirt and filth. This man had died, and his body had been dragged along the ground, and now his hair was filthy. He was missing and his people would never find him.

The dog man decided to bury him where he lay. He couldn't move the corpse of a man whose face was mincemeat; bits were sure to fall off into the bottom of the cart or onto the road, and one of the stray dogs might gnaw at him when the dog man wasn't looking. Gazing sadly at the dusty hair, he took a small comb from his pocket, gently patted the scalp, then ran his hand over the head, flicking away specks of dirt, and began to comb. He would not be buried with unkempt hair.

The dogs dug a small hole next to the tree, then backed away a little and started tearing at the roots that snaked out underground until they had made space enough for the body, and then they resumed their digging: they dug and dug. The dog man had finished combing the corpse and brushing off all the dirt that clung to it. He lifted the body, climbed down into the hole, and laid it out on the earth, then he got out and waited by the graveside while the dogs heaped the earth back in.

This was just one of thousands whose fathers and mothers would suffer torment in the years ahead, would live on false hope, would be tormented by the waiting. They would hang photographs of the missing son or brother on the walls of their apartment, would place them at their building's entrance or in their cars, would tuck them beneath their clothes or in their bags. Some would die of grief while they slept, and some would die more gradually—would gradually lose the ability to move or talk, then beg off food altogether and slowly expire. One and all, they were worse off than the dead, no doubt about it. Those left behind would be quite certain that the son or brother had died, but they would be kept awake at night by their ignorance of where he'd been buried, their suspicion that he wouldn't have been interred as he should be, without the rites of washing and being laid out in a casket. When it occurred to them that he had been buried far from his family, alone in a grave with no one to keep him company, they'd panic. Slowly but surely some would go mad, imagining that their son, their brother, might not have been buried at all, but left out in the open to be eaten by the kites and dogs. They would come to believe that abominable men had killed him, and butchered him, and sold him as cheap meat to fools. They would swear off meat, picturing every joint as a cut of the son or brother. *My son was not buried in the soil, he was buried in bellies. People killed him and ate him.* And with time, many more would go mad, slowly but surely, those who had never before tasted loss. "Martyrs?" they would say. "My ass! That's enough from you. They died and we'll never know who killed them. They're not martyrs. Deserters die in war as well. They flee in the face of the enemy and they're not martyrs." There would be others, equally extreme, on the other side: "They are the slain," they'd say, "not true martyrs. Martyrs aren't shot down from rooftops. They would lose their claim to vengeance. There can be no vengeance for martyrs. No, they were killed and we know who killed them. We saw who killed them." Father and brother would go mad, slowly but surely. Their loss would remain, throttling all subsequent desires and dreams, and they would think: *Why did this happen? Where do we go now? What path do we take?*

The dog man stood among his dogs. For the first time in years, his eyes filled with tears. This was too much. This was a torment he hadn't seen before, a grief before which he could only concede defeat, a fear worse than any he'd ever witnessed. Even the dog man felt this fear, for all that he knew everything, or thought he did.

179

He had to move now. There was still much work to be done. He must hunt out the bodies that lay everywhere. The road ahead was long, and bodies beyond number were falling still. His mission was no easier. At last, he moved off with his dogs.

Years from this day, the dead man's father would lie dead himself, and this body would have been drenched with water many times and dissolved completely, and the tree which sheltered the body all that time would have forgotten the roots that had been severed to make way for the grave, would have watched as the body disintegrated and grew smaller day by day, would have sympathized with humans, and their puny, fleeting bodies, and the torment of their souls. The mutilated skull and combed hair would remain beneath the ground as witnesses to the terror of his death and the delicacy of his burial. Years later, his brother might pass this tree one night and drunkenly piss against its trunk.

There were crows in the tree, watching what was happening, hidden in the darkness in their black cloaks. Not moving, not cawing—watching what was happening and shuddering. Their dread was like a blackness.

By dawn, many had been buried in public parks, beneath the asphalt on the roads and beneath trees, beside ruined walls, behind the pillars propping up the overpasses, under loose paving stones on sidewalks. The night before, there had been a new body every minute, all of them without ID, all killed, and not one bled to death, not one dead from a drop in blood pressure, but all of dread. The chaos had laid waste to everything upon the earth.

The dogs were in a state of indescribable physical exhaustion, but their spirits were high. They were perfectly content. The dog man longed for death. He wondered when his time would come, and he received no answer. But he knew it would be a long time coming, and that he would see what he had never seen in all the years gone by.

*

Insal carried Zahra on his arm.

He stood outside the entrance to the morgue with dozens of others, all shouting and swearing. Their eyes would roll to the ceiling and they'd proclaim God's greatness; they would look to the floor and beg mercy. Then one would start shouting with rage. He wanted to go in, he'd bellow. He wanted to see who was inside. Each time someone plucked up enough courage to approach the door, their steps, despite themselves, would falter. A quarrel that flared up between one of those waiting and the morgue attendant was quickly smothered by the gravity of the situation. Most were men. There were just three women, standing over to one side of the hallway, not talking, silent—as one would expect from those awaiting the worst—while the men jetted smoke from their cigarettes and shouted out at regular intervals.

No one who went into the morgue found what they were searching for. First, they would go through the register, looking for the name of the missing person, and if they didn't find it then they would enter the morgue and hunt through the nameless bodies, and then leave, the anxiety eating them alive. Not one thought to take comfort in the fact that if they couldn't find him then he must be alive, because they knew he could be dead somewhere else. Indeed, those who emerged from the morgue thought only of the shortest route to the nearest hospital. All were convinced that the missing would be missing forever.

Insal wrote out Zahra's full name on the waiting list and returned with her to the attendant. The attendant seemed more masterful today, more confident, a change evident in the sharp gaze he turned on those standing before him and the decisive tone with which he answered questioners. But he trembled when his eyes fell on Zahra.

Zahra mumbled, her face creased up, and she started keening in a low voice, readying herself for tears. Perhaps she'd been alarmed by all the people or the disorderly commotion that surrounded her.

181

The chaos of smells was oppressive and bewildering. Zahra could make out fear, anxiety, anger, and sickness. She sniffed out sweat and feet and hair. And over these lay the powerful, heavy odor of antiperspirants and fragrances, while the reek of formaldehyde and disinfectant blanketed the lot. From some unseen spot, some corner Zahra couldn't quite locate, came the faint scent of uncertain hope. This was a memory of her father's smell. He was here. Or had been. He was so close. All his smells now washed over her: his distinctive sweat, the jasmine water he always wore, his newly washed cotton clothes, his constant concern for her, his contentment when he held her. Other smells, also peculiar to her father, were absent, and in their place were more she didn't know. This confused Zahra.

She turned to Insal and asked, "We'll see Papa?"

This was the first time she had ever addressed Insal. The first time, in fact, that she'd engaged with those around her as human beings who could be spoken to and questioned. And Insal could think of nothing to say. He didn't know for certain whether Zahra would find her father or not, nor did he know if she would understand what had happened. Would she accept the idea of death? But he must say something. "Yes, we'll see him today," he said. Then he thought for a moment and added, "Or maybe tomorrow. . . ."

Their brief conversation was overheard. Some people had been chatting with their neighbors, others stared silently at some feature of the hallway, but all heard what had been said and gradually they fell quiet. They understood what this was: the girl was looking for her father. Insal and Zahra were at the center of things now, the most important two people there. Would she find her father? And who was he, the fellow holding her like a daughter? And when the attendant called out the next name on the list, the man stepped up to Insal and told him to take his place. For a few seconds Insal hesitated, embarrassed, but the smell of his trepidation pressed in on Zahra and, without warning, she burst into tears.

Insal's eyes lingered on everything he saw, on those around him and their clothes, on the tiled flooring and the color of the walls. This was a place for warehousing the dead and cold, not for the living to wait. He walked up to the door, patting Zahra's back in an attempt to soothe her, patting her mechanically in a daze, and she became even more agitated and tearful. Everyone assumed she was crying because she understood what she was about to see. They were wrong. She was weeping at the stifling stench of fear.

At the very moment the door slammed into Insal's shoulder, the smells hit Zahra and she realized that the fear had not been coming from outside, but from here—from behind the threshold she'd that moment crossed, where the silence was broken by the incessant buzzing of a white neon light.

Not fear exactly, but an ex-fear. The memory of fear, clinging to the bodies. This was the smell of dread taken to its furthest extreme. There was no hope, or anger, or any other emotion, but there were other smells: heavy sweat and gunpowder, steel and brass, many tears. And two penetrating odors: one artificial, that burned the eyes and made you cry, the smell of a wind freighted with stinging dust, and another that Zahra couldn't make out at all: of a dark, viscous, living liquid. A new smell.

Refrigerators of gleaming metal were stacked in rows inside the spacious room, their depthless lengths sunk into the wall. The attendant stood by the metal door of the first fridge, grasped the handle, and asked Insal if he was ready. Insal didn't answer, just stayed silent and stared at the door. The attendant opened it and there was the darkness of the box's interior. He slid out a narrow tray on which a pair of bodies had been piled: a man in his sixties, eyes half-open and a still-bloody wound in his head, sprawled on the corpse of a fifteen-year-old with no evident injuries but a very pale face, exceptionally fine features, and carefully combed hair.

Insal was worried that Zahra might cry, but she didn't. She began staring at the bodies. Obviously her father wasn't one of them, Insal thought. Zahra's silence encouraged the attendant. He said nothing to Insal or to her, but slid the tray back in place, shut the door, and opened another. From that moment on, the actions of the attendant, of Insal and Zahra, too, had a kind of mechanical repetition about them.

Twenty bodies in, Zahra began to moan: a whine, on and off. The sound of mewing cats. The sound of a sadness too exalted to be expressed in tears.

After thirty bodies, Zahra turned, pushed her face into Insal's neck, circling it with her arm. In this position, she stopped fighting the smell of the bodies and started searching for her father, letting in the corpse's smell without the need to look. She seemed calm, her faint moans somehow no indication of either grief or fright. Though Zahra was certainly frightened. Not from seeing the bodies, but because of their smell.

It was there that Zahra came to know the smell of blood. At last, she made the connection between the smell of the dark fluid, the living liquid, the familiar smell of her father, and the smell of the red substance she saw—sometimes flowing, sometimes dry, and many times in a state between the two. Zahra saw fresh wounds and blood that had leaked from mouths and noses, always with a different smell, slight variations that marked each instance from the others—but that thick, liquid smell common to them all.

The attendant would open a door and the faint trace of a body's odor would materialize around her. Behind the many metal doors lay many bodies, none of which were her father's. This she knew from the smells leaking through the doors. None belonged to her father.

The little group went on looking at bodies. Some of the trays held three bodies, while the rest contained two. The number of the slain was staggering. All of them were unidentified, all were waiting for someone to recognize them. In the ledger outside, there were the names of twenty dead, while more than two hundred bodies lay in here. Those were identified, and these were unidentified, and the fates of them all were unknown beyond these walls.

At last, the tour was over. Insal was delighted because the mission was at an end, because Zahra had not found the body. As he left the hospital, he was thinking how many other hospitals contained the bodies of people killed over the last few days. Tomorrow he would search in another hospital. He would carry Zahra as he had done today, and together they would search through the bodies. It no longer bothered him as it had before. Zahra had been calm. She'd moaned a little, as though in pain, had wept softly, had spent most of the time buried in his shoulder. The day had passed with an ease he'd not anticipated and when, in the taxi, he asked her if she'd been afraid, she nodded her head and fell back onto his shoulder.

As the taxi passed through one of the city's squares, three brothers were felled, killed by the bullets of a single sniper. The first dropped, so the second tried dragging him away and he, too, collapsed, at which the third brother approached and also fell. For two hours they remained as they were, anyone attempting to go over to them warned off by others. People knew the snipers occupied the rooftops and were moving easily back and forth between them. They knew, too, that the snipers soon lost interest: they'd take down a target, then leave their position, moving around in search of a new one. They weren't after anyone in particular. They fired at random.

But the sniper who shot the three brothers didn't lose interest as quickly as the others. He preferred to hold position and observe events through his rifle's scope, to keep a proper watch over his victim—before the shot and immediately after it—and then to stay put that so he might see what happened when people found the body bundled up on the ground, to see how they touched it, how they hesitated before covering it with newspaper, how they stood before it, staring motionless at the scene, not brave enough to lift the

185

sheets of newsprint, just staring at the vaguely human form beneath the words and images.

The sniper knew that this time he must claim three victims. He didn't know they were brothers—he didn't care if they were brothers or simply friends: he just had to kill them. By chance, the second brother fell onto the first. A one-in-a-million shot, thought the sniper, and resolved to shoot the third brother so as to drop him across the others. This is how the sniper liked it: for the body to freeze in midair for an instant, a moment of joy for both sniper and victim. Then he'd be sure that the soul had left the body. You couldn't appreciate the moment if someone died in their bed or while sleeping. When a person was killed in motion, their body would always freeze for an instant, for the tiniest fraction of a second, just enough time for the soul to break free before gravity reclaimed the lifeless corpse.

During the course of his work over the last few days, the sniper had wished that his scope might register, if only once, the soul's ascent or even its departure from the body. He thought to himself that his victims' souls must be standing over their bodies and fixing him with their gaze, that they had to know where their liberator was hiding. He'd gazed upward into the sky above the prone bodies and peered into the darkness, but had seen nothing. He'd widened the scope's field of vision and swept the heavens, but had seen nothing. Picking up his gun and aiming it aloft, he'd scampered about, in danger of exposing himself to everybody—but all precautions were pointless and a waste of precious time. He might have failed to carry out a mission or two at its scheduled time, but that was how this sniper was: his victims mattered to him, the human condition mattered to him. For some reason, the sniper thought of himself as a species one step above mankind.

At last, the sniper moved. He trotted over the rooftop to the other side, overlooking a street busy with pedestrians. He steadied his rifle, took aim, and began to fire.

5

SO FAR, INSAL AND ZAHRA had visited three morgues. A morgue a day, each time poring through the registers—first the lists of the wounded and those in comas, then the books of the dead— then entering the morgue and searching among the bodies. Three morgues, and not a trace of Zahra's father. Even the memory of his smell, which had brushed Zahra in the Qasr al-Aini morgue, was gone. The man had vanished.

If only Insal had known: that the dog man was burying the dead; that thirty-five corpses lay heaped in a room on the rooftop of the Mogamma in Tahrir Square; that three hundred and fifty-five bodies had been interred on the city's outskirts.

The cramps gnawed at Leila's belly. Too late, she realized that the baby was coming now, that she was miscarrying. She told herself that the four-month-old thing would be emerging alive, and that made her think of her milkless breasts, and she called her mother to ask her advice. Fluids and blood were flowing out of her. She couldn't remember when the pains had begun. A shiver ran right through her body. Her soul was slowly being taken from her. She told her mother to call the pharmacy and order powdered milk for the child. While the milk was being delivered and the baby was emerging, the mother must come to the apartment and prepare for the birth. When she heard this, her mother gathered herself and told Leila not to worry. She played along, understanding that the miscarriage was in its final stages, but unable to account for Leila's sudden detour into irrationality. Who would have imagined that a clear-headed woman her daughter's age would act like this? Her mother put on her clothes and hurried downstairs.

Leila tried calling Insal. She wanted to let him know what was happening. The lines had been down for days, but she'd heard they'd been back up since yesterday. She tried calling his phone, and failed. She tried many times, and she failed each time, and when she gave up for good she sent him a short text message: *I'm giving birth*.

At that very moment, Insal was standing before the morgue's door. Between the thick concrete walls and the inundation of attempted calls, the networks had all jammed solid. Insal's phone was dead, and in his temporary absence his child was coming dead into the world.

The fetus slipped slowly from Leila's body. She stared at her surroundings—the chair next to her, the bedside table, the ceiling, the curtains—then fixed her gaze on the empty place in the bed where Zahra had been sleeping just hours before. Leila went utterly still. By not moving, she thought she might be able to hold the fetus inside her. Maybe her movements were the reason she was losing it. But the fetus had slipped out, leaving a void in Leila's soul.

The fetus lay on the bed below her. She nudged it with her finger. She touched its indeterminate limbs. She tried to guess its sex. She could only make out the legs and a narrow waist. At last, she understood it was stillborn.

Leaving it like that wouldn't do, she thought, and she took a little towel, itself no bigger than a grown man's hand, and wrapped the fetus up in it. To protect it. Its arm tangled with the arm of the Mickey Mouse printed on the towel. Mickey was leading him away to a make-believe world far from the present. Leila wished she could join them both wherever they were. She heard the clatter of her mother coming in through the front door, and Mickey's make-believe world vanished. All

188

fondness for the fetus vanished, and nothing remained but sorrow. She gathered up the wrapped scrap in the palm of her hand and inspected its reddened, bloody features, the tissues that had started to take shape months before.

As she covered the short distance from the front door to the bedroom, the mother called her daughter's name. When Leila didn't respond to her initial greeting, she shouted her name in fright and hurried forward in fretful silence. She came in as Leila was examining the fetus. Leila was thinking about her final duty: should she recite from the Quran? Say prayers over the dead? Had it died, or had it never lived at all? Would Insal have to get a certificate issued for a death or a birth? Can one pray covered in blood?

Her mother was as remorseless and angry as she ever got. She didn't ask about the absent Insal. The question never occurred to her. She knew the answer. Insal wasn't shouldering his responsibilities. He was busy with that girl and her missing father, and had no time to take care of Leila. She didn't ask Leila how she felt. She knew how a woman feels just after she's miscarried. She knew that she wouldn't be able to stand a single word of reproach, that she wouldn't speak for days, and that the shock was greater than Leila could have anticipated. Leila's mother gazed at the dead fetus on the towel. She saw Mickey's arm, his hand hidden in the white glove and, her mind completing the picture, his smiling face. Mickey's face was hidden beneath the fetus.

All Leila had to do was wash. She must clean off the sweat and dried tears, and then dress in clean clothes. No, not the house-robe: she must put on a loose-fitting dress and come to her parents' house. She wouldn't live with Insal any more. Insal was finished the moment the fetus slipped out. Leila would have a new start, away from him. Leila looked at her mother and she was all hope. "Take me with you," she said.

Leila got changed and her mother started to pack a little case with the necessities: medicines and a few clothes.

She took Leila's gold jewelry from the bedroom where she contemplated the fetus lying in the little towel. This was her revenge on Insal. Her grandson, sure—but her daughter mattered more. She left everything as it was and went to the kitchen to fetch a little dish. She lifted the fetus from the towel and placed it on the dish. The fetus looked extraordinarily tiny and frail against its colorful surface. Big-headed. Red. Only if you knew it was a fetus could you tell, otherwise you'd assume it was something else. Who would put a fetus in a dish as revenge against its father?

Insal's fetus, lying motionless in a little dish on the dining table, was the most extreme revenge she could conceive of, and in years to come she'd boast to one and all that she had put his son on a plate, so that it would be the first thing he saw when he came through the door. She would declare that she had never regretted what she'd done, no matter how long ago it had all been. "Insal did wrong," she would say, "and he had to be punished."

The pair of them left the house, Leila thinking nothing. Many strings had been severed in an instant. The fetus was no longer her son. Insal was not her caring husband. This was not her home any more. Her mother hugged her, clasping her tighter with every step to help her walk, restoring her rights of ownership, and transmitting to her the great energy of her hatred. *Insal doesn't deserve to be living with you. Insal will wear himself out trailing after you, and he'll never see hide nor hair of you again. Insal's insane, and he lost his kid because he neglected you.* And Leila wondered if this was unfair to Insal. But the hatred stopped her mouth.

The apartment was deserted.

Insal turned the key and pushed the door open. He let Zahra down off his arm and she walked forward a few paces, then caught the metallic smell filling the apartment, the strong reek of blood she'd identified just days before. Striding to the bedroom, Insal called Leila's name, while Zahra clambered onto one of the chairs around the dining table and stood up to find herself facing the little dish. There was no one in the bedroom, and as Insal came back out he saw Zahra attempting to touch the fetus with her little fingers. Her forefinger came away with a fleck of the soft matter and she lifted it to her mouth to taste the musty liquid. Insal stopped dead. Tried to understand what this was. When Zahra said, "Is this dates?" he grabbed the dish and brought it up to his face. What was this tender red lump lying there in the dish? He wanted to know. And even before he'd fully grasped what had happened, he knew that what lay in wait for Zahra would be terrible indeed.

Insal moved through the apartment as though drugged, unaware of his surroundings but still carrying out his daily routine. He fed Zahra and changed her clothes with a beginner's clumsiness. He watched her as she began to play with a little ball, but the fetus lying in the dish was distracting him. Every so often, he'd go over and stare at it. He couldn't believe that this was his child.

When she answered his call, Leila's mother was straight to the point: "Your son's on the table. Eat him."

He kept quiet, didn't utter a sound, and she fell silent, waiting for just one word so that she could rail at him. When she heard nothing, she said, "Eat your son. You hear me? Eat your son!"

Insal lay beside Zahra until she fell asleep.

When he'd realized what was in the dish, Insal had been stupefied.

"No, it's not dates," he'd answered her, and she'd asked, "What is it then?"

The little corpse couldn't stay like that forever. Ants might swarm and eat it. He wrapped the body in a little blanket that he'd bought especially for the newborn, placed the bundle in a plastic bag, and went out.

191

There was hardly anyone in the street, just the odd pedestrian here and there. People had grown tired of standing around questioning everyone who walked past. He went on, ordering his thoughts. Where would he go? What would he do with the body?

About a hundred meters away, there was a large park. Maybe he could reach through the railings and dig a little hole, then lay the bundle in it and cover it with soil? The body would lie amid the trees and flowers. But his arm would only reach a few centimeters into the soil. He'd be buried near the surface and that was a risk. A dog might dig down and eat him. No, the park was no good.

Halfway down the street, another park began, running down to the overpass. Perhaps he could bury the body in that park. There was no fence and he'd be able to get to a much more secure spot, dig deep, and bid the body a safe farewell. But dogs still posed a threat. That pack staggering down the street could still dig. The dogs were the only thing Insal was afraid of.

So where then? In the vast heap of garbage, like other people? Whenever he heard of someone dumping their child in the trash, he'd be astonished. It was claimed that the new towns—the great city's far-flung satellite suburbs whose names were all variations on the one event (October 6th, The Crossing, The Tenth of Ramadan: names of victory)—were home to whores who were always falling pregnant and giving birth. Insal had heard of one girl who'd chucked her baby out of the window the minute she'd delivered him, dropping him expertly on the garbage pile beneath. She'd had a lot of practice: she threw her trash out of the window every day. He'd heard of the notorious whore from October 6th City who'd broken down in tears before throwing her newborn away. The baby had still been alive. Maybe her heart hadn't let her dump him while he'd lived and breathed, so she'd set him on the sidewalk and sat on him until he was dead, then tossed him in

192

the cart. A woman walking by had been suspicious. She had reached into the cart and come out holding the baby's hand. People had gathered around and shouted, and the whore had said, "Even cats eat their young."

Insal wasn't going to sit on his fetus. He walked on through the darkness, the little dish with its tiny red contents a vision hovering before him, swelling until it was as wide as the street itself. On he walked, and however far he went the dish went with him, and then it swelled further until it covered the whole neighborhood. Insal could not go on. Walking was exhausting, and the body weighed heavy in his hand. He sat down on the sidewalk, and beside him sat the whore, a white bundle like his own beneath her rump.

"Next time, I'll eat it," she said.

The dog pack went by. They were walking down the empty center of the street. Not one of them was following a scent— they just stopped, staring at him and the bundle resting on his thigh. This was the first time they'd come across a tiny body accompanied by an adult male. They were alarmed; their howls might scare him, might anger him. Then the dog man arrived, pulling his cart, and came to a halt before Insal.

Insal saw the bodies heaped in the cart, some featureless, all with visible wounds, some covered with scraps of newspaper, and some without anything to hide them. The cart wasn't yet full and it rested lightly in the dog man's hands. Insal estimated the distance to the tree in the neighboring street. He looked at the whore next to him and saw her lips moving, but no sound came out. He turned back to face the dog man. He was sweating despite the cold, his hands huge on his scrawny frame, and his clipped hair was uncombed—it looked like he'd just gotten out of bed. The dog man drummed his fingers against the cart's shaft, tapping the keys of a piano, awaiting Insal's move. It occurred to Insal that the dog man passing by was no coincidence—that he'd come looking for a body that could find no grave.

He raised the hand that held his child in a salute, thanking the dog man, who waved goodbye. Insal's gaze fastened on the cart as it lurched away.

The dogs barked: "Another dead one! Here's another! He must be buried! Over there, by the big building! A young man's body! Just died! He must be buried!"

AH 455

I WAS IN THE MARKETPLACE when I heard that Sakhr al-Khaz-arji had died.

We expected him to die a young man. All who saw him as a child expected it. The southerners in particular were in accord. They said that he was marked, a Son of Death. They said he would die a boy and would not see out his twentieth year; and when he turned twenty and that year went by, their disquiet grew. They said that his crossing the threshold of his twentieth year would bring him to a terrible end. His death would be a sign for our times, so they said, and thus it became an event that all awaited. Women wept for sorrow at what would befall him, and men grieved at the sight of him, and some went further and said that what awaited him was an injustice, yet not one of them truly knew what that thing was. But a strange knowing laid its shadow over us all. We knew that the day of his death would be a great day. The people would repeat this at all their gatherings, and the young man would hear them and with every passing day become more resigned. He became as the angels—without sin.

All were asking, "Where is the body?" and the question moved among the people until each man was inquiring of his fellow, "Where is Sakhr?" to which that man would answer with the same question, "Where is Sakhr?" and in this manner we became a throng of fools, repeating the question over and over. Then the people began to weep and wail in the streets,

197

and when I heard the lamentations of a woman carrying her infant girl, the daughter patting the weeping woman's cheek to reassure her, I took fright, and I said that today was a terrible day, more terrible perhaps than any we had known before, and I bethought myself to pray that God might lift from us the trials of this day, yet I knew that God would answer no prayers.

And I knew that I was dead that day.

I left the neighborhood in a daze, not knowing which road I walked, my chest paining me even though I felt myself to be hollow, without innards. I was reeling from the pain, and in the streets I saw men reeling, too, and some lay on the ground, exhausted or dead, motionless or twitching, while others fell without warning where they stood, and I knew that they had died that very instant.

Then I heard the people saying that Sakhr al-Khazarji was laid out for burial at the foot of Muqattam and for some minutes I stood bewildered, for I had forgotten in which direction the cliff lay. I had forgotten which road I must walk to get there, and I was alarmed by the strength of the wind, by a whistling that was everywhere yet whose source I did not know, by a yellow dust that filled the air around me and which I breathed in. Then I spied people walking with great deliberation all in one direction, and I asked them where it was that they went, and they said that they made for Muqattam, and I walked with them.

I sought shelter in the houses' shade. I walked pressed to the walls, taking refuge in their lee from the wind and the dust, and I blocked my ears with my fingers, affrighted at the ceaseless whistling, and though the sun had vanished behind a yellow veil the air was hot and stifling, and shade was scarce.

And I looked about me and saw the people were consumed by their fear of what befell us, as I was. The houses cast a short and insubstantial shade upon them, though the sun's rays were quite disappeared, and I wondered to see these shadows thrown against the walls even though the sun was in its setting, and I knew that I should not see the terror to come.

Then the number of people grew, from dozens to hundreds, an ocean of people before me, and another ocean behind, and myself in their midst, the fear claiming my body limb by limb. And one of the people cried out, "Sakhr is dead, the Son of Death has died!" and one by one the people took up his cry, and the cry became a chant broken every minute by the sobbing of the men. All were shouting, "Sakhr al-Khazarji is dead, the Son of Death has died."

For the first time, I saw women in the street, wracked with grief and weeping. They seemed young and slight, with heads bowed and their eyes filled with tears. Then they grew more numerous, all of them dressed in black, rivers of women flowing into the ocean of men like an arrow that pierces the neck and passes through it. They were much faster than us, much fleeter—or perhaps it was that they grieved more. I had not known that grief could make man fleet.

And one of our number would look toward the river of women, and he would weep and shield his eyes with his palm, as though concealing the world from his sight, as though afraid to gaze too long on the women's sorrow lest the sorrow claim him and he weep. As though he did not weep himself. We were proud, but the weeping slew us.

As I walked along with the people, my chest grew heavy and the dust gathered in my hollow trunk. All of a sudden, my heartbeat quickened—I was surely affected by the dust and fear—and everywhere around me lay those struck dead from terror. I slowed my pace and turned to the side of the road, where I sat on the ground with my back against one of the houses.

Then I tried to rise, but my body would not move, and I looked about me in search of aid, but the people were concerned only with what was happening. They stampeded onward, noticing nothing and nobody. I felt a great thirst and my throat did dry so quickly it were as though all the water in my body had boiled away, and when the door of the house where I sat opened and women came out, I raised up my arm and with all my strength cried, "Water!" but my voice was weak and went unheard.

The people walked along, all headed for the Barqiya Gate near the foot of Muqattam, and I was with them, running when they ran and wailing when they wailed. Muqattam showed clear against the horizon as the crowd encountered the men of the guard at the far end of the street. The guard tried to turn them aside. They beat them with staves so that they would fall back, and some of them did fall back, afraid, then they pressed forward once more, pushed on by the mass at their backs, and I was held fast in their midst, wanting to go on to Muqattam, fearing the guard and defying them, with the mob around me.

Then the guard brandished swords and lances in the faces of the people to cow them, each officer waving his sword in the air and making it dance that the hesitant crowd might see the sun's rays glimmer on its blade, but the people continued to gather until there was but a fabric's thickness between each man and his fellow. And as the crush grew, those at the front were forced forward toward the guard, for all that they struggled and pushed back at those in the rear, and of a sudden we found the air filled with dust, and the wind—wailing as we wailed, answering our grief like with like—and with a fearful whistling.

And I knew that this day was my last.

And then our front ranks gave in to the press of those behind and advanced, unresisting, to receive the sword thrusts in their breasts and brows, and then to trample down every officer who stood in their path together with those of their number who had been struck and fallen, and thus was the ground paved with those who struck and who were struck, and for a short while the people broke out in a cry and tumult, and the guard disappeared beneath the feet, and their horses fled, bloodied and nearly fallen down from exhaustion, and I trod upon a dead man, and sought to avoid another, but then I bethought me of revenge and I trampled a third and a fourth, and so did stamp upon every corpse in my way. No man would prevent me going to Sakhr. No man would bar me from vengeance.

Now the Turks appeared, flogging the necks of their mounts in wild haste, slicing through our ranks, crushing breasts and heads with their horses' hooves, maces in hand, their long lances spearing all who stood on their right hand, determined to check the people's advance.

And I came forward step by step until I could see the horses passing between the people's heads and trampling all who stood before them, and I saw the people standing transfixed, unmoving, in a swoon of shock and fear, and I saw others—as though they were awakening from this trance—advancing to face the horses and lances, and not fleeing to the roadside as they ought.

I had drawn very near to the Turks when a horseman passed to one side of me and speared me in the shoulder, and then a second came, who struck my head with a whip, and the blood covered my face, and as I felt it dripping warm from my brow to my cheeks, a horse's hooves struck me in my chest.

The horse must have trampled over me several times. There I lay, feeling nothing but a faint pain.

A continuous screaming filled the air, and I knew not what it was. The sound of a thousand birds perishing? My breath left me and the air emptied from my chest.

In the distance, the Barqiya Gate appeared—and behind it, Muqattam. The crowd hurried toward it and I thought to myself that the jostling bodies would raze the gate or that it would collapse on our heads, so great was the crush.

Then the Barqiya Gate was fast by and the guard were setting our backs aflame with their whips, each horseman raising the hand that held his long whip, then lashing it down so that it passed over the bodies of us all, and the people cried out, "Cover your faces, cover your eyes!" and not one of us thought of coming forward or impeding the guard.

And I squeezed my eyes shut and shielded them with my palm, and I felt my body moving, borne along by the crowd without my feet supporting me. I was a fist's breadth off the ground. And I spread my fingers, and opened my right eye, and saw that everyone had done as I did and were shielding their eyes with their hands, and I saw that the whips of the guard had become ropes of light, no sooner striking one of our number than he lay dead, and then the whips burst into flame and with each whip stroke a little of this fire was left on the dead man's body, and I saw people that were slain, bodies limp and heads lolling, and so great was the crush that I could not see their arms dangling by their sides. The corpses were packed upright and moving with the crowd, their heads all swaying together in time with every step.

Then I raised my hands aloft and I shouted to the people, "Beware the whips! They are death! They are fire!" and the people lifted their hands from their eyes and found the whips whirling above their heads and the corpses pressed in beside them, walking as they walked.

I saw my body lifted two arm-lengths in the air and I saw the people filling every space about me—and had the heavens rained, the earth would not have felt a drop. And we were but a few arms' distance from the Barqiya Gate when the crowd suddenly slowed, and I felt my chest being squeezed, and I could not draw breath. And I was borne along against my will, and I knew that in moments I would be dead.

I was but an arm's length from the Barqiya Gate when I found the crowd ascending, and me with them, and the people raising their arms aloft and crying out, then their heads swaying all to one side and their arms dropping down. One man brought his arm down upon my head, and the arm of another came down on the head of the man in front of him, and I did not realize that they had been taken until we were passing beneath the arch.

As I was carried through the Barqiya Gate, the clamor faded from my ears and the pressing weight upon my chest was gone.

For some moments, I stood beneath the arch of the Barqiya Gate and studied the scene to my left, where the crowd did cry aloud and wail, raising their arms in what I thought supplication. And the people were pressing in on either side of the gate, powerless to do otherwise, perishing beneath the great crush and the weight of terror. Then I turned to my right and there in the distance I spied Muqattam and the people who had escaped the grip of the crowd making their way there in great haste, caring nothing for those who fell to the ground and trampling them as though they were dust. And I knew that thousands had died this day and that thousands more would die, and that I would live to see and to know, and I knew that death was better than knowledge.

I came to where Sakhr's body lay. He was laid out on a stone platform, a mighty outcrop of Muqattam rock rising four or five arm-lengths above our heads, and they had covered him in thick white cloth. And as the air swirled about him, stirred by an angry wind, they carefully secured the edge of the cloth beneath the body.

The people left a great empty arc about the body, as though they feared to approach it, and at the edge of this arc stood his uncles, his father's siblings and his mother's. I arrived after they had agreed to wash the corpse together, and I heard from those around me that a great many had fallen dead while the uncles had been in dispute, and that fear had stricken all those who claimed the courage and strength required to lift his weight—that those who approached the platform had fallen straightway upon the ground, and that those who were wont to offer their services as corpse-washers had been unable to lay a finger on the body. Then I heard that his uncles, who had arrived before me, had spent much time quarreling over which half of the family should wash him, each group insisting that it was the most deserving, and after much debate they had agreed that the father's family should wash his left-hand side and his mother's siblings the right.

Then the wind picked up, bearing a yellow dust behind which the half-set sun vanished utterly, and the people began to cry out, "Lord!" pleading to be saved.

And I moved forward, brushing every shoulder in my way and grasping every arm, all those I passed either touching my shoulder, or gripping it, or slapping my back, until I came to the empty arc about Sakhr's body, and I saw him, raised up on the platform, the body right before my eyes, and I saw those who stood around him.

And I stared at the crowd who stood on the other side of the arc and I saw that the people's shadows had vanished. The sun was behind them, starting to set and hidden behind a veil of dust suspended in the air, and I prayed God it might set quickly.

Sakhr's father's brothers gathered themselves and advanced upon the corpse, followed by his mother's kin, and they all vanished behind the veil of dust, and one man cried, "Wash him now! The dust hides his unclean parts!" and everyone raised their eyes toward the corpse and the corpse-washers, and we saw their shadowed forms lifting the cloth from him, and his recumbent body lay naked before us, surrendered to death, and the people began to fall down dead.

And we saw one of the washers draw back in trepidation, in fear of the body that but a short while before he had approached and made ready to wash, and we saw him fall down in an excess of fright, and then he began to crawl and creep like an infant and he disappeared into the midst of the crowd. And we saw those who remained resting their hands against the platform in search of support, and the sound of weeping was on every side, louder than every other sound. Then the uncles gathered themselves, and the first of them touched Sakhr's body and the rest took heart.

And we saw one of them take Sakhr's right arm to lay it out from his side, and we heard the cracking of his joints, and every person in that crowd began to strike his face, weeping and crying out, and some ran through the ranks of people, colliding with everyone in their path.

And now a new fear seemed to have taken hold of the people, an unexpected blow, for I heard their screams behind me, the distant screams of men in torment, and then the screams grew louder, and one of those who screamed approached until he was standing almost at my back, yet not one of those around me turned. We all stared forward at Sakhr's body. We were all afraid to turn.

And I knew that I had lost the power of speech, and I turned to the man who stood next to me and tried to ask him, "What art thou?" but I could utter only sounds without meaning, and I took to bellowing like a man whose tongue had been cut out, and I struck at my face with my fists.

And in place of men stood fear.

The washers hurried, each man finishing his work in haste, then standing there waiting for Sakhr's coffin and the litter that would bear him. I could no longer see anything save a mass of yellow-black about the body, and then the dust cleared and settled on the ground, leaving fine motes suspended in the air, and the figures around the corpse showed plain, and their shadows fled away, but the shadow of the platform remained, its darkness a stain upon the earth.

And we saw them drawing back from the body, some retreating and running in fear, one falling motionless, and the remainder rooted to the spot as though they had died on their feet.

*

I came to the foot of Muqattam and heard the crowd reciting the two shahadas, the recitation given to the dead man who awaits the Angel of Death, as though imploring the angel to deliver them from a grievous torment.

And as this went on, the screaming gradually stilled and I looked to their faces and found that every man had laid his dagger or sword aside, and had ceased to beat his face with stone and fist, and had turned as one toward the body laid out on the platform over the people's heads.

And I looked to where the people were looking, and I raised my face, and I clung to the shoulder of the man who stood before me.

Sakhr al-Khazarji was sitting on the rock, feet hanging down and not touching the ground, leaning his arms against the platform's edge, his head bowed down to his chest, which rose and fell with great breaths. And water soaked him and flowed down over his body, and then I understood that this was not the water in which he had been washed, but his sweat, streaming from his skin to coat him and dripping down from his toes.

The people around me muttered, every one of them in a daze, "Sakhr is risen."

After a march of many hours, I came at last to the foot of Muqattam, where I found the people standing and not speaking, and silence hanging over the place.

And I saw Sakhr sitting on a raised platform. Had he not died? Had we not gathered here to wash him and place him in a casket? And one of those standing by told me, "He has this instant risen."

And at first I did not understand what was happening, for how could someone, even Sakhr, be risen again after he had died? A life after death? And what of all those beneath the dust who had not risen this day? A strange day indeed. Had the Hour come with no signs to proclaim it?

206

And I bethought myself that these were drunkards, that this could not be the Sakhr who had died, or else that he had not died and the drunkards had just thought him dead. And I resolved to return from whence I had come.

And a voice in the crowd cried, "I die!" and sprawled out on the ground, and his companions read the shahada over him and he repeated it after them, the agonies of death writ upon his face, until he ceased reciting and his eyes widened in fear, and he stayed thus, trembling and turning his face from one companion to another, and death did not come. Then he cried out, "Lord, take me!" and repeated his cry, trembling all the while, his breath quickening, until we said that surely he was being taken, but his breathing only quickened and quickened as he continued to plead, so that one of our number cried out, "Die!" and beat at his temples. Drunk on fear, these men, pleading for death and death not coming, and I could not understand how a man might plead for death and death not come to him, when just moments before people had been dropping dead on every side.

And I knew that we were in hell.

Then Sakhr arose. He stood on the rock and gazed down at us, and his shadow stretched out before him, nor was his face visible, though the sun was setting at our backs and illuminated him, and we saw his eyes roaming around, searching for something in the crowd, and we saw his right arm raised above his head, held out as though he wished to cover the people with its shadow.

The people were stricken and they did not speak, and he who spoke could not be understood. The resurrection had blotted out their wits.

My wits are sound: the corpse did move his head—an illusion, yet he nodded and was dead.

*

207

We were standing like men in a stupor when Sakhr al-Khazarji spoke.

He said, "You were not, nor did you live. You are the sons of guile. You lived in hope, and hope there is none."

Then said Sakhr, atremble, "What were you? How did you live? You are my first-born sons. You are they who ruined all, and hoped, and hope there is none." Then he fell silent for a long while, and we betook ourselves to examine what he had said, and one of our number wept as women weep and mumbled through the groans and tears: "He rebukes us, for we brought ruin to the earth, clinging to the hope of God's pardon, and yet there is no hope of Him pardoning our crimes." Then another spoke and said, "He measures us by our first-born sons, as though, like him, we had never brought sons into the world at all." And the people began to argue back and forth, each claiming that he had heard him speak thus, and that his meaning thereby was this. . . .

And in the sudden silence that drowned all things, I saw Sakhr's voice entering my breast. I was near to him, and I raised my face to him and found that his lips were fixed and did not move, and that his face was unbending as stone; yet his voice reached me as clearly as though it were I who spoke. He said, "What are you? What were you? You are the first-born sons. You are they who suffered in hope, and hope there is none." And I thought upon his words and saw that I was nothing, that I had lived and lived not, that I had been and knew not how I had been, that I was my father's first-born son, and that I had suffered much, that not a day had passed without suffering, that I had always believed that there was hope for a better life—a happy day, just one hour of joy from a whole life—and should it not come, then there was another life for the patient. God's promise. Yet in that instant, as Sakhr denied the existence of any hope, I beheld the true promise, and I knew that we were in hell.

*

Then Sakhr lifted up his arms, and shook his fists in the air, and cried out to the people, saying, "I am not as you supposed," and the people pleaded for death and in that moment death abandoned them, and on every side the prayer rose up, "Lord, take me."

Sakhr's cry rent the air, "I am not as you supposed," and those who stood there longed for death and each one said, "Lord, take me." Then a cry rose from the crowd, "I am giving birth!" and we said that it was a woman crying out in the manner of a man, and I approached the one who screamed and the people did likewise, pushing and shoving, as eager as I to see. I came to where a few men stood gathered together, staring down at their feet, and on the ground between them I saw a man, sprawled out with his unclean parts exposed—and, emerging from his anus, a pup, still and lifeless, and the people shouted words that made no sense. Then one pointed to the creature and cried, "Dog!" and he repeated the word twice or thrice again, and I looked to where it lay and saw that it was like any male newborn, a son of Adam, and I asked myself, "What is wrong with this man who calls it a dog? There it is, a newborn child before our eyes, and nothing to wonder at." Then the man began to howl, "A dog! It is a dog!" and we saw that he had lost the power of speech, and he continued to howl, not knowing what had happened to him, and the people about him said, "God be praised!" Then some of them turned to howling, and their numbers grew until all were howling like dogs— like dogs, they howled, "God be praised!" not realizing what had happened to them, and then I bethought me that maybe I had lost the power of speech like them, and I resolved to test my tongue, and I spoke and heard my voice uttering the speech of men, yet I knew I howled like them, and knew that I heard it not.

*

The people were asking for death, saying, "Lord, take me," or "Lord, kill me," or "Lord, claim me," and then their prayers became a single phrase and all together, in great wretchedness, they chanted, "Lord, take me! Lord, take me!"

Then Sakhr said, "Silence! There shall be no death this hour, but only eternity." He was naked, his body trembling as though wracked with fever, and I heard him say, "You are dead. We are all dead," and I recalled hearing something like these words before, its meaning clearer. Then one of those standing there asked him, "How is it that we are dead when we are here, standing before you?" and Sakhr replied, "We stand in hell," and the cries of the people rose up, and the dispute between them grew, and their voices became louder and much was said, and the men trembled and shook. And we said that the day had gone on for many hours and wondered when night would come—as though night could deliver us.

Then Sakhr cried, "There shall be no deliverance this day! We are in hell!"

I awoke from my swoon and leaned myself against the bodies of those around me. I stood without the strength to stand, and I saw Sakhr—dead but a short while ago—alive, and the people all about me wept and hid their eyes and faces as though they had not the courage to behold him. Then Sakhr cried, "The Hour has been and gone, the people have been set in the balance, and we remain here. This is the hell of the evildoers!" And he was silent, and we said to ourselves, "If only he had stayed dead."

And I knew that I was here forevermore.

Then Sakhr pointed to the dead before him and said, "Arise!" and all those laid out upon the ground rose up as though they had never fallen, and I saw those fallen in a swoon awaken, and the dead brought back to life—and some had cut their throats and I saw them standing, not bleeding, their throats open to the wind and their speech a bubbling, and Sakhr said unto all:

"You have died, and been judged, and fallen here, into hell. Where you shall be tomorrow, I know not; another hell, or paradise."

Then he said:

"The world ended an age hence. The Hour came. The people rose again."

Then he said:

"He who lives today is in hell or heaven, forevermore or for a time—and hope there is none. Your only hope is patience."

And the people, affrighted, cried out and wept until their breasts were wetted.

Sakhr was silent, and we told ourselves that he had said his piece, and his eye wandered over our heads, aimlessly roving over the crowd.

Then Sakhr's shadow stretched out over the people, a great shadow fallen toward the setting sun—as though the sun were setting before us, not behind us—and not one of us took note of Sakhr's inverted shadow, for the horror we saw and heard was greater than any shadow.

Then the shadow moved, turning slowly over the crowd as though it were a ray of darkness whose source was Sakhr, and we heard sighs of relief from the mouths of those who stood there as the shadow passed over their heads. The shadow passed over the people and they were taken in a rapture. Then it passed on, and each man sat down on the ground, his head bowed, and mumbling.

And I saw the shadow approach the place where I stood.

The shadow engulfed me and I saw the blackness.

There was no light about me, no glint, nothing save the dark, and I remembered a saying that made play of darkness and the dark of heart, and I knew that I was an evildoer and that this day I would see those I had wronged and how I had wronged them.

The shadow claimed me for mere moments, but my former life passed before me in a flash, and I saw that I had been a tyrant in the world of men, and that those I had killed unjustly were reckoned up and they exceeded a thousand thousand souls, and that my prayers and fasting were not placed in the reckoning, as though they had never been, and I knew that I was in the fire forevermore.

And I saw that I had killed a woman in the world of men— and then I saw her approaching me, and standing before me, and striking me with a length of iron until I fell down dead, and I tried to remember who she was but I could not. Then I saw myself in another body, speaking another tongue, and I saw her striking me with a length of iron until she slew me. Then I saw myself in a third body, and a fourth, and a fifth, and in each I saw her striking me until I fell down dead, and I knew that I was in the fire forevermore.

And I saw that I had lived eight lives in hell, moving from torment to torment, and never knowing that I was in torment, and I knew that I was in the fire forevermore.

And I saw that I had been entrusted with vast territories and had been at the center of great affairs, and I saw that I had killed not because I was unjust or just but because I had left every man to do what he would. And I saw that I had been complacent. I had chosen idleness, and flown from duty, and abandoned the storehouses to thieves. I saw that a man had been born in my time to a mother full of fear, and that as he grew, he, too, came into fear, and when he died, died fearful. And I saw that I had lived numberless lives in hell, and I saw

212

that I was tormented with fear, living in fear of all things, and I knew that I was in the fire forevermore.

And I knew that I had been a judge in the world of men, and I knew that I had lived two thousand lives in hell, in which I had been a length of firewood by which men warmed themselves, then ashes, then risen again as firewood by which men warmed themselves once more. And I knew that the torment had changed and that I had become a hearth on which men lit their fires.

And I knew that I was in the fire forevermore.

And the shadow had almost disappeared from atop my head when I heard the screams of Amer al-Jowhari, whom I had murdered in the world of men, screaming as he had done the day I killed him, the very screams I hear here every day, and I knew that I was in the fire forevermore.

Then the shadow went from me—and my visions, too—and the people on my left appeared resigned, the shadow having passed them by, as on my right they surrendered to the shadow.

Then the people fixed their gaze on Sakhr, until we saw none other but him.

Sakhr said, "We have reached the end. There must be punishment."

And I heard Sakhr say: "This hell of yours will endure many years yet, many years more terrible than those you have seen. This hell will end and another hell follow it, just as another hell came before."

He said: "After I am gone, you will see seven years of darkness in which everything will perish before your eyes. You shall grow hungry and eat the flesh of dogs, then you shall die and devour one another's corpses, then you shall despair and eat your children."

He said: "Then two-thirds of you will be no more. They are living the last of their lives in hell. For he who dies during these seven years shall be free, and he who lives shall be here forevermore."

He said: "Hope shall be set in your hearts, and hope there is none, and hope is your torment."

He said: "And the mindful among you are those who see that your hope is false."

He said: "All who have died this day are now risen, and all know the inner truth of what is and will be. I leave you for all eternity. I shall plead mercy for you, for that which is to come exceeds all limits."

He said: "Set aside all hope. Know that the end is an illusion."

Then I saw Sakhr falling back onto his platform, and we saw the last rays of the sun setting at our backs, and all were waiting for the uncles to make their move, and all were content with what they had that instant learned. And the fear had gone, and in its place was certainty.

And I bethought me that I had lived a just life in hell. And I looked to that which delighted me and found it to be the cause of my travails. I remembered carefree days and saw that they were the path to my misery, and I understood that every hour of joy had brought me days of sorrow.

And I considered my prayers and my fasting and I laughed, for there is no prayer here, nor fasting, nor ever any lightening of the torment. All that I possess is patience and all that I fear is hope.

AD 2011

1

MANY TRAGEDIES HAD BEFALLEN THE garbage man. Thirty years ago, he had lost his eye, and the memory of that day had never left him. He'd been sitting at a café in al-Daher when a fight broke out beside him, so he'd gotten to his feet in order to steal a leather wallet that one of the men had left on his chair. The man had spotted him just as he'd grabbed it and made to flee, and had shouted a warning to the others. The garbage man had fought fiercely. Even after his eye had oozed out and he'd known he'd lost it forever, he had still fought on. They'd never seen a thief fight like he did, which is why they all decided to let him go on his way without turning him over to the police.

Working in a plastics factory, he'd slipped a disc, which had put him on his back for a long time, and because of the close ties between plastics and trash he'd been able to leave work at the factory and get a job at a garbage plant—that's what he called it: a 'plant'—where household trash was picked and sorted into plastics, paper, and organic waste. Work you only needed one eye for, and ragged clothes—for those who sorted garbage didn't matter.

There, amid the mounds of trash brought in each day, the garbage man had found plenty of food. He'd turned his nose up at it back then: he was earning nicely, and eating well, and living fine, lots of fucking the women he worked with and even more with the neighbors' wives. He was a bull: a massive body, a face disfigured from his many battles, and a blank white eye. When he fucked, darkness was the perfect cover for that face.

But the food people threw in the trash kept him up at night: fresh fruit, pieces of chicken still with their meat and skin, stale loaves. He saw millions of scraps of bread. Food a man might pass on, but real food nonetheless. He'd toss it to the pigs and it would be killing him, though this was the best way to get rid of organic waste: pigs would eat anything.

Then they had said that the pigs had a dangerous disease that would infect people and kill them, and the garbage man had dug a deep pit. The plant's owner had dug with him, weeping bitterly, and when the time had come he'd asked the garbage man to finish the job on his own because he wouldn't be able to help him. The garbage man had shattered the skulls of the small black pigs with an iron bar, and whenever one had run from him, he had let it go. He'd known another worker would kill it within minutes. It was just a body he wouldn't have to bury. The garbage man had tossed the pigs' corpses into the pit, then heaped dirt over them. A few days later, the owner had let him go. He was going to get into another trade, he'd said—there was no future in garbage without pigs—and he'd advised the garbage man to find other work. He had said that garbage was finished.

That day, Insal and Zahra visited two morgues. They viewed hundreds of bodies, and with each one Zahra would turn her head away, would see the dead face and hide hers in his neck, or turn it away to stare out over Insal's shoulder, her way of signaling rejection or refusal. Then Insal would pass on to the next fridge—or the metal table in the corner of the hall, the simple cot—and stand before the corpse to ask her for the thousand-and-first time: "Is this Papa? Is this Papa? Zahra, is this Papa?" And Zahra would not utter a word. She just turned her head away.

This was supposed to be the last morgue of the day, but Insal still had to stop by Qasr al-Aini, where he'd been told that two new bodies had arrived. There could be something there for Zahra, although she was worn out. It had been another long day: two morgues already, and the return to Qasr al-Aini would be the third. Zahra might fall asleep on the way from sheer exhaustion, but Qasr al-Aini it must be, no getting away from it.

Zahra was limp on his shoulder. Insal stopped for a moment outside the door, staring at the morgue attendant.

Visiting hours were over and many people stood outside the door pleading with the attendant, who was turning them down with a face of stone. They were ready to hand over small bribes, but he refused all the same. He felt no indignation, but he was tired of the way people around him were acting, of their desperation to come in. He had corpses piling up and dozens coming in each day to peer at them, but the number of bodies kept rising: only a few of the missing were ever found. One or two a day, perhaps. The morgue never emptied; the number of bodies arriving just went up.

Zahra had woken up a little. Insal put her down and they walked slowly along at a pace suited to her little legs. They approached the morgue door. The attendant followed their progress, and when they got to the door he opened it.

Inside, Insal launched into the standard preliminaries—"We're going to look for Papa, Zahra, got that? Okay? Is this Papa? Is this Papa?"—and at each body Zahra turned her face away. Her father's smell was not here. Not here, except for a very distant trace, a memory, as though he had been present many days ago.

At the last, as Insal approached the final refrigerator and the attendant opened the final metal hatch, as Insal asked, "Zahra, is this Papa?" the girl stiffened before the days-dead face. It looked uninjured, with no traces of congealed blood. Zahra did not move her eyes away as she usually did. Again, Insal asked her, "Is this Papa, Zahra?" and she replied, "Papa."

219

Insal signed many forms without reading a single one of them. He wanted the whole business done with, and signed over all responsibility to the hospital. They would wash the body, would arrange for prayers to be said over it, would bury it in a pauper's grave. The only thing he learned was that it would be going to the Imam al-Shafei cemetery. Zahra leaned her head against the wall while Insal was busy with the papers, and when he was done he picked her up and walked out.

The attendant had seen many bodies and he remembered them all. He never forgot what his eyes had seen. His memory preserved everything. It could summon up anything that he'd stored away over the years. He would create images of the dead in his mind, would gather the images together, would sketch them out with faint, translucent lines—lines described in the air against a white background—then lay them one over the other, in as many layers as there were pictures in his head: right eye layered over right eye, nose atop nose, lip on lip. And one lip might be askew if the face was torn up, and parts sometimes missing from the head; and then again, the face might be whole and perfect. The attendant stored thousands of faces in his memory, image on image, layer on layer, and had no idea himself where it would all end, or whether there was an end. His memory now held a single image made up of many images, of thousands: a neutral face with no clear features, just two eyes, a nose, and a mouth, all sketched in loose, indeterminate lines. Now, when a new face was laid down over it, the composite image did not change. Unchanging at last. One face. But of whom the attendant didn't know.

He would watch the youngsters come happily into the hospital, laughing as they noisily recounted the exploits of the day before—when someone had fired tear gas at them, or when one of them had run away or rushed over to attack the hired thugs. He would observe their delight as they talked about the progress they were making on the street, full of zeal as they walked the corridor to the morgue. One might get overexcited, hopping in the air as he described how he'd caught the canister of tear gas. These kids were plucking canisters out of the air. Their torment was truly terrible, the attendant would tell himself.

As they approached the door, the kids would frown, would slow their pace, would look at their feet. Their voices would grow quiet. One would ask about their missing comrade, then in they'd go and hurriedly look around, snatching glances at the bodies, then on their way again, recounting their absent friend's heroics. He must be shacked up with his girlfriend, they'd say, in clover, while they were here, beside themselves with worry, searching for him. The attendant would follow their progress down the corridor. Slowly, they'd fade from sight, their bodies becoming identical little flecks, moving dots in torment. They were driven by hope, these ones. They were being tormented as none had been before—the greatest dose of hope the attendant had seen anyone take in his life.

2

THE GARBAGE MAN WAS GENTLE with the girls. They had done his bidding all day. He'd never have imagined that the older girl would respond so readily. He hadn't bothered with the younger one at all. The older girl would act like a grown woman, would grasp his cock, squeeze it, play with it. The garbage man tried to take the young girl's hand and teach her how, but she didn't pick it up like the other one, she wasn't a pro, and most of the time the older girl would take her place and lead him where he wanted to go. But there was something missing. His pleasure wasn't complete. The girl's body was too young. Didn't do the job. But he treated it as though it were a proper body—better than any image he could dream up, better than the fantasies he'd lived with—and he made himself a little promise: in a few years' time, she'd have a real body, would be a real woman for him to own.

But the garbage man was thinking ahead. Circumstances could change. She might find herself a handsome, strong, young man with an undamaged face and two good eyes, who walked erect and didn't stumble. A fellow like this might come along, and they'd fall in love, and she'd leave him. But the young one here would tie her down. They wouldn't leave together unless two young men came along at once. At this point, the garbage man became truly angry. With all the losses he'd suffered before, the thought of a future without either of the girls enraged him. They were all he had now. Even the trash he ate from every day, piled up in pyramids in the middle of the road, didn't belong to him.

The garbage man was fed up with his home beneath the bridge. It wasn't a home, just a place to sleep. What he dreamed of was a place in one of the many heaps of garbage here. He'd dig into the side of one of them, would excavate a tunnel into the center of the pyramid. Nothing to worry about: it wouldn't fall down and he'd grown used to the smell long ago. He was careful to keep a little rotten food beside him—when he slept, when he sat on the sidewalk, as the older girl was playing with his cock; at all times, in order not to forget that smell. So that he could never smell anything but it. He also made sure to imprint it in the girls' minds. How could they live with him if they weren't used to the stench of decay?

When he reached the pyramid's dead center, he would set about widening the tunnel. A tunnel no longer: he would carve out the middle of the pyramid into two bedrooms and a large lounge. Of course, he'd need planks to prop up the ceiling and walls. He'd steal them from the building site next to the pyramids or from the lumberyard nearby.

He'd be able to dig the tunnel quick enough, four to five months say, though then again maybe a year was more like it, then another year to carve out the bedrooms and living room. Two years after starting work, he would be living in this house of his, and the big girl would be fully grown, and he'd sit on the floor in the living room, leaning against an empty box and waiting for her to fetch him his food. Two years was a long time, true, but the garbage man was in no hurry. What mattered was that no one could know what he was up to. If people found out what he was doing, they'd dig in the other trash pyramids—there were many pyramids, but they'd all be used up in the end—and the whole place, repellent to nose and eyes alike, would be transformed into a busy neighbor-hood like those around it. And then, any one of them might overextend his living room, and the pyramid would collapse

224

on his head and those of his companions. The garbage man came here to get away from people and from their buildings, which he loathed. He wanted to live in one, but he loathed them all the same. Living here was his idea, and his alone. No one else would ever get a piece of it. He was prepared to kill anyone who threatened the success of this idea.

The garbage man dreamed. A dream of his one and only trip to see the pyramids of Giza. This scene from years before replayed itself, and it was only after he'd woken that he remembered he'd been a boy when he'd visited them and could begin to unpick reality from his dream. He recalled visiting the pyramids with classmates: walking along in a double line of schoolboys, two by two, a teacher at the head of the line and another at the tail. But the dream passed hazily over the reason for the visit and the faces of his companions and skipped straight to the tour guide's speech: "Pyramids are huge tombs. Dwelling places, too, perhaps. Pyramids could be anything and everything." So the tour guide had said, and the garbage man had never forgotten his words. And when he woke and emerged from his little house beneath the overpass, he saw the pyramids of garbage ranked neatly and pleasingly in a single line, and birds aplenty circling over them and alighting, and he said to himself, "Those are truly pretty pyramids, fit to live in."

He finished his daily rounds. He scavenged food for lunch and someone gave him a cigarette. He begged eight pounds and someone gave him another cigarette. He pictured the older girl holding the cigarette and breathing out smoke. He smiled and blood coursed through his veins. He was aroused, his cock stood up, and he looked forward to a fun-filled night.

Beneath the overpass, the garbage man sat on the ground. The two girls lay beside him, and the sounds of the cars that passed by a few meters overhead head were clearly audible. The light of the setting sun bathed the overpass's metal frame, and it

225

stored the heat away, ready to discharge it into the air once the sun was gone. He was so thirsty. He lifted a bottle of water to his mouth and drank, then went outside to piss against the nearest of the bridge's columns. When he turned to go back to his little hiding place, he saw a group of young men approaching the overpass. They stood by his house and started peering in at the two girls through gaps in the planks and cardboard sheets. A second group came toward him, watching him very carefully and leaving their laughter behind with their companions, who were now trying to open the little door. They formed a barrier between the garbage man and his home. They were holding wooden staves, short lengths of piping, and cables.

They made him sit down. The sun had set, few cars drove overhead, and there was nobody in the street. Each and every one of them went into the little house and did as he pleased, raping the older girl, who submitted to them all, while the young one in the corner mostly hid her eyes. And the garbage man was outside, and afraid. He wanted it all to end without trouble—for them to get bored or for them to finish fucking her. He could hear her faint squeals and could now anticipate exactly when she'd make them. He felt no sorrow for her.

One of them was penetrating her and she cried out. The garbage man heard the sound and told himself that the cry was surely a cry of pain, but he did not get up and chase them away. They would get angry and might overpower him. He wanted it all to be over quickly. The girl wanted the one on top of her to be done quickly. The men wanted the same thing themselves.

And now the men waiting their turn began to beat him. The garbage man received their blows in silence. Fighting back, he knew, would only provoke them. They were in raptures. They had decided to beat him until they were too tired to go on, and he told himself he'd take it—the garbage he ate each day had left him strong and able to endure. The blows to his head were very painful. After several of these, he could no longer feel the pain or the blood that flowed down his face.

Even after they were done and gone, the garbage man stayed seated. He wasn't strong enough to stand. From within the shack, he could hear the girl weeping softly.

A maimed tomcat stepped past him. Decrepit, its face blank and tail filthy, it stalked past him very slowly. Very slowly indeed. There were smears of dried blood in its fur. The garbage man reached out his arm and struck it with his fist. It didn't shy or jerk away like a cat would normally do. The punch shifted it sideways, but it went on walking without giving him a glance. On it went, leaving behind the man, and the house, and the soft weeping, and stepped down off the sidewalk to cross the road, heedless of the cars flashing by before its nose—heedless of the car that tried to stop before it struck. The driver stamped the brakes and the tires screeched. He almost managed it, but then another car struck him from behind and rolled him over the cat.

Wreckage from the two cars scattered, the drivers got out, and each started blaming the other. The tomcat had disappeared completely. The garbage man peered over, but he couldn't see it. Then he started crawling toward his little house, the blood running from his head and into his eyes.

At night, Zahra began to talk to Insal in her childish voice, and he did his best to answer her questions. She constructed her sentences with difficulty and her tone of voice would lift at the end of each statement to lend it the stamp of inquiry. Zahra had learned to question—and at an age when other children asked questions of their fathers, she was asking hers of this stranger.

So his wife Leila was gone, his stillborn child was as safe as could be, and Zahra's father was dead. No one at home but Zahra and Insal, who stretched out on the bed and thought: *I'll adopt her. She'll be my daughter, mine alone.*

Insal drifted away, gazing at Zahra's sleeping face beside him, sketching out a happy future for them both, father and

227

daughter; and maybe Leila would return or he'd convince her to come back and raise Zahra with him.

In the morning, Insal woke to Zahra's moans. He was lying down, and he sat up, and by the faint sunlight filtering between the shutter's slats saw that something was wrong with her mouth. She was crying bitterly. He got up and switched on the light, then came back to bed to find that the skin on her face had spread and was growing over her lips. A strange, wrinkled skin. He saw Zahra's skin creeping out from either side of her mouth and covering it, spreading out and covering the lips; sealing up the mouth.

But what was happening wasn't causing her pain. It only constricted her mouth. Her fingers felt an unfamiliar thickening when she tried touching her lips. Insal started to press down on the delicate membrane in an attempt to understand what had happened. The skin hadn't spread over the lips as he'd assumed; the flesh was fusing. The two lips were slowly joining, the mouth's muscles and internal tissues slowly cleaving together. Even as Insal was dressing, was counting his change, was getting ready to leave the house and take Zahra to the doctor, the mouth was joining up and the open hole growing smaller. It looked to Insal as though the mouth would close up completely in a matter of hours.

He picked her up, her body tense and trembling, his hot with distress. Her face was damp with tears. Insal's happy dreams fled away. Zahra might never be cured; maybe the doctor wouldn't know what was wrong with her. Insal tried to remember if anyone had ever been afflicted with something like this. A disease he'd heard of, perhaps, that an acquaintance had had? He tried to recall if he'd ever seen something similar. He couldn't think of anything. He signaled for a taxi and set off for the nearest hospital.

All day long, Insal traipsed around the hospital carrying Zahra, from nurse to doctor, from bed to bed. They snipped away a small sample of the self-generating skin from over

228

her lips and took some of her blood, and at least a dozen doctors examined her face—all of them silent, their expressions unmoved. What was happening was quite normal, Insal thought to himself. *If everything that's going on around us these days is normal, then what's happening to Zahra is normal, too. This is no disease.*

At the end of the day, in the evening, they asked him to go with Zahra to a room. They would both stay there overnight.

They had been feeding Zahra mashed food, which she very nearly refused to take, only her hunger prompting her to accept it. She hated it, particularly since she had to spoon it in through the small gap that remained of her mouth, chewing it a little, then swallowing. They gave her a sedative, and a few minutes later she surrendered to sleep.

Insal slept fitfully. Every few minutes, he opened his eyes to peer into Zahra's face and check that she was sleeping. Then he'd close his eyes once more and drift off. When he opened them and found her twisted over in the pose of someone lost in oblivion, he was reassured. At least she was feeling no pain now. She was deep asleep.

The next morning, he saw that her mouth had closed completely. The little opening at its center had disappeared, her lips gone forever, and in the daylight that came in through the window Zahra began to mewl. The sound escaped her nose and Insal wondered if he was dreaming. He must be. He sprinted screaming from the room.

The doctors were very sorry. What was happening was most unusual, they informed him. They'd never seen it before. They knew that once human organs stopped moving they gradually died, the muscles withering and then disappearing altogether. Even before that happened, the limb was usually done for, incapable of functioning. Yet what was happening to Zahra was different: a film of tissue had grown to seal the space between her lips; the lips had melded together, and the mouth's opening had vanished without cause or reason. But analysis of her blood and endocrine functions confirmed that Zahra was quite all right. She was in no real danger.

There was a solution, one doctor said, but it was as unconventional as Zahra's condition. A surgeon could open her lips, passing his scalpel down the old line of her mouth and forcing it apart, then suture the edges to stop the bleeding. A quick, effective, surgical solution—much better than hunting through books and trying to treat the condition with drugs.

But Zahra was not his daughter, and he would have to hand her back to her people one day. His dreams were all forgotten now. She wasn't going to live with him forever—she would never be his daughter. Insal wished it were so with all his heart, but he knew deep down that he was taking her as a replacement for his dead boy, and when he found her relatives they would never forgive him for acting on the doctor's suggestion. Her father, unjustly killed and buried in a pauper's grave, would not forgive him either. They would meet in the afterlife, unclothed, and the father would chastise him for what he had done: *How dare you? How could you disfigure Zahra's face?* He would never forgive him and would demand that he be punished. Insal clung to hope—one day, he thought, she would return to normal. One day she would wake, her mouth parted in a beautiful smile, her lips whole, without the scalpel's scars and the marks of the surgeon's thread.

Zahra submitted to everyone who milled around her. The doctors fetched a thin silicone tube. They carefully introduced one end of this into her nostril, pushing it a few centimeters in, and when it stopped as if encountering an obstruction they leaned her head back and gently resumed the attempt, persisting until they had passed it through her nose and down her gullet to her stomach. This was Zahra's new mouth. They fetched a bowl of purée of indeterminate hue, and with a syringe began to squirt it slowly into the end of the tube. Zahra put up no resistance. She stopped crying. Something strange was inside her, a foreign body, and food was passing through it into her insides. Lots of people stood around her. The reek of illness. Its stench was everywhere here: the smell of a young man who'd passed away just a minute before; the smell of two more who'd burned to death; from the nurse who stood over her the smell of blood she'd come to know in recent days; sweat from the exhausted doctor who moved back and forth before her, his body numb from the powerful tranquilizers he took each day and without which he was unable to do his work.

Then, as the purée slid through the tube into her belly, another fleeting smell filled the air, soothing her. A lovely sensation enveloped her as her stomach filled. The taste of what she'd eaten was gone, but the smell was there.

The doctors, the nurse, and Insal departed, and Zahra remained behind on the bed. The end of the tube dangled from her nose, sealed by the nurse with a flexible, see-through cap so that nothing inside her would seep out, but the smell of illness continued to fill the room.

Insal broke down before the doctor, told him he didn't want to see her fed like that for the rest of her life; that he'd prefer for her to die than live like that; that it would mean constant torment for her and for him; that what was happening was rank injustice; that she had never done anything to deserve all this pain.

The tranquilizers that flowed in the doctor's veins left him feeling weightless, sure of himself and sure of his performance, and Insal's pleas were absolutely standard. He'd heard them dozens of times before from patient's relatives on the brink of nervous breakdown, and these were no different. The same words, the same pain, and the tranquilizers made it all ridiculous and repetitive. As the sentences followed one after the other, the doctor was thinking, *Yep. . . Whatever. . . . Sure. . . Get to the point, please. . . . No cure. . . . No food other than by catheter. . . . It's called a catheter, yes. . . . Forget a complete recovery. . . . Illness is sent to try us. . . . I know. . . . I know, I know. . . . Aren't you going to shut up, friend . . . ? The girl'll be dead in days. . . . Give me a break. . . .*

231

After just a few months on the job, the doctor had become certain that everything happening around him was utterly meaningless, that he must not allow himself to be affected by the death of a patient; he might even take pleasure in the death of one of the long-term inmates—the sufferer relieved of his cares, the relatives relieved, the doctor too. Some cases were terminal, and he had to go to extraordinary lengths to treat them. This girl, for instance—her case was far from usual, the first recorded case in history, it seemed, and yet it was up to him to deal with her.

People were being killed out there. Dozens a day, he'd heard. They were truly at peace: no more suffering for them. The doctor reflected that nothing they would encounter in hell could be worse than what they'd seen on earth. And then, on top of it all, along comes this man and his daughter to waste his time and the hospital's. A simple calculation told him that the girl had just days to live. She would be unable to survive for long fed through a silicone tube. Soon she'd be needing solids. Her poor mental state would affect her physical health. Perhaps she'd get an infection from the tube that sat inside her. Then he thought of his alternative solution, not to relieve the girl's suffering, but so that he might be shot of her and her father. He would get a surgeon to open the mouth. A mutilation, no two ways about it, but she would at least eat normally. Her lips would never be the same again, though, and maybe they had even turned into tissue of a different kind.

At the end of the day, following an intensive examination, one of the surgeons decided that he would perform the operation the next day. Cost no object, he said: he'd do it for free because it was an exceptional case. Insal wouldn't pay a penny.

Insal agreed.

They lay together on the bed, waiting for tomorrow. In the darkness, Zahra passed her palm over his face. She felt his mouth and nose, brushed his closed eyes, and touched his eyebrows, reached out and pinched the lobe of his left ear before returning to his mouth and nose. Her father's smell had receded in her memory, and that of Insal was carving out a place for itself inside her.

This permanently fearful man, this man in pain, this man loves me and does not know me. I can smell his love but his fear upsets me. Don't be afraid. You know, fear is not for grown-ups, fear is for us little ones alone, and when I grow up I shall not be afraid. I shall no longer know the smell of my own fear.

Asleep, Insal saw that he had become a volcano, a volcano called Krakatoa. He was walking across a vast expanse floored with glowing white tiles, and on all sides thin iron columns rose into the air. Krakatoa was walking between the thin columns and not understanding what they were, and after a while he came across Zahra, who had turned into a naked wooden doll. All her joints seemed to be made of cheap wood and her hair was synthetic, but the face was hers. There was this metal rod sticking out of her, a kind of tail, which emitted sounds whenever she moved, like vast machines turning over in a factory. The doll was wandering all here and there between the thin columns, gazing over at Krakatoa for moments at a time, then averting her face and drifting away again. And every time she moved, her metal tail would thrash with its sound of vast machinery.

Krakatoa saw a thin whip in the doll's hand, and then he saw her cracking the whip over her head, striking at something he couldn't see, something above the columns. He decided to find out what was up there, and calmly and slowly he rose up, flew up, until he saw that the columns were the legs of many beds with white quilts and coverlets laid out over them. He saw that the beds were scattered around at random, and that was why their legs had seemed like a forest of thin trunks.

On the beds, men lay on their backs—and the doll's whip floated out over them, then down in quick, short strokes. And then other whips rose up to strike at other men, and when Krakatoa drew near to one and peered at him, he saw that the man was missing a face, missing the skin on his face, and he knew that someone had peeled the skin off all these faces with surgical precision. The face had been cut from hairline to chin, and from ear to ear, then lifted away to leave the head faceless. The delicate muscles showed bloody, the teeth white and lipless, and eyes stared upward without lids, their gaze unwavering despite the stinging whip.

Krakatoa started screaming at the wooden doll: "Enough, Leila! Zahra, enough!" And why Krakatoa was calling her Leila when he knew she was Zahra, he couldn't say.

Then he knew that those stretched out were dead, and that even so the wooden doll was tormenting them. The doll was tormenting the dead.

Krakatoa wanted to understand what he was. He knew that he was a famous volcano. Many years before, he had exploded in a mighty eruption, the sound of which could be heard far away. But he thought that there must have been some kind of mistake, that he wasn't Krakatoa. That he was something else. Then, in the far, far distance, he spied a mirror, so he flew toward it to look into it and to know what he was.

The sound of the vast machines swelled and the whip strokes gathered in intensity, while the men stayed as they were, lying on their backs, and as Insal drew near to the mirror the sound of the machines increased greatly in volume, and Insal awoke.

It was dawn. In the dark, Insal wrapped Zahra's body in a blanket and took her away. He knew that hospital security would try to stop him, and when he got to the entrance he sprinted out and away from the guard, who chased after him for a few yards and then fell back.

He wouldn't leave Zahra with the doctors to be opened up by knives. He ran, picturing the scalpel passing smoothly over skin and making a small opening—a little bleeding—and then the wound closing up a second later despite the efforts of the doctor, who, amazed, reopens it again, only for it to close once more, obstinate and unrelenting. Zahra would stay dumb forever, would never speak or eat, would take her food from a tube through her nose.

Insal dashed on, Zahra in his arms, and when he grew tired, he walked. No one was about. People were fed up with chasing gangsters and standing guard over their buildings, and the streets stood empty with only a few exceptions: those returning from the square with a blend of hope and fear—and, somewhere not far off, the dog man, hard at work, gathering bodies into his cart as he did each day, while his dogs combed the neighborhood in search of more.

3

THE GARBAGE MAN RAPED THE girl as violently as he was able. It hurt her, and the pain grew and spread, accompanied by tearing flesh and flowing blood. There had been many rapists before the garbage man, but none had been quite like him. She tried to get free, but he held her to the ground and went on with what he was doing, the blood from his wounds covering his face and covering her. The bleeding had almost stopped.

Around the little house, the dogs had gathered, watching what was happening through the gaps between the wooden boards with lifeless eyes and mouths held shut, their silence undisturbed but for the garbage man's mutterings and groans, and the girl's repeated, rising cries. And when the stink of blood and shit was suddenly and unmistakably present, the dogs' ears pricked up and a nervous thrill ran through the pack, transmitted to the dog man who stood behind them. He stood at a distance of two meters from the garbage man's shack. He could see nothing through the narrow cracks, but he knew what was going on—had known it long before it happened—and now he knew that human tissues had just ripped apart; that a heart was thumping out of control, about to stop; that moments earlier the younger girl who lay beside the two entwined bodies had died of fear. And, as was his wont, he stood there, waiting.

All he could see were the planks stacked carelessly beneath the on-ramp and the sparse light behind them filtering through the cracks, and when the garbage man was done, and his body was slumped in absolute surrender atop that of the girl, and his limbs had begun to relax in readiness for what was to come, the dog man approached the flimsy door on one side of the little house and opened it to see the garbage man lying there, unresisting. The garbage man raised his head and stared into the dog man's face with lost eyes, then signaled for him to come closer.

The garbage man couldn't move. The girl was pushing up beneath him, his huge body crushing her ribs. The dog man stood next to him and tried to shift him off her, but the garbage man struck him a glancing blow. His words scarcely audible, he said, "There's a knife in the corner. Fetch it." The dog man searched for the knife and found it. He handed it to the garbage man. The garbage man's arm could only move slowly; he couldn't even grip the knife properly. He held the handle and brought the blade to his bloody mouth, then clamped his lips down onto it. He closed his eyes, tickling the blade with his tongue, then he stopped and said, "The steel's so cold."

He tried to cut his own throat, but the blunted blade in his weak grip couldn't pierce the skin. With a great effort, he held the knife upright, resting on the ground beside the girl's neck, and laid his throat against the pointed tip. He looked one last time into her eyes, then leaned into the blade. Blood gushed out.

The dogs gathered around the three bodies lying on the ground. Many pungent smells spread through the air: they didn't need to sniff at the bodies. The reek excited them and, aroused and confused, they padded around the cramped shack. The smell of rage, of thick blood, of the semen of the man who was taking his final steps toward death, and the exceptionally powerful smell of the raped girl's shit. She'd shat in the extremes of the final assault. And the smell of an emotion, too, one the dogs were encountering for the first time. It was something stronger than fright; a smell to stop the heart, to freeze it dead. The dogs barked, "This man is dead! This man is dead! There's a girl! Dead, too! The little girl has died! They must both be buried!"

The garbage man's body was enormous, still hot and supple, wet with sweat, and spit, and sperm, sprawled out atop the older girl—of whom only a thin arm could be seen, stretched out on the floor by the man's head. The knife had sunk into his neck. It had missed the spine, but its handle protruded plain to see, and behind the handle, the girl's eyes, staring in terror at the dogs. In one corner was the little girl's body: cold, sat upright in the fetal position, her head buried between her legs, tucked away as if trying to escape her surroundings. The older girl gave a soft moan, and coughed, and with everything she had, attempted to heave the man's body off her. The dog man helped her. He rolled the corpse over onto the floor, and she stretched out beside it. Her shattered body, its many bloody wounds exposed to view : marks blue and red, a torn lip, one nipple missing and in its place a patch of blood-red flesh, blood pooling at the ear and congealing in her hair. A chaos of blood and semen, shit welling from between her thighs and spreading into a great stain that fouled the floor and the rest of her body. The dog man lifted the two corpses and placed them in his cart, then pushed it out of the shack. The dogs were barking: "She shall not die! This one will live! Two have died! Enough for now! They must be buried!"

The dog man knew that the girl would live for many years, and that she would see much, much more; that what had happened here was just a small part of what was to happen to her; and that the radiant justice never erred, though it might seem that way. And then he shut the hovel's door and hefted his cart, testing its weight and its wheels, making certain they were sound for the road ahead was long.

He went to the sidewalk, pulling the bodies in his cart, the pack trotting all around him.

Once home, Insal laid a sleeping Zahra down on the bed. He saw her face shining out from the edge of the blanket. She was wrapped up like a caterpillar in a cocoon awaiting its

239

imminent transformation into a butterfly, but unlike the caterpillar she was closing in on herself. Insal thought to himself that her eyes would soon close as her mouth had done. Maybe this was a new disease that nobody knew about. Zahra looked like she had just come down with a fever. He wrapped her tight to protect her from gusts of cold air, then felt uneasy: this was a coffin, not a bath towel or a cocoon. He hastily opened the towel to leave her whole body exposed, to show her face. It had altered considerably. But Insal couldn't say exactly what it was that had changed. Something was missing. Some imperceptible reordering had occurred. Then, at last, he saw it.

Insal saw short, fine hairs on her cheek and others on the blanket, and when he shifted her body to one side he found more. He found a brown worm between her body and the blanket, trapped there beside her head. Had it come from the hospital? Had it dropped from a tree as he ran along with her in his arms? He peered at Zahra's face, trying to understand what had happened.

It was Zahra's ear.

He held the cup of the little ear between his fingers. It was a different shade of brown from the pale skin of Zahra's face: shriveled, a little desiccated, and so light as to be weightless. It really did look like a worm in Insal's palm, and when he examined the spot where it should be on Zahra's head he saw a pinprick hole. An ear without a cup; an opening where the sound could enter. The cup had fallen off on the other side as well, and there the hole had healed, grown over with skin like the mouth before it.

At last, he saw the reason for the face's transformation: Zahra's eyebrows were falling out. They were very sparse now and soon, it seemed, they would be gone completely. In the end, though, it didn't matter. She'd lost her mouth and ears, and they surely mattered more.

Without lips or ears, and with her two eyebrows disappearing, Zahra was slowly but surely losing her face. Nothing left

240

but the nose and eyes, and he now knew she'd soon lose those, too. Insal didn't know how he knew it, nor did he understand why this was happening. When he stared at her eyes, he saw the two orbs swiveling beneath her lids. It was a sign of light sleep, this slight flickering, and soon Zahra would wake.

If Zahra had been able to speak, she would have said, "I can't hear! I can't hear!" but the look of panic in her eyes was unmistakable. Insal understood that she'd registered that her hearing and her ears were gone.

Zahra began to mewl. Yesterday, she had been completely silent. Despite the long hours spent in the hospital's corridors, the sedatives she'd taken had seemed to work and she hadn't cried once. Now she wept, but the sound came soft and low as it passed through throat, and skull, and flesh, and bone. She tried stretching her mouth wide to scream, but the formation of flesh and skin prevented her. She could see Insal moving his mouth to talk to her, but couldn't hear his voice at all. She heard only her voice, a muffled buzzing from within. Like a mewing: waves of sound that rose and fell with every breath. She exhaled through her nose, and a whistling accompanied the mews.

Insal peeled a banana and mashed it with a spoon, then slowly stirred in a little milk and introduced the mixture into the large syringe.

Zahra tried removing the tube from her nose and felt it hanging there, motionless. When Insal prevented her she cried, mewed, and on seeing the syringe in Insal's hand, she became afraid and mewed harder and harder, and then when Insal made to take hold of the tube, she snatched it from his hand with uncharacteristic roughness. She didn't understand what was happening, though she wasn't in pain and the silence that enveloped her might even be called agreeable. But she was afraid.

Gently, Insal took the tube. He freed it from her quivering fist, and began to pat her back and hug her. Then he described an expression of cartoonish excitement on his face. He lifted his brows and opened his mouth in astonishment. He looked at the syringe filled with food and licked his lips. He plugged the nozzle into the end of the tube, got ready to push, then slowly squeezed out the food. Zahra enjoyed the sensation of the food sliding down into her stomach. She could feel the tube passing it through her body. She could see Insal's hand gently depressing the plunger and the thick paste sliding into the tube. This was eating, she recalled.

When her stomach was full, she relaxed. She calmed down. She was sated. Zahra smiled, a smile without lips or teeth.

A little later Insal signaled to her to try it for herself. He left her to peel the banana. He helped her to mash it with the spoon. Zahra forgot herself and raised the spoon to where her mouth had been, but it bumped against skin. Her eyes smiled and she tipped her head back. Then she started pressing the spoon into the remaining chunk of banana and deliberately letting the loose piece slip away, as though it were sliding around the bowl out of control: press after press until the chunk flew from the bowl and her eyes smiled all the more. Insal filled the syringe with the paste, attached it to the tube, and guided Zahra's little hand onto the plunger. She took it and began to feed herself, with the clumsiness of a child learning to eat for the first time.

Zahra now had a way of feeding herself without mouth, or teeth, or tongue. She would never taste food again. Instead, it would travel straight from syringe to stomach. She would smell it, though; its odor would reach her as other smells did, and soon Insal would teach her how to introduce the thin tube into her nose, then how to pass it through the little nostril, then how to lean her head back to get it past the kink in her nasal cavity, then how to gently push it on its way so as not to damage the soft tissue inside, then to see how the passage was easier after that, with no further obstacles or kinks, until the red mark halfway down the tube had reached her nose. Only then would the end of the tube be in her stomach. Insal was sure she'd learn how to eat by herself. This was the first day, the first step, on the path of learning.

By noon, Zahra was finally awake, Insal asleep beside her after the many exhausting hours of the previous day. She left him and began roaming around the locked apartment.

She took Leila's little mirror and stared at her face. Peered at her shut mouth. Turned her head to better see the ears. Their absence baffled her, maybe more so than her missing mouth. She hadn't spoken much, she didn't know many words, and had had to think for several seconds while she put her sentences together, but she had been able to hear without any effort at all—and today the sounds were gone, and nothing remained but the smells that surrounded her.

Zahra's eyes were almost closed over. Her lashes had all dropped out. Her upper lids sagged and she couldn't lift them. She couldn't open her eyes to their full extent today. She laid her forefinger on the mirror, traced over her nose and eyes, pointed to her mouth, trying to speak, but there were no words, just a honk from her nose, a snort to signal her contentment.

Insal awoke and sat up in bed. He watched Zahra, not moving so that she wouldn't see he was awake, and noticed the lashes spilled on the pillow. He picked her up, and stared into her eyes. He saw the eyelids drooping, slowly readying themselves to fuse.

Zahra would go blind—Insal knew that now for a certainty—yet he would go on teaching her to eat by herself, and then he would teach her how to read. He'd need a specialist for that, to teach her Braille and the use of hole-punched pages that Zahra could touch with her fingertips.

Her lids fused slowly before his eyes. Slowly, slowly, over the course of the next two hours, her field of vision narrowed, and she began to cry softly. This was the last time the tears would be able to run down her cheeks. The lids would instead become pouches for her tears.

243

All day, Zahra ran her hands over Insal's face—when he fed her, when he undressed and bathed her, when he laid her down next to him at night.

Insal had convinced himself that there was some reason for what was happening to Zahra. This was no torment, as he'd first thought, and gradually he arrived at his own private understanding: it was to isolate her from everything that was taking place. Zahra would grow and age detached from her surroundings. She would never see or hear a thing. She'd never get involved in human relationships at all. Thus she would remain, and he would look after her.

Early in the morning, the pair took the metro to the Qasr al-Aini hospital. A call had come inviting Insal to go. He knew that no one would be able to help Zahra. The doctors at the hospital would be unable to treat her. They'd check and recheck her without the slightest hope of a cure: this wasn't a disease to be dosed and dismissed. Even so, he wrapped her in a blanket to protect her from the cold and held her in his arms as he sat in his seat on the train.

The smell of hope mixed with that of fear: they were created together. Zahra was well acquainted with the smell of fear. Her father had been afraid most of the time, only at ease when he held her. But the smell of hope was new, and it was strong here in the carriage—many hopeful people got on and got off, leaving it hanging in the air. It didn't fade easily, but rather filled the space, infecting the other passengers, who sketched out a bright future for themselves in their minds, who hoped for a better life: a happy marriage in the not too distant future; a beautiful young son who'd grow into a successful man. They wished to kill the fear that worried at their souls as they walked the streets. They would replace it with a successful nation that would astound the world. The hopeful ones imagined that they were writing history; the illusion of history possessed them in the same way that it possessed the mad, and in the end they would vie with lunatics for a place in history—the things they had done would be passed on and taught to their children and grandchildren.

For others, though, the fear grew. They assumed that there was no escape, no way to walk without the possibility of terror waiting at every bend in the road, and so they walked hardly at all, fleeing the long, high road for shorter, less troublesome paths. Their fathers had taught them that the equal distribution of injustice lay at the very pinnacle of Mount Justice, that peak they'd never scale, would never reach, though they trudged forward for the rest of their lives. And those who'd not been taught to sway with the wind by their fathers took their lessons from the storm's blasts: they avoided them as much as possible, but the storms came anyway and came hard, outpacing their attempts to flee. No choice but to bend when the storm came. When it caught them, they had to give in, and then they might emerge, minutes or years later, and the fearful among them would have no conception of what kind of future lay in wait—unable to draw themselves a path, for they'd never seen a path before. People here were born afraid, lived afraid, and died in terror, and hope only appeared toward the end. That was how it was. The equal distribution of injustice is the very pinnacle of justice, but there is another form of divine justice: no injustice at all—and better yet, the presence of mercy. Even those who had strayed from the path, who had deliberately done wrong and sunk themselves in darkness, assumed that mercy would save them. Not in this world, though, not in this time of ours, but in the one to come.

A foolish assumption, thought one of those who knew. He was sitting at one end of the carriage, watching the happy discussions. He almost wept at their foolishness. How could they not see what was happening? How was it not one of them had looked closely at what had been happening all these years and centuries? These ones were yet to realize that they were in hell. These ones would be tormented by hope. And, as occasionally

245

happened with those who knew, the sight of Zahra and Insal swamped the man with grief: the girl wrapped in her blanket and seated on Insal's lap, her face shielded from view, and then Insal moving to make space for a man to sit beside him, and the blanket slipping from Zahra's face, the absence of her features plain to see. The one who knew told himself that this was what hurt him most: the children being tormented. He knew that they didn't realize what was happening, and that their torment was a torment, too, to those around them. One that might intensify until their relatives grew to hate them, while their horror prevented them from seeing what was really taking place. For some—the children, say—the torment might be lessened. They might go deaf and not suffer what the rest could hear, or go blind and be spared the sight of what went on around them. Or they might be paralyzed and unable to feel anything at all. All these things were a lessening of the torment. Madness was a complete deliverance, a way out of hell—although no one truly left. The mad remained here: instruments of torture turned on others.

The one who knew told himself that any relief granted those in torment was a further torment to those around them; a limitless pain wrung them. *Aren't I being slowly slain by this deformed child and her father, almost dead from grief? And toward the end, the adults realize that the child is unaware of what's happening— will never be in torment—and they recant, and beseech, and beg that their torment be lessened, knowing at last that they are the ones being tormented. Yet even so*, the one who knew reflected sorrowfully, *even so, they do not understand this hell they're in. They do not understand that just a few short years separate them from this hell coming to an end—just so that a fresh hell might begin.*

The morgue attendant had assumed that once he knew he was in hell he would not be tormented. Torment, he'd told himself, was to remain in hell without knowing it, hooked on hope of a better life soon to come, or clutching to the promise of heaven

246

in the next. When you knew where you were, the torment came to a stop: however much you were tormented, it would have no effect. But now he was caught in a vicious circle of suffering, no different from the ignorant. He sat, facing the morgue door, and reflecting that the ignorant might even be better off.

The sound of distant footsteps reached him. He waited for the newcomer, and turned his gaze to the far end of the corridor where the hospital's main hall met the passageway leading to the morgue. He trembled in an excess of apprehension. The newcomer brought good tidings, that much was certain, but not for the attendant. Good for others, good for someone else. Insal approached, carrying Zahra, almost nothing of her visible beneath the blanket, and suddenly the sound of his footsteps ceased; the quaking of the attendant's body blotted out all other sounds.

Insal explained what had happened as Zahra sat on his lap, her head against his chest. He could feel her breathing, calm and regular. The attendant heard him out and said nothing. As Insal went on, the attendant became confused, astonished that all this could have happened. What good could he do now? How could he help Insal? He could guide the seeker to what he sought—he was a caretaker of bodies and corpses, a custodian of those who had died. As for the living, he had nothing to do with them.

Zahra's breathing grew disrupted. Was that a cough? She rubbed her face, and the cover finally slipped from her face to reveal her features: scarred skin in place of lips, eyes with lashless lids slowly sealing up but still just open, surrounded by secretions like thick tears. The attendant noticed fine, discarded lashes on the blanket.

The attendant had seen many things in his life. He had been able to understand everything going on around him. He would take pleasure in penetrating the secret of the torment that hid behind the loud laughter, grins, and shy glances. The sheer variety of what befell people left him in awe, and when he saw

247

what was happening to Zahra he was amazed. This torment was pure and direct, uncomplicated by trickery. He asked for the wisdom and knowledge to do what was required of him.

The attendant ran his thumb over what had once been Zahra's lips, evening out the wrinkled skin, smoothing it as a baker smooths his dough. The skin where her ears had been was soft beneath his fingers. He stopped up the remaining right-hand hole and smoothed the skin on the left, then he pinched the lids of her right eye shut between forefinger and thumb, and ran the ball of his thumb along the empty line of lashes. The lids fused completely, with no holes or cracks through which the pupil could be seen, and no line now to differentiate one lid from the other.

As he completed the process, the attendant shook. He knew that this was the most splendid thing he had ever done in his life. He had been part of something magnificent, though he didn't understand its import: was he bringing her relief or torment? He knew, too, that his knowledge was deficient, and that the knowledge of all those who knew was incomplete like his, and that he would never have a perfect understanding of hell.

4

ZAHRA'S ISOLATION WAS COMPLETE, HER features almost completely sealed off. Only her two small nasal openings remained, permitting the tube's awkward insertion and allowing air to pass in and out.

He prepared many kinds of food for her: vegetables, beef soup, chicken, and stewed fruit. Realizing that she could still make out smells, he started lifting the food to her nasal openings, waiting for the skin to wrinkle in appreciation. He bought her flowers and held them where her mouth had been. He picked basil and jasmine from the neighbors' little garden, rubbing the basil between his fingers, then smearing it over her missing mouth so that the smell might reach her. He couldn't see her smile, just a slight creasing in her cheeks, but he knew that she was happy.

One sunny day, Insal understood that he was in hell. He was slicing up an apple when he saw what he had done in the world, and for a brief moment he trembled, then understood that this was his final lifetime in hell, that though he must remain here for a few more years, he would go to heaven when he died. Reassured, he resumed his slicing.

He realized, too, that what was happening was too great for men to comprehend, and that what was to come would be no less than what had gone before, but more violent still, and that the fortunate were those who would die before this hell was ended. Then he understood that the attendant had shown Zahra mercy when he'd extinguished her sense of sight, and he understood that she would live in order that others might see her—and not because she was to be tormented by them.

He had given Zahra her breakfast and was thinking that today he might continue teaching her to walk unaided. He remembered the past few days, helping her to walk down the passage leading to the living room, calling out a warning whenever she looked like stumbling and then smiling to himself, at his own spontaneous reaction: how could he have forgotten that she couldn't hear him? He heard the sound of her footsteps emerging from the bedroom. She was holding onto the doorframe with her left hand as he had taught her and feeling her way with her feet, when the doorbell rang.

Insal opened the front door to find two women there, one wearing a niqab and the other unveiled. The unveiled woman said she wished to speak with him, and told him that the woman in the niqab was Zahra's aunt, her father's sister.

Zahra's aunt and her companion sat on the sofa. The moment they were seated, the aunt clasped her companion's hand in hers and pressed her fingers into the palm. She wanted to see Zahra, the companion said. Insal was at a loss. How was he to tell them what had happened, especially since their first request was to see the girl? How was he to prepare them for the shock? He replied that Zahra was ill, that she was suffering from a strange disease. For a few moments, the companion tapped at the niqab-wearer's hand, pressing her fingertips into the palm and the underside of her fingers as though typing on a tiny keyboard. The woman in the niqab appeared to tense and began pressing quickly on the palm of the other, who told Insal: "Never mind. Bring her."

They know about Zahra's illness, Insal thought, but how could they know what had happened? And where had the aunt been all this time? Many days had passed since Zahra's father had disappeared, and it made no sense that a strange woman

250

should suddenly appear and ask to see the girl. If this was her aunt, then she'd take her away for sure, but how did he know she really was her aunt? The woman in the niqab anticipated Insal's thoughts. His silence and stillness, communicated to her by her companion, made it clear. To her, Zahra's illness had been expected, had been likely, but the timing was unusual and painful. Unhurriedly, she started undoing the covering over her face. She lifted the niqab, and her face was the most eloquent confirmation of her kinship.

Her head was devoid of all features. Just two holes in place of a nose and nothing else besides. An undifferentiated sheet of skin, without crease or fold.

The companion explained that they communicated by tapping their fingers. Zahra's aunt touched her fingers to tell her what she wanted, she repeated it to Insal, and what Insal said was passed back the same way. There was no other way: the woman hadn't spoken, seen, or heard a thing for many years.

Insal asked her name. "Zahra," said the woman. "Zahra's father named his daughter after his sister."

Zahra came into the room, walking slowly and feeling her way along the wall. Insal fell silent, as did the companion, who stared woodenly at Zahra. Slowly, very slowly, she advanced across the part of the room without any furniture until she reached the chair next to the sofa. She leaned on it with her hand, and came to a halt before the three of them: a dazed Insal, a woman she didn't know, and her aunt, whom she hadn't smelled in a long time.

This is how it came to her:

At first, the aunt's smell seemed to have altered slightly. Zahra's two nose holes detected a tremulousness, an anxiety mixed with fear. Her aunt was worried, and Zahra did not know why but neither did she care and, turning her body toward the source of the smell, she walked in a straight line until her knee touched her aunt. Zahra thought her sense of smell must be deceiving her and that this lady couldn't be her aunt. She wanted to be sure, to be certain of her aunt's presence in front of her.

As her knee hit her aunt, the smell of fear and confusion rolled over Zahra. The elder Zahra lifted her up and sat her on her lap. The girl was now face to face with her at last. For a moment, their breath mingled—the older woman's feelings crept across to the girl, and then a powerful force, an irresistible urge, raised the child's palm to the aunt's face. Gently, Zahra felt across the place of her missing right eye, delicately brushing over the eyeball as though unable to credit that it was gone: this really was a missing eye; this was her auntie's eye, for sure. Then her fingers crept toward the brows, to check if they were missing, before descending the slope of the temple to the ear. For this, Zahra had to come very close to her aunt. As her hand touched the site of the absent mouth, a sense of profound equanimity enveloped both girl and woman and—for the first time in a long time— Zahra relaxed and became still.

Zahra kept running her hand over her aunt's cheek. Slow, even passes, testing out her favored sense: touch. At the nasal openings, she stopped, lifted her head, and stuck the tips of her first and middle fingers into the holes. There was a momentary lull, then the aunt released a sudden blast from her nose and Zahra snatched her hand away in feigned alarm. The aunt rocked her head back, as did the girl, then the two foreheads met once more. They were laughing.

And all the while, Insal was moaning and as the moans swelled into wails it became more than the aunt's companion could bear—the feeling fingers, the muffled laughter, Insal's grief—and she stumbled away, looking for somewhere in the unfamiliar apartment where she might cry in peace, then stood sobbing in the corridor. Insal wept, too.

The companion returned more composed. She sat next to the aunt and gave her her hand, then asked Insal if Zahra's father had been found. He told her that he'd died. He told her

252

that Zahra had identified him before she'd lost her sight. She asked if he had identified the man himself. Insal explained that he and Zahra had searched long and hard for the body, that she'd accompanied him on every trip to the morgues, that they'd finally found the body in the morgue at the Qasr al-Aini hospital. He told them that the body had been moved around from morgue to morgue, and that it had ended up at Qasr al-Aini—they'd found it by chance. Zahra had recognized the face at first glance. Insal said that the father had died in the demonstrations, that he was a martyr—no doubt about it—and that he, Insal, was sorry. Sorry because he'd exposed Zahra to all that suffering, but he hadn't been able to identify the man on his own.

The companion asked if there'd been any distinctive mark on the father's face. Insal thought for a minute, then confessed that he'd noticed nothing out of the ordinary. The man had had a black, fairly thick mustache and slightly protuberant front teeth.

The aunt raised her arms in the air, then slapped them down hard against her thighs. That wasn't Zahra's father, the companion said. Zahra wouldn't mistake her own father. That man had been a stranger. Zahra's father was just like Zahra's aunt, and like Zahra, too: without face or senses.

Through her companion, she said that her brother's features had disappeared long ago. He'd been a young man when his eyes and nose had closed up and his ears had dropped off, and he'd lived without his senses from then on. Zahra's father loved people, was a friend to many, and the older Zahra had learned that he had indeed participated in the demonstrations and had gone missing on a Friday. The aunt was briefly still, and busied herself patting little Zahra and playing with her hair. Then she grasped her companion's hand again and continued.

The aunt lived abroad, the companion told Insal, and had come to Egypt when Zahra and her father went missing. They had asked a lot of questions until at last they'd reached Insal.

253

The woman told Insal that from now on he wasn't to worry about Zahra or her father. The aunt couldn't go looking for him, and the living trumped the dead.

The aunt stood up with Zahra in her arms. She lifted her right arm and took a step toward Insal. Insal reached out and touched the outstretched palm. The aunt took hold of his hand, then his forearm, then pulled hard, bringing what had been her mouth closer until it was touching his forehead. Then she let her niqab fall back over her face and wrapped up Zahra's face and head to hide her from prying eyes.

She walked the short distance to the car that was waiting for them with her companion beside her and together they sped away.

AD 2025

1

I WAS IN SHOCK, UNABLE to move, and it seemed to me as though everything had suddenly collapsed on top of me: people, buildings, the whole wide world. There, beneath the metal sphere, with Burhan settled on my chest just below my face, I was visited by an absolute certainty: I knew that we were in hell.

And I forgot the anticipated revolution, the people gathered in the street, the piles of corpses, and the tearful cries imploring me to open fire once more. I abandoned the rooftop, feeling my way through the darkness, and hurried downstairs. The street was dark and many bodies were scattered on the ground—more real now than they'd seemed as images through the rifle's scope—while a crowd of the living stood around, weeping and groaning, miserable, raising their faces toward the sphere and screaming out words, most of which I couldn't follow. They were demanding that I go on shooting, all of them still hoping for a bullet from the sky.

I had no idea where I should go, but I headed for Opera Square, fleeing the screaming people behind me. There was not a soul on the street between the two squares, and a mob of dogs, three packs together, were roaming about, sniffing the ground and the air in search of something. As I passed them by, they stopped and stared at me as though I were a ghost. As though they knew that I knew where we were.

I saw a man standing on the sidewalk, a pile of short metal pipes stacked in front him—a hundred pipes or more, each one about a meter long. I walked up and asked, "How much?" And as I was looking at him and his wares, he answered me, "A pipe? A pipe's one pound." I went on walking, asking myself where we truly were, and I tried to reason logically: how could we come to be in hell and not know it? Had the dread day come? Had we been judged, and then come here? Was Cairo our hell, or was all of Egypt? Was the whole world hell? And I thought that I must be raving, or that this must be the effect of the karbon I'd taken over the last two days, and I remembered the tower, and Cairo spread out before me, and me sniping whomever I chose. But the certainty was stronger than all the questions and all the answers. Yes indeed: despite everything, we were in hell, and all the worldly semblances about us were but an illusion.

I walked until I came to sprawling Opera Square, to be greeted by the sound of moans and the staccato thump of muffled blows. I saw hundreds clustered about the plinth of Ibrahim Pasha's broken statue. The square was crowded—hardly room enough to place your feet—with everyone shoving their neighbors, trying to make more space to stand or move. The streetlamps were out, and the light was very faint and came from far away, and it was only when I'd drawn closer and was standing on the edge of the square, just a couple of meters from them, that I understood why the people were gathered together.

Each and every one of them was clutching a short metal pipe, making space to swing with their left hands, then striking the person nearest to them. The blows were random, undirected; they might fall on a head, or arm, or chest, and then the pipe-holder would keep going, raining blows on another, even as he in turn might be receiving them from someone else, without making any effort to protect himself. All of them, without exception, were taking part in a massed battle of one-sided assaults—each attacking those around him—and yet there were no parties to this conflict, but that each man was a party unto himself. And it seemed to me as though victory was not the object, and that self-defense was not the purpose, and that all that concerned them was to kill the greatest number possible. These were not the operatives on the ground of whom the resistance leadership had spoken, the ones who would finish the job. These were regular citizens murdering one another.

In the gloom, their features were lost. Whenever one of them fell to the ground, others would leave off their private battles and batter him with killing blows, finishing him off, then going on hitting, crushing his skull to nothing and tearing his body apart. The sound of the blows would be muffled at first, then slowly but surely would grow sharper, accompanied by a metallic ringing, and I realized that the battered body had been completely broken up, and nothing was left save shreds of flesh, and that the ends of the pipes were clinking off the exposed marble of the plinth's surrounds. Amid the dense crowds, the bodies themselves were invisible, but I could picture the scene—ragged flesh, crushed bone, dark flecks of blood—and when more had fallen, and the open spaces around the statue grew, and the marble could be seen again, I saw no red flecks on the ground, but rather great black heaps of no definite shape or form.

I did not leave. I was paralyzed, incapable of movement, too unmanned even to take the decision to go. Alone, I witnessed them falling, one after the other. The distant lights outlined the bodies as a single mass of flesh, and nothing could be clearly seen but the night-black pipes—rising, then whipping down to rise again—and as the bodies fell, the smell of chopped flesh floated out: the smell you catch, mixed with the tang of blood, outside the butcher's shop. After a few minutes, their arms became heavier and their numbers started to dwindle until five were left, staggering about. Slowly, they came together at the statue's plinth and began hitting out listlessly at one another. They were exhausted and had bled profusely, but their proximity to death spurred them on, pushed them to keep going until all was done.

At length, only one remained, clutching a pipe in his left hand. His right arm had been severed and its shredded remnants dangled down, visible beneath his long and bloody shirtsleeve. He sat on the ground panting, surrounded by bodies. Feebly, he lifted the pipe over his head, but he couldn't hold it there and let his arm fall to his side. He tried to lift it again and failed. At last, he saw me, and with trembling intensity he raised the pipe to his face. He didn't utter a word, but moaned instead, as though addressing me, and I gathered that he wanted me to come closer. My feet slipped in the blood that coated the white marble and I tripped through the bodies and bones bundled on the ground, but I kept walking until I reached him. I was very close now, but in the darkness his features were absent. And in the midst of all this, the lights in the square suddenly flared.

I saw him plain, unshadowed. Masked in blood. What teeth remained gleaming in his shattered face. I saw many cracks in his skull, a chaos beneath his scalp. Then he turned his bulging eyes toward me, imploring. The bodies filled the square. One solid mass, not bodies stuck together; if I hadn't seen what had happened just minutes before, I wouldn't have known that these were the corpses of the slain. I took the pipe. It was covered in layers and layers of sticky, congealing blood, and it was hot. Despite myself, it fell from my hand. I hunted for a piece of fabric between the lumps of flesh, bent to rip a rag from a shirt, and wrapped it around the pipe, and then I stood motionless before the man for a long time, not believing what was happening. He was breathing slowly, without the strength to lift his gaze to my face. For a few moments, he held his head up, then gave in completely, and it slumped, staring down into his lap. The first blow came in hard from the side and took off part of his skull. He toppled to the ground and I continued hitting him, though I was sure he was dead. Why I persisted, I don't know, but I went on hitting him until his body lost all definition.

Silence filled the square. All was calm: no cars or pedestrians, every window shut and darkened. On the statue's plinth, someone had written 'Mankind has failed,' and I thought to myself that whoever had done this knew where we were, and perhaps there were many others who knew it, too. And I asked myself where all these dead were going. Where do you go when you die in hell?

My hands, and arms, and shirt were all spattered with blood, and I didn't like to touch my mask to check if it was clean lest I mark it, too. As was his habit, Burhan showed up after the event, circling me, then settling on my shoulder. The Saint had been right: I no longer needed him. I picked him up. In my palm, he was light and motionless, totally surrendered to the heat of my skin, and it took no effort. After the violent blows, it was the simplest of feats. With my thumb, I prodded twice into Burhan's underbelly. He didn't resist and made no move to fly away. His underbelly and delicate legs caved in, and I pushed further into his body until I'd split him in two lengthwise. He was weightless as a butterfly.

I lifted my gaze to the towering white marble plinth. Nothing remained of the statue save three legs of the horse that once had borne Ibrahim Pasha on its back.

And now I was walking home, stripping my clothes off piece by piece and my shoes. The blood that soaked me was unbearable, and there were shreds of flesh and bone shards beneath my fingernails and in my hair. I looked around for a tap, but could find only a water jar on a windowsill beside the road. What little water there was I poured over my head and its coldness took my breath away. This was a moment from my former life, no doubt. I was treading barefoot through the broken glass, and gravel, and trash that filled the street, sidestepping the bodies lying randomly on every side and not knowing if a fellow sniper had killed them or if they'd killed each other.

Outside the apartment door, I remembered that I'd taken off my clothes and that my money, and keys, and ID had been in them. I knocked until Farida woke up and asked, "Who is it?" from behind the locked door, and when she opened it my nakedness alarmed her and she screamed. Panicking, she asked what had happened to me, what had happened outside: "Are they really killing people?" I made straight for the bathroom and tried to remove the blood that clung to my body. Farida came to help. She removed my mask and I almost wept when I realized that my face was uncovered. Without asking me a single question, she started rubbing at my skin with her bare hands; when I looked into her eyes, I saw none of the terror there had been at the front door. She had the steady calm of a woman washing her husband or her child. She removed her pajamas, which she wore with nothing on underneath, and at that moment, beneath the harsh lighting, the water in my eyes multiplying her image dozens of times over, she seemed as alluring as ever. She lifted my arm and bent her head to wash my armpit. I knew Farida had seen more shit than I could ever imagine, that she'd lived many, many days in terror, and that others had merely seen what she'd seen, let alone experienced what she had been subjected to, yet they had lost their minds. And I knew that she would see more soon enough, and I trembled, for suddenly the veil had been drawn closed, and I did not know what Farida had done in her mortal life to deserve such torment.

Beneath the water that fell on us, I wept and told her: "We are in hell, Farida. We are in torment."

2

TODAY MARKED THREE MONTHS SINCE Evacuation Day. It was all over—the troops of the Fourth and Fifth Armies of the Knights of Malta had left the country and we had reclaimed every inch of Egypt; had reclaimed, too, after great but short-lived celebrations, all our hardship and all our torment.

The ice cube melted quickly.

I rose from the bed and opened the fridge, took out another ice cube, and enclosed it in my fist. Every time I wanted to escape this idea of hell, I held an ice cube to assure myself that there was biting cold here, the polar opposite of what I knew of hell. In the end, though, the ice would always melt and confirm that hell was where we were.

How was it people hadn't noticed? How did I not pick up on it before? Perhaps we were too caught up in creating paths, taking certain actions and avoiding others in order to escape hell once we'd died, never realizing that we were already here, for real, in torment.

Farida would be here in a few minutes. She'd finished work at the hospital an hour before, enough time to get here from Abbasiya via al-Azhar Street. We'd thought a lot about relocating to an apartment in Abbasiya to reduce the distance between work and home, or even a little pad in New Cairo. An hour on Cairo's public transport was a long time, ultimately twice as exhausting and grueling as a full day on the job. But

Farida had taken a drag on her cigarette and said that she liked it here. I wondered whether Farida knew that we were in hell, whether she realized that every day we were being tormented in a thousand different ways. Farida no longer had any choice over what she could wear, and the money she'd put away during her months on the game would soon be spent. The hospital salary wasn't enough and she was forced to withdraw a sum from her bank account every few days. She hadn't withdrawn a single pound when she worked as a prostitute, she told me: her income had covered her needs and more. I quickly worked out what she'd been making—fifty pounds per client, and an extra fifty for any special requests; when business was good, that came to five hundred pounds a day. No need for detailed comparisons; this figure was more than her entire monthly salary. True, she'd left behind the heavy bodies, the sweat and stink of strangers, but now she faced a torment of a different kind.

Farida had abandoned medicine early on—a few days before I'd met her, in fact. She had finished her postgraduate year of training and had immediately taken off for one of the brothels on Sharif Street. This was just after the prostitution law had been passed, and she'd walked into the brothel owner's office weighed down with her hatred of human bodies, of all bodies. Later, she told me that she'd made her mind up months before she ever set foot in that office—after one hundred days working at the hospital, to be precise. Her colleague in the emergency ward had been a little older than her and thus more experienced, and on that hundredth day more than sixteen individuals had died beneath his hands. A man had been brought into the emergency room on the verge of death, then his heart had stopped and her colleague had tried reviving him. He'd failed. He'd failed every time. Not one of the dying had been wounded by a bullet or hit by shrapnel from a resistance bombing. Some turned up after falling from scaffolding on building sites, following car accidents, or in the wake of heart attacks. The last one had been like that: Farida said that she had been a young and extremely beautiful woman, a fine tracery of veins showing through her white skin. She had been dead, actually dead, but Farida's colleague had asked Farida to massage her heart anyway. The girl was young, he'd told Farida, her heart might start working again, but Farida hadn't had the courage and so, without directing any blame toward Farida, the doctor had attempted to revive her instead.

Fifteen dead bodies in a single day had been more than enough for her colleague, Farida said, and he had been determined to bring the girl back from the brink—and, when he'd lost his mind and begun ramming down on her chest with all his strength in an effort to get her heart started, several of her ribs had been crushed by the sheer force. Farida had heard the sound of breaking bone and had been unable to stay on her feet. The doctor must have heard it, too, but he had continued pressing down and crushing the ribcage, and then the broken end of one rib had thrust through the skin of her chest and jutted out, white and lightly smeared with blood. Farida said that the girl had looked like she was sleeping, not the slightest trace of death in her face, but the protruding bone and the twisted lines of the smashed ribs beneath her skin told a different story.

Farida told me how all of a sudden she had perceived how terribly weak the human body was—an unbelievably fragile machine—and in a flash, everything she'd learned at medical school had come back to her, each detail confirming what she'd just that minute understood: that skin is easily cut; that everything runs off the heart and there is no alternative mechanism; that the neck vertebrae are quickly broken; that eyes stop functioning at the smallest injury; that if the brain suffers the slightest damage, the limbs and senses stop working; that brain cells are never replaced; that any one of thousands of viruses can bring a body to a grinding halt in mere hours. It took the sight of the rib's broken end to bring these simple facts home. In that instant, she understood that this body of hers could earn her stacks of money without any call for mental exertion, for desperate efforts to help the sick cling onto life, to keep these clinging cases happy, for anything else that might remind her of the body's great frailty.

The brothel owner had been very practical, she said, hadn't seemed like a brothel owner at all, in fact—more like the well-heeled director of a private company. As she came in, he had been poring through a pile of documents, and she'd noticed that the pages in his hands were covered in tables, stats, and graphs, that she'd assumed were related in some way to the trade and projections for its future potential. He had asked her for her date of birth, whether she was able to work long hours, and about her previous experience; and when she'd told him, shamefacedly, that she'd just left the hospital, he'd said that it happened a lot, and that he always welcomed doctors and nurses because they could work under pressure: they were fine with things that other women felt were insulting, they didn't treat their bodies like they were precious objects. And, of course, most importantly of all, they knew exactly how sexual diseases were transmitted and how to protect themselves. He had asked if she'd had any experience with clients, if she'd ever slept with a man for money, and then if she could cope with unconventional requests. And when she'd said that she would do anything, he'd replied that that was excellent, that conventional was so rare these days it qualified as a kink. Did she understand what he meant? She had understood perfectly. He'd asked her to remove her clothes so that he could inspect her body, so she'd stood up and taken it all off.

He hadn't looked at her for long, but said she would have to try first with one of the professionals—as a little test, no more. He had been very polite, had said that she might find she didn't like doing it with strangers, that she might not care for the fetish that was the fashion back then. And then they'd set a date.

266

Farida had been tormented in the hospital, and her colleague with her, and it was the patients who had come in on the verge of death that had tormented them. They were all cogs in an endlessly complex, highly efficient, astonishingly precise machine: a torture device far greater than the human body. And it seemed that the cog that was Farida had not been turning as it should and had been moved to another section of the same machine, where it might turn with maximum efficiency—for the machine could never stop.

The ice cube melted. Was this the tenth? The sting had gone and my hand no longer hurt.

Farida came in, worn out as always. She removed her lightweight hijab and hugged me for a long time without speaking, then let me go and headed for the bed, saying she was going to take a nap.

Is there still hope in the streets, Farida?

My phone rang, and an officer said that there'd be a small raid tomorrow on the karbon plant in Port Said Street. A police unit would rush the place, round up five or six bodies, and confiscate everything they found. I put a call through to the lab owner, told him everything, and advised him to leave behind a full barrel of scarabs and one each of ants and cockroaches. If he cleared the lab out completely, I said, that could leave me and my informant in the Interior Ministry exposed. Then I asked for seven thousand pounds in exchange for the tip-off. Of course, the man had no option but to do as he was told, but in any case, the seven thousand wasn't just for me: my source would take three and would pass on maybe a thousand of that to whoever had brought him the info. The lab owner said he'd leave behind three guys he wanted to get rid of, and asked if it would be possible for him to bribe the officers later in order to recover some of the confiscated karbon. I didn't care about the details any more. I told him that that wasn't going to happen: the quantities involved were too small. As I ended the call, I

267

wondered whether we were supposed to be trying to make a living in hell or whether this was just another torment.

I hadn't smoked a karbon cigarette for three months and I didn't need one now, or rather I no longer felt the same delight escaping into the nothingness. Generally people would stop using karbon for a few weeks, then go back to consuming it in far greater quantities. At first, the police had mounted entirely genuine surprise raids and had confiscated what they found, and then, with time, information about each raid had started leaking out to the dealers and lab owners. I and others had played middlemen in these leaks, and everything had more or less gone back to how it had been. I thought to myself that though I might one day return to karbon, I'd never touch hash again.

Farida confessed to me that karbon had saved her from suicide on several occasions. She used to karbon before she went to work; who knew, maybe she karboned in the taxi without caring what the driver taking her to Sharif Street thought. The months she'd spent as a prostitute had left her relatively unaffected and it was all thanks to karbon—plus it was the karbon that had compensated her for my two-year absence up the tower. Living on karbon had been much more pleasant than she'd imagined. She'd only been physically aware of her body for a few hours a day, and her disappearance into what she called 'the night' was a flight from everything that took place in her room at work. She couldn't remember a thing from those days. Now that she was back working at the hospital, she might occasionally come across patients who'd been clients. She'd recognize them from the look of surprise on their faces when they saw her. Surprise, turning to a shamefaced grin that would have become a leer were it not for the fact that there were other people about—not to mention her stern demeanor and hijab, which halted any such developments in their tracks. The patient who'd been her client would put her out of his mind and leave.

268

The day would come when Farida would go back to taking karbon at work. She would turn into a tirelessly functioning machine, her mind escaped into her 'night.' She would return home to sleep until the effects had worn off, would flee from the patients who slowly but surely passed away—though death was the kindest form of mercy in this hell of ours. But Farida preferred karbon. It helped her.

Tomorrow, a force from the ministry would raid the karbon lab. I knew just where it was; I'd visited it many times. They'd confiscate the goods and arrest those they found there. And maybe, if they wanted to make the play perfect, they'd shoot one of them, and the officers would testify that he'd raised his gun, and fired two shots, but missed. And maybe the lab's owner would get angry, and things would snowball, and he'd return the favor, killing an officer or two. And so the wheel would turn and the whole thing would get completely out of hand, the cops and lab owners going at it tit for tat until the dealers were nearly wiped out. And then one of the heavyweights might intervene, might demand that the pressure on the labs be slackened given their importance, and one generation of dealers would be replaced by another—smarter and better organized—and then things could move on some more, members of parliament legalizing karbon just as they'd done for prostitution; in any case, these weren't drugs being smoked, but insects, and the smoker wasn't left listless and idle, quite the opposite—and nor did they hallucinate. Plus, it offered a little relief from ceaseless torment.

3

It had been an effortless progression.

Twenty-four hours after the Day of Martyrs, we watched Field Marshal Paul-Pierre Genevieve in his medal-bedecked uniform address the people in elegant French, with an Arabic translation at the bottom of the screen for their benefit.

He had many words of praise for the Egyptian people who had played host to the Fourth and Fifth Armies of the Knights of Malta in recent times; he proclaimed his forces' victory in the battle for Egyptian national liberation, and the country's deliverance from the corrupt mob who had ruled before; and he saluted the contribution of the ever-responsible Egyptian people to the Knights of Malta's mighty struggle. He addressed the persecuted Egyptian people, reminding them that the Knights were the first rulers ever to treat them kindly, to clap them on their broad backs, to take them by the hand and lead them down the path to civilization—the first step being the new laws that freed them from the ignorance, blind error, and despair of the twentieth century. He stressed that the Egyptian people had every reason to believe that they were evolving and progressing to take their place in the ranks of civilized Western nations, and stated that from now on Egypt should not be spoken of as the East, but rather as a part of the West—respected and held in high esteem by all the world.

The speech lasted two whole hours. None of those listening to it on the radio understood a word he said and of course the translated subtitles were indecipherable to the majority of those who were sitting in cafés watching wall-mounted television sets. About an hour in, a few individuals volunteered to read the translated lines out loud using microphones so that those sitting further away from the television screens could follow. Slowly their voices swelled, warmed by the zeal with which the field marshal doled out his praise of the Egyptian people. But by the end of the second hour, everybody had tired of the exercise. The volunteers abandoned their mikes, and those at home switched off their sets or changed to other channels, following the example of the radio audience, who'd done the same just minutes into the broadcast.

Finally, after one hundred and nineteen minutes of Arabic-subtitled French, Field Marshal Paul-Pierre Genevieve declared the start of operations to disperse outside the borders of the country, and issued an order for the re-banding of the Egyptian armed forces and the promotion of Niazi Orabi al-Gamali from major general to lieutenant general. This was followed by an order promoting Major General Niazi Orabi al-Gamali to the rank of colonel general, then an order promoting Colonel General Niazi Orabi al-Gamali to the rank of field marshal, and finally an order ceding control of the country to the Supreme Council of the Armed Forces under the leadership of Field Marshal Niazi Orabi al-Gamali.

Through the window came the accustomed clamor of the street. I was lying on the bed, following the speech on my television's little screen, and struggling to read the spidery lines as I attempted to work out what was going on. Quarter of an hour in, the noise outside gradually started to swell, and transformed into a joyful and spontaneous celebration, a happy chaos with shouts and patriotic anthems ringing out. This people, the cries affirmed, does not know the meaning of impossible: Egypt's golden sun has risen once more, stronger than ever before, and all creation has ground to a halt— stopped breathing, stopped working, stopped everything—to

272

witness how the foundations of glory may be laid without any outside help at all. Then they all surrendered to cliché, crying that they loved their country, that it was more than love—the homeland claimed their very hearts.

And though no one knew who this General al-Gamali was, all rejoiced because an Egyptian would be ruling Egypt once again; and when we saw him, short and squat, head tilted back to salute the towering field marshal, we smiled the smile of those who catch sight of their beloved child—weak and flawed, but beloved—and we told ourselves that in his short-ness lay his guile and cunning. The man was the least among us, and it seemed that we were simply waiting for someone to lead our country—anyone—and I thought to myself that a short-assed patriot in hell was preferable to a foreign occupier in the selfsame hell.

And the people disregarded the absurdity of the whole thing—of the field marshal's ridiculous speech, of his unprec-edented promotion of General al-Gamali—and instead rejoiced greatly at the return of the Egyptian Army to the fray, all convinced that the army had taken part in the resis-tance operations. I was reading comments online and thinking back to the things I'd done during my years with the resistance (and what I'd experienced of the army's total absence and the absolute control of the police), and whenever I caught myself wondering where my letter had got to—my message from the resistance leadership congratulating me on our victory and welcoming me back to the Interior Ministry—I'd immediately remember that nothing mattered any more. We were swal-lowed up into hell, and we did not know it.

Following the speech, events moved fast, for the Knights of Malta departed the country as quickly as they had occupied it. They moved their weaponry and gear from Cairo and the Delta down the Nile and its branches, through the narrow roads that linked the heartland with the north, and out into the Mediterranean Sea. They cleared out of their bases, and out of our bases that they'd occupied, and offloaded damaged equipment and most of their light arms, handing them over to seed the rearmament of the Egyptian army. They met no resistance to speak of—unflagging assistance, rather—and the whole thing was wrapped up inside a week.

For that week, people walked the streets full of hope. Smiles returned to faces. And I walked among them, awe-struck by the sheer scale of what was afoot. All of them would soon be back in torment, I knew. I didn't know how it would happen, but I knew that it would, and I spent most of my time at home, only rarely going outside. I was no longer able to bear the sight of those faces; no longer able to avoid imag-ining their fates. And on Evacuation Day itself, the day the last soldier departed from the quay at Dakhila port in Alex-andria, I refused to emerge. Farida went down into the street alone, happy as could be. She begged me to go with her, but I pled exhaustion and was lying on my bed when I heard the sound of the march out in the street—a regular occurrence in those days. Patriotic chants to a fervent rhythm, bidding the last occupier leave, rejoicing in the evacuation, celebrating all true patriots, thanking the resistance, the army, and the Supreme Council of the Egyptian Armed Forces, and gener-ally being appreciative of everyone's efforts. It was as though I'd left hell and returned to the mortal coil: no torment, no ignominy, and people optimistic enough to march along and chant from sheer joy. I moved to the window and saw dozens of people gathered in the small street, marching, and chant-ing, and carrying signs, one beating on a drum to keep the chants in time, and at the edges of the procession people wav-ing at those standing on their balconies and at their windows, summoning them to come down and join in. And I noticed that their numbers were growing, that many were joining the march, and from somewhere nearby I heard another chant, overlaying the chanting down below, and then, suddenly, a second, larger procession appeared out of a side street and joined the first, the pair of them fusing and unifying beneath a single chant, cried out to a melody I shall never forget, and I thought to myself how many hours they must have practiced to get it so perfectly in tune. "O Egyptian!" they chanted. "Mighty Sayyid! Dervish's son! Does the Nile not flow, does it not run?" And I wept.

No, no, we had not returned to the world. We were still in hell, still in Egypt, and this great coming together of hearts in song was but a prelude to the black anguish that lay ahead. In days, in months, these hopes and dreams of theirs would flay their hides. They would be burned to death. Would be tormented and would repent of what they had this instant been chanting. There were no masters here, no dervishes—and the Nile flowed by, but it flowed in hell: red, and black, and blue, the hues of blood, and shit, and dead flesh. I wept, because for the first time in this life of mine I pitied the people. They imagined themselves to be laying the foundations of a great edifice, yet the truth was that there was no country, no state, no law, nor anything real at all. All this was but an illusion they lived that their suffering might continue: elegant, profound, capable of dealing the severest damage to their souls. I wept because I saw that we were in hell and did not know it, that we tormented one another and knew it not, and that there was not the slightest hope of even a single day being better than the one we lived through now. I clutched the window frame as I wept, and someone in the march observed my weeping, and waved to me, and wept in turn; then those around him noticed what was happening, and they waved to me, and stopped marching, and some of them smiled and some of them wept, and others covered their eyes with their hands. They thought I wept for joy at what we'd done, and in that moment I did not know what we could have done to deserve all this. Would it not have been better to grill us in our skins, as we'd been told would happen, so that we might know that we were being tormented and repent of what we'd done in the mortal world?

275

Yet what was happening evinced a genius far beyond anything we'd conceived. This was a truly divine punishment.

How can a man live in hell once he has realized this fact? How could I still be in torment now that I had no hope in tomorrow?

And for the thousandth time I wondered: does Farida know that we're in hell? Don't all these people sense that there is no injustice, no justice, and no mercy here? Do they not realize that all hope is a sham, that every expectation of a better life to come is error, and that things were getting worse and never, ever, better?

On Evacuation Day, General al-Gamali tasked Dr. Khalifa Sidqi with forming a new government and, as always in times of great upheaval, *al-Ahram*'s lead was sonorous, full of hope, and inscribed in elegant cursive: *Dr. Sidqi prime minister for the twenty-first time; reports that the Information Ministry is to be abolished.*

Over the course of the next three months, the media, the people, the birds, the street dogs, the stones scattered in the streets, the trees, and their songbirds chewed and savored every last speck of shit spoken about the new constitution, and the new ministry, and the new regional boundaries, and the new parliamentary system (or the new presidential system), and the new army, and the extent to which the people were being apprised of the new budget for the new army, and the new laws, and the new judiciary, and the new fast-track courts which would punish the new criminals who threatened the new secu-rity, and the new fifth column, and the new traitors, and the new political parties, and, finally, the new Muslim Brothers.

Of course, there was still humor in hell. I saw this for myself in Talaat Harb Street. A seller was monotonously crying his wares, his voice raised high and his tone mockingly self-aware. Beneath his arm, he held a cardboard box full of shiny golden spoons and around his head was a thin bandana in the colors of the Egyptian flag with some of the same spoons tucked between his forehead and the strip of cloth, sticking upright like a rickety crown. He cried his wares in short sentences, all to the same rhythm, over and over and never tiring, a wave of happiness radiating off him and washing over those around him, so that they smiled and even laughed, not at his idiosyncratic salesmanship, but at the sly insinuation in what he said. It was just before the referendum on the new constitution, and debate was raging and turning to shouting and shoving, a few even beating up those who saw things differently. Outside a shop, by a banner which read 'Yes to a New Constitution for a New Egypt,' the spoon-seller drew to a halt and fixed the passersby with the look of a man about to impart a great secret. He was dark-skinned, sweating, and skinny, his huge mustache out of keeping with the small face and bald head, and I told myself he was going to say something about the constitution. We were going to find out if he was for it or against it. But he genuinely caught me by surprise when he resumed his monotonous sales pitch, the short sentences now slightly altered: "Shit spoons! Buy your shit spoons! A present for Mama and Papa, for Hamada and Miyada! Shit spoons for everyone!"

Naturally the new constitution was approved by an overwhelming majority amid fresh scenes of celebration only slightly less effusive than those witnessed on Evacuation Day. The date of the parliamentary elections drew nearer, and in their wake the presidential elections, which it seemed that General al-Gamali would win, sweeping the other candidates aside.

This time around, though, people abandoned hope very quickly indeed.

In just three months, everything turned upside down: the smiles vanished and violence reclaimed its place in people's lives. They were throwing themselves off rooftops once again, stoning each other to death in the streets, and the vast majority couldn't care less about what was happening, accepting it all as they'd always accepted it, without the slightest objection.

Three months of false hopes and silky words: a short breather in preparation for a greater torment, but without an occupation this time around.

One day, Farida came home downcast because cholera and donkey influenza had broken out again; and because she'd read the Health Ministry report that confirmed that while average life expectancy had risen under occupation, the rates of child mortality had also risen; and finally, because an old disease, once in abeyance, had returned with a vengeance, robbing those under ten years of age of their sight, and hearing, and power of speech.

That day I decided that many must know where we were, but that they were unable or unwilling to speak about it. That they must have found out, as I did, by means of a revelation, its source unknown. That no other man had told them. That everyone wanted to shout the truth of where we were living to the rooftops, but were afraid of being judged mad or unbelievers.

And as for trying to inform people, there was not the slightest point to that. What was the use of people knowing they were in torment? Better, it seemed, to leave people with the illusion intact, to figure out that it was an illusion on their own. And I understood that the suicides were simply doomed attempts to escape. Doomed because suicide is never a way out of hell. You don't get out that easily, with the stroke of a razor blade, or by jumping down with your neck caught in a noose. That's just self-deception, as the Saint had said. Even so, I still wondered to myself where people went after they had died or killed themselves.

That very day, Farida said she would go back on the game. The decision had been taken then, although it seemed to me as though she were waiting for my approval, or for my opinion if nothing else, and after a short silence I said that I would support whatever she did. Farida appeared considerably relieved.

Where had the Saint gone? Where had all my colleagues gone?

Every day, I'd go to sleep trembling with fear—knowing that my fear was a torment to me, yet unable to avoid it—Farida lying alongside me, me waiting for her to go to sleep so that I could cry noiselessly and without screwing up my face, weeping for what she would encounter before long: the thing I neither knew nor could see, though I understood that she would be tormented somehow, and that she would torment me with her.

I had to try to get in touch with the Saint again.

4

YET, FOR ALL THAT, THERE was happiness. Farida was joyful, practically flying around the apartment most of the time, where before she'd come in each afternoon depressed and it would be an hour before she'd start to interact me, before she turned back into the regular human being who joked, and smiled, and wanted to go outside and walk among the people in the street.

They were all idiots, she said, and we were idiots just the same. Then she'd start dancing in the living room, spinning on the spot like a ballet dancer, or shaking her belly in the lewd Oriental style, or getting down like a disco dancer from a seventies film. Always something different, and always without music. When I proposed putting on a tune, she said her way was better: she could hear the music in her head and switch genres whenever she got bored, changing dances as she liked. She looked odd, turning and turning—and me hearing only the whisper of her feet on the bare tiles—then occasionally getting carried away, clapping and moaning without realizing she did it. And sometimes she'd smile at me. But most of the time her dance was hers alone. She'd close her eyes and wouldn't see me, enjoying alone the music that played in her head.

I tried convincing myself that she knew everything, so that I might explain away the things she did: while I escaped by submerging myself in despair, she was trying to fashion for herself another world outside this hell of ours. When she wasn't working, she danced, went out, and aimlessly wandered the streets.

When she told me that she wanted to go back on the game, I considered returning to the Interior Ministry. Kamal al-Asyuti was now deputy minister for general security, the number two man at the ministry, and he would surely remember me and find me a cushy posting. Maybe he would give me a rifle so I could go back to sniping people from the tops of tall buildings. I was a former officer, and every month I went to the bank to withdraw my pension from my private account. The money I made from leaked information was more than I needed, and for the first time I understood why it was that some people went without, doing just enough to ward off hunger in what they regarded as a fleeting, impermanent world, forswearing their desires in hope of an immortality in the afterlife. Going back to the ministry would have its advantages. I'd have a daily routine to distract me from what was happening, to get me away from melting ice cubes in my hands. More excitement, for sure; maybe more of the killing I'd missed so much. I longed to create an illusion that I could live in, like Farida did. Like they all did.

And at the same time, I was looking for the one way out, for death, but I just couldn't see how it would work. And though she must have sensed, too, that death was the ideal solution, she constantly avoided it, tunneling deeper into the illusion of the world she'd made for herself, intensifying it to wall herself in.

Before leaving the hospital for the second time, she talked to me at length about a sick boy who was staying there. She talked on and on, and I knew that I was being tormented without a finger being laid on me. I would listen to Farida talk about the boy and summon him to mind over and over again, would dream of him when I slept. And I'd relive the sight that

I'd seen through my scope of corpses being robbed, of the death throes that came before complete stillness. I would close my eyes, desperate to escape these scenes, but still they would come—more manifest, sharper.

Someone had left the kid outside the entrance to the hospital. He had been sitting on the ground, naked but for a loose-fitting robe. Terrified security guards had brought him inside. Breathing was regular and pulse likewise. Blood tests showed that there was nothing wrong with him. But the boy had no eyes. No mouth, no ears. His face had been smooth and featureless except for a nose, and a few days later that nose had turned dark brown and dropped off. He had been hooked up to a feeding tube that ran into his stomach, and they had had to cut out a section of the tubing to remove the fallen nose. Despite it all, the boy had managed to live a normal enough life. Let out into the garden one day he ran off carefree between the trees. Farida said he would sprint forward a few paces, then change direction and dash forward a few paces more, and so on, managing not to collide with the trees and other objects around him.

They didn't know his name, so they'd called him Samir after the doctor who'd first examined him and insisted he be kept in the hospital to receive the care he needed. They had found an unoccupied bed for him on one of the wards—and when they had to take the bed for another patient, he had been transferred to the medicine storeroom and laid out on a mattress they'd put down on the floor. In time, they noticed that Samir had lost all his senses, even touch. He no longer twitched when a needle pricked his skin or moved his head when they brought an alcohol-soaked cotton swab to where his nose had once been. Farida told me that one day she'd gone in to see him and found that he'd removed his robe and was lying there, naked, his blue penis lying shrunken and lifeless where it had fallen between his thighs, and in its place a tiny, pinkish hole. Samir's knees were raised and he was slowly

283

rubbing his heels against the mattress, back and forth, feeling the rough fabric for the last time. But Farida did not cry.

Eventually, Samir had died, she said, and then many more came just like him, all children. Samir had been about ten years old, but the new patients were three, and four, and five. They came accompanied by relatives, who would be weeping with fright, while the patients themselves were always calm, only growing agitated when the tubes and needles came out. When they were brought in, maybe only one of the senses had been lost—they had no eyes, say, or nose, or ears—and then the others would close over or drop off, one after the other, in no fixed order and at no fixed interval. In the end, there was nothing for it but to set aside a whole ward for the sense-deprived children.

Farida wanted to hasten these patients toward death. She knew that they weren't suffering or in pain, but their families were wrestling with indescribable agony. She said that she had met a mother who'd been ready to be cast into the fire if it would cure her son. At first, Farida had thought the mother meant being burned alive, but then she realized that the woman was giving up her afterlife in exchange for her son's life in this world.

But the epidemic hardly made a ripple: it wasn't written about in the papers and no one from the ministry moved to investigate the matter. Numbers increased with every passing day, news came through of cases breaking out among children in various governorates, and doctors began calling up their colleagues, making inquiries about any similar cases in the past only to discover that indeed there had been: fifteen years ago, thirty years back. They found that a female patient had passed away just months before, after living without her senses for nearly forty years. They discovered that there were many people living with the condition who had never once stepped into a hospital.

One day, shortly before the boy Samir had died, Farida had come across a huge crowd gathered in Abbasiya Square. Having waited ten minutes on the stationary bus, she got down and walked the rest of the way to the hospital. Beneath the overpass, before the left turn that would take her to the hospital, she found Samir, standing there stark naked. The last of his face had vanished just days before, and he had become a skin-wrapped form with no features worthy of the name. Two thin metal tubes prevented his nostrils from closing, and if those who stood staring had looked closely they would have seen two more fine tubes, one in his anus, the other in what remained of his penis, to stop those holes healing over, too. Samir stood there, cut off from his surroundings, and Farida had no idea how he had gotten there, nor how she would get him back through the crowds to the hospital.

She tried pushing past those in front of her. After enduring swearing, kicks, and much groping, she made it to the front ranks of the mob, where Samir stood calmly. He grasped the thin silicon feeding tube dangling from his nostril and started pulling it out with a series of quick, but measured, jerks. The tube must have been caught on something. Samir's jerks became more vigorous and the crowd started muttering, not understanding what he was doing, patently amazed by his appearance, his nakedness. And then he seemed to tire of his measured approach and gave the tube a single, violent yank.

Blood spurted thickly from his nasal opening, and clumps and long, dark crimson ribbons of half-clotted gore fell to the ground. Samir cupped his hands under his nose and they filled with blood, which he promptly heaped back over his head and chest. At this point, the crowd started bombarding him with anything they could lay their hands on.

I could not figure out if this was a suicide or not.

The only thing that pained Farida was what happened to him at the end. She said that people like Samir didn't deserve to die beneath a hail of stones, and empty bottles, and split shoes. Farida was hit several times as she tried to rescue him. She picked him up, carried him along for a minute or so, then got tired, lowering his body to the ground and dragging him as the crowd scattered, gathering up anything they could throw and then pelting him again. It was only a few minutes' walk from Abbasiya Square to the hospital, but the journey left the boy on the brink of death.

When an injured Farida came through the hospital doors covered in blood and dragging the boy by his arms, the doctors proved hopelessly stupid. They took him straight to Emergency, where they did all in their power to keep him alive: stopped the bleeding, stuck a drip in his arm and electrodes on his chest, pumped medicine around his veins, measured his heartbeat. Farida washed her hands of it all, refused to help her colleagues, and sat next to Samir in the operating room waiting for what was to come. She'd had a powerful sense that what they were doing was wrong, she told me. The boy wanted to die, and they wanted him to stay alive at any price, and she thought to herself how wrong she'd been to defend him and bring him back to the hospital. Grief-stricken, she watched his pulse stop as the injected drugs surged around his body. She watched as his brain died, and as his body was hooked up to the artificial respirator. She watched the stony-faced doctors' determined efforts to keep the heart functioning normally. Samir's body had grown much thinner, and amid the machines, and tubes, and beeps he seemed not of this world. Seemed, she told me, like another kind of being altogether, not a person at all. And she had wished one of the doctors would see it, too, and uncouple him from the machines, and leave him to die without wrecking what was left of him. But their faces were stone, she said, and they weren't thinking.

The boy passed, but not peacefully. He suffered greatly from the doctors' determination to keep him with them, and as they worked, Farida said, she had remembered him playing in the garden, his few scampered steps in each direction as though he'd been trying to find a way out of our world and couldn't. But at last he passed, and left them his body, and they meddled with it, opening up his chest and skull to examine his motionless heart and the brain they claimed had caused it all.

Farida said that they failed to find a cause for the disease; and for this reason, and this reason alone, they came to the exceptionally inadequate conclusion that whatever had happened could not be considered a disease. Even so, they continued to monitor those cases that were being looked after inside the hospital, and tracked down several outside it. When they received no response from the Ministry of Health, they asked the hospital staff to visit these people and note down any pertinent observations: how did the patient cope with the condition? Had it been transmitted to another person or not? How long had the patient been affected?

This was Farida's final job at the hospital: paying a home call to one of the afflicted.

5

AT FIRST, I REFUSED TO enter the villa, but Farida insisted I accompany her. I'd come as far as the gate, she said, and it made no sense for me to wait outside in the street.

She was very anxious. She had never visited a patient at home before, and said that meeting someone who'd lived with this disease for fifteen years would be tough for her.

I had always thought of Farida as the strongest person I knew, but recently she'd weakened. She'd stopped organizing anything, had asked the Ministry of Health for unpaid leave, and had been told that her leave was approved without reservation. That had been easy, but her final job would not be. I told her that she could excuse herself, that she could spend her last month going to work as usual without any outside visits, but she said she didn't want that. She wanted to go and see the case. She was prepared to visit her once, even twice, but it would be tough.

I'd told her that I'd come with her. She could say I was her husband or her friend; a doctor or a nurse, even. I wouldn't be able to make it any easier, of course—but I'd be there, and maybe that would help. She didn't hesitate—she agreed on the spot—and it struck me that if I hadn't offered to come she would have asked me herself.

The street was narrow. Despite the line of parked vehicles on both sides of the road, it was clear that cars hardly ever came down here. There was a row of small villas all joined

289

together, and a little garden outside each one. We found the place after asking for the street name, and Farida hesitated for a moment before pressing the bell mounted next to the metal gate. Grasping one of the gate's railings, I found that it was hot from the sun, and suddenly I felt the sweat gather on my forehead and brow. I saw Farida take two paces back into the street, then turn and take two paces toward the gate. Her brown feet looked bare in her flat sandals, and I imagined what she'd look like walking barefoot over the scorching asphalt: hopping about and breathing hard as the ground burned the soles of her feet. She was nervous, waiting for someone to come and open up. I saw their shadow. I saw the arm stretch out behind the gate to swing it open, and then I saw the face of a woman in her sixties. She smiled, greeted us, and asked us in. We walked through a neglected garden, shaded by tall trees that seemed older than the building itself.

There were two entrances to the villa: a higher entrance, reached by a short flight of stairs, and a second, down below, where we went. We descended two stone steps and walked into a wide hall with a low ceiling, that felt strangely familiar. The first thing to catch my attention was the seated body, small and pale in the far corner.

Farida had talked to me a lot about what the disease did to them—how their eyes and mouths were sealed—but I had never met one face to face. The girl's skin covered the entirety of her hairless skull. There were no features. All I could make out by way of a face were two small, dark nasal openings. When we entered the hall, she turned her face toward us. We'd paused for a moment out of respect for the silence that filled the space, but the girl's turn in our direction startled us. All we could see was her head slowly revolving, sweeping the hall with its missing eyes until it came to rest, calmly pointing in our direction.

The woman invited us to approach the girl. She sat down beside her, and Farida and I sat facing them. My eyes fixed on

290

the blank face—a statue, a mannequin in a shop window—and when her head swiveled slowly around I held my breath and asked myself how she could be alive. What was the purpose of her being here with us in hell?

The woman said she would translate what the girl said. She'd lived with her for many years and could translate back and forth quite easily. All we had to do was ask a question and wait for a reply. Then she held out her hand to the girl's lap and unfurled her palm. The girl took hold of it and lightly tapped it with her fingertips, then started tracing them over the palm as though tickling her.

"Zahra bids you welcome," said the lady. "She says that talking like this might seem strange, but she hasn't spoken for years—ever since she fell silent, I have helped her. She is now ready to answer any questions you may have. Perhaps, with her answers and a medical examination, you'll be able to find some cure for her condition."

The girl was pressing delicately at the woman's palm, her four fingers sketching what might have been the shapes of letters, maybe emotions, hints, opinions, expressions.

"Zahra would like to be introduced to you both."

I couldn't think what to say. I'd come to keep Farida company. I hadn't imagined I would be getting caught up in something like this, and the shock of the face-to-face encounter had robbed me of words. Farida, however, said: "I'm Dr. Farida. I called a couple of days ago to set a time for our meeting. This is Ahmed, my friend."

The hands switched—the girl's palm now lay open, the woman's fingers gently tapping away—and then switched back. The girl traced and traced, a great outpouring of words, and at a certain point the woman began to speak even as the girl continued to touch her palm.

"The symptoms first appeared fifteen years ago. All I remember is a lot of visits to various hospitals trying to get treatment, but nothing came of it. My father and my aunt

291

were like this as well. They both developed the same symptoms when they were in their twenties, and I'm only a little younger than they were. My father died right before my symptoms appeared, my aunt died four years ago, and now I live with Aunt Fawziya. I don't know anyone else."

She looked to be just ten years old. So slender and wan: more a skinny kid than a grown woman. I could barely make out the shape of her body beneath her baggy, concealing clothes, and just for a moment I forgot all about hell and its torments. In this hell, Zahra was the very acme of torment.

Farida asked her many questions. I didn't hear any of it; I was staring at the slender body and the butterfly-light hand, and trying to puzzle out the system of delicate strokes she was tracing on Fawziya's palm. Sometimes the strokes came quicker, sometimes they'd revert to their lazy curves. She moved her fingertips off the palm to touch the lady's fingers—the pair's fingertips often touched, but never linked together—then they moved away, still in motion, back to the palm, then retreated as far as the wrist and brushed the forearm with silken softness. A second slipped by and the hand dropped, to settle in the girl's lap. Her hand and fingers were like a separate being under orders: independent, but unable to abandon her. And with every minute that passed, she grew closer and closer to me. She was reeling me in, at an imperceptible pace that couldn't be fought, couldn't be escaped—or rather, it wasn't that I couldn't leave her, but that I didn't want to. If there was anyone in the world closer to me than Farida, then beyond doubt that person was Zahra. And suddenly I longed for her fingertips to stroke my face.

Fawziya took out a briefcase containing a considerable number of documents and handed them to Farida. These, she said, were the test results, the names of the medicines and doctors, and images of every inch of Zahra's body spanning the years. She said that she had prepared these copies especially for Farida, and that Farida must find a cure for the girl's condition. She said that Zahra had lost hope long ago, but that she did not want the disease to spread through the population and was ready to welcome Farida around at any time.

I could sense Farida: a body without a soul. Asking questions and not listening to the answers. Forever on the verge of bitter tears, like the man I'd seen months before in Sharif Street. She wasn't confused, but rather in a state of abject surrender. "Yes," she was saying. "Sure." Mechanically, without thinking. Where was the butterfly I'd met trotting upstairs at that brothel?

The conversation between the three of them dragged on. I was waiting for Farida to ask me to check Zahra's pulse or put the stethoscope on her chest, but instead it was Fawziya who asked Farida to give her an examination instead —she'd felt pains in her hip that morning and didn't know what the matter was. The woman got up and begged my pardon; Farida rose to her feet, too, dazed and empty-headed, and the pair of them went over to a door at the side of the hall and pushed through it, revealing a flight of stairs to the first floor. Farida told me she wouldn't be gone long, and Fawziya asked me to wait there with the girl, because she couldn't be left alone. I thought to myself that I made a poor guardian: I wouldn't be able to help her if anything happened. But then again, what could happen to her that would be worse than this?

She looked terribly gaunt, as though her companion's absence had revealed her true dimensions: her head the size of a smooth coconut on her stalk of a neck. She was silent, but I knew her mind was raging with thoughts.

Calmly, she held her hand out to me, palm heavenward, her fingers so very thin with pink, translucent nails. I waited, not sure how to proceed, though what was being asked was clear enough. I reached out and took her whole hand into mine: a tiny, docile bird in my palm. Would she say anything with her fingers? Would she talk in the language I didn't understand? However, what came wasn't speech. Zahra didn't say a thing. I didn't hear her breathe a word. And yet she spoke to me, speechlessly. She spoke secret words, unheard but perfectly understood: clear not in my ears, but in my head. If humans could impart revelation to one another, then this was revelation:

"I know that this is hard. . . ."

I snatched my hand back and leapt to my feet in fright. An unanticipated jolt of electricity had run through me. What had come into my head hadn't been a voice but words, clearer than any voice—what I'd experienced beneath the metal sphere hadn't been half so clear—and though it felt as though these words had come from within me, they were hers, no doubt about it. And then, while I stood facing her, fighting back a shudder, she spoke without touching me.

"This is the first time anyone's talked to you this way. It's frightening, of course, but you've seen much that is frightening, Ahmed. You would never have known we were in hell if it weren't for the terror that possessed you. This is the essence of hell, its alpha and omega: terror upon terror."

I froze completely. In that instant, I was a statue made of stone.

"You keep your knowledge to yourself, because you must. No one who knows what is happening ever speaks of it. But you have abandoned your post, and you must return. Don't feel bad on account of what the people suffer—for it is justice, and you are the instrument of mercy. Why did you lay your weapon down and stop killing?"

What to do? Should I scream to rid my mind of this thing that was devouring it? Should I run outside?

"You have penetrated the veil. It seems that you do not know everything, and in this there is good cause, though I myself am presently ignorant of it. But it is your duty to go back and kill. You are not yet aware of your importance: this hell cannot function without you."

I was still standing, trying to free myself from what was happening, but then I collapsed onto a chair in complete submission.

294

"People assume that hell is a place, but they are wrong. We are presently in a long and unbroken passage of time, an era out of which many have passed and within which but a very few remain, so few that you and I will see their end. And after this, another hell will begin, in which the people shall be tormented—the ones who will be here forevermore and who shall never leave. These you shall not kill. They shall not be burned in fire, they shall not die by drowning, they shall not leave this hell of ours but to another hell."

Having frozen, my muscles now relaxed. I was like a sleeper, shoulders slumped, unable to move my hands in my lap. I was fully aware of everything she said, and I trembled in fear.

"Those that you kill shall go away. They shall face no path or journey, no obstacles of any kind—they shall simply be gone away from this hell of ours, and will find themselves, each one, in heaven. You send people to heaven."

Terror upon terror, she had said.

"But you have stopped, and this is not permitted. You, who know that we are in hell, have broken off, while your colleagues, most of whom do not know, remain ever active. Many years ago, I cut all ties with you all. I never learned your speech and I do not know how it is that you describe yourselves, but I know that you are a mercy to all those you kill, just as your colleagues are a mercy to all those they have killed and shall kill shortly."

I slumped further still and leaned my head against the chair's back. I hadn't realized it until now, but I was drooling; I could feel its warmth against the cold skin of my chin.

"I am here to make you and others understand what is taking place. I am here with you; one of you. I have seen my torment before me, so clear that I might reach out and touch it. Just imagine: I remember nothing but my torment. No images or sounds but those I saw and heard in my torment. This is what occupies my thoughts, and nothing else besides, yet I know that what is happening around me is terrifying, as befits a hell that is coming to an end. I smell it in the absolute despair of the people, just as I smelled it on you when you entered. You are in the depths of despair, and this is good. I have not smelled hope for so long now, you know."

My head lolled to one side. My body was heavy, like a dead man's. Slowly, I began to lose consciousness.

"I know that this knowledge brings you pain. You keep it in and are afraid to pass it on to others. But your knowledge is your own. You cannot pass it on, not even to Farida. What you know, many others like you know. They learned it the same way and all for different reasons, but no one ever speaks of it. Even I do not speak of it if I can help it. Be comforted therefore. Be at peace with what is happening."

I woke to Farida shaking me by the shoulder, and immediately everything Zahra had said to me came rushing back. But Farida was looking at me accusingly. She asked how I could go to sleep, and her not gone ten minutes; how I could nod off in my chair, a guest in a stranger's house. And for a moment, all Zahra's talk seemed like a dream. Farida was telling me off for forgetting my manners, my duties as a guest. Silently, I got to my feet, Zahra's words in my thoughts, at peace with everything.

At the end of the narrow street, I saw a dark-skinned man energetically addressing a woman selling vegetables. He was raising what remained of a right arm lopped off at the elbow, supporting it with his left hand and telling the woman she'd "done the girl wrong" by "consenting to the marriage."

Farida and I stood side by side, waiting for a taxi. The street was empty save for a few pedestrians and passing cars, and in the space between the two cars parked next to us, I spotted three cats. A little kitten, barely aware of what was taking place around her; a second, bigger cat, clearly agitated; and between the two of them, a third, its mouth agape and tremors running through its body every few seconds. It was dying.

The kitten started licking itself, without a thought for the dying cat. The middle cat, meanwhile, licked furiously at the dying cat's fur, at a speed quite out of keeping with death's solemnity. I looked for signs of a wound or blood on the dying cat's fur, but couldn't see anything. Out of the corner of my eye, I kept a watch on Farida. I didn't want her to see what I saw, but she was staring out in the direction of the approaching traffic, waiting for the taxi. As I turned back to the cats, the big one moved around the dying cat, stepped over its body, and resumed its licking; then, as the dying cat bucked violently upward, the big cat opened its mouth wide and closed it over the other's head, then proceeded to take the head further and further into its mouth. The dying cat was shuddering, neck twisting as its head disappeared into the big cat's maw, but then the big cat choked and coughed the head out. For a moment, the dying cat was still, then it started to tremble once again. A taxi pulled up in front of me, hiding them from view.

I sat in the back seat, struggling to keep the big cat in sight as it tried to get the dying cat's head back inside its mouth. This time, it managed to get the whole thing in; and though it looked like it was gagging, it didn't let it go. The dying cat was in its final throes, the big cat rigid as a statue, and the kitten still licking itself.

6

THERE WAS THIS FEELING OF blankness. Maybe I'm exaggerating—it wasn't a feeling—but I remember being in despair and then shrugging off that despair.

I called everyone I knew, looking for a pistol. They all told me that getting hold of a gun was impossible right now. The police themselves were short of guns and ammunition. Anything and everything the Knights of Malta had left behind had been scooped up by the army. They hadn't left a single bullet or gun for anyone else, and I was told that even officers from the Interior Ministry were carrying backstreet zip guns instead of automatics. Fine, so I'd find myself a zip gun.

If I had been any good with daggers or knives, I wouldn't have hesitated. It was far easier to get hold of them than firearms and all the fuss that came with them: no ammo, no cleaning, no bullets jammed in the barrel, no fear of accidentally shooting off a round or the firing pin exploding. All I needed was a strong arm and a familiarity with the locations of the body's vital organs.

Farida was late home every night, not getting in before 2 a.m., always very tired and falling deep asleep in no time. Despite her approaches, I wouldn't talk to her. I would even snap at her, quite out of character, if she tried to snuggle up. I couldn't touch her when she was karboned. What would be the point of pleasure that she wouldn't remember?

And so I took to going out before she returned. Walking the streets by night and not coming home until I was sure she'd be asleep.

A few days previously, I had passed a street sweeper. He was proceeding painfully slowly, sweeping nothing, just pushing his broom over the dust-free sidewalk. As though he were waiting for someone, or working merely to satisfy anyone who might be watching. I barked at him, but he didn't move—and when I punched him in the back, he turned to me with a blank, expressionless face, then resumed his sweeping. I snatched the huge broom from him and threw it to one side, and he went over, picked it up, then returned to the same spot in front of me, sweeping the ground as though issuing a challenge.

The wooden pole I was carrying was too kind to him. It would bounce right back each time I smacked it into his head. Metal was heavier and more rigid: so much more effective. I had to hit him a lot before his skull was fully flattened out. It was utterly draining: a hundred or more blows. What hurt my hands were the misses, when the pole smacked into the asphalt. It really hurt, and it occurred to me just then that three or four rounds—or just a single bullet to the head—were infinitely preferable to a hundred blows with a club. Faster.

I thought of the rifle I had hidden by the Cairo Tower, but that wouldn't do: its extra-long barrel was cumbersome, and I had no desire to go back to sniping. It wasn't to be arbitrary like it had been before. Now, I had to choose whom I would send to heaven. But how? Was there some list or some instinctive understanding of those who deserved mercy? I mustn't complicate things unnecessarily.

I snatched a plastic bag from the hand of a woman in her fifties. I needed it. A big bag, full of tomatoes and cucumbers. I emptied the contents onto the ground. She screamed at first, a short yelp that died straight away. I covered her head with the bag in an effort to suffocate her. It was a particularly tricky maneuver, and though I was calm and was asking her

300

to remain calm she wouldn't settle, even when I told her that we were in hell and that I knew she knew this. She fell still for a second, then flared up again, gabbling words that mostly passed me by. She was asking me to give her an hour. *What? An hour? I tell you you're off to heaven, and you say wait an hour?* I ignored her request and, lifting the bag off her head, found no alternative than to stick my fingers in her mouth and wrench out her lower jaw. Dislocating a jaw didn't turn out to be too difficult. Wiggle it left and right a bit, a series of sharp downward jerks, then more wiggling, rougher than before, and the bone gives way completely and you're left with only tendons, skin, and flesh, and ripping through those is easy. Her whole jaw came away as she fell forward. I tried disposing of the blood-slicked mandible, but its teeth were sunk deep into my palm.

At last I heard from the Saint. I spoke to him with real affection. I was genuinely happy, and it struck me that for months now I hadn't clapped eyes on anyone I knew except Farida. True, I didn't know the Saint well, but even so we'd been through a lot together. From a mutual acquaintance, an officer at the ministry, the Saint had heard I was looking for a gun. He said he'd be able to get hold of a brand new Beretta and two boxes of 9-mm ammunition, the best news I'd heard in a long time. Even when I'd been an officer myself, laying hands on a Beretta had been difficult. Oh, Saint, what a saint you are. Being who he was, he asked for two kilos of karbon in exchange for the gun and rounds. *Really, Saint? You can't get hold of karbon?*

We met at the intersection of Galaa and July 26th Streets. I was standing on the sidewalk, waiting, and he drove by in an old car. He handed me the bundle containing the automatic and the ammo, and I passed him the karbon. Not a word was said. He looked at me for second before we both burst out laughing. Then he got out and we embraced. *Saint, where are the golden days of ignorance now?*

Barter was best these days, he said. The country was in a state of permanent decline, but there was no inflation and

301

"that whore was valueless." And when I asked him who this whore was, he answered, "The pound," and I laughed.

But the meeting wasn't going to end that simply. The Saint hadn't asked me why I wanted the gun, and our bargain was extremely unfair on him: a kilo of karbon was worth much less than a new Beretta.

Sitting in his car, testing out the automatic and loading rounds into its magazine, I asked, "So when's the big day, Saint?"

I had no idea that I was going to ask a question like that. I'd never dreamed that I'd have the courage to declare my knowledge to anyone else. The Saint, fiddling with the bag of karbon, froze for a couple of seconds, then closed the bag, reached out, and felt under the seat. "You'll be getting another pistol in two days," he said, "and next time it will be a gift from me. I'm rationing the bullets, so don't go shooting them off at random. Now, you'll have to excuse me. I must be going."

I got out, having filled two clips with bullets. The Beretta was at my waist, tucked between trousers and underpants: my preferred carry. It suggested massive indifference. The Saint started the engine and, leaning over the passenger seat, craned his head until he could see me: "No man knows when the Day shall come."

The Beretta was a really lovely piece, American-made, not Italian as the Saint had told me. He was already long gone when, still standing on the same spot on the sidewalk, I depressed the safety catch and loosed my bullets into the passersby. They screamed a bit. Some wept. Others stampeded. But the rest just plodded glumly along as, all around them, people dropped, thrashing and keening. I didn't kill many, since I wasn't aiming for heads and chests. I swapped a full clip for the empty one, and this time I took aim, but in my haste I missed a lot. Then I pulled myself together and started pointing the gun at people's eyes. Close range.

302

I was wandering along in no particular direction, not bothering to conceal the pistol but brandishing it in their faces, and whenever I saw someone I wanted to kill, I would block their way—menacing them until they stopped—then raise the Beretta and shoot straight into their eye. No room for error that way. The bullet can't deviate like it does when it strikes the outside of the skull, but instead it penetrates the eyeball and the delicate bone behind it, then on through the brain and the back of the skull. The exit wound is, of course, bigger, and the brain scatters out, and after all that the chances of the victim still being alive are nil. But the certainty came at a price. I had to stand upright, face to face with the target. Had to make him fear me and hold still for that single second.

Before I reached the apartment, I'd emptied both boxes; one hundred rounds, and I'd killed less than forty. Not my usual efficiency. I'd have to be more careful from here on. I was walking down al-Azhar Street, and I knew I had to kill those around me, but I was letting them go on their way unopposed. Then, about a hundred meters before my building, my resistance crumbled. I beat two people to death with the Beretta: smashed a hole in the skull of the first with the barrel, and gouged out the eye of the second the same way. I worried that the gun might break from the repeated impacts, but I needed to kill them.

I got home. Farida was sleeping, and the most terrible thought urged itself on me: to kill her now, right now, no dragging my feet. But the thought seemed truly evil, not fit for one sent to deliver folk to heaven. I wasn't sending them to heaven because I wanted to, but because their time had come.

But I didn't sleep. That I'd run out of bullets bothered me, and I called up the Saint again, asking him for any amount of ammo he could lay his hands on. I heard him laugh loudly as he asked whether I'd really shot off all one hundred or just lost some. I mustn't worry about lack of ammo, he told me. I mustn't worry about anything at all. But he asked me to wait

303

just two days: he'd meet me, and bring another gun and a large quantity of rounds. Better than a Beretta this time: a Glock in prime condition.

The Saint's words rang in my ears. He didn't know when the Day was coming, but this attitude of his suggested that it was already upon us, had been for quite some time. What if it had come thousands of years ago? Our whole history a fantasy: all these prophets and messengers, all the wars, and states, and cultures, all these ideas, and all these words, all these beings and creatures—born in hell.

Maybe the real world had been completely different from the one we lived in now. Had we lived on another planet, on other worlds? Had we been humans there, or were these bodies of ours, too, a cryptic torment?

7

A KNIFE, I DISCOVERED, WOULD stay cold for minutes, a little longer than it took an ice cube to melt. I'd taken to putting several knives in the fridge and taking them out to hold the blade against my palm until the chill stung me, then moving the knife to temple and cheek, to brow and neck, then around my body: chest, and arm, and armpit, and thigh. And I'd hold it beneath my balls, to feel the cold almost gone, the blade so close to slicing the sensitive flesh. After doing this a few times, I deliberately cut my foot. No blood came out, nor did I see any blood when I made the wound deeper. The flesh showed dark blue.

I left the knife and the wound, and sent a text to Farida—*Is human flesh blue? I thought it was pink or red*—then set the phone aside to take another look at the wound. A few seconds later, I got her reply: *Of course it's blue, and dark as well. Who told you it was red?* Farida wasn't busy, it seemed.

Are you free? I wrote. *Do have any clients today?*

Two sweet ones. One of them comes before he touches me.

Such variety in hell! There are still beginners!

The johns aren't what they used to be . . . , I wrote.

I might be back late today. I'm staying up with the girls.

Girls? You filthy little bitch!

Hahahaha! That's no way for an upstanding officer to talk!

I hadn't thought of myself as an officer for a while. All the years on the job had become meaningless, and the months up the tower, too, had slid from my memory. Everything I'd done

305

had no importance now—was as though it never had been at all—and I tried to recall the last time I'd given a thought to public affairs, but couldn't. The people had elected a whole load of military men and police officers to the first parliament, then more to the next, and now they were thinking of forming a third parliament for no other reason than to bring in yet more officers. There must be a whole lot of people fighting over the shitheap outside, each grasping his golden spoon and jostling for a glob.

I had soon tired of my work—just two years and all the zeal was gone; my faith in the resistance had ended the day I came down from the tower. As for what I was doing now, it was what I was here for. I didn't want to sleep a wink in the days that lay ahead. I wanted never-ending ammunition and guns without limit. My primary mission: to deliver people by killing them. I'd done it as a cop, and I'd done it in the resistance, and now I was doing it full of zeal.

Some of us would be leaving for heaven, and others would not leave at all, but would merely return to hell.

But who would deliver me?

Had I been a slaver in the world of men? A brothel keeper? A judge? A killer? A mercenary? A terrorist?

The only ones I crowed over were those who blew themselves up in the hope of heaven. They had outbragged everyone, claiming to be striving for a better life and a fairer world. But the others . . . ?

The Saint knew a lot. I'd be meeting him again in two days' time and I must ask him about everything.

Farida was carrying the Glock when she went to work these days. She'd learned quickly and the gun had become a comfort to her. Truth be told, it reassured me, too. I'd only taught her to shoot in the air so that she wouldn't kill anyone. The sound of a gunshot was enough to keep people away. But I told her that if she saw one of those shirtless guys, she should shoot at him without hesitating. That lot would be killed and return to hell once more, for certain. Farida didn't have the strength to fight them off, and protecting her—even if we were in hell—mattered more to me than their lives. But I wouldn't kill them any more. They were either custodians here or, like me, were sending people to heaven. I had realized that they were too important to be killed.

A few days earlier, just before dawn, I'd been in Bab al-Luq, walking without purpose. I hadn't wanted to kill anyone that day, but I had the Beretta with me. A few people had left early for work. I saw them, with their combed hair and clean, pressed clothes; and others, too, dragging their feet on their way back home, staring at the ground with exhausted faces, or sitting at a café at the end of a night out, finishing their last drinks, or sprinting wearily to catch the last bus. The streets branched beneath my feet until I came to Abdeen, and from there I tried to find that side street where I'd had my first and last meeting with the leadership of the resistance. But I couldn't find it.

I shouldn't be walking around so aimlessly, I told myself, and I remembered that there was a karbon lab on the roof of a building at the end of Abdel-Aziz Street. I'd known about the place for a while, and I knew its owner. I'd only called in a few favors from him in exchange for services I'd rendered, and had never taken any of his karbon without paying the full price. He would give the karbon that Farida needed upfront—he'd be fine with me putting off payment for a few days, or weeks, even: I would say I'd pay later and he wouldn't object. But there'd be no later, now. I knew that the end was very near.

On one corner, a fuul cart was set up, very early indeed. The cart's owner had his work overalls on and was getting ready for the customers who wouldn't be coming for at least another hour. He was muttering something I couldn't hear—prayers, perhaps, or entreaties—with a fool's optimism, shielding himself with supplications amid all that was taking

307

place, stirring the fuul in its pot with the long-handled ladle, looking over the bowls of taamiya, fried potato, and pickles laid out atop the cart, making sure they were full and in good condition, checking the little bowls beside him were clean, making a quick call to the bread man, asking him not to come late like yesterday, lightly tapping the bottles of oil to see that they were full and in place, then turning his back on the lot and resuming his humble, muttered pleas. Someone who truly deserved to live in hell. If I was killing those who knew where we were so that they might go to heaven, if I really was a mercy and not a torment, if I was so very important, then I must leave this man to live.

I was walking toward the karbon lab when I heard a disturbance behind me. I turned and saw a group of cockroaches. As usual, they were all wearing just their trousers, and their heads were wrapped in sheets of newspaper. They quickly came to where the man stood by his cart, and the racket they made swelled in the dawn silence.

They didn't touch him, but immediately fell to smashing his bowls of food and tossing the contents in the air. They removed the huge pot of fuul and emptied it onto the ground. They didn't hit the man at all, but when he grabbed his big knife in a trembling hand they circled around and started baiting him. It wasn't an all-out assault at first, just pinches and jabs to various parts of his body; then things developed, and they were slapping him hard on the back of his neck. He was turning around and around inside the circle they'd formed about him, trying to answer his captors' attacks or escape them, and when he started to bleed, I made my move. No way would I leave this man to die.

I shouted at them and swore, pointing the Beretta at their faces and threatening to shoot, and when I got close I slipped the magazine in. The sound of metal on metal excited them and they made for me, their bodies radiating evil. This was the first confrontation I'd been involved in for a while, the first ever with men in masks, and it was then that I knew what it meant not to see the expressions of agitation on your opponent's face. I opened fire on them, one after another. As each one fell, the rest kept coming on with quick deliberate steps, and I held one round back for the fifth and final youth, who advanced with incredible assurance until he was just a meter away. He pulled a knife from his pocket and raised his arm to strike, but I shot him in the head.

The fuul seller was very angry, shouting and asking me why I'd done it. He walked up to me in a rage, scolding and swearing, then grabbed the barrel of the gun—which was still in my hand—and, holding the muzzle against his temple, said, "Shoot." He started abusing me, growing more and more upset as he said, "Shoot!" over and over. Then he let the gun go and wept with a bitterness I hadn't expected. I couldn't understand the strangled words he spoke as he wept and groaned. His face had switched from rage to sorrow in an eye-blink, and between the sobs I managed to make out that he wanted to die, for everything to be over.

I left him sobbing and went on my way. It would have been easy for me to have killed him, and then everything really would have been over, but I had immediately vetoed the idea. This was a man trying to come to terms with his surroundings. He surely knew that we were in hell, but he still had the remnants of hope: he cared about his work and he was trying to succeed, even though it was only selling fuul; he'd defended the cart and his fuul, and he'd raised the knife, playing the part of the man clinging to life. Was this what they called schizophrenia? And not only that, he even got up early to earn his crust! *You've certainly surprised the custodians of hell, my friend, and now you'll have to live your illusion until you die a natural death—no one's going to kill you so you can cheat your beautiful dream.* The thing that upset me most was killing the five kids wrapped in newspaper. They had been custodians of this world, one of the sources of the terror heaped on terror, and killing them was a

309

loss indeed. I was genuinely sorry. It hadn't been accidental: I'd shot them deliberately. So I thought of the great victory I'd won for hell when I saved the fuul man, and I weighed that gain against the loss of the young men, and I found that I'd come out ahead.

Maybe I would have to choose my targets with more care from now on, guided by nothing but instinct and my victims' acquiescence.

8

FARIDA HAD GONE OUT AN hour ago, and now I had to go to work as well. I got the Beretta ready, filled two clips, and took along a box of ammunition, to be ready in case a sudden burst of enthusiasm came over me. My phone rang.

I heard a voice—"Otared?"—which I couldn't immediately identify, but it was deeply familiar and when I answered in the affirmative it wasted no time: "It's Kamal al-Asyuti."

The major general seemed less exhausted than before. His skin was softer and the paleness had gone; he had even put on a little weight. Deputy minister for general security was a comfortable post and an important one, too. He rarely left the ministry and didn't carry a gun: others carried them to protect him. He could get the details of any case in minutes thanks to a team of helpers and hangers-on, and the files containing the really red-hot scandals were always on his desk.

Kamal al-Asyuti had been appointed deputy minister following the evacuation, during Khalifa Sidqi's first government, and when the minister had been ousted, al-Asyuti had held onto his job. Then the promoted general had been elected president, and in Sidqi's third government the minister and most of the Interior had been moved on, yet still al-Asyuti kept his post. It didn't take a genius or some expert in the backroom machinations of government to get it: al-Asyuti was the real minister and the man sitting in the minister's office was window dressing. Both were comfortable with the situation. His Excellency happily took the massive salary, the well ordered way of life, the wary bodyguards, the lavish convoys, and the media glitz, while his deputy made do with a somewhat reduced share of the same, coupled with limitless powers. When he got it right, the minister got the glory; and when he got it wrong, it was the minister who was charged with coming up short. And this, I believe, suited al-Asyuti down to the ground.

The man didn't stop smiling from the moment I entered the room. He greeted me effusively and left his desk to sit beside me with an ease of manner I hadn't anticipated. I had only met him the once—the time he'd given me my final mission to kill—and yet he was being very affectionate.

"Where have you been, my friend? What are you up to?"

It seemed as though he knew just what I was up to; the way the question was phrased carried not the slightest trace of blame.

"Nothing," I said. "I'm living with a girlfriend, and God bless the ministry's pension."

The answer didn't appear to satisfy him.

"And you're happy, are you? That's no kind of life for a man who's served his nation and joined the resistance against the occupier. You deserve a lot better than this."

By his own world-bound, patriotic logic, that was certainly true, but what use was all that now?

He smiled and went on: "I want you to come back to the Interior. I want someone like you who can be relied upon. Every man who knows how to respect orders and carry them out to the letter is vital if we're to restore security to the country. If you'd prefer an easy job without too many difficulties or duties, it's there for you. If you're exhausted, or fed up, or you just don't have the desire to work any more, then at least let us find you a nice desk to sit at and a fat salary."

I could think of nothing to say. I remained silent and, when he saw I was going to stay like that, he became irritated. The man genuinely cared about me. He wanted to make me happy any way he could.

"I know you're in a somewhat complicated situation. Your girl's job is perfectly legal, but it's not what many would choose. I also know you're the middleman in lots of deals involving karbon—and the truth is, I can't turn a blind eye to this much longer. You might find yourself caught up in a case, and I won't be able to help you, and that's just what I don't want. Of course, it wouldn't happen on purpose. No officer would ever seek to get a colleague thrown into jail, and you know it. But don't you think all this is a dead end for an excellent officer?"

A question. I would have to find an answer, even if there was no meaningful answer to be had. But how to reply to someone who was talking to me about a world that was only an illusion?

Seeing me silent, he continued: "I've really got no idea what's bothering you. I'm assuming you're over the shock. You killed a lot of people for Egypt's sake, and I had taken it as read that the people you shot in Ataba must have affected you considerably. The man's had enough and he's not coming back, I told myself. Of course, I completely understand that you might feel like this. Any one of us might see something criminal about such killing. Even me! I might change my mind tomorrow, leave this job of mine, and go home. That's why I never asked to talk with you, or blamed you for getting out. But what you've been doing these past few weeks has stunned me."

Finally, we had gotten to the point.

"Prior to the evacuation, we were killing people as part of a master plan, which, as you have seen, succeeded. But your recent killings are meaningless, motiveless. I can't understand why you're doing it."

A real dilemma! Why had I come here? I could have ignored the invitation and run off somewhere to hide.

On he went, genuinely bewildered: "Have you lost your mind, my friend? The occupation's over and you've started

313

killing people at random, without a system—and what's more, you're doing it out on the street, not hidden away like the trained sniper you are. Has the lust for killing robbed you of your reason? Tell me, Otared, what happened?"

Otared. It had been a long time since I'd been called by my last name. My silence stretched out. The major general would be convinced of my insanity; there was no other explanation for what I was doing, no other reason for this silence of mine. After this meeting, my mission would be that much more difficult, perhaps impossible. I was a cancer abroad in the street, spreading and killing people without mercy, and the Interior must root it out as quickly as they could.

There was no point in denying it. If I denied it, the major general would certainly be angry and accuse me of stupidity. But was there any way to duck his questions? Could I tell him I was on a mission, just as I'd been on missions in the past?

It was only then, sitting in Major General Kamal al-Asyuti's air-conditioned office, that everything became clear.

Zahra's words, not all of which I'd understood at the time, now made sense. We were on a mission to send people to heaven, she had said, all of us: myself, the Saint, al-Asyuti, and the rest of my colleagues at the Interior. We were a mercy to those in torment here. The tragedy was that they did not know.

I remembered the message delivered to me on the Day of Martyrs.

"Who wrote the order I received on the Day of Martyrs?" I asked him.

He was extremely upset at this—a change of subject that conveyed my indifference to what he'd said; a question about a trifling detail that didn't concern him in the slightest. But whoever had sent that order to me had known the truth for certain.

Brow furrowed, he said: "What kind of question is that? You know we weren't officers back then; we employed complex routes to deliver orders to members of the resistance. Do you even remember how the orders reached you?"

314

"I certainly do," I replied. "A man wearing a horsehead mask came around and gave me a piece of paper that said, 'At 7 p.m., send them to heaven. The Tiring Building, Ataba,' and nothing else."

"That's not the way orders are written, and you know it—but the time and place were perfectly correct. You found the gun and ammo there, and you successfully performed your mission."

He paused for a moment, then said: "The Saint was responsible for distributing orders, and what you've just told me fits with his sense of humor. Then again, maybe he meant to ensure that he wouldn't get in trouble if he was arrested, so he used a code to get the information across . . . but then again, the sentence is perfectly transparent—the code wouldn't serve its purpose."

The Saint! That explained everything.

"Well, I don't understand how it can have happened, but it hardly matters. The result you can see for yourself, my dear man: we've taken back the country and the occupier's been expelled."

He grew more agitated and shifted to the edge of his seat, body tilted toward me and eyebrows raised: "We're trying to rebuild Egypt, to repair the damage done to the state in recent years. This damage didn't just happen under the occupation. No, it's the product of decades of improvisation, lack of planning, repeated failure, of correcting mistakes with mistakes more destructive still. The only way to safeguard the security of the state is to increase punishments and speed up the processing of court cases. This is what we've been doing in recent months. Delayed justice is fatal, and the state's on the brink of death for many reasons. We're putting pressure on everyone here to try to secure it. Soon, we'll be able to stop hanging criminals in police cells because we don't believe the law deters them, and because we know there are a million loopholes through which they can escape, and because

315

we know how hopeless, and ignorant, and utterly stupid the judges are—we can forget all this, because at last the lawmakers and judges have realized that the only way to bring Egypt back to life is by tightening our grip, by fast-tracking court cases, by handing out severe punishments and implementing them with even greater rigor. We'll keep executions public to deter people. We'll devise new forms of death sentence to make anyone considering committing a crime tremble at the thought of it. If the Knights of Malta did anything for this country, it was making executions public. Do you want us to become a shambles like those African states? Don't you want Egypt to rule once more? To become Mother of the World again? Greater than the world? If that's what you want, then stop what you're doing and come back to us."

A powerful desire to applaud the big man's speech swept over me. I was on the brink of laughter, and how I managed not to mock all that shit he'd just spouted I've no idea. *The state? You fool.*

On he went, unperturbed: "As I said, we've taken back the country, and there's no time to relax. Now's the time to go to work, Otared. Having done your duty so well on the Day of Martyrs, what you're doing now makes no sense."

"But the people didn't rise up," I said. "The occupiers left without a revolution."

He cut me off sharply: "That's enough! The Knights of Malta feared a bloodbath. They never dreamed we'd do what we did. Their soldiers and officers presented their superiors with petitions requesting to leave this insane country. Ultimately, your actions had the greatest possible impact on the Knights of Malta."

Carefully, and still harboring some small measure of respect for him, I said, "You're not listening to me, sir. I'm trying to tell you that the people didn't run from my bullets; they welcomed them with open arms. I was shooting at the passersby and they didn't run, sir, and afterward I realized

316

that they'd been deliberately standing in the line of fire so that I would kill them."

He waved his hand. "Pure fantasy! You're imagining it. Why would anyone want to die like that? Or want to die at all?"

He paused again, then raised his eyes to the window where the light came bright into the room.

"Unless, that is, he was escaping some torment?"

I was momentarily stunned. *He must know, too, but he can't say. Kamal al-Asyuti knows!* This was my chance to speak.

"Perhaps they were fleeing a torment we don't know about: high prices, a terrible life, the occupation itself. Perhaps you and I are both fleeing the same torment without realizing it, escaping it by staying put in an air-conditioned room or clutching ice cubes."

Was that a foolish thing to say, or did he really know? His face was wooden, unmoved and expressionless; my words, my hints, had taken him by surprise—I must strike the final blow and bring an end to this conversation once and for all.

"Sir. We are in hell. You know this. And what I am currently engaged in is of a piece with all our missions—your mission and the mission of everyone who works in this building. We really do send people to heaven, and it makes no sense to obstruct me or stop me working. All that's happening is that I'm operating outside the structure of uniforms and official orders, and truth be told, I'm doing it absolutely perfectly, maybe better than ever before."

There. It was out.

He could have said many things, could have given any number of dishonest responses, could have twisted and turned, but he did nothing of the sort. He was silent for a long while. I had nothing to say; he had nothing to say. The time for talk was over and there was no longer any point to me apologizing for my bluntness or excusing myself. No longer any point to continuing the meeting.

317

I rose from my place and walked to the door. For an instant, I paused, grasping the door handle, waiting for him to say a word, anything at all, and I glanced behind me to see him sitting there, head bowed, elbows resting on his knees, and his fingers locked together.

I opened the door and walked out.

I'd walked these corridors years before. There's a sense of awe that fills every young officer who enters the building; as I walked now, that awe was still present, but it was not awe at that imposing sanctuary of the Interior's majesty and influence, nor was it that blend of pride at belonging to this fortress of courage and disquiet at the vast responsibility placed on one's shoulders—that mixed emotion that dwindles until it disappears in middle age or midway through one's career to become, by the end, almost preposterous. No, it was awe at not knowing, despite all that I knew.

I was wondering whether those who walked with me, those around me, the guards and the officers—some tormented, some tormentors—were they custodians of this hell or angels of mercy? Both? Or were these names, and labels, and titles imaginary, unreal? Our understanding of hell was very limited. Were they here in hell for all eternity, or would they at some point go to heaven? And the question that continued to bedevil me until it became a mocking refrain: did they know? But even if I answered them, the questions would never end: every answer was a wrong one, even if it appeared to be right, and it seemed to me that everything bothering me was a part of my torment, from which there was no escape.

The place was properly air-conditioned, very cold. I took the stairs down, though I could have used the elevators: I was trying to stay here for as long as possible, though for no real reason. Quite impossible that I'd bump into anyone I knew here—the building was too vast to allow for chance encounters—but I was still uneasy; not at the prospect of their questions and their predictable insistence that I return, but at the delusion in their eyes and, even worse—as with al-Asyuti—the expressions on their faces as they devotedly carried out their appointed roles in hell.

What happened in the police stations was certainly a torment of some kind, as was the grim existence eked out in prisons and the cells of state security where many had died, their corpses tossed into the trash. And then there were the others, the ones who'd gone missing in transit, and us not knowing for sure if they'd vanished into jail's dark maze or whether they'd escaped into the light of day. . . . The light? There'd been no light outside the walls, just the illusion of it. Even those who'd dropped from the official record and out of sight had been in torment. How was it, then, that I or anyone else could be a mercy, come to send people to heaven? Did we torment them, then later bring them mercy?

I picked my gun up at the entrance. I was sticking it into my trousers the way I always carried it when the sergeant gave me the thumbs-up and said, "Lovely little gun that, sir."

The Beretta has an irresistible magic which works on everyone who sees or shoots it.

I walked away from the ministry down Sheikh Rihan Street, then turned into Mohamed Farid, making for Sharif Street. Following my frank exchange with al-Asyuti, hell had retreated to the edge of my vision and the world's illusion was plain before my eyes—as though by telling him that I would not return, I had freed myself from the shackles of reality. What was happening was absurd to the utmost extent. How could illusion free us when we were living such terrible lives? Sometimes I thought that the knowledge I'd been granted was the true punishment, for all that I couldn't be sure the revelation was genuine or not. I had been lying on my back, a faint pain coursing through my limbs, my forefinger tingling, when I had seen and known, and not a minute's peace since, and me at first assuming that this knowledge would lighten my torment. Yet those who knew

319

were tormented more than others, it appeared. This knowledge, trapped in my head and in the head of Major General al-Asyuti; Zahra's few memories that came back to her to open old wounds; our shared desire to escape it all; my burning need to be killing people all the time that had grown stronger after I'd met Zahra—all this, and not a moment's peace.

And I asked myself: who shall send me to heaven?

Sharif Street was on edge. Lots of police vehicles and lots of police in black balaclavas carrying automatic weapons, walking the street in groups of three and looking highly agitated, waiting for the slightest excuse to start shooting. Approaching the brothel where Farida worked, the cops and guns increased: some crime had just taken place here, for sure, and they were here to arrest the criminal. Though there was a chance that Farida might be in danger, I was perfectly composed—the worst fate she'd meet would be deliverance.

I tried calling, but her phone was off. I tried getting to the building, but the police were firm and stopped me coming closer. As you always do at such scenes, I overheard snatches of conversation: about a murder, about a whore who'd shot at one of the officers and killed him on the spot, about others who'd been killed the same way in the same place. And it was clear to me that Farida had done this. Then I saw a person emerging from the building's entrance, making for the police van and surrounded on all sides by a great press of officers and troopers. I could not see the person, but I was sure it was Farida.

The van took off at high speed and passed me by, its lights blinking blue in the blackness. But I was not alarmed, was not the slightest bit shaken. I was tired of hell, I was tired of what I was doing, and perhaps I was happy now that the end was near.

The case was sewn up tight.

Farida had shot two clients in her room, who subsequently turned out to be police officers. For some reason, she had then

320

decided to come out of her room and shoot some more people. Fifteen rounds at six different people, and she'd hit them all. The Glock's lightness and rapid fire had certainly helped. The case was sewn up tight because the two officers had been regular customers, because she'd had a dispute with one of them a while back, and because she'd brought the Glock with her from her apartment. For all these reasons, the prosecutor's office concluded that this was a case of premeditated murder. The investigators recorded in the case file that the two officers had been killed in the line of duty (which certainly wasn't true), so the prosecutor appended a charge of aggravated circumstance.

It happened so quickly: drawing up the case files, turning them over to the prosecutor and on to the courts, and then the start of the court proceedings—all of it accompanied by an hysterical media campaign calling for prostitution to be banned and for officers to be more heavily armed. I was meeting with officers and former colleagues and asking if there was any way out, and they'd grin at me and say that the case was too big now, that it had become a matter of public interest, and good luck. The Saint said that a death sentence was a certainty, and there was no getting around it. It would be a public execution, broadcast nationwide—a confirmation of the authority of the judiciary and the strength of the Interior's grip. To frighten people.

I encountered a total lack of sympathy for those condemned to death and executed in the public squares. I heard tales of the impaled and strung-up corpses being subjected to mob stonings, of bodies robbed while they dangled from their ropes, or being dragged through the streets and dismembered—tales more suggestive of savage hordes than of citizens of a modern state. But the state supported it all and quite conceivably the draggings and butchery were being carried out by officers in plain clothes.

It was alleged that Farida had fired fifteen rounds, then continued to press down on the trigger, aiming the gun at those present inside the building. Down she went, squeezing the trigger in the face of everyone she encountered on the stairs, then out into the street, squeezing and squeezing, and when they forced the Glock from her hand, and threw her to the ground, and beat her so hard they broke two of her ribs, she kept her right arm raised, forefinger crooked, firing from an imaginary pistol as children do.

She had fired her imaginary pistol at the officers in the Qasr al-Nil police station, at the prosecutor, at the prison guards, at the judge during the opening session of her trial. She squeezed and squeezed that trigger at everyone she met.

During the third hearing, I approached the cage. I saw her level her fist, finger ready on the invisible trigger, waiting until her eyes met someone's gaze, then blazing away. Despite all my attempts to do so, I hadn't seen her since she'd first opened fire. She was as thin as always, her expression innocent. She started playing, firing at random into those present. They were all concentrating on the judge and the lawyers standing before him, and ignoring her completely. She turned her head, her gaze sweeping the room, until she came to me. For the first time in a long time, I trembled, and she stopped firing, and stared long and hard at my face.

She wept quietly, her tears flowing, knowing full well that I couldn't help her any more. I wouldn't be taking her in my arms, wouldn't be concealing her face with my mask and escaping with her, just the two of us together. That wouldn't happen. And she didn't shoot at me. She just kept staring. I left the courtroom; I had no need to hear what would be said there. I knew that the death sentence would be issued and carried out.

I wandered for hours, wearing my mask, shooting everyone I felt deserved to go to heaven. Doing my job with matchless dedication, and thinking about Farida's fate and what would soon be happening to her—and never for an instant did I feel that she had been hard done by. I was possessed by an absolute conviction that an eternal justice was guiding Farida's destiny, cleansing her of the sins that had once defiled her in a hell that was not this hell of ours. I wished I could have been a reader of palms, that I might know what was hidden from both of us concerning our past lives: how many times she'd been raped, how many times murdered, how often her body had been ill-treated after death—and these things done not to torment her, but that she might torment others. I longed to see what she had done in the real world. I had once believed her to be the victim of great injustice, believed that what she had done in the world could not possibly justify everything that had happened to her here, but she must have done things too terrible to conceive. And despite all that had happened, and all that would happen, my faith in this justice grew.

Would those whom Farida had wronged in the world witness what would happen to her? Or would they gain their vengeance without being aware of it? Some surely must be here with us in hell. Perhaps someone she wronged was standing as the judge, looking through her case file, carefully poring through the pages in search of proof and evidence. Maybe he, too, was being tormented, because he was reading so carefully, because he was afraid to be unfair. Maybe those she wronged were even now tormenting her in prison and taking their revenge—or maybe it would be her executioner. And maybe I was one of those she had wronged in the world; I was tormenting her and I did not know it.

The breeze was light and chill, a contrast to the day's sapping heat. If only I could hold an ice cube now.

Once again, my clip was empty—I no longer counted the rounds I carried or those I fired—and I longed for my mission to be at an end, and for rest, rest by any means. For I would be going to another hell to play the same role: an executioner, and a mercy to the people.

9

I HAD AN APPOINTMENT WITH the Saint. He'd called me up and asked to meet at the Baron Palace in Heliopolis. I had objected, told him that the place was too far away and it wouldn't work out, but he had insisted and said that I was going to like what I saw very much indeed.

The taxi driver told me that Salah Salim Street was blocked for some reason and that traffic was being diverted into Heliopolis itself. He would get me as close as he could to the palace, he said, and I'd have to walk the rest of the way. Nothing I could object to there: it was an excellent opportunity to do a bit of shooting.

We came to the outskirts of Heliopolis. I had only walked these streets a few times before and I didn't know them. I was outside the zone of my favored and familiar haunts now, as though I was back on the ground during the resistance: vague missions in strange places. And I remembered how, despite everything, we had arranged conferences and meetings to discuss what we'd be doing in the days ahead, and I remembered al-Asyuti, and the Saint, and many other colleagues, and the endless gunfire.

Perhaps it was the Saint who'd informed al-Asyuti what I was up to. The fellow had a soft spot for old comrades, and he preferred to meet up away from prying eyes to keep me safe from arrest. The silence with which he had ended our last encounter had been an unspoken blessing, an agreement

325

to keep me doing what I was doing free from restrictions. But I was out in the open now; if I was arrested, neither al-Asyuti nor anyone else would be able to protect me. Indeed, the ties that bound me to Farida—in jail, her story splashed across the papers—might very well come to light. The journalists hadn't been able to find a single unattractive picture of her, so they'd added spots to a lovely old photograph and turned her wide eyes into slits, and the shot had run in every paper and news site in the land. If they caught me, they'd say I was taking revenge for what had happened to her, but who cared? Nothing mattered to me except roaming the streets and killing at random. The Saint had sounded nervous when I told him that what I was doing was upsetting the ministry, that I was a threat to public order, undermining security. But that wasn't what was worrying him; he wanted me at liberty to carry out my mission unobstructed.

I fired off all my bullets in Korba, very close to the Baron Palace. I went into a jeweler's and killed everyone inside. The broken glass and diamonds mixed together until I could no longer tell the two apart. I walked through the dark of night toward the palace, thinking of killing people with my bare hands.

A vast crowd stood outside the building, hundreds of people, some wearing masks that covered the whole of their faces, others with surgical masks over their mouths and noses. A few wore gas masks. Were we going to be taking on the police? The Saint was going to get me into trouble. But these people weren't assembled here to fight the cops. They were dressed comfortably and presentably in the kind of clothes you wear when you go to the park to lie on the grass. There was a celebratory atmosphere and even before I crossed Salah Salim, I could hear the sound of ouds and guitars. I was walking through the crowds, making for the palace wall, and the music was coming at me from all directions, and the sound of many voices raised in song—jarring, fervent, full of laughter—grew louder.

326

From somewhere nearby, I heard the Saint call my name, and I turned to see him coming toward me, smiling as always. He shook my hand and we embraced, without my having the faintest idea what all this was about. He was affectionate this time, more so than I was used to from him, wearing nothing on his face but carrying two rubber gas masks in a black bag, clearly identifiable by the reinforced plastic panes at eye level. Inside the bag, they looked soft and crumpled.

Our conversation was most enjoyable. He chattered about all sorts of things, none of them important, as though discussing what was truly important was a taboo among those who knew.

The crowd began moving toward the palace. They were gathered in little knots, keeping close to the outer railing. Then, quite how I'm not sure, planks of wood and lengths of corrugated iron materialized in their hands, on which they drummed frenetically as they sang their happy song.

But the Saint took me aside.

We walked off, leaving the palace behind us. He was silent, gazing out at the horizon and thinking I knew not what. To our right was the entrance to a long tunnel that dipped down below the road, and a line of classical villas that by worldly standards might suggest luxury, but which appeared to me as empty hulks, glaring out at us. I had met up with the Saint several times over the past few weeks and we had talked a lot, but it was only as we walked down that street that he answered my question.

Without preamble, he said, "No one knows when the Day will come, but many now believe that the whole of human history has been written in hell."

"It all happened in hell?" I asked. "All those lives, lived in hell? I assumed that the Day had already come but our torment was so great that we'd forgotten, or that we'd forgotten it so that we could be tormented with the illusion of the world."

He fell silent for a moment, then said: "That's true. Our memories are dead to us, but closer to the end we shall recall

327

all that we have lived through. Remembering is our true torment, not what is happening to us right now."

I didn't speak. Once again, I thought to myself that we must come from a world quite different from this place we were in now, utterly unlike our illusion—without streets, or buildings, or walls, or trees—and yet we did not recall a second of our time there, and everything we lived through now was but a hell that we'd been warned of in that former world.

"The whole business is deeply painful," the Saint said. "You've no doubt wondered whether we deserve this, wondered what we did in the world to deserve to live in this hell. I don't know if you've come to the conclusion that this is justice, but if you have, allow me to reassure you: you're almost out."

I was to leave. At last!

"But don't get too excited," he went on. "You will be going soon enough, but no one knows if he will be departing for heaven or to pass another life back here."

I said: "That doesn't matter in the slightest. Living in hell and being ignorant of the fact is a thousand times better than this knowing. I understand now why people kill themselves."

This time, his warning was serious: "That is the greatest error the tormented can commit. Whoever kills himself here shall never go to heaven. He shall cycle through hell after hell and never leave. The suicide is here forevermore."

"But it's still better, Saint. What's happening is more than anyone can bear!"

The Saint laughed.

"You thought living here would be easy? People must show patience. Maybe this time they will leave for heaven."

He said nothing for a while, and his smile vanished. Then:

"I think that people here have come very far indeed. . . ."

"What do you mean?"

"I mean that the damage done to the souls here cannot be effaced by entering into heaven. These souls will remain weakened forever. I don't precisely know what will happen at that point. Perhaps we'll remember everything, and the memory of it will continue to torment us. Maybe we'll forget—but if we forget, then what's the point of it all?"

I could think of nothing to say. He halted, and I halted, and from afar came the sound of metal being struck. No, not metal: the sound of bare feet thudding on the ground.

"Otared," the Saint said, "be sure to kill as many as you can. The end is very near now, you can't imagine how near. Don't waste any opportunity to kill, for what is coming is worse than you can conceive."

"How will it happen?" I asked.

The sound grew louder as it approached. He raised his head, trying to see if anything was moving off in the distance, and I did likewise, but we saw nothing.

Speaking rapidly as he peered down the length of the street, he said, "I've no idea, of course. Maybe those who witness the end will see what no man has ever seen before. Maybe the end will be kind to us both. Maybe we shall stay in hell forever. All that's certain is that you are to send people straight to heaven."

"Will we see the end together?" I asked.

Rushing his words now, he said, "I'm sure we will see everything right up until the final moment. Maybe we won't see it together, but we'll both see it for sure."

The sounds were very close now and the Saint's body tensed. He started jigging up and down, little hops, staring at the nearby intersection on our left. Then he looked at me and said, "Can you run?"

A pack of dogs appeared, running at great speed. As they exited the intersection, their momentum carried them straight ahead, but they quickly altered course and made directly for us, six or seven of them. And no sooner had that happened than a second pack appeared at the very same intersection: much larger, it seemed, endless, all the dogs of Cairo running together in a single stream.

The Saint clutched my arm.

329

"Run! Run for the palace!"

We ran, the dogs closing on us very quickly. Our walk hadn't taken us too far from the palace. I could hear the dogs closing on us as we ran, and it struck me that I hadn't heard them bark once.

Before us was a group of people gathered behind a wall that they'd constructed from wooden planking and short lengths of corrugated iron—enough cover to hide behind but sufficiently low to see over—into which they'd opened plank-lined passages leading to the palace. The knots of people were like tongues of flesh in a black ocean of asphalt. As we drew closer, those behind the wall removed two boards from the front of the structure and waved their arms, inviting us inside. Together we ran for the entrance, and so great was our speed that we collided with those waiting on the other side. Then they replaced the boards and the barrier was restored, a wall to keep the dogs from touching us.

At first, a great number of dogs smashed into the wooden wall. The boards shivered in the hands of those standing behind them and almost broke apart, but in less than a minute the dogs had figured it out and were running down the passage-ways toward the palace. The torrent of dogs was tremendous, thousands of bodies rushing by as I stood behind the boards, pouring out of Heliopolis and Salah Salim Street and whipping past, caring for nothing, not stopping or turning, not barking, noiseless but for the scrape of their paws on asphalt.

The head of the river breached the palace's outer railing and entered the building itself, even as its body still roared down the passageways between the knots of people, and then they were through the entrance and inside in their hundreds, dogs spilling from windows and balconies, tails and heads pil-ing up, the rooms on the ground floor full to bursting while more dogs ran past us outside.

A long time passed, maybe half an hour, before the great torrent of dogs began to slacken and the last groups of stragglers appeared, sprinting toward a palace that was now completely crammed, the remaining dogs thronging around it.

Silence descended and many of us put on our masks in readiness for whatever was coming next—everything was unexpected. I looked around for the Saint and spotted him a few meters away. I called his name and he came toward me, and I to him, and as we met I asked, "What now?"

"This is what I told you about. Now the palace will collapse."

I lifted my eyes to the old ornamental façade and said to myself that a building like this must be indestructible, that it would never come down.

"Everyone around us knows that this will happen," the Saint went on. "They've all come to see the show."

His words seemed strange, but I'd grown accustomed to all the strange things happening around me. Patting my shoulder, he said, "Don't worry. They all know. You're among friends, Otared."

And indeed I did feel much better. I was among those who knew; one of them, standing with them. I was about to ask the Saint if this was to be the end, but the roar of the palace's collapse prevented me from talking. The internal walls and ceilings were the first to fall, then the dome caved in, then the outer walls subsided onto the dogs milling around the outside of the palace. As the ground quaked beneath our feet and a tremendous noise stopped our ears, a cloud of dust rose dozens of meters into the air. Then the dust cloud reached us, smelling of rain, and enveloped us completely.

I wasn't the slightest bit interested in the fate of the dogs. No doubt they'd all perished beneath the rubble.

The crowd calmly dispersed, walking off with a bare minimum of handshakes and clipped farewells, and were gone. The Saint lit a cigarette.

"The dogs are dead, my friend. Tomorrow's the end."

*

I walked away in the direction of central Heliopolis. I walked and walked, got lost down streets that all looked alike and amid old houses, until I came to a place with a great park and tall buildings. There, I followed the metro's tracks, before deciding to risk a detour into the maze of side streets. I was getting lost on purpose.

But these streets weren't entirely unfamiliar. I'd seen them, or ones like them, before, though I couldn't remember the names. This was a dark street with spare little trees hanging over the walls of the houses on either side. The streetlamps were off, and the light from a shop door shone white and uncommonly brightly in the distance. There were no pedestrians here. No cars. I thought that I might sleep there on the sidewalk and nobody would bother me. I would sleep deeply and wouldn't wake until tomorrow morning, to witness the end. There was a man sitting on a wooden chair outside the shop. He was very far away, but even so he looked perfectly at ease, his arm hooked over the back of the chair with a native indolence dear to my heart.

I was walking down the sidewalk toward the light when I noticed a window set into the high wall on the other side of the street, pure darkness behind its vertical metal bars and unlit white candles melted and fixed in place along the sill. The whole frame was illuminated by the lightless, glowing white of the candle wax. If there was any way out of this hell, then the window was it.

The man sat calmly, waiting, drenched in the strong light spilling from the shop at his back. I looked through the shop window and saw only wooden shelves holding nothing but a few old watches, and no one inside despite the dazzling glare. The moment he saw me, the man gave a smile of joy and waved his arm in greeting, but he didn't move from his chair. I drew closer, trying to recall if I'd seen him before, but unlike the street he wasn't familiar at all. Overcome by curiosity, I went up and greeted him.

332

He said that he had been waiting for me for a long time. Many years had gone by, and he had sat out here each evening at the same time. He knew that I would come one day at precisely this hour. I wasn't late, he said, glancing at his watch—I had it down to the very minute—and then he told me that he had been given the hour, but not the day. And gently he chided me, but he also said that he had never been bored, that he would have waited many more years and never lost his faith that I would come.

I asked him if he would rather we went inside, but he said it would only take a couple of minutes at most. He wasn't going to get up. I must finish it all now.

On the sidewalk opposite, I saw the silhouette of a woman carefully setting a lit candle on the windowsill, then grasping one of the thin bars and murmuring to herself, the light unveiling her lined face.

The man never spoke a word to prompt me, but his expression and his smile said as much: an invitation to come closer, and closer still. I drew up to the chair, circled his neck with my hands, and started to squeeze, and before I could increase the pressure he reached out, and gripped my wrist, and croaked something I couldn't understand. I let him go. He coughed a little and rubbed his neck, then asked if he was supposed to resist, so that the death wouldn't count as suicide. I had no ready answer to that, but after some hesitation I told him that it would be considered a regular death. He shivered with delight, and smiled once more, and this time he turned his face away, toward the window. And, docile as anything, he laid his hands in his lap. The candle was out and the woman was gone. I clasped his neck again and started to squeeze with all my strength.

10

THERE WEREN'T MANY PEOPLE IN Ataba Square, no more than a hundred perhaps, wearily looking on as several individuals were hanged on the high stage. It was a procedure performed as pure routine: the condemned stood beneath the gallows, then the executioner placed the noose about his neck, took a few steps back, and opened the trap, and the body dropped away, suspended from the rope. A few minutes later, the body was slowly lifted back up, listing a little, but with enough slack in the rope to let the knot be loosened. The executioner approached and removed the head from the noose, the body was gradually lowered into the base of the stage, and the next convict stepped forward to take his place.

I walked down Adly Street. They had impaled a large number of men outside the synagogue and left them there, their blood smearing the stakes. It was a far bloodier spectacle than the hanging, but people were passing by without giving the bodies so much as a second glance. A number of officers sat there, their shoulders beneath the corpses' feet, fiddling with their phones and reading the papers.

On Talaat Harb Street, two men had been strung up from lampposts. The legs of each man had been roped together, while their bodies dangled free, arms hanging straight down. From the neck of one of them, a sign had been hung. I couldn't make out the words, so I went right up and peered, and though the letters became crystal clear, I still couldn't read a thing.

Close by Talaat Harb Square, the soldiers had stacked a great quantity of corpses into a small hill. I walked by the hill with the other people, but only two or three turned to look.

I couldn't decide: should I enter Tahrir from Qasr al-Nil Street or from Talaat Harb? I didn't want to go the long way around and enter the square from the far side. As I stood there on the corner of Talaat Harb Street, I could clearly see the great edifice of the Mogamma in Tahrir. I walked down the street, which had started to become crowded. On the corner of Hoda Shaarawi Street stood blue barrels containing severed heads and a great green skip full of headless bodies. There was much blood underfoot, still slippery in some places but mainly dried; when my foot struck the solid, clotted lumps, the crust peeled off to reveal layers of a dark, sticky red. By now my shoes were disgusting, and I paused for a moment to contemplate the fact that I had never before walked in such dirty shoes.

Coming into Tahrir Square, I turned instinctively to look at the Cairo Tower. I pictured a sniper up there, watching the square, watching me, tracking me through his scope as I walked toward its dead center. I grinned and waved, looking toward the balcony where I used to stand. There were a huge number of people in the square, and the sheer scale of the vast stage suggested that many more would be along soon. The stage rose up in the middle of the square, about three meters high and running away either side of a black-clad executioner, who was lifting boxes up from the interior of the stage through a trapdoor I couldn't see. Then he opened the boxes and took out his tools, which he laid out on a table that stood at center stage, the black of his outfit broken only by three stars gleaming on either shoulder.

I pushed through the standing spectators until the dense crowd around the base of the stage prevented me from going further. There were no women where I stood. Only a few wore masks; the rest had left their faces uncovered.

We were silent, waiting for what would happen. A suffocating reek of sweat rose off the crowd. They looked exhausted

336

and unshaven. Many were barefoot, their clothes ragged and ill fitting. I was a stranger among them.

Teams of cockroaches spread through the crowd, muscles quivering, their chests, and arms, and shoulders tensed. At first, I assumed this was a show of strength, a display, but none of it was intentional. Their youthful bodies surged and bobbed unconsciously, out of control.

A doctor climbed onto the stage, dapper in white coat and spectacles. From his capacious bag, he took flexible tubes, monitors, syringes, and pouches containing a colorless solution. These he laid out on the table alongside the executioner's tools.

I felt shudders run down my arm and beneath my armpit, and a great weight pressing down on my shoulders. I had difficulty breathing. Then the pain struck my back and my muscles convulsed.

A hatch in the floor of the stage was opened and the executioner brought Farida out from below. I knew her body immediately—I didn't need to wait for the executioner to lift the black hood from her head.

She was dressed in red, her head held high, and was looking into the executioner's face, studying him. They had cut her hair, and the neck I adored seemed terribly thin.

The executioner took her by the arm and led her to the front of the stage, facing the crowds, then he made her turn around, showing her off to them, and they went wild: howls, and whistles, and cries, arms raised high in celebration. And all the while the sky pressed down.

The executioner stripped the red dress off her—she had been wearing nothing else—and began gesturing at her breasts. He looked out at the crowds and lifted his hand to his chin in mock wonder. He thrust out his forefinger, alerting them to the missing nipple.

Then he took a scalpel from the table beside him, sliced away her other nipple, and tossed it to the crowd.

337

The people behind me surged forward, their expressions dazed and lifeless. They wanted to grab the nipple at any cost, but it was lost underfoot. The stink of sweat enveloped us, rank and overwhelming.

The executioner brought her back to center stage, her breast bleeding. He tied her to a stout post that stuck up out of the boards and shackled her neck with an iron ring fixed to the post.

The doctor stuck a needle in her neck, attached it to a pouch of the colorless solution, and hooked up a monitor to her chest. Then he bound her arms together just above the elbows with strips of white cloth.

The executioner was merciful: he decided to cut her hands off in one go, not to snip the fingers off one by one. He cut quickly and without much blood, then threw them to the crowd. Their excitement increased and they swarmed around the hands.

With the same scalpel, he sliced the skin and flesh off her right elbow, then started cutting through the joint with a saw. He threw the arm to the crowd. Then he cut off another piece and threw that, too.

At the executioner's direction, a second man emerged from inside the stage and stood behind Farida. He grasped her breasts and held her against the wooden post, and now the executioner worked fast. He cut off both her legs at the knees.

I was injured several times—people were squabbling violently over the body parts being tossed down to them. The second exe-cutioner released Farida and left her to thrash about, suspended from her neck and trying to get free from the iron ring, and all around me were many people standing stock still, faces raised. They had dropped their trousers and were masturbating.

The two men now settled what was left of Farida into a raised chair. The executioner cut in a circle around the base of each breast, digging deeper and deeper until he'd removed them both. Then he threw them to the crowd. The powerful smell of sperm mixed with that of the sweat, and I could no longer feel the pain or the great weight pressing down. I was free at last.

338

Men were standing around me, utterly naked, with sperm dripping from their cocks. One of them began to club the heads of his neighbors with a short metal pipe that rang with every blow, yet no one paid him or his blows any heed. Even those he was assaulting didn't move.

Then I heard the sound of gunfire, and many of those standing by the stage fell down. Someone was shooting from beneath the stage to clear space for themselves. A group of masked men dressed in black with bulletproof vests emerged. They waved their guns at the crowd, and three of them brought out a vast, polished mirror. It gleamed in the sun, and at its base I could see huge wheels. They rolled it over the fallen bodies, wobbling and almost falling, until it had passed over all those lying there.

They made a quarter turn in front of the stage, the mirror turning with them, and I could see the buildings and the blue sky behind them reflected in the surface facing me—as though I were looking into another hell.

Then they stopped in front of Farida and the executioner lifted her head to face the mirror. Her eyes locked on it. Farida was still alive, and she smiled.

Then the executioner unclasped the iron ring and, with his colleague's help, he lifted her up and threw her to the crowd.

Hundreds descended on Farida. I fell down, feet trampling every part of me, and I grabbed at a passing leg and brought down its owner, and many more who were coming after him fell down in turn. And when the crowd's rush had subsided, I was able, with difficulty, to get to my feet.

I looked for Farida, but she was too important for them to have left her behind. The crowd stampeded to the edge of the square, and I ran with them, and I caught glimpses of Farida's body being tossed from hand to hand, the crowd tossing it back and forth, soaked in blood. It would be visible for an instant, then vanish for seconds at a time, then appear again, growing bloodier and bloodier every time.

At last, they hoisted her aloft and ran with her toward Mohamed Mahmoud Street. I could see her terrified face. Terror upon terror, as Zahra had said.

Wasn't there to be a moment of unconsciousness? Wasn't my torment to be lessened?

And Farida—wasn't she going to die?

A cold wind gusted over us, blowing in from where Farida could still be seen, and I knew that this was death's mercy, come to us at long last. And I wept, for I had given up hope that death would ever come.

Then those carrying Farida fell down at last, and she fell with them.

And death passed between the people, like a wave taking them, raising up souls and casting bodies down. They were dying in mid-motion, then dropping. And then the wave approached me and passed me. It passed me by, and ran away behind me.

And in not more than a single second, the great uproar was turned to total silence. Even those who remained standing were silent, gazing stonily at the fallen all about them.

Then those who were left joined battle, weeping bitterly as they pounded heads with their fists. A man gouged out another man's eye and tried to pull out his jaw. A man bit into another man's neck and the blood spurted forth. Two men were throttling one another, each gripping the other's neck with his hands and yanking upward, and then one died and released the neck of the other, who still held him upright by his neck, continuing to choke him even though he had passed, keening, and shrieking, and shaking the body left and right.

Why do I not die?

I walked toward the spot where Farida had fallen, my feet stumbling over the freshly dead, avoiding those who fought all around me, forced to drop to my knees and to crawl on all fours to reach her, to lay my hands on the flesh and on the heads. The wind was blowing in my face, carrying the full stink of the rotting corpses and the fevered cries of struggling men.

Farida had gone to ground at the beginning of Mohamed Mahmoud Street. I made it there and looked for her body, but I couldn't find it. It had vanished beneath the others and nothing of it could be seen, and I thought to myself that hell would end now, and that there was no point in burying her.

And I turned back toward the square and the setting sun, to find that all the bodies were gone away. They were gone, along with the stage—there was nothing at all on the ground and nothing behind me.

My knees were touching the asphalt. There were no bodies beneath me, not even Farida's.

I studied the streets on every side—Qasr al-Aini, and Mohamed Mahmoud, and Talaat Harb—and there was nothing in any of them: no cars, no people. I was alone.

And slowly but surely, I saw hell come to an end.

Every sound around me was gone away, except for the sound of the wind that blew and stirred my clothes. Then even that slackened, until it was no more and the sound of it was gone from my ears.

And I heard no sound save my own heart beating in the midst of the silence—nothing around me now save the buildings of hell, its streets, and lanes, and shop signs, no trace of man at all. And then my heartbeat slowed, and its sound faded until it was gone.

I no longer heard anything at all.

Then I saw that I had been a policeman in the world, and I saw that I had been a policeman in many different lives in many hells, and a million million images passed before me in which I saw everything: how I had tormented people and been tormented by them.

And I saw that hell was eternal and unbroken, changeless and undying; and that in the end, all other things would pass away and nothing besides remain. And I knew that I was in hell forevermore, and that I belonged here.

341

SELECTED HOOPOE TITLES

No Knives in the Kitchens of this City
by Khaled Khalifa, translated by Leri Price

The Longing of the Dervish
by Hammour Ziada, translated by Jonathan Wright

Time of White Horses
by Ibrahim Nasrallah, translated by Nancy Roberts

*

hoopoe is an imprint for engaged, open-minded readers hungry for outstanding fiction that challenges headlines, re-imagines histories, and celebrates original storytelling. Through elegant paperback and digital editions, **hoopoe** champions bold, contemporary writers from across the Middle East alongside some of the finest, groundbreaking authors of earlier generations.

At hoopoefiction.com, curious and adventurous readers from around the world will find new writing, interviews, and criticism from our authors, translators, and editors.